Praise for *USA TODAY* bestselling author

KASEY MICHAELS

"Kasey Michaels aims for the heart and never misses."
—*New York Times* bestselling author Nora Roberts

"A multilayered tale.... Here is a novel that holds attention
because of the intricate story, engaging characters
and wonderful writing."
—*RT Book Reviews* on *What an Earl Wants*,
4½ stars, Top Pick

"Michaels' beloved Regency romances are witty and
smart, and the second volume in her Redgrave series is
no different. The lively banter, intriguing plot, fascinating
twists and turns...sheer delight."
—*RT Book Reviews* on *What a Lady Needs*, 4½ stars

"The historical elements...imbue the novel with powerful
realism that will keep readers coming back."
—*Publishers Weekly* on *A Midsummer Night's Sin*

"A poignant and highly satisfying read...
filled with simmering sensuality, subtle touches of repartee,
a hero out for revenge and a heroine ripe for adventure.
You'll enjoy the ride."
—*RT Book Reviews* on *How to Tame a Lady*

"Michaels' new Regency miniseries is a joy.... You will laugh
and even shed a tear over this touching romance."
—*RT Book Reviews* on *How to Tempt a Duke*

"Michaels has done it again....
Witty dialogue peppers a plot full of delectable details
exposing the foibles and follies of the age."
—*Publishers Weekly* on *The Butler Did It* (starred review)

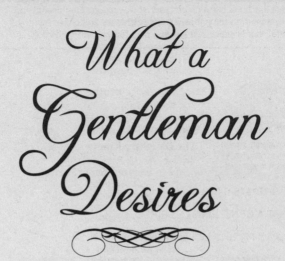

What a Gentleman Desires

KASEY MICHAELS

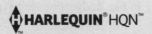

HARLEQUIN® HQN™

Recycling programs
for this product may
not exist in your area.

ISBN-13: 978-0-373-77783-9

WHAT A GENTLEMAN DESIRES

Copyright © 2013 by Kathryn Seidick

Printed in U.S.A.

Dear Reader,

As you may know by now, many of my favorite Regency Era heroes are fops. Well, not *really* fops, but as is said nowadays: "But he plays one on TV."

Valentine Redgrave, youngest brother of the Earl of Saltwood (*What an Earl Wants*), enacts just such a part in London society for his Regency "audience." Boon companion, nary a serious bone in his well set-up body, Val is loved by all if admired by none, as he is, after all, only a younger son, currently without prospects; outwardly dangerous as a dandelion.

But not without wit, or else he couldn't so quietly and successfully serve the Crown…and now, the Redgrave family in particular. Because there is trouble afoot, and the Redgraves are in it up to Valentine's exquisitely tied cravat.

Did I mention Val has a weakness for ladies in distress? Oh, yes. His sister Kate (*What a Lady Needs*) vows his penchant for playing knight in shining armor will land him in deep trouble someday.

So to prove Kate's point, I couldn't resist plunking down Miss Daisy Marchant, governess-on-a-mission, in his path…and in his way.

Or in other words: here comes trouble!

Let's go have some fun, and romance, and danger as these two mismatched creatures—much to their mutual surprise—stumble their way into love. And please visit me online on Facebook or at my website, www.kaseymichaels.com, to catch up on all my news.

Kasey Michaels

To Ruth Ryan Langan and the memory of her sweet Tom-babe—theirs was a love story for the ages.

What a
Gentleman
Desires

Being a man would be an unbearable job—
if it weren't for women.
—O. A. Battista

PROLOGUE

ENGLISH PIGS. FRENCH DOGS.

Roasted beefs! Frog eaters!

Sworn enemies. Temporary truces.

The histories of England and France can be plotted out on a time line of wars between the two countries: a legacy of insults, envy and, paradoxically, smatterings of admiration.

But, mostly, the populace of the two countries heartily disliked each other, which did not keep them from occasionally *using* each other for their own gain.

English gold and wool for French brandy and silks, for instance; the boat traffic across the Straits of Dover was never ending, both in times of peace and when the two countries were at war. In peacetime this was called *trade;* in times of war the term was *smuggling*. This dance of advance and retreat, peace and conflict, had gone on so long many seemed to believe the pattern was some sort of natural order, and merely accepted the ever-changing status quo.

It was left to more inventive minds to see the larger picture, and seek a more permanent solution to this near-constant conflict. One, as it would naturally follow for some of those clever minds, which included immense personal gain.

Charles Redgrave, Sixteenth Earl of Saltwood, was just such a man. He understood enough of history, of the vulnerabilities and peculiar appetites of men, of the way the world works, to believe the unpopular French king would assist him in his dream of being named at least nominal ruler of Great Britain. He felt himself qualified for this role thanks to a thimbleful of possibly illegitimate royal Stuart blood flowing in his veins, his immense wealth and the ruthless pursuit of enough land in Kent to proclaim it his own kingdom if necessary.

When a man like Charles Redgrave dreamed, he did not dream small dreams.

In return for this assistance, Charles believed, all he had to do was assassinate the bumbling George III (and probably the Archbishop of Canterbury, as well), and hand over a large part of the English treasury to Louis XV. Louis would be popular again, and Charles happy beyond his wildest dreams and ambitions. And, at last, there would be a permanent (and mutually profitable) peace between the two nations, all thanks to Charles IV of the House of Stuart.

Really. Even if most people would agree the Earl of Saltwood had more than a few slates off his roof. Either that, or the man was so thoroughly insane he was, in fact, dangerously brilliant.

To give the earl some credit, somewhere in this

idea was perhaps a kernel of a chance for possible success, although it should be pointed out that rarely is it a particularly splendid notion to begin any Grand Plan with the words: "Off with his head!"

In any event, both men were called to their final rewards before things could get out of hand, one still hated, the other unfulfilled.

Decades later, Barry Redgrave, Seventeenth Earl of Saltwood, learning of his father's ambitions—and of his unique and titillating *modus operandi*—also set his sights and hopes on France, and Louis XVI, who was proving to be even more unpopular than his papa. Barry's plan was to convince England (by fair means or foul; hopefully foul, actually, because that was much more delicious) to intercede on Louis's behalf.

He pointed out that revolution in France could just as easily become revolution in England. Louis and his queen, the lovely Marie Antoinette of "let them eat cake" infamy, would be *so* grateful, and in return support Barry's *coup d'état*...again, a plan ending with a Saltwood on the English throne.

But just as the Bastille fell, Barry was lying dead on the dueling field, shot in the back, purportedly by his unfaithful Spanish wife. Not that much later, the embattled Louis lost his head, literally.

Both earls had employed a rather strange route to their hoped-for success, that of gathering together secret groups of wealthy, politically and socially powerful men, in point of fact forming a corrupt and sexually deviant hellfire club known only as the Society. Whether through ambition, sexual appetite or even discreet blackmail, the Society moved beyond its original devil's dozen thirteen members, all of whom quickly went to ground when Charles died, and most certainly repeated their ratlike scurry for the exits after the scandal of Barry Redgrave.

After nearly a half century of on-again, off-again existence as a haven for seditionists and easily-led sexually promiscuous devil worshippers, the Society was as dead as Charles and Barry.

The world could heave a collective sigh of relief, even if it never knew it perhaps should have been holding its breath.

The Saltwoods buried the history of the last two ambitious and possibly mad earls under the deepest carpet at Redgrave Manor and moved on, Barry and Maribel's four children eventually reaching adulthood and going into Society (no, not that Society!). The scandal of Barry's murder and their mother's involvement, along with never quite quelled whispers of the possibility of some deliciously naughty hellfire club, moved on with them.

But that was all right with the family, who rather enjoyed being referred to as those scandalous Redgraves. The dowager countess, Lady Beatrix (Trixie) Redgrave, fairly reveled in the notoriety, actually. She certainly did nothing to discourage it at any rate, and had bedded more lovers since Charles's death than many Englishmen had teeth left to chew their roasted beef.

And then one day about a month in the past, the Eighteenth Earl of Saltwood, Gideon Redgrave, was shocked to learn that the Society, the tawdry creation of his sire, his grandsire, intended to be the instrument of their success, was back in the treason business, this new devil's thirteen conspiring with none other than Napoleon Bonaparte.

The Redgraves looked to each other, but only for a moment, as none of them were the sort to drag out the Society for another airing, and then began the race to identify and stop whoever in blazes was using the methods of the Society for their own gain.

The protection of England was, of course, the Redgrave family's immediate and main concern. Of course!

But, yes, there were also all those unknown, sordid bits of Redgrave history that needed to be safely kept beneath that deep carpet....

CHAPTER ONE

1810

LORD SPENCER PERCEVAL, serving as both Prime Minister and Chancellor of Great Britain during these troubling times, sank into his favorite tub chair in his private study behind the imposing ebony door of No. 10 Downing Street. He had just moments earlier successfully concluded his most important mission of the day: seeing the last of his dozen children off to bed.

They'd been lined up like proper little soldiers, to bow or curtsy before him, and to smile as he kissed them each square in the middle of their foreheads. His wife had then adjourned to their bedroom, a twinkle in her eye—the same twinkle that had caused him to convince her to elope with him so many years ago, when her father had considered a younger Perceval unsuitable matrimonial material.

A small silver tray was placed before the prime minister. "Your evening refreshment, my lord? And I must commend you. Quite the brood you have there—or is that clutch? No, that would be hens, or ducks, or some such *fowl* thing. A thousand pardons. Lovely children, all of them. Stellar, really."

Perceval relaxed the sudden death grip he'd clamped around the arms of the chair. "I should have known immediately it had to be a Redgrave. Although I would have been less surprised was it Saltwood himself. How the devil did you get in here?"

"I'm quite certain the earl sends his regards, or would, if he'd known his rascally brother planned to, as it were, *drop in* on you tonight. As to the how of it? A valid question from your vantage point, I'm sure," Valentine Redgrave said, putting down the tray and taking up the facing club chair, quite precisely crossing one well-shaped leg over the other, his long-fingered hands folded in his lap. After all, he was in evening clothes, and it wouldn't be polite to slouch, comfortable though he was in his surroundings. "But if I told you, I'd be reduced to begging your starchy under-secretary to allow me a private audience, as has been the case these past two weeks. Have you by any chance been *ducking* me?"

"Absolutely not," the prime minster declared, although seemingly unable to look Val directly in the eye as he said it. "I've been otherwise involved."

"As have we Redgraves, not that you seem interested in our progress."

"*Our* meaning *your?* Now, why do I doubt that? As it is, Lord Singleton will soon be reporting to me."

Remembering the nearly giddy communication

sent to him from Redgrave Manor by his sister and tucked in with Simon Ravenbill's official report, Valentine only smiled. "My soon-to-be new brother is otherwise *engaged,* I'm afraid, and forward his apologies. Behold me, his trusted messenger."

Ah, now the prime minister was paying attention.

"Egads, you must be kidding. You Redgraves have managed to corrupt the Marquis of Singleton? I wouldn't have thought that possible."

"Most anything is within the realm of possibility, my lord, if one simply applies oneself. But it wasn't all of us. Just the one, the pretty one. I'll be honored to pass along the delightful news that you wish them happy. But now, if we've finished with this amicable yet hardly germane chitchat, shall we get down to cases? We've got serious business to discuss."

"I know that, you insolent puppy, but this is no way to go about it. You mean to tell me Ravenbill's so besotted he put nothing in writing for me?"

"Not knowing friend from foe, would you have done anything so potentially dangerous? No, of course you wouldn't," Val rejoined smoothly, as there wasn't a Redgrave born who didn't know how to speak the truth in order to avoid lying through his teeth. Their sister, Lady Katherine, had rather elevated clever evasion of the truth to an art form, actually. "It's all those sweet children, isn't it? They've turned your mind domestic tonight, when you should be attending to business. Quite understandable, really. Very well, I'll recap."

"You do that. And then I'll have you clapped in irons for daring to accost me in my home. We're agreed?"

"That seems only reasonable," Val said, getting to his feet. He looked quite presentable, sitting. But standing? Ah. Few were more impressive than a tall, dark-haired Redgrave, standing, be it Gideon, Earl of Saltwood, or any of his trio of younger siblings, including Kate! The English in them seemed to recede then, and the Spanish side of them came out to play, to remind all of their mother's fiery blood singing through their veins. Their mother, who had so disgraced the family as to shoot their father in the back in order to save her French lover on the dueling field. One couldn't be faulted if one imagined a pistol in Valentine's hand; after all, it was in the blood.

And then, in the space of ten even, silently counted heartbeats, Valentine bowed, as if to acknowledge the prime minister's power over a lowly creature such as himself. "I can but humbly submit to your command. Only do be so kind as to make certain the irons are clean. This is a new jacket, you understand."

"Bah," said the prime minister, clearly immune to both Valentine's physical presence and his nonsense. "Sit down, Redgrave. I'm not to be taken in like some raw schoolboy. You're as cooperative as a room full of cats. What have you and our unexpected Romeo discovered?"

"Not me. Oh, no, not me, just as you so cleverly surmised. I'm afraid I was busy elsewhere, on a mission having much more to do with the simpler pleasures in life."

"A woman. Perhaps several—an entire *clutch* of fair females. Your reputation precedes you, carefully constructed as it is, to cover your occasional work for some high-ranking government idiot who actually trusts you. But friend to that someone or not, a dank cell awaits you if you don't soon drop this charade and come to the point."

Ah. Spencer Perceval wasn't stupid, and he knew about Val's occasional service, even if he didn't know the man or the department. Hell's bells, he probably didn't know the department even existed. Such was the amount of secrecy these days, what with spies everywhere from the low to the high, working for either political belief or pay, it didn't much matter. But a too-interested Perceval was a dangerous Perceval, and to be avoided at all costs.

"A thousand apologies, I'm sure, but I find myself totally at sea. Me, *working?* I hardly think so. That was the answer you expected, wasn't it?" When the prime minister smiled at last, Val neatly split his coattails and seated himself once more, this time leaning his forearms on his strong thighs and clasping his hands together between his knees, his posture all business. "All right, then, now that we're through dancing about, *fruitlessly* hoping for ripe plums of information to drop out of each other's mouths, let's get to it. Thankfully, I do have some progress to report."

"Spencer, darling, I thought you'd be— Oh. I didn't realize…"

Valentine rose immediately and took his handsome, ingratiating self across the width of the intimate room, to bow over the lady's nervously offered hand. "How very good to see you again, dear lady. I vow, it has been an age. Too long…yes, yes, indeed. Wherever has this brute been hiding you?"

"The… That is, our two youngest were ill with the measles, and I didn't wish to— Mr. Redgrave, you can release my hand now, for I've been married to this good gentleman long enough to know not to quiz you on why you're here. However, Spencer, if I might see you for a moment?"

Perceval was already beside her, and glaring at Valentine. "I'll return directly. In the meantime, Redgrave, sit yourself down again—and for God's sake, don't touch anything."

Valentine managed to look crestfallen, abashed and wickedly amused, all at one and the same time. It was also an art, this ability of his to play many roles at once for his audience, and if his brilliance didn't impress the crusty prime minister, it still worked wonders with his lady wife, who scolded, "Spencer, that was rude."

"Yet, alas, dear lady, a verbal spanking well deserved," Val said, bowing once more.

He waited until the pair had adjourned to the hall-

way before helping himself to the wine he'd first offered the prime minister and re-taking his seat as
ordered, planning to use this unexpected interlude to
align his thoughts. There were things Perceval knew,
things he could never know and things he needed to
be told. It was all a matter of carefully—keeping to
the *fowl* theme of the evening thus far—lining up
his ducks in their proper rows.

Valentine began with a mental listing of things
the prime minister knew: The Redgraves had "stumbled over," as Gideon had so obliquely put it, the existence of a group within the government plotting
to assist Bonaparte and help overthrow the Crown.
As proof of his words, Gideon had handed over evidence supposedly found near Redgrave Manor that
supplies meant for the king's troops massing on
the Peninsula were about to be diverted elsewhere.
Gideon also had given the man two names: Archie
Upton and Lord Charles Mailer, both employed by
the government. Upton was dead now, Mailer was
being watched. Perceval was also gifted with an entire bag of moonshine about both men being part of
a "secret society" possibly operating in the area, and
the prime minister had assigned Simon Ravenbill to
go to the estate to investigate.

Perceval knew there was more to it than that,
must be wondering about the depth of the Redgrave
involvement, but had prudently not asked. Yet.

Then there was what the prime minister could
not be privy to: this particular secret society could

be traced back to the time of Valentine's father and grandfather. A hellfire club with a carefully concealed history of attempted treason mixed in among the seemly mandatory satanic rites and naughty sexual antics so in vogue with such groups of powerful and ambitious men. Men who believed themselves both entitled to such pleasures and immune to discovery and scandal (until they were proven wrong, on both counts). The Redgraves wanted to help, not be thrown into prison as likely suspects!

Then there was the news Simon and Kate had sent to him, which had to be told: information, gold coin, spies and quite a bit of opium made the crossing between the beach at Redgrave Manor and France... or at least it had done until Simon and a band of unnamed local smugglers had put a stop to this traffic a scant two weeks ago.

Unfortunately, the prime minister would also have to be told the Redgraves had learned nothing more about the identities of the current members. No names, no other locations had been found. The Society had definitely *used* the estate, its caves and handy beach, but they hadn't left their mark there.

There was one name, that much was true: one Society member who had acted as leader of the smugglers. But as the captured man had chosen suicide over confession, his body quietly disposed of at sea, Valentine had decided Perceval didn't need to know of that small failure, or of Simon's dire warning: "A leader who can convince others to kill themselves in order to protect him is a deadly dangerous man surrounded by worshipful fanatics. Be alert at all times, strike first and, for God's sake, don't bother attempting to capture any of them alive. If you hesitate, you'll die, and Kate will be exceedingly out of humor with you."

An unlovely thought all-around, Valentine believed, excluding the leavening remark about his sister, and advice he'd committed to memory. Perceval would scoff at such dramatics, being the coolheaded logical Englishman to his core, but the fiery Spanish blood in Val's veins believed nothing impossible when it came to his fellow man.

As to the Redgraves themselves, their own family history? Ah, much had been learned there thanks to Val's brother Gideon, their sister, Kate, and Simon Ravenbill, and even the dowager countess, who'd had the misfortune to witness the first two incarnations of the Society.

But none of that more sordid history would ever be shared with the prime minister. It was certainly true that, because of that family history, the Redgraves were better armed to defeat the Society...but they were also more vulnerable to having that salacious history made public knowledge. That would never do!

And so, with the Crown's help—and, truthfully, preferably without it—the Redgraves would put a stop to the Society, for reasons both patriotic and personal.

Gideon had done his part, uncovering the existence of the Society in the first place, and Kate and Simon had put an end to the smuggling. Now, with their brother Maximillien on the Continent, tracking clues on that end, it was up to Valentine to take up the trail that, once followed, could destroy the Society forever, protect the Crown from the greedy Bonaparte, and tuck the scandalous Redgrave history away once and for all.

One, two, three. As simple as that. Three paths, three goals. Except they also were three giant steps, none of them easily taken, and with deadly pitfalls strewn along the way to trap the unwary.

With scarcely any solid clues to follow, the main purpose of Val's visit tonight was to dazzle Perceval with news of the smuggling and then quickly gather information about one thing that had been bothering him. Hopefully, Perceval would be so happy to see the back of him he'd give it to him.

And so it was a scant few minutes later, after feeding carefully selected information from columns one, two and three to the prime minister, that Valentine asked: "Who ordered the construction of more Martello Towers along the southern coast? There were to be no more, the threat of French invasion long past. And yet now, amazingly, more are popping up. Why? Is there something you haven't told us? For shame, sir, for shame, when my brother has been so exceedingly honest with you."

"Only a fool would believe that last statement.

Besides, I'm certain I was asking the questions," Perceval said smoothly.

Val sat back at his ease, crossing one leg over the other once more, his forearms resting lightly on the arms of the chair, indicating he was now in charge. They were both actors on a private stage, with nothing said or done without careful thought. Politics was a battle of sorts, fought with innuendo...and sometimes great fun, actually. "You were. Now, having been so marvelously cooperative, it's my turn. *Quid pro*—whatever the rest of that is. I'm the second of two younger sons, and not expected to be brilliant."

"*Quid pro quo.* This for that. An even exchange, although I highly suspect the latter isn't true in this case." Perceval's neck turned rather red above his collar. "Very well, although this has nothing to do with you."

"On the contrary. Redgrave Manor is located quite near the coast, if you'll recall, and a prime spot from which to launch an invasion. If we're to have uninvited visitors from across the Channel, we should be laying in large quantities of truffles and snails." Valentine smiled his most mischievous smile. "Lord knows we already have enough French brandy."

"How amusing. But very well, if you'll promise to go away."

"Reluctantly," Valentine lied smoothly. "But, yes, I will go, never to darken your door again. Or would that be window?"

"Again, how amusing," Perceval said blandly. "The additional towers are merely a precaution. A spy was discovered some months ago, thanks to a loyal subject of the Crown. Although he escaped capture, a discreet search of the man's abandoned rooms disclosed, among other things, a communiqué written in code, detailing new plans for an invasion."

Valentine's mind was racing, even as he leisurely plucked an imaginary bit of lint from his coat sleeve. "My, my. And oh, dear, as well. Such disturbing news, although if memory serves me, Bonaparte has been setting his eyes eastward of late, with his presumed eventual target being Russia. Does he even have the ships and troops to attack us here?" He looked at the prime minister quizzically. "Hmm, and here's a thought. Easily deciphered, this conveniently discovered communiqué, would you say?" Val asked quietly.

"I'll have you know the government employs only the most talented..." Perceval sighed. "Yes, easily deciphered. I'll admit that worried me, but not enough to disregard the information."

"You had no choice but to react prudently." Valentine kept his expression blank. It wouldn't do to embarrass the prime minister by telling him, if the Redgraves were correct in their conclusions as to the reason behind the renewed construction, he and the Crown had been badly hoodwinked. So he contented himself by asking his intended question, the one that had brought him here this evening: "Who warned the government of this suspected spy? Do you know?"

Perceval was rubbing at his cheek, hard, as if to ease some pain in his now tightly clenched jaw. "Yes, not that it helps. I personally received the information via a letter penned to me by one of the king's coterie of chums, one Guy Bedworth, Marquis of—"

"Mellis," Valentine finished for him, knowing another hope had been dashed; he would learn nothing from the marquis. "The *late* Marquis of Mellis. Also, if I recall correctly, a great chum of my father's." *And known by us to have been a member of the Society during Barry's time...and perhaps again now, or at least until his death.* "Sudden, was it?"

"Sad, that. Although perhaps fitting. He was found slumped in his favorite chair in his favorite club, you know. There aren't many better ways to go."

There's one, Valentine thought, prudently lowering his eyes, *that of being carefully dressed and placed in his favorite chair in his favorite club after expending his last energies in the bed of one Dowager Countess of Saltwood—Trixie Redgrave, mine own grandmother. To hear Gideon tell it—which he'd done only with the most reluctance—the worst, other than pulling Mellis's drawers on, had been attempting to rid the man's face of an unholy grin.*

"He was also a bosom friend of my grandmother," Valentine managed at last. *Literally.* "A pity then. We'll learn nothing from him." *Only what Trixie learned concerning the Society before old Guy cocked up his toes (among other things), and that, Prime Minister, is included in Column Two: things you will never know.*

"Are we through here?" Perceval got to his feet, indicating he clearly thought so, and since this was, at least for the length of his term of office, his home, Valentine rose, as well. "Please convey the Crown's sincere thanks for all your family has done, most especially for thwarting that nasty business of shipping troop supplies to the incorrect ports. Although, when it comes to the smuggling of spies and secrets, I suppose this clever group will only find themselves another landing beach, won't they? These are serious, frightening times, Mr. Redgrave."

"Downright terrifying, some might say. I realize I'm being given the boot, but are you at the same time dismissing *all* the Redgraves?"

"How astute of you. Yes, I am. I won't say the earl hasn't been helpful, and will not say he has his own personal interests in mind as well as those of the Crown—"

"Ah, but you just said both."

Perceval motioned toward the hallway. "Let it go, Mr. Redgrave. This business about the *Society,* as you insist on terming this particular gang of traitorous thugs, is of no especial import to anyone save your family. We are interested in much larger game now, that of thwarting Bonaparte."

"And you see no connection between the two,

even after being told about the smugglers on Red-grave land. Amazing."

"You're wrong again. I don't *care* about the con-nection. There's a difference. Of course these men must be found, and stopped, stamped out, along with any other pockets of traitors, and unfortunately, there are several." The prime minister was beginning to look testy, not a good look on the man. "You've ad-mitted you learned no more names, and in fact, by confronting the men on the beach yourselves rather than contacting me, you may have sent them all to ground, which is the very *opposite* of helpful, Mr. Redgrave. Do you understand now?"

"Yes, I was afraid you might come to that conclu-sion." Valentine retrieved his hat, gloves and cane from a dark corner of the study. "So, in other words, thank you awfully for bringing the sticky matter of a group of powerful men out to hand England over to the French to you on a platter, but now please go away?"

"Or else find yourselves brought to task for in-terfering in Crown business? Very good, Redgrave, that's precisely what I'm saying. Kindly convey my like sentiments to Lord Singleton. We will take mat-ters from here."

"Having made such whacking great progress in unmasking these traitors on your own." Valentine placed his hat on his head at a jaunty angle and then gave it a solid *thump* to secure it. He knew he really should shut up now, before he truly was clapped in irons. He'd gotten what he'd come for: the information about the Martello Towers, and his *congé,* which freed all Redgraves from being in the sticky position of having to report to the Crown (or conduct themselves within the rules, which often got in the way of progress).

But, at the end of the day, no Redgrave wished to hear he'd been *dismissed.* It was a matter of pride, or something.

Perceval stepped back as a clearly confused uniformed guard opened the door for the exit of a man he hadn't seen enter. Valentine gave him a short salute.

The prime minister followed him, to stand in the open doorway as Valentine hesitated on the marble step, to pull on his evening gloves. "You're not going to leave this alone, you Redgraves, are you?"

Valentine debated between truth and evasion, deciding it wouldn't be polite to lie to the prime minister directly after insulting him. "My apologies again to your lady wife for having disturbed you."

"Just go, Redgrave," Perceval said wearily.

"Yes, within the moment. Only one thing more. Only a trifling thing, but I must ask. The guns on the Martello Towers, my lord, they're bolted into place, correct—strong, immovable? Which way do they face?"

"Now you're wasting my time. You know which way they face. They face the enemy."

"A sterling defense, although not a great help if

attack were to come from inland. They're rather defenseless in that situation."

"That wouldn't happen. The towers were built, are being built, to prevent the enemy from ever landing on our shores, let alone moving inland."

Valentine leaned in closer, and spoke quietly. "Unless the enemy, helped by, oh, say a band of highly placed traitors calling themselves the *Society,* found a way to slowly bring over and hide trained troops to capture the towers, including those you've so conveniently recommenced building. More than one hundred of them, marching along the southern coast. Imagine that, my lord, if you can. Then the enemy those guns would face would be *our* Royal Navy, as we attempt to stop an invading army brought to our shores under the protection of those same guns."

"That's not how wars are fought."

"The gentlemanly rules of warfare only work if both sides agree to them. Or have you never read of the Trojan horse?"

He then smiled, satisfied his parting shot had given the prime minister a lot to think about, bowed and quit No. 10 for the damp of a foggy London evening.

He walked to the corner and the Redgrave town coach that had been awaiting his arrival. A groom hastened to open the door and let down the step, and was therefore able to then carry the whispered direction of Valentine's next destination up to the coachie on the box. With any luck, he should find his quarry in the card room. Lord Charles Mailer, a man whose acquaintance he'd been carefully nurturing for the past fortnight.

Because no Redgrave worth his salt was ever caught without an alternate plan.

CHAPTER TWO

AFTER A FORTNIGHT spent carefully cultivating the man's interest and friendship, Valentine had come to the conclusion Lord Charles Mailer—crude, mean and profane—was an idiot, but he wasn't stupid.

Although that description of the man seemed to contradict itself, Valentine meant it. If he could suspend a sign above Mailer's head, to remind him of his conclusions, it would read: *He's a Buffoon, But Tread Carefully!*

In physical appearance, Lord Mailer was... unimpressive. At least when held to Valentine's high standards. The man dressed importantly, impeccably, but without flair, sans any real style. When it came to fashion, he followed the crowd, and if the crowd arbitrarily decided to suddenly begin rolling up its cravats and tying them about its foreheads, Lord Charles Mailer would be trotting through Mayfair resembling nothing more than a rather puffy, pale-faced, red-haired American Indian.

This second son of the Earl of Vyrnwy, and carrying one of that powerful man's merely honorary titles, Mailer had until recently volunteered his services at the Admiralty, until leaving town quite suddenly after his friend Archie Upton had stepped (been pushed?) under the wheels of a brewery wagon. But Mailer couldn't seem to stay away from Mayfair. He'd returned only a single day after Valentine had arrived in the metropolis, planning to visit with his grandmother before moving on from there to chase his target down on his small estate. But Trixie was not in London. Mailer was.

Valentine considered all of this to be serendipity, or perhaps even a heavenly blessing on his plan. The seeming duet of coincidences might also be traced back to the devil, he supposed, which was why it was never a good idea to dig too deeply into such things. Trixie would only have *deviled* him with questions about Mailer, anyway, since it was she who had discovered his and Upton's association with the Society.

Simon Ravenbill had earlier attempted to break down Upton and Mailer in order to gain more insight into the Society, but Valentine believed Simon had been too heavy-handed in his pursuit. Valentine... well, he rather prided himself on his finesse. He wouldn't say he had Mailer landed in the boat quite yet, but he had fairly well seated the hook in the man's mouth. It was simply a matter of playing his fish now—feeding him line, then reeling him in again, all while inwardly despising him, another of Valentine's talents.

Really, he should consider a whirl or two on the stage, except Gideon would most certainly not approve, and Trixie would embarrass him by shouting

"Bravo!" over and over and perhaps even personally driving a wagonload of roses onto the stage.

But back to Valentine's new chum.

Lord Mailer believed himself a wit, and, remembering his crude and mean nature, his humor often took the form of ridiculing his fellow man. His mind seemed never to stray far from sex—when he'd last had it, how much he longed for it, when he would next have it—and he delighted in publicly recalling his most memorable encounters.

Lord Mailer had arrived in town with his shy, blonde and unfortunately sallow-complexioned bride of less than a year—his second, as the first had perished in a sad accident involving a fall from a cliff (highly suspicious, that, to a man like Valentine), leaving behind two motherless children. He alternately ignored or teased Lady Caroline unmercifully, so that she kept her head down in public, seldom spoke above a whisper and rarely lifted her eyelids above half-mast.

As Valentine had led the woman into the dance at Lady Wexford's ball the previous Saturday, Lady Caro had physically flinched when he'd taken her elbow, and then hastily explained she'd stumbled on the stairs that morning, and bruised her arm.

The woman couldn't lie worth a damn, and Valentine, with his well-known weakness for ladies in distress, now had another reason to enjoy bringing Mailer down. But at least until the fact the man drew breath was no longer of importance to him, Charles Mailer would not know any of this.

Then he would.

Valentine looked forward to that day.

"You're smiling beneath that hat, aren't you, and not asleep at all," the man who should by rights be measuring every breath commented as the well-sprung Vyrnwy coach smoothly rolled along through the countryside. "Good. Saves me the bother of having to elbow you awake. We're nearly at Fernwood."

Valentine eased himself upward out of his comfortable slouch, his booted feet no longer deposited on the facing seat, and tipped up the brim of his dove-gray curly brimmed beaver. He raked a hand through his nearly black, thick and overlong hair, which then tumbled in soft waves about his forehead and ears, the result a good rendering of a handsome, perfectly dressed and endearing ragamuffin. A look he knew suited him. "You said something, Charles? Good God, don't tell me I was snoring. I'd never again be able to stay the night in any ladybird's bed, if I knew that."

"Is that where you went last night, after you left me at Lady Wexford's? To rut? Who was she? Titled slut, paid whore? Either way, the older ones are always more grateful, ain't they, if you take my meaning."

"A gentleman never tells," Valentine responded evasively as he slid a slim silver box of pastilles from his waistcoat pocket, flicked it open with one hand

and popped a scented tablet into his mouth. "Here, for God's sake take one. It will be an improvement over the sausages you swallowed down when we stopped for luncheon."

Mailer glared at the contents for a moment, probably considering whether or not he'd just been insulted, and then fished out two pastilles for himself; the fellow was a glutton even in the smallest things. "You want me to tell you first, is that it?" he asked, clearly not letting the subject drop. "Very well. I had to content myself with my own wife, curse the luck. I'd do no worse sticking my cock through a knothole. That would be a *large* knothole."

"As you say. Please don't be too disappointed if I'll not tease you for a personal inspection," Valentine said, longing to choke the man.

"Yes, so I say, blast you. Stiff as a board, that woman."

The silver lid snapped shut. "Then why bother?"

"You're not leg-shackled, so you wouldn't know. Got to keep them in line, that's why. Because they're women. They'll do the damndest things if you ever slacken your hold on the leash."

Like be so desperate as to step off a cliff to be away from you? Or perhaps she tugged too much on the leash and had to be pushed, and that's why, for wife number two, you chose such a timid mouse? Valentine yawned behind his hand, having grown tired of his role of avid satyr, but sure it was time to trot it out for yet another airing.

"This is why I'm so grateful for our friendship, Charles, and for this invitation to visit your estate. All this wisdom you shower on me. Although, not to insult Lady Caro, if you don't mind I think I'll choose my own wife if that day ever dawns. Which I highly doubt. I've no need of an heir, for one, and much as I enjoy indulging myself in their anatomy, as a species I find females to be uniformly loathsome and inferior."

"Enjoy their anatomy. Ha! If you ain't a card, Redgrave. Believe me, you'll have plenty to choose from, just as I promised. I knew I liked you, from that first night, even if you took Madame La Rue's three best dollys up with you, and kept them busy for, what was it—three hours? I heard none of them were fit for service for days afterward."

"Rumor only, Charles. Only two weren't fit for service. The third damn near killed me with enthusiasm." *Gad, this is nauseating, especially since the man's breeches are showing a decided bulge.*

In truth, Valentine had treated the three ladies of the evening to several hands of whist and a supper he'd ordered up from the kitchens, and then paid the madam generously so that she'd keep the ladies out of service for a few days, claiming they were *too worn for work.* Two had napped on the bed until he'd left, but the third had offered herself, an invitation Valentine had turned down as gently as possible, his dedication to Crown and family not extending to a possible bout of the pox.

"As for the other, no insult taken," Mailer said with a dismissing wave of his hand. The one with a gold ring on the index finger, fashioned in the shape of a fully opened rose.

Valentine couldn't resist; he would let out a little more line, even while setting the hook deeper. "You know, Charles, I've been longing to ask. Barry, my late father, had just such a rose depicted in his portrait at the Long Gallery at Redgrave Manor, only his was in the form of a stickpin. Although the diamond may have been larger."

"You don't say?" Mailer held up his hand to inspect the ring, fingers spread, frowning at the diamond at its center. His hand trembled slightly, and he quickly lowered it again. "Gift from my maternal grandfather, actually. M'brother Geoffrey wanted nothing to do with it, said it was gaudy."

"I think it exquisite. A bit of a stick, your brother, I suppose?"

"Too holy by half, yes. And dotty over his wife and kiddies, just like some commoner. M'father, too, for that matter. But Grandfather said I had just the right twinkle in my eye, and should get the rose and all once he'd stuck his spoon in the wall."

And all? What was all? *Could the fool be referring to the costume the Society members wore for their disgusting rites? One like Simon found with his late brother's belongings? Yes, yes, the plot thickens.*

Mailer's pale eyes narrowed, but when he spoke again his tone was light. *Not intelligent, but clever.*

"I don't often wear the ring, actually, but only resurrected it to remind myself to be more careful in my pleasures."

"And doesn't *that* sound intriguing. You must tell me about this happy lapse. Perhaps I wish to make the same mistake."

"I didn't say it was a mistake, other than in shortening my pleasure." Mailer smiled as he attempted to remove the ring, but it was stuck tight around his pudgy finger. "Who's got old Barry's, do you know? Seems to me I heard the earl himself was seen sporting a rose stickpin for a day or two."

"Really?" *Damn. Gideon only wore the thing to draw out the Society, and only a few times before prudently putting it away again once he understood its true meaning.* "As Earl, the bugger inherited a near Midas treasury of geegaws and such. And we all know how vain he is, blast him. I doubt he wears the same stickpin twice in a decade. All while keeping me on a budget that would starve a mouse."

"Older brothers can be the very devil," Mailer agreed, dropping the subject in favor of pointing out the coach was about to arrive at his estate. "Ah, and would you look at that. There's my planklike wife, arrived ahead of us as ordered, and the two whelps, all at attention, awaiting their lord and master. That's all well and good, but there'd best be ice from the icehouse on the drinks table, or heads will roll."

Valentine looked out the off window of the coach to see Lady Caro and two young children standing

at attention on the drive directly in front of the doors
to the place, a double row of servants behind them,
lining the steps on either side. Ran a tight ship, Lord
Mailer did, and didn't everyone look so happy to
see him? They all (save a pair of yapping dogs, who
probably greeted everyone with near-insane antici-
pation) could have been facing a full firing squad
for all the joy in anyone's eyes.

How wonderful he'd thought to position a plain
coach at the inn they'd last passed along the roadway; he'd seen his coachman, Twitchill, lounging
on a bench just outside the inn door. The man had
put a finger to his slouch hat as the Mailer coach
rolled past. Valentine considered it prudent to never
enter into anyone's front door without knowing a
quick way out the back, as it were. Having to rely
on Lord Charles for return transport to London held
no appeal.

His gaze slid lastly to the tall, slender, plainly
dressed, rather round-shouldered young woman who
stood off to the right, darkly scowling behind her
spectacles while doing her best to control the two
small white dogs on their leashes. He may not have
seen her at all, were it not for the yapping dogs, and
the way a thin, watery sun seemed to find and catch
at streaks of gold in her darkly red hair. Hair she had
scraped back tightly into a bun thicker than his fist.

Was he the only one who noticed she seemed to
be in costume? Damn Perceval for an interring nui-
sance, clearly sending a watchdog to spy on him.

And to prefer some barque of frailty over *him?* Or was she only in disguise thanks to his reputation, so that he wouldn't pursue her? Insulting, that's what that was, either way.

"Lovely family, Charles, and clearly a well-schooled staff," he said, leaning back against the squabs once more. "But who's the drab?"

Mailer poked his head front and peered out as the coach door was opened and the steps pulled down, then laughed. "Ah, the redoubtable Miss Marchant. A piece of work, that one, but she seems able to control m'wife and the brats. Pity she's plain as a pikestaff and nearly as skinny. Can't abide a woman without tits. Tits and hips, and the more the better, right? A man deserves something soft to land in, I say."

And as he'd said all of this, Mailer was stepping onto the gravel, his words clearly heard by everyone. Miss Marchant, his children, his staff and, most certainly, his painfully thin little wife. The dogs, whose yapping might have been helpful, had instantly quieted and were even now lying hunched on their fat bellies, as if hoping to disappear into the ground.

"My lord," Lady Caroline said, dropping into a curtsy, tugging at the female child's skirts so that she did, as well, while the boy bowed to his father. "Mr. Redgrave. Welcome." She then turned to the governess. "Daisy? If you'll return them to the nursery, please?"

Half dragging the reluctant dogs, the woman

shuffled over to the small gathering and gave a quick, eyes-averted curtsy to the gentlemen before bringing the children to heel with a discreet clearing of her throat.

"Daisy, is it?" Valentine drawled, leaning his head slightly forward to attempt to discern the color of her downcast eyes. "That won't be difficult to remember. My sister's mare is named Daisy. Oddly enough, she's also a chestnut. Do you *ride* well, Daisy Marchant?"

Mailer gave a snort of laughter and pounded Valentine on the back in glee, nearly sending him reeling, even as the governess raised her eyes for a moment, a split second, no more, to glare daggers at them both.

Ah. Blue. Huge, and blue, and intelligent...and you'd enjoy nothing more than turning my guts into garters. Miss Daisy Marchant, you've done it now... and we will meet again.

"I CAN ONLY apologize again, Daisy," Lady Caro said miserably as she sat in front of her dressing table, bony shoulders slumped and eyes threatening to spill over with tears yet again. "His lordship never thinks to mind his tongue."

Daisy pulled the pair of silver-backed brushes through her ladyship's long blond hair. She'd been summoned to minister to her mistress, not an uncommon demand. Seven-year-old Lydia and three-year-old William had been tucked up after their porridge and left in charge of the nurse an hour earlier, and now it was time for the mistress of the household to go downstairs to play hostess again for her guest once the men left their brandy and cigars behind them in the dining room.

If Daisy could only get the woman to move. Lord knew she couldn't seem to get her to eat this past month. And when she did force down a few bites, as when taking her meals with guests, she more often than not, like tonight, then ran upstairs to vomit into her chamber pot.

She'd believed the woman ill, or increasing, but after overhearing Lord Mailer this afternoon, she was now nursing another theory. The woman had begun starving herself in order to avoid her husband's attentions. In Lady Caro's place, she knew she might have done the same thing…although she felt fairly certain she'd be more inclined to bounce a brick off his flaming red head. Perhaps she should suggest…?

But not now. First Daisy had a few questions she'd like answered before hopefully convincing her to return to the drawing room. "And Mr. Redgrave? I suppose we can say the same about him for his remarks?"

Lady Caroline looked into the mirror at Daisy's reflection. "I don't know. That was all so confusing to me. He was ever so kind to me in London. Perhaps it was only because you're a servant, although that shouldn't make a difference, should it? Not if he's a real gentleman."

"Perhaps that's the answer. He's no real gentleman."

"Although quite well set up, don't you think? And clean." The woman put her hands to her pale cheeks. "Oh, dear, I shouldn't have said that. Because I'm not in the least interested, of course. Still, if one has to, at least he's…" Her voice trailed off on a sigh.

Daisy let Lady Caroline's mind go off on whatever tangent she wished, giving herself permission to reflect (not for the first time), on the physical attributes of Mr. Valentine Redgrave.

She wondered first at his age, as she was all of two and twenty, not that such a fact would ever come into play, seeing as how he'd just hours earlier compared her to a horse, and then added that unspeakable innuendo about *riding.* Still, she thought he was probably no more than a few years her senior, as time had yet to carve a single line in his definitely handsome face.

His hair was a marvel, in such complete opposite to his finely cut clothes that seemed to caress his slimly muscular body, showing off his straight shoulders and strong thighs. From the neck down, he was the compleat gentleman, the pride of his tailor, but from the cravat up? That amused slash of mouth, that faintly foreign aquiline nose, that thick riot of nearly black hair that blew about his face? He appeared a paradox, his perfect features softening, making him look younger than his years. Approachable. Touchable…

But it was his eyes that had intrigued her most. They were not simply brown, but amber, long-lashed and—had it been her imagination?—sympathetic. She could actually imagine his eyes apologizing for the humiliating words coming from his mouth.

But that was ridiculous. He had come to Fernwood in Charles Mailer's company, hadn't he? That was really all Daisy needed to know.

"I'm feeling better now, thank you, Daisy. I suppose you can stop now."

Daisy shook herself back to attention. How long had she been brushing the woman's hair to help ease her headache? Long enough to feel a cramp between her purposely stooped shoulder blades. "Very good, madam. Shall I call Davinia now to put up your hair once more?"

Lady Caroline's sigh was audible, almost trembling: nearly a shudder. "Yes, I can put this off no longer, although it's just Mr. Redgrave this evening. Tomorrow there will be others and it will only grow worse. Charles hasn't even told me any names. Which could be more terrible, do you think? Knowing, or not knowing? Oh, now I'm saying too much. Perhaps some few drops of laudanum sprinkled on my handkerchief…?"

Daisy patted the woman's shoulder, wishing there were some way she could protect her. But there wasn't. Not yet. "And have you falling asleep, your nose in your teacup? Wouldn't that be a silly thing? You'll be fine, I promise you. Do you remember what I told you?"

Caroline nodded. "Speak only of the weather and my stepchildren and everyone will go away, believing me a dead bore. Which I am, you know. I don't understand the half of what anyone says, and seem to laugh at all the incorrect times. They make me *so* nervous. They're all so hard, so brittle."

And they show up every full moon, just like some mythical beasts risen from the depths, claws and fangs out and ready to pounce. Ah, Rose, how frightened you must have been when you realized your fate. But this time, sweet sister, this full moon, perhaps I'll be able to learn more....

"Daisy? Daisy, you're hurting me."

Daisy quickly removed her hand from Caro's shoulder, unaware she'd begun digging her fingertips into the woman's soft flesh. But she felt so useless. She hadn't been able to help her sister. She couldn't help this woman. Not yet. Not until she fully understood what was happening. Because there was more happening than she'd first been forced to believe.

"Forgive me, ma'am. My mind must have gone off wandering."

"And clearly not to a pleasant place," Lady Caroline said, rubbing at her thin shoulder. "I'm sorry if I upset you. I'm much better now, I promise. Yes, decidedly better. It must be my monthly flux that has me so upset."

Such intimate talk never made Daisy comfortable, especially Lady Caroline's seeming obsession with her monthly flux. "Is it so very painful?"

"Only in that it has not yet arrived," Lady Caroline said as Daisy lifted a small silver bell and rang for Davinia, who was doubtless already listening at the keyhole.

Daisy didn't care for Davinia, a sour-faced old woman who may be her ladyship's maid, but clearly knew her quarterly wages emanated from his lordship's purse.

"She tells him, you know," Caroline whispered quickly, as if able to read Daisy's thoughts. "I can't lie, because she tells him. *Shh,* here she comes. You go back up to the nursery now, Daisy, and don't bother to think you need must be here when I return." She raised her voice slightly. "Davinia takes very good care of me   don't you, Davinia?"

The older woman said nothing, but merely waved Daisy away and began twisting Caroline's hair back into its original topknot, ready to be strung through with paste pearls.

Daisy curtsied, wished her mistress a good evening and gratefully escaped the dressing room, stepping into the hallway without first checking to see if it was empty, and rolled her shoulders a time or two to relax them as she straightened her posture. Not a mistake she would have made if her mind weren't so otherwise occupied.

"Well, hello there, Daisy. And where would you be rushing off to?"

Redgrave.

She dropped into a quick, shoulders-front curtsy, keeping her eyes down. "I'm needed in the nursery, sir," she mumbled quietly as she rose once more.

"To teach them sums while they sleep, I suppose. But only after leaving her ladyship. Got your fingers in more than one pie, do you? Clever."

Daisy nearly raised her head, but managed to remain quite still in her subservient pose. "I'm confident you know what you mean, sir, but I do not. If you'll excuse me…?"

He stepped in front of her. "Curiosity compels the question. So, what is it? Impecunious orphaned child of some village vicar? Well-schooled but penniless daughter of a teacher? Or perhaps neither of those, but something more? The possibilities are nearly endless. Your mother married beneath her, your father was disowned, *you* were disowned, naughty puss? Please, must I go on?"

He wasn't the sort to give up easily. His smile told her that; he wasn't going to let her pass until she answered his question. If she moved to her left, he would move to his right; if she moved to her right, he would step to his left. The last thing she wished was to be caught up in some awkward dance of moves and countermoves, one he seemed eager to engage in with her.

"Impoverished daughter of the late Reverend James Marchant, Hampshire," she said, raising her chin. "He also taught Latin to the village boys, if that doesn't confuse the issue. In any case, *fere libenter homines id quod volunt credunt.*"

"'Men willingly believe what they wish.' Julius Caesar. So you're a bluestocking, as well. No wonder he steers clear. Very well, you may go."

Mailer; he meant Lord Mailer. Daisy, not about to pretend she didn't understand who *he* was, was instead about to point out that Mr. Redgrave did not have charge of either her comings or her goings. She quickly thought better of it. The man was already too interested by half, not that she could understand why. None of Mailer's other *guests* these past months had ever paid her the least attention.

"Thank you, sir," she said, curtsying yet again, hoping there was no sarcastic edge to her voice.

But as she moved to make good her exit he grabbed at her elbow, eased closer. She looked up into his odd amber eyes, and nearly flinched. She could see flecks of gold in them, and the intelligence, the humor. "You're more than welcome, Daisy. It's too late now, but in hindsight, considering the man doesn't have a discerning hair on his solid-as-a-plank head, do you ever think those hideous spectacles may have taken the thing a step too far?"

Really? She'd been rather proud of the spectacles. Plain glass, but thick as windowpanes, so that anyone would think she was half-blind. She'd been wonderfully overlooked for three months, by everyone. But not, drat him, Mr. Valentine Redgrave. He couldn't have shocked her more if he'd suddenly grown horns. Her stomach plummeted to her toes. Her blood ran cold, sending tiny pinpoint prickles to dancing on her skin. She wondered if she might faint.

"Forgive me, Mr. Redgrave. I have no idea what you mean by—"

He released her arm. "No, of course you don't. I won't even ask whom you work for, because I'd like to cherish the notion that even those hare-brained idiots in Downing Street wouldn't insert anyone so obvious. Just remember this if you will, as I certainly make it a point to do so. Appearances are often deceiving."

Whom did she work for? Goodness, whom did *he* work for? What on earth was he talking about?

Still, she took a chance. Perhaps it was the eyes... or that she was as foolish and gullible as her sister. Or that she so needed an ally that, like some drowning sailor, she would reach desperately for any floating straw. Because lately she'd been feeling as if she'd stumbled into something very much over her head, and if Redgrave had shown up here for some reason of his own, well, maybe he knew what was going on. "And behavior can be deceiving, as well, Mr. Redgrave?"

"Good girl. I loathe long explanations, but if my instincts are correct—and they very nearly always are—one may be needed here, from each of us. Where can we meet tomorrow?"

Meet? Daisy hadn't expected that. Then again, she didn't seem to expect anything that came out of the man's mouth. "We…um. I insist Lydia and William be out-of-doors at least three hours a day, one directly after breaking their fast, and another two after luncheon. Dependent on the weather, naturally."

"Naturally. Wouldn't want the little dears to catch a chill. Then we'll be well chaperoned, if that worries you," Valentine said, nodding his approval. "Very well, I'll be certain to be on my best behavior so as to not shock the kiddies. Until then, Daisy, I suggest you don't attempt anything foolish, such as searching my rooms. You might startle Piffkin."

She blinked. "You brought your dog here?"

When Valentine Redgrave smiled in real amusement, it was as if the sun had just come out, to burn away any remnants of a cloudy day. Daisy could fairly fancy she felt its warmth, and had to fight a ridiculous urge to bring herself closer to the intoxicating heat. She'd been forced to depend on her wits on her own for so long…had she actually come to hope for help in any port?

"My valet, Daisy, although I see your point. But, contrary to what his name might imply, unlike Mailer's pitiful specimens, he doesn't bark. He bites." He glanced toward the door to Lady Caro's dressing room, as if he'd heard something. "And now I must go, and so must you."

"But we don't even… That is, I don't see why we should— Oh, hang it," she ended to his departing back as he headed for the main staircase.

What had just happened?

But she knew what had just happened.

A pair of soft amber eyes had just happened. A warm smile. That thick mane of hair her fingers itched to touch.

Was Valentine Redgrave a badly needed ally, or an exceedingly clever foe?

Or was he simply the most beautiful man she'd ever seen up close? Perhaps she was just as gullible and needy and soon to be disillusioned as poor, doomed Rose.

CHAPTER THREE

"JUST THE TWO of us for breakfast, Charles?" Valentine asked as he was ushered into the morning room by one of the footmen. "How cozy."

His lordship looked up from his plate of coddled eggs, a bit of yolk clinging to his chin. "You were observed speaking with Miss Marchant yesterday evening," he said without preamble. "Why? Making some late-night assignation after all you said to the contrary?"

So he'd been correct; that door had opened a crack.

Hmm. Take umbrage? Look puzzled? What to do, what to do? Valentine knew he needed a reaction, quickly.

He spoke while making his way along the sideboard, loading his plate with a steady hand, his back to Mailer.

"Daisy? Although she'd be more fittingly named after some noxious, prickly weed," he said, having decided on a course of action. He would—for the moment—ignore the fact that Mailer's servants reported to him, and concentrate on keeping Daisy's secret safe. "I fear my gentlemanly conscience belatedly got the better of me. When I chanced to see the sad creature slumping down the hall on my way downstairs, I felt bound by good manners to apologize for my earlier remarks. Lord knows she's got enough *problems* on her own, without me adding to them. One can only hope the poor woman doesn't now decide to take me in affection, for that would only lead to sorry disappointment. She couldn't raise my *interest* were she to fling her naked self at my feet."

Adding a single slice of buttered toast to his plate, he turned about to face his host, his eyelids narrowed. "Now if you'd care to explain *why* my movements are being watched, I'd own to being quite curious to hear your answer."

Perfect. Admit to something—mea culpa, mea culpa—and then quickly turn the tables so that the other person is cast into the role of wrongdoer. Kate's advice did come in handy from time to time. Look at Mailer—the wind seems to have entirely gone out of his sails.

"I—I only thought to ask if she'd bothered you in any way," Mailer said, not precisely a master of improvisation. "My wife took her on a few months ago while I was not at home. She's no thief, I tempted her by leaving my ring on the hallway table…"

Valentine sat himself down and flourished his serviette before placing it on his lap. "That ring? Perhaps it simply wasn't to her taste."

Mailer held out his hand, the diamond at the center of the golden rose catching the sunlight. "There's nothing wrong with this—you don't think it isn't *masculine* enough, do you? I mean, a rose?"

I could skewer that damn ring through his nose and lead him around by it, no question. A true follower, nothing remotely resembling a leader. A man we need, but not the man we seek. "Nonsense, Charles, I've already told you it's a fine ring." Then, unable to resist, he added with an indulgent smile, "If you favor that sort of thing."

Mailer twisted the *thing* around his finger, and this time slipped it off and into his pocket. "The thing is, I believe Miss Marchant may be *smart*." He said the word as if this were somehow vile, to be avoided at all costs.

Valentine coughed into his hand, to cover a grin. "Really? I would have thought that preferable in a governess, perhaps even mandatory."

"They're just nursery brats, what do they need of a governess? Companion is more like it, that's what she is. I don't like it. I didn't mind, not at first. But she makes my skin crawl somehow. I catch her looking at me, and I—"

"Look back?" Valentine asked as he cut into a thick slice of ham; who would have thought sparring with idiots could so increase his appetite. Then he looked up, pulling a face. "Charles, you must be jesting. Nobody could be *that* desperate. It would be like seducing a broomstick."

"God's teeth, no! When I have— No! She's in

the way at times, that's all. Besides, I've never been partial to red hair."

Valentine took a bite of ham while keeping his amazed gaze on Mailer. "Really?"

"I know, I know. I've red hair, and I loathe it. But it's on top of my head, so at least I'm spared having to look at it."

Valentine threw back his head and laughed. "Charles, you're a complete card. It's no wonder I like you so much as to bury myself here in the country," he said, and watched as the man preened. "Now tell me again about this amazing party you dangled in front of me, as I only see the two of us here. And your lady wife, of course."

Mailer frowned. "Yes, I know. I received a note earlier. It seems there has been a delay of some sort, and the remainder of the party won't arrive for another few days."

Valentine considered this dollop of news. Perhaps the rest of the *part*y was still out hunting for their missing shipment from France? Searching for their goods, and for one Honorable Ambrose Webber, who had so foolishly put a period to his own existence rather than be captured, and who now was most probably nothing more than a skeleton lying at the bottom of the Straits of Dover, bits of him having filled the bellies of a variety of marine life.

Valentine rather hoped there wouldn't be a fish course at dinner.

"That's a pity, then, isn't it? Do these tardy guests

have names, or are they to be a surprise? I rather dislike surprises, Charles. You said I was in for elevated political conversation and some entertainment that indulges what even the most lenient fleshpots in Piccadilly refuse. I suppose I could deal with the loss of the former, but if you've been exaggerating the latter, well, then, Charles, shame on you, and I'll be leaving."

"No, no, you can't leave— That is to say, you'll miss all the fun! As to the other guests? Well, you see now, that's the thing," Mailer said, pushing a split, smoked herring around his plate with his fork. "It's all true, just what I said—beyond your wildest imaginings, I promise you. But…but I explained this, didn't I? No, I suppose I didn't." He looked across the table at Valentine, his expression hopeful. "I didn't? Are you sure?"

Valentine imagined the herring shoved halfway down Mailer's throat. Nasty, but the image helped him tamp down his temper. "No, you didn't, and yes, I'm quite sure. Why don't you do that now, if you're done dissecting your kippers. I admit to being highly intrigued."

Mailer put down his fork. "The thing is…the thing is, I'm not certain who is coming. It…*varies*. Yes, that's the word. Varies. Variety being the…the something of life."

"The very spice of life, the thing that gives it all its flavor. Cowper said it first, I believe." Valentine sat back in his chair. "I see." Then he sat front again, glaring at Mailer over the candlesticks. "No, that's a lie. I don't see. Are you host of this *party* or not?"

Mailer dismissed the servants with an abrupt wave of his hand, then leaned forward toward Valentine, not speaking until the door closed behind the footmen. "Look, sometimes it's…well, the guests are known, and we meet here at Fernwood. But at other times we meet somewhere else, and the entertainment is more…anonymous."

"Here, perhaps there—and you say you don't *know?* Not the time, not the place? My first instincts were right, weren't they? You're all talk, Charles, boastful talk and wishful thinking. I should simply hire a coach and head back to town. I've already explained my appetites, and you assured me—"

"Oh, but I meant it, I meant every word! Anything and anyone you want, anything and anyone you desire. London's brothels are but pale imitations of what you and I deserve, just as I told you that night after we left Madame La Rue's and you complained yours all objected to the restraints."

"Love knots, and not for long," Valentine corrected, remembering with extreme distaste the *sharing* of experiences Charles had insisted upon after they'd departed the brothel. "Compliance. It's all in the way you present the thing."

"Yes, if you're into begging," Mailer said, his eyes gone flat and hard. "If it's pleading you want to do, it can be arranged, but why beg when you can demand, hmm? Did I tell you about the time I—"

It was time to take charge of the little fish.

"Again with the boasts, and all as you continue to tell me I must be patient," Valentine said, tossing his serviette on the table and getting to his feet; if he took one more bite he might just cast up his accounts in Mailer's face. "Two days, Charles. I can almost enjoy being bucolic for two days, but no more. Understood?"

Mailer rose, as well. "Yes, yes, do that. Anything you wish, anything at all. The grounds are lovely, you know."

"But your wife isn't. I do not want to see her at table again while I'm in residence. Do you understand?"

Mailer nodded furiously. "She's sadly indisposed as of this moment. Is there anything else you require? One of the maids? I can personally recommend—"

Valentine cut him off. "A man of my name and reputation doesn't so lower himself as to diddle the servants." He took a line from his grandmother's verbal arsenal and asked, "Were you raised by wolves?"

"I—I—I say, Valentine, that wasn't called for."

Valentine bowed, figuratively feeding out more line. "You're correct. Forgive me, Charles. I'm embarrassed to say my hot Spanish blood doesn't deal well with delays. If you'll excuse me now, I believe I should take myself off outside, perhaps to walk away my foul mood, partake of a liquid lunch at some nearby pub. We'll speak again at the dinner table. Perhaps by then you'll have more news on your other guests. Should we call them guests? Fellow participants, perhaps?"

"Ha-ha," Mailer laughed nervously, and waved him on his way.

At the doorway, Valentine turned to see the man once again attacking his kippers, seemingly confident the conversation had gone well, that he'd ridden over some rough ground and traversed it all to his satisfaction.

What a total ass.

Valentine returned to his assigned bedchamber, running down Piffkin in the dressing room. The valet retrieved his master's newly brushed hat and smoothed gloves before handing him a carved ivory-topped sword cane.

"Really, Piffkin? It's not as if I'm to be strutting up Bond Street, now is it?" Valentine asked, refusing the hat and gloves. He did accept the cane, but only to prop it against the wall. "As for the cane, I'm taking a leisurely country stroll over my new bosom chum's estate, not facing a Piccadilly alley alone at midnight."

The dour-faced man of uncertain years merely shrugged and turned back to the pressing iron he was employing to smooth one of a pile of pristine neckcloths currently residing on a tabletop. Piffkin wore white cotton gloves at all times, even when pressing neckcloths or laying out towels for the master's bath. This, more than anything, described Piffkin. The gloves, and his fatherly concern for *young Master Valentine*.

"There may be bears in the woods, sir," he said in way of explanation.

"Piffkin, there haven't been bears on this damp island in a thousand years. All right, except those brought here from Europe for bear-baiting, a despicable excuse for sport."

"Indeed. One or two may have escaped a cruel master, and even now lurk close by, eager to revenge themselves on any passerby so foolish as to stumble about in unfamiliar woods, unarmed."

Piffkin turned to smile broadly at Valentine, showing a remarkable gold tooth Valentine had always admired but never dared to inquire about since he was seven, and the valet, then nursemaid, had told him he'd been given it as a reward for saving a princess in a tower. If the man didn't want his charge to know the true story, then so be it. Valentine had secrets he wouldn't care to share with Piffkin, either.

"Observe me as I dutifully tuck the cane beneath my arm, thankful to have such a caring friend concerned for my welfare."

"Concerned? I simply don't wish to have to clean up the mess in an effort to make you presentable for the dowager countess. Sewing your ears back on and such before laying you out," Piffkin said, the gold tooth in evidence once more.

"How much does Trixie pay you over and above

what I do, Piffkin? How often do you report to her? I've always wondered."

"Her ladyship worries over all her chicks. Be on the lookout for those bears, Master Valentine. I do believe they are plentiful here," the valet said, and returned to his pressing, the conversation obviously over, his charge dismissed to go bear hunting.

Valentine was fairly well pleased with himself as he made his way downstairs and was bowed out-of-doors by a small boy in preposterously gilded livery.

For one thing, he knew for certain now that coincidence had nothing to do with his new friendship with Mailer. As he had been cultivating the man, the man had been cultivating him, most probably on orders sent to him at his country estate, which had brought Mailer hieing back to Mayfair. Purposely seeking him out, being amenable, testing him as to his politics and his pleasures, hanging the bait of unlimited debauchery while Valentine pretended an avid interest in both.

That was why he could run hot and cold with Mailer, threaten to leave and be indulged, insult and be smiled at in return. Mailer was acting on orders: get the fellow here and we'll see what we've got. It hadn't hurt that, while feigning drunkenness, Valentine had babbled about collapsed tunnels at Redgrave Manor and dirty little books full of wild tales that would put the ancient Kama Sutra to the blush.

Valentine knew he wasn't Gideon, but he was a Redgrave, probably appearing as the easiest target for the Society. How did they plan to use him? So far, he'd convinced Mailer he was a kindred spirit, both in sexual tastes and politics. He'd waxed poetic about the glorious Bonaparte over a half-dozen bottles of wine, extolling the freedom of men and the injustice of this English folly concerning titles and younger sons. Being the first to push free of the womb took no special talent, it was sheer good luck, and deserved no special rewards, Bonaparte would reward endeavor, not birth order, et cetera.

He'd been brilliant, he thought, but he wasn't foolish enough to believe he'd got here on his own; he was here at Fernwood because the Society wanted him here.

And if they wanted him dead?

It was going to take more than a swordstick to protect him if he made a misstep. More than the stiletto tucked in his boot or the small pistol stuck into an inside pocket of his hacking jacket.

At least he had cleared one possible distraction out of his way. The so timid and sad Lady Caroline would be confined to her rooms. She was safer there, he hoped, and at least she wouldn't be looking down the dining table at him with pleading eyes, or sadly staring at the wall, her mind gone somewhere else, making him want to forget he still needed Charles Mailer breathing. He contented himself by thinking the woman would make a much happier widow.

Now to get rid of Perceval's so-obvious agent. He worked most effectively alone, without having to worry about anyone else getting in the way and muddying the waters. Especially a woman, damn it.

Leisurely swinging his cane, Valentine set off across the scythed lawns in search of the patently false governess and her charges, telling himself he was merely interested in rousting the woman from the estate.

But perhaps he wouldn't shoo her back to Downing Street quite yet…not before he had satisfied his curiosity to see Miss Daisy Marchant with her hair down.…

"I WANT TO go inside, Daisy," seven-year-old Lydia complained. "My boots are pinching. Why did we have to wear boots? I don't like it here. It's muddy, and it smells."

Daisy gritted her teeth, inwardly cursing Valentine Redgrave for a slugabed. Did he really think children slept past the first crowing rooster of the morning? They'd been up, and fed, and dragged into the fresh air before the dew had left the grass, and she would soon be at her wits' end to keep them amused…and out of doors.

"I told you, sweetheart, I've decided upon a lesson in botany, and that's why we're in the greenhouse, to learn the names of all the pretty flowers." *And to stay out of sight of the windows of the house, and Lord Charles Mailer, not that Mr. Redgrave seems to be a man of his word.*

Lydia grinned rather evilly. "Willie doesn't care

about botany. He's eating dirt out of that pot over there."

"Oh, laws—now I remember why I take care my usual charges are all above the age of ten. William, stop that!" Daisy hastened across the hard dirt floor to where the child was happily smearing dark, rich soil over his chubby cheeks. "What on earth do you think you're doing, young man?"

Willie looked up at her, his small baby teeth and round blue eyes shining in his otherwise muddy brown face, and shrugged.

Clearly, Daisy thought, the boy was a prodigy. He didn't answer her because it should be obvious to her what he was doing. Either that, or the child would eat anything that even vaguely resembled food, which was more likely.

She picked him up at the waist and held him at arms' length in order to carry him to a nearby trough and pump, where she made short work out of cleaning his hands and face, which didn't mean her plain morning gown came away from the exercise in pristine condition. Her cuffs were soggy and there were a few splashes of mud on her bodice. William's little face, however, shone.

"You didn't find any pretty pink squiggly things in the pot, did you, William?" she asked, more than slightly concerned as she bent to go eye to eye with him. "You didn't eat any?"

"You mean worms, don't you? Willie eats worms,

Willie eats worms!" Lydia trilled, dancing about in her glee, her pinching boots forgotten.

"He does not!" Daisy protested, lifting the boy down from the wooden table and standing him on the dirt. "Stay," she warned tightly.

Willie began to cry.

"Willie eats worms, Willie eats—"

"For the love of heaven, Lydia, *stifle yourself.*" Daisy winced. She was being a bad governess. A bad, bad governess. Clearly the children had no place in the greenhouse, and should be taken inside for a midmorning snack. William was always up for a snack, and Lydia could be easily bribed with the promise of a special story before bedtime. One having to do with dragons, or perhaps man-eating fish. Any sort of monster or ogre would do, as long as they died horribly in the end and the princess was saved by the handsome knight.

And speaking of handsome knights, she thought even as she pointed out a particularly fine rose to the children, *I'm more now than ever convinced there aren't any in my immediate future. I picked the one perfect spot for us to meet and talk without being observed, and all I've gotten for my genius so far are two filthy children and my hair misbehaving badly in all this humid heat. Where* is *the man?*

"Now, children, this is a rose," she said, holding on to the tail of William's small jacket so he couldn't wander. "I'm convinced it has some intricate Latin name, but for now we'll simply call it a rose. A…a pink rose. Why don't you sniff it, Lydia? It should smell delicious."

"Ow! Ow, ow, ow!" Lydia cried out a moment later, holding on to one hand with the other and hopping about in circles. "I'm bleeding, I'm bleeding!"

William began to cry. Again.

"You must have grabbed a thorn," Daisy said, reaching for Lydia. "Stop hopping and let me see. Ah, yes, there it is. Let me just pluck it out."

"No! Don't touch it! This is all your fault, Daisy. You made me hurt myself."

"Yes, of course," Daisy bit out as she attempted to hold the child still. "I thought making you cry would be the perfect topping for my morning."

"My, my, my, what do we have here? I was drawn inside by what I thought was a voice raised in song, a song of worms, no less, only to find a pretty princess, *crying.* No, no, this cannot be countenanced."

Daisy's spine went stiff at the highly dramatic, definitely mocking tone in Valentine Redgrave's voice. Now *he bothers to present himself? Just when I'm at my worst? How wonderful.*

There was one thing to say, however: Lydia was definitely all female. The child took one look at Valentine and her cries were cut off as if by magic. *The magic of a smile.* "Are you a prince?"

"Indeed I am, fair lady, late from the kingdom of Redgravia," Valentine said, bowing as if to a queen.

"Oh, good grief." Daisy longed to murder him, and she'd always believed herself to be a calm, carefully controlled person. Perhaps a tad sarcastic when pushed too far, a failing her father had never been reluctant to point out to her, but she was by and large, she thought, a reasonable person. "Miss Lydia's got a rose thorn stuck in her thumb and refuses to let me dislodge it," she said, which was the only greeting he would get from her. A prince? Indeed!

"And I can see why she refused you, Miss Marchant," Valentine said, going down on one knee in the dirt. "Clearly this is a magical thorn, and only a prince of the blood can remove it."

"Then perhaps you'd be so good as to toddle off and fetch us one," Daisy said sweetly, her blood boiling now. Did he have to look so much like a fairy-tale prince?

His smile made her feel petty. After all, he was only trying to help. The thorn had to be removed, and she didn't relish chasing a screeching Lydia all over the greenhouse to get the job done.

"Your hand, fair princess, if you please," he said, holding out his own.

Lydia curtsied and offered her hand (both done rather saucily, which made Daisy wonder if some females were simply born to beguile the opposite sex—a gift from the gods she herself had not been granted).

Valentine looked deeply into the girl's eyes, complimenting them on their sky-blue brilliance, and at the same time managed to remove the thorn—which wasn't all that deep in any case. He then dabbed at her thumb with a pristine handkerchief he'd produced from somewhere, neatly blotting away the single drop of blood.

"And now to banish the pain with a kiss," he said. "By your leave, my princess?"

As Daisy opened her mouth to protest, Lydia nodded furiously...and Valentine bent, pressed a kiss on the child's thumb.

"You've mud on your royal knee, prince," she said as he stood up once more.

"Better than on my nose," he countered, and then laughed as Daisy instinctively raised her fingers to her face.

"There's no mud on my nose."

"True. But your reaction tells me if I'd told you not to turn about because someone is standing behind you, the first thing you'd do is turn around. That's the trouble with women. You're too curious. I can't have that."

He couldn't have that? The nerve of the man! She'd thought he'd be serious today. But here they were again, as they were last night, with him hinting at something she didn't understand. It was a game she had no interest in playing at the moment. "Children, it's time to go inside," she said quietly. *As far away from this genial madman as we can get!*

But Lydia, who minutes earlier would have leaped at this suggestion, was too busy staring at her thumb in some bemusement. "I don't want to go inside. I want to look at the pretty man…the pretty flowers. Don't we, Willie?"

Since William was sucking on one of a handful of pastilles he'd inexplicably come in possession of, he neither agreed nor disagreed. He was too busy smiling up at Valentine.

"You're incorrigible, and all your children will grow up to be entirely unmanageable," she accused him quietly.

"You can't ruin a child by encouraging their imaginations, my dearest grandmother always said, you can only achieve that by breaking his natural spirit to suit your will." Valentine grinned. "She raised the entire current crop of Redgraves, you understand."

"That explains so much. Your sisters were allowed to revel in fantasies and you and your brothers were given anything and everything you wished."

"Two brothers, and we learned life has its responsibilities, as well, and one younger sister, who variously dubbed me her shining prince or the ogre at the gate, depending on her mood. Luckily for the young lady here, I suppose, I mostly was cast in the role of rescuing hero. With Kate, you rather had to be."

Daisy shifted her feet in slight embarrassment. "Well, you certainly took to the role."

"Thank you." He gifted both them with an elegant bow. "Your humble servant, ladies." Then he straightened, and called out to a young servant who'd just entered the greenhouse. "Here, young man," he said, already reaching into his pocket, to extract a coin quickly slipped into an entirely new pocket. "The young miss wishes to have you assist her in gathering a large bouquet for the nursery, if you please. As for young Master William, he would very much desire a small trowel, a pot of water, an apron of sorts and a low table he can use to make pies. Mud pies. All young gentlemen enjoy patting out mud pies. Isn't that right, Master William? Why, I can nearly feel the pleasurable experience of Redgrave mud squeezing out from between my fingers. Pure heaven, I promise you."

For a child who seemed to never understand much of anything Daisy said to him, young Master William showed a quick intelligence in grasping what Valentine had offered. He grabbed the servant's hand and began tugging him back to the trough.

"And a second bouquet, my prince, in thanks for your rescue," Lydia gushed, dropping into her best curtsy before following after her brother.

Daisy opened her mouth to protest, but just as quickly shut it again. He was making the children disappear, and she was about to learn why, whether she wished to or not. She probably really wished to, much as she tried to tell herself she did not. She'd just have to stand here with her hair twisting itself up into ridiculous corkscrew curls and attempt to prove she was reasonably intelligent in spite of the mud and her damp cuffs.

"They'll be safe enough, and near enough, for the

few minutes we need, Miss Marchant," Valentine assured her. He reached out and touched one of the errant ringlets hugging her nape, and a shiver ran down her neck, skipped across her shoulder, as if anticipating his further touch. "Almost alive, isn't it, winding itself around my finger. I should like to see it all down."

A lesser man would have burst into flame as she glared at him in her most stern governess manner. "Then it can only be hoped your grandmother also taught you how to deal well with disappointment."

"Sadly, her one failing. Yes, well, down to business, I suppose," he said, crossing his arms and leaning one hip against a potting table. "Now, who are you?"

"Who are *you?*" she countered, taking a precautionary step backward. "I already told you who I am, although I'm still at a loss to know why I did anything so foolish."

"And your name is Daisy," he said, shaking his head. "Really, Miss Marchant? That's all you could come up with?"

All right, now she reversed direction, and took a step forward. "And what's so terrible about Daisy?"

He shrugged. "For one, as I've already mentioned, my—"

"Your sister's mare is named Daisy. Yes, I remember. How very droll. Nevertheless, that is my name, and I'm fine with it, thank you very much.

How is it for you, lugging about a silly romantic burden like Valentine?"

He touched a hand to his forehead in a rather negligent salute. "I suppose we're even now. Very good, Miss Marchant. Now tell me why you're here."

She decided to be deliberately obtuse. "Because you demanded we meet, and I agreed, figuring you for a madman who must be treated with some care." *And because I'm afraid you're going to tell me something I already suspect, and much as I don't want to hear it, I probably need to hear it before I'm forced to finally believe it.*

"Again, I salute your attempts at wit. But much as I'm enjoying our sparring session, I don't believe we have time to indulge ourselves much longer, so I'll keep this brief. I want you gone from this estate, now, and you can tell whomever it is who sent you that only the luck of having a shortsighted idiot as your quarry has stood between you and a rather messy end. Oh, please add that the Honorable Mr. Valentine Redgrave sends his regards, and if he is ever so fortunate as to discover your employer's name, the man can expect a visit from him. One he won't care for, tell him. Sending a female here. Madness."

"Because…?" Daisy asked, hoping if she pretended to go along with his nonsense he'd at last say *something* that made sense about why *he* was here. Right now, all he was succeeding in doing was alternately frightening and confounding her.

"You know damn well *because,* and I'll be damned if I'll be put to the blush explaining the obvious. We warned them, but clearly they only half believed us, otherwise they wouldn't have put a woman within ten miles of this place. They told you something, as you've already disguised yourself, not that any but a fool would be deceived, so you'd have to at least be able to guess at what could happen to you if—"

He stopped, blinked and whispered something under his breath. From the look on his face, she was glad she couldn't hear what he said.

Her heart was pounding now, whether in dread or confirmation of her worst fears, she couldn't be sure. One thing was certain, she couldn't allow him to stop now. "Yes? What could happen to me if—?"

"I can't believe this. I can't believe those idiots didn't warn you."

This conversation was going nowhere, and she was finished being his audience. Clearly he was convinced she was someone she was not. She would give him one more chance to untwist his tongue, but only because she didn't seem to have a choice.

Daisy jammed her fists against her hips. "That's because there are no id— There is no *they.* There's no *he* or *him,* either. Can't you please endeavor to get that through your thick skull? I'm here because I'm employed here. I'm a governess, and I dress as I dress because a governess does not seek out the attentions of husbands and sons or the wrath of wives and mothers, not if she wishes warm food in her belly and a dry roof over her head for more than a fortnight. Please let me know when you want to stop speaking in circles, and perhaps we can meet again. Otherwise, this conversation is *over,* Mr. Redgrave. And if you have not only lately escaped a straitwaistcoat and a cell in Bedlam, then I suggest you consider being measured for both."

"All right, we'll play it your way, mostly because I'm beginning to believe I've made a horrible mistake, God help me. You're nothing more than a vicar's innocent orphaned daughter, making her way in the world as best she can. Not here to spy on his lordship, not here to spy, God forbid, on any of us Redgraves who might have shown up. Whatever's true, whatever I'm beginning to believe, you'd better believe this. Gloves off, Miss Marchant—you've fallen into a den of monsters that gather here monthly to play their terrible games. A hellfire club, Miss Marchant, if you've ever heard the term. Devil horns, hideous costumes, sacrificial altars, the entire gambit of debauchery. They rape women like you for sport, pass them about among them—and that may be the least of it. You have to leave. Now."

This was worse than she'd thought, worse than anything she could have ever imagined. Daisy staggered where she stood, nearly lost her balance. "What?" She couldn't locate the strength to speak above a strangled whisper. "*What* did you just say to me?"

"At last, your full attention. You heard me. Take women, use them, perhaps then kill in their excitement or simply to cover their crimes, something I've just recently begun to suspect of the imbecilic but dangerous Lord Mailer. *They,* whoever they are over and above Mailer, consider it their right to use and abuse women in pursuit of their own pleasures, among other things. If that isn't enough to convince you, take a good long look at your mistress. She lives in terror, doesn't she? How long have you been here?"

"Still, if one has to, at least he's..."

At least he's clean. Daisy heard Lady Caroline's words whispered again in her ear.

She wanted to scream, to run. But she had to stand her ground, hear the rest of it. She had to know, truly, why Valentine Redgrave had come here. Was he really here in the role of rescuing prince? No, of course not. He was here on some sort of mission of his own, not on orders from the Crown. He certainly hadn't come here to help *her.*

"How…how long have I been here? You asked that, didn't you? A few—" Daisy had to pause, attempt to catch her breath, for she seemed to have forgotten how to breathe. *Rose. Ah, God...Rose. Maybe I'm finally getting closer.* "Near…nearly three months."

"Then at least two full moons. Good. Since you're not deaf and blind, Miss Marchant, you must have seen something during that time, must suspect something odd going on. Think a moment."

He knew about the full moon? How could he know that? It was only by keeping her diary that she had eventually realized how different things were at Fernwood leading up to the first night of the full moon. Just as they were now, with another full moon in the offing. Six months ago, Rose had left London, just before a full moon.

"I don't know what you mean by that. I haven't— Oh, all right, all right. Don't look at me that way. Yes. Yes, I've noticed things. People. Mostly gentlemen, but some of their wives, as well. They stay for a week or less. Coming and going at strange hours while they're here, sometimes gone all night. But what you're saying is so utterly preposterous that I—"

"All right, that could be useful. Did you happen to hear any names? It would be an immense help to me, Miss Marchant, if you remember any names. There's much more to this than men indulging their fantasies."

"Downing Street," Daisy breathed, a tight fist squeezing her heart as her supposition was confirmed. "You teased me with Downing Street. You… you thought I was some…some sort of *spy* for the government? Spying on Lord Mailer? On *you,* for pity's sake?" She clapped her hands to her chest. "A spy? *Me?*"

"Presumptive, assuming fool that I am, yes, I did.

God's teeth, everything you've said is the truth, I can see it clearly now. You're a governess and I'm...I am who I am, let's say that, shall we—an interested party. But let's buck up and get past all that, shall we?"

"Buck up? After what you've just said? You ask a lot, Mr. Redgrave. But you do believe me. Finally. *Why?*"

"Like one of my dogs with a marrow bone. All right, but quickly. I believe you because no one could feign the pure shock and horror I just saw in your eyes, not even me. Forgive me for frightening you needlessly, but in my defense, you did refuse to listen. And forgive me yet again for now begging that we meet once more, tonight, to give you time to prepare a list of any names you might recall. Don't ask Lady Caro or any of the servants—that would be needlessly dangerous—but rely only on your own memory."

"I...I've been keeping a journal."

Valentine sighed audibly. "Many do. I hope you keep it well hidden. I'll have already arranged transport for you to London, or wherever you wish to go. Do you have adequate funds?" He shook his head at that. "No, of course she doesn't, and she certainly can't apply to Mailer for her quarterly wages. I'll provide that, as well. She can't even risk emptying her cupboard, carrying a traveling bag. But we'll manage it."

Daisy was rapidly getting her feet back under

her. "I'm standing right here, Mr. Redgrave. Please cease in referring to me as *she*."

At last he smiled. "My apologies. I often think out loud."

"An unfortunate habit you should do your utmost to curb."

"Yes, definitely a governess. I don't know how I could have mistaken you for anything else. Just believe this. Things are about to get messy, Miss Prunes and Prisms, so you leave here tonight, do you understand? If you've nowhere else to go, I suppose I can turn you over to my sister at Redgrave Manor until this is settled. Can't have you just roaming about, not once they realize you may know too much. Plus, frankly, you're very much in my way and I need to devote my full attention on keeping my own self safe."

Daisy's senses were whirling and she struggled to hang on, not fall into hysterics. Banish her, toss her away? Just when she was at last making some progress? "But— but what about the children? Lady Caroline? If even half of what you've said is true, they're in danger, aren't they?"

"No more than they were in before your arrival. Besides, I'm here now."

Now she fought a sneer. "Oh, yes, *you're* here now. Why didn't I realize that at once? I'm in the way, but it's nothing at all for you to protect Lady Caroline and two fairly unruly children. The brave

Prince of Mud Pies. I see your point. Everything will be so much better now."

"I'll ignore the insult, and assume you aren't overjoyed by my plan for you. I suppose I should be grateful you aren't in strong hysterics, actually."

"I considered them, but discarded the idea in favor of marveling at your arrogance."

"Ouch. And may I say, if Kate had had you as governess Redgrave Manor would have been even more interesting. You ruffle, Miss Marchant, but your powers of recovery are astounding."

He couldn't know how she had long ago learned to guard her emotions; being set loose on her own into an uncaring world at the age of seventeen had taught her to hide her feelings behind an ironclad facade. Tears were a waste of time and aided nothing, and appearing vulnerable was dangerous. She was a survivor, and she would survive this most horrible truth; but she would not leave this place until she had somehow located her sister. Oh, God, what remained of her sister...

"You refuse to leave, don't you?"

"My congratulations, Mr. Redgrave, that's the first correct assumption you've arrived at since you first stepped out of the traveling coach yesterday, that wretched insult on your lips. No, I'm not leaving."

He looked at her for a long moment and she felt as if he'd just stripped her naked, all the way to her soul.

"But not in any misguided idea of protecting the children or her ladyship, although that may play some part in it now that you're here. Women take ridiculous ideas like that into their heads all the time."

"Are you thinking out loud again, Mr. Redgrave, or just being insulting?"

"I'm sorry, but truth is truth. If you'd been there to see my idiot sister when Simon slipped into the— Never mind. You came to Fernwood for reasons of your own. I was right as far as I went. I merely went too far, including Downing Street in my theory. Perceval meant it when he said he wasn't all that interested in what we Redgraves uncovered. But then why? Why are you here, why do you stay where you're clearly unhappy?"

She had no quick answers for him. At the moment, what she wanted most was to be alone. To think about Rose, come to grips with what she'd suspected since her very first weeks at Fernwood. Valentine Redgrave had given her more answers than he could possibly know, but there were still so many questions. "Children! It's time to go!"

Lydia came scampering back down the pathway, clutching a small bouquet of roses she promptly thrust at Valentine. "Here, my prince. Tobias snipped off all the thorns for me."

Lydia's girlish lovesickness was palpable. Daisy rolled her eyes. This was why, throughout history, men retained such swollen heads: women persisted in foolishly adoring them for no good reason. *Just*

*like poor, poor Rose. I have to get away from this
man. I have to think. I don't want to think...*

Daisy turned to the child in near desperation.
"Where's William, Lydia?"

"His mud pies aren't dry, and Tobias says they'll
fall to pieces if they aren't allowed to dry. They're
very nice. Tobias showed him how to push colored
pebbles in them to make faces, and tiny leaves for
hair." She looked up at Valentine. "Not that *I* would
enjoy doing anything so young and silly." She then
quickly hid her hands, caked with drying mud, behind her back.

"I'll come back for them later," Daisy promised,
shooing the girl ahead of her.

"Farewell, dear prince!" Lydia called back to Valentine, who once again demonstrated his finesse
with a courtly bow—young, handsome, carefree—
just as if words like *rape* and *hellfire club* had never
passed his lips.

Then he turned about, to depart the greenhouse,
without setting a time or place for them to meet
again. He'd probably just pop up like some jack-in-
the-box when she least expected him. She watched
as he took up a cane he must have rested against one
of the other potting tables, gave it a twirl or two before tucking it beneath his arm.

Truly, the man was insufferable. Yet she felt safer
knowing he was here. Safer, but oh, so very much sad-
der. And even more determined to confront Charles
Mailer, now that she knew what to ask him. Not *where*

did you imprison my sister? but *what did you do with her body?* Because there was no more room for hope now, was there? She'd known that from the beginning....

Willing her hands not to shake or her voice to waver, Daisy proceeded along the center pathway determined, and dry-eyed, to make an appreciative fuss over William's mud pies.

CHAPTER FOUR

VALENTINE TOSSED THE bouquet on a table and the cane onto the bed before lightly hoisting himself up onto the high mattress and flinging himself down on his back to glare at the light summer canopy above his head.

"Pouting, sir?" Piffkin said blandly, retrieving the cane and putting it, it would seem to the casual observer, out of harm's way. "Lovely flowers, though. Shall I order you a sweet to help boost you out of the doldrums?"

"You could fashion me a gag and then tie it tightly while you're at it," Valentine muttered, putting his hands behind his head and crossing his legs at the ankle. "Piffkin? Why have you never told me I talk too much?"

"Couldn't get a word in edgewise, I suppose," the valet said, shaking his head. "You've drying mud caked on the soles of your boots. I'll have them, please."

Grumbling under his breath, Val pushed himself upright and turned so that his legs hung over the edge of the bed. "Before you rail at me, there's also a smudge on my left knee, rightly earned as I rescued a young princess."

"Huzzah. And may I add it is an honor to be in your employ," Piffkin commented as, with Valentine's foot in his back to assist him, the boots were removed. "I'll have the buckskins now, sir."

Valentine complied, and was handed a dark blue silk banyan in return, tying it tightly about his waist. He did all of this without conscious thought. He'd been taking orders from Piffkin since he was in short coats, and some things shouldn't change or else the entire world order could be turned upside-down. "Don't you want to know why I was pouting?"

"You're done, then? Good. I would imagine, since you were heading out to confront the suspicious governess, that you were met with failure and, worse, may have given yourself away in the process. Should I be packing, sir, or do you wish to dispatch Lord Mailer to his dark reward before we go? Your stiletto, sir," he ended, handing over the blade that had been secured in a special sleeve inside the right boot. "I suggest a swift, straight cut across the windpipe, but from behind, please, as bloodstains are the very devil in the laundry."

Valentine rewarded the valet with a lopsided grin. "You speak as if I go about routinely killing people."

"No, sir. I speak as if certain you will be forced to dispatch at least one someone before this week is out. I doubt you'll have a choice."

"Peeking at my correspondence again? Because

that's pretty much what Simon told me I'd have to do. Rest assured, Piffkin, if that does prove to be the case, I won't spend weeks agonizing over the deed. This is war."

"More than war, Master Valentine. Hellfire."

Valentine deposited his long body on what he hoped would prove a comfortable chair, and then raised his stockinged feet up onto the low table. "Is there anything you don't know, Piffkin?"

"Yes, sir. It would appear I remain at a loss to know why Miss Marchant has so upset you."

"I suppose I could quote Lord Mailer and say it's because I suspect she may be smart. Because that's certainly true. Smart. Too smart not to have noticed something strange is going on here, and too smart to attempt to deny she has some suspicions. On the other hand, she may also have some names for me, which would be an immense help."

"How gratifying. However, I believe we're still missing the bits that contributed to your pout, sir," Piffkin said, taking a brush to the dried mud on his master's buckskins.

"I'm getting to them, if you'll allow me to first say I believe I shall never enter another greenhouse. The strangest things seem to happen in them."

"You're not dirty enough to have fallen into a pit."

"There are pits and then there are pits. In this case I suppose you'd say a human pit."

"You're in danger of falling into Miss March-ant? That hardly seems proper, Master Valentine."

"You're such a wit, Piffkin," Valentine said dully. "Consider her more of an enigma. I don't think she just happened to find herself employed here. From what I deduced from Mailer, I'm not inclined to think there was an advertisement placed in the local or London newspapers. I believe she sought out a position here in particular. I think she's come here with some motive of her own, showing up unbidden to worm her way in as governess to a pair of infants who have as much use for a governess as you have need of a comb."

The valet raised a hand to the sleek, polished pate above his bushy brows. "I am experimenting with a new wax. However, it does, sadly, cost you one pound six per pot. Not an extremely large pot."

"But worth every groat, I'm sure. I could probably read by the glow from your head in a full moon. Speaking of which—our Miss Marchant has confirmed my information that the Society have been gathering here during the full moon. She's seen them, at least the ones who stay here at Fernwood. But I was forced to tell her more than I wished in my attempts to get what I thought was the truth from her, and now she refuses to leave, even after I handed her some rather unlovely information that would have had any reasonable woman hot-footedly racing for the nearest posting inn. I never should have said a word to her, not a single word."

"You do at times reveal a penchant for needlessly complicating matters, Master Valentine."

"Putting my foot in it, you mean. As I told her, it was the disguise, mostly, that steered me in the wrong direction, if I'm to have any excuse at all. She was shocked to hear what I had to say, genuinely shocked. But her reaction fell far short of what I would have expected. She already knew, or at least suspected something havey-cavey going on beneath that inquisitive little nose of hers. Now it's left to me to learn why she's here. Then I should be able to convince her to leave."

"Would you go if someone asked you to leave, especially after you'd taken such pains to get here in the first place? You know, the way you have done?"

Valentine spared a moment to recall the warm, silky softness of Daisy's ringlets against his hand. "She's in the way, Piffkin."

"Females are always in the way, it's their nature. It's more than that. You're intrigued."

"I don't have the luxury to be intrigued, for God's sake, or the possibility of being distracted while making certain she doesn't get herself into trouble. As you so brilliantly pointed out, there could be bears."

"So she goes."

Valentine got to his feet. "So she goes, if I have to tie her up and personally toss her in the coach. I'll have her taken to the Manor, where Kate and Simon can watch over her."

"Until you have the leisure to be distracted,"

Piffkin said, neatly catching the banyan Valentine tossed at him.

"Until the Society is exposed and destroyed. No matter why she's here, her abrupt departure will be suspect and she could be marked for elimination."

"Yes, of course. While I am already charged with removing her ladyship and the kiddies to the hide-away inn Twitchill and the others have adjourned to whenever you think it appropriate. Thus burdened, I couldn't possibly take Miss Marchant along with us. Shame on me for thinking anything else."

"Miss Marchant is quite concerned about her la-dyship. Remember, I caught her out last evening, departing the woman's chambers. Hardly the action of a governess. I believe Lady Caroline indulges in laudanum, or perhaps hides in it. Lord knows she doesn't eat. She spent the entire meal yesterday vari-ously staring at me or the wall."

The wall. Just the one, when there were four to choose from, not to mention two gaudy chandeliers. Valentine closed his eyes, attempting to mentally re-construct the Mailer dining room: sideboard, foot-man, door, bank of windows, footman, one of those depressing paintings of dead game, door, another sideboard, more windows, fireplace, painting above the fireplace.

Ah, yes, now he had it. The painting above the fireplace. Lady Caroline hadn't been just idly star-ing, she had been attempting to send him a message. But why would she do that, if she believed he was about to become a member of the Society, either happily or as a result of some sort of blackmail, as Simon's brother had been, to his damnation? Had she been trying to warn him away, or draw his attention? It would be a hell of a thing if she had seen through him when her husband had not.

"A young woman forced to seek the solace of opium. How very sad. Would you care for your breeches back now, sir? I've managed to banish the smut, and it will only be the work of a moment to brush up your boots so that you can partake of an afternoon ride, and perhaps a luncheon at the new inn, where you can surreptitiously have some sort of contact with our men. A reconnoiter of the area is in order, isn't it?"

Valentine pulled himself away from his thoughts. "Always a prudent move, yes, and thank you for once again anticipating my next step. Mailer boasts of his stable, so it would be mean of me not to take advantage of his offer of the best he has should I care for a ride. Frankly, anything would be preferable to spending the afternoon looking at his face. I nearly had to stuff his neckcloth down his gullet twice on the way here yesterday in the coach."

Valentine heard Mailer's voice again in his head, their conversation of just a few hours ago. Something about some of the parties being *here,* while others were held *there.* Could the so-called satanic rites of the Society take place *here,* and the treasonous conversations *there?* Or were there several meeting places, with Mailer's property only one, perhaps simply the one closest to London? Anything was possible. Not every arrangement could be as extensive as his grandfather and father had accomplished at Redgrave Manor. This incarnation of the Society might simply have to make do the best they could. Lord knew they were *making-do* to have a buffoon like Charles Mailer as one of their members.

"You're smiling, sir. Is that a good thing?"

"Possibly. I do believe a few more pieces of the puzzle may just have fallen into place inside my thick brain. Tell me, Piffkin, if you were to host some satanic rite, where would you do it? Indoors or out? Remember—not to influence your answer— the weather is fairly warm, and it would seem a full moon is mandatory."

"And perhaps a convenient church ruin somewhere close by, in order to take full advantage of that moon?"

"Perhaps. Convenient or specially constructed, just as many of our more romantical citizens have ordered ruins built on their estates. Coincidently, there's a large oil painting of the ruins of a stone circle holding place of honor in Mailer's dining room, so such things may intrigue him."

"It sounds as if this particular painting intrigues you, as well."

"Possibly, possibly. A ruined stone circle mimicking Stonehenge or Avebury or any of the others would hardly be remarked on, and even if truly ancient, stories about bloodthirsty Druids and such would be enough to keep the local population from seeking it out during a full moon. However, it wouldn't appear out of the ordinary for a guest new to Fernwood to stop to admire the thing in the daytime, walk about a bit, kick a few of the stones. If there is one, that is."

"Try not to scuff your boots." Piffkin rescued the discarded bouquet and snatched up a vase as he headed for the water pitcher. "There may even be posies, and benches for the ladies to sit and paint watercolors."

"Before you paint too rosy a picture, remember, we're only being wishful here right now."

"And where would this sorry world be, without wishes." The gold tooth shone for a moment in the sunlight streaming into the bedchamber. "Enjoy your ride, Master Valentine."

Valentine considered a dismissive *hrummph* at the man's hopeful words, but only said, "Thank you, Piffkin." After all, *he* hadn't been raised by wolves.

DAISY SAT CURLED up in the window embrasure in her small attic room, alternately looking out through the dusty window and turning pages in her diary, reading snippets here and there.

The children were with their nurse, partaking of their luncheon and, after pleading the headache thanks to the bright sun this morning, Daisy had escaped the schoolroom. She would not be needed again until Lady Caroline summoned her for what had become a regular late-afternoon chat. The meetings were outwardly so that Daisy could report on the children's "progress" under her tutelage, but the children were rarely mentioned. At times Daisy wondered if the woman even remembered their ages.

No, Lady Caroline would talk about her childhood home, her deceased parents, her older sister, who now resided in Canada with her soldier husband.

Sometimes, she simply asked Daisy to kneel with her and pray.

She dreaded meeting with the woman today, could not imagine how she could even look at her without hugging her, telling her how sorry she was... and then grilling her about a small, blonde woman with a beauty mark just at the top outside corner of her mouth.

Unlike herself, especially in her drab brown governess trappings and glasses, Rose had favored their mother and was—had been—an angel, and hardly forgettable. If Lady Caroline had seen her, she would remember her.

If only Charles Mailer had never seen her...

Daisy turned another page in her diary, beginning to read at the place where it had all begun. And ended.

...Rose has written that she has met a gentleman in the street. An inauspicious meeting, for

he'd nearly knocked her down with his um-
brella while racing to avoid the rain, but his
apology and offer to allow her under his brolly
as he walked her back to the ribbon shop had
made up for this. She seems taken with the gen-
tleman, which both cheers and worries me, as
they were not formally introduced. Papa would
not have approved, but Papa is gone. If she is
to find happiness again after Walter's death,
my heart can only remain hopeful.

...I think it may be time I leave here and travel
to London. Increasingly, Rose's letters are
filled only with this man, Chas, as she calls
him. I know she is lonely, and that she frets at
her straitened circumstances as she attempts
to survive on Walter's small army pension, but
those same circumstances could be coloring
her judgment. My own purse grows increas-
ingly thin as I await my last quarter's wages,
having had to augment my wardrobe with the
purchase of materials for a new gown. A hor-
rible expense, but not to be avoided, as I'd al-
ready turned the collar and cuffs twice on the
old one. One must look genteel, not shabby,
according to Mrs. Beckwith, who is suspicious
of me at any rate, certain I'm casting sheep's
eyes at her pudgy husband.

Reluctantly, Daisy continued to turn the pages.

...Ah, Rose, dearest sister. My heart overflows
with joy for her. It would seem her Chas has

*proposed marriage, and she is off to the coun-
tryside to be introduced to his mama. So giddy
is she, I can barely make out her scribbles as
she crosses her lines on the page, but I do wish
I knew more of this man. I can only rejoice for
her. Mr. Beckwith is becoming a problem. My
wages can't come quickly enough, and then I
will return to London to see Rose.*

*...Where is she? Three weeks without any
word. Why has there been no letter? This is
so unlike her, especially when she must be
over the moon with happiness. Did the man's
mother not care for her? How could she not?
Rose is the sweetest creature in nature, and
her manners are all that is pleasing. Oh, she
is driving me mad with worry!*

*...The penny post has at last brought an an-
swer from Miss Hopkins, who shares Rose's
flat above the ribbon shop. Rose has not returned, and there has been no word from her.
Only a servant, sent to gather the remainder
of her belongings. He told her some faradid-
dle about Rose having decided to emigrate
to America. That can't be, Rose would never
leave me, not without a word! Miss Hopkins
knows no more than I about this Chas, save
that she did manage to ask the servant where
he was taking Rose's possessions. Unfortunately, she can only remember that the man
wore green livery and said they were heading*

south, with nearly twenty miles to cover before nightfall to be home and dry, and to an estate with the word wood *in it somewhere. Burnwood? Oakwood?*

Daisy closed the diary. She knew the remainder of the entries by heart. How she had searched the maps in the Beckwith library whenever she could, and then collected her quarterly wage and left at once, not giving a second's thought to Mrs. Beckwith's "good riddance to bad rubbish" and the lack of a reference. She'd ridden as an outside passenger on the posting coach, haranguing the drivers, begging them to dredge their memories for estates with the word *wood* connected to them. She ate little, slept even less and had been soaked to the bone more than once. She'd stopped and asked questions at villages nearby estates dubbed Laurelwood, Fleetwood, Inglewood, Far Woods, Birchwood—had Englishmen no imagination at all? But, at long last: Fernwood, owned by one Lord Charles Mailer. *Chas.*

Inquiries at the posting inn extracted the information she needed: Lord Mailer had two children living at home, yes. The Mailer livery was green. No, his lordship was not in residence at the moment, but his lady wife and the children were on the premises.

Finally, after a month of searching, crisscrossing the countryside within the perimeters of the large rectangle she had drawn on a map pilfered from Mr.

Beckwith, Daisy had found what she was looking for. Now to breach the walls, as it were.

She'd paid down nearly the remainder of her small purse for a room and a bath, brushed her most presentable gown clean, wrote three letters of recommendation in differing handwriting (Mrs. Beckwith's letter was particularly effusive in its praise) and set out on foot for Fernwood the next morning.

And here she'd been the three months since, learning nothing about Rose, but every day growing more suspicious that something terrible was going on at Fernwood, and if she only watched, and waited, she would learn what it was. Then she would confront Lord Mailer and demand he tell her what he'd done with Rose.

But it was left to Valentine Redgrave to give her answers she didn't want to face.

She should go, just as he'd demanded. There was nothing more she could do here. There would be no rescue, there could only be more dreadful, damning answers. Rose was gone. Not to America, not horribly deceived and then abandoned, too mortified to return to London, too ashamed to confess her mistake to her very own sister. No, even if now those two fates seemed to be wished for events. If Mr. Redgrave was correct, and Daisy still longed to disbelieve him, Rose had moved beyond the powers of her sister to save her.

"Oh, God, why do You allow such things? I don't

understand. Why does the devil so often win? Papa raised us to believe good follows good, the righteous will have their reward. It was all so easy to understand as long as our lives ran smoothly. But this… this is too much. This is all so senseless and wrong."

Daisy wiped at her damp cheeks in an attempt to collect herself, looking out through the window once more onto an unimpressive view of several outbuildings and the rear of the horse stables. Crying never helped anything, most especially a broken heart. She had to stiffen her backbone, retrieve her resolve. She had come here to find her sister, and that's exactly what she would do. If she had to break every Commandment along the way, she would find Rose, and take her home, see that she was laid to rest beside their parents.

She watched as Valentine Redgrave appeared on horseback, heading away from the stables. He was alone: no Lord Mailer with him, no groom. She experienced a moment of panic before realizing he couldn't be leaving; he had arrived in Mailer's coach. Besides, he was here for a purpose, and Daisy doubted he was simply off to have himself an enjoyable gallop. She didn't think anything Valentine Redgrave did was that uncomplicated.

When he turned away from the gravel drive that led to the front of the estate house and the direction of the gates, she decided his ride would keep him on Fernwood land, which wasn't all that extensive outside its plowed fields, all of them already planted. Lord Mailer was rarely seen on horseback, and mostly used the pony cart when he did go out on the estate. His major recreation when in residence, she had learned, other than the monthly *parties,* consisted of sitting in his study and drinking himself into a stupor. By all rights, he and his family should be living in genteel poverty, but that didn't seem to be the case.

For an inquisitive sort, as she felt sure Mr. Redgrave was, that left little of interest save for the stream, the penned cattle and sheep, the spit of dense trees, the cliff and the stones.

Daisy had seen the remains of standing stones before, and it had been obvious to her from the first that this particular construction definitely did not have its birth thanks to long-ago Druids or other worshippers. It wasn't nearly so sad as the Gothick Ruin Mrs. Beckwith had ordered constructed at Beckwith Park. Poor woman, no matter how industriously the gardeners tried, they could not succeed in coaxing moss to grow on the stones of the supposed ancient chapel. In fact, the only embellishment at all remained the generations of doves who inhabited it, leaving their drying nests, molted feathers and nasty droppings everywhere.

There was moss growing on the standing and toppled stones at Fernwood. Daisy knew that because she'd taken her charges there several times, as they enjoyed running along the supposedly fallen lintel stones lying in deep grass populated by wildflowers. A few of the tall lintel stones had been set in place, age and weather not yet softening all the chisel marks. It may not be an overwhelmingly accurate construction, and quite a poor imitation of Stonehenge, but as it perched very near the cliff, at the topmost rise of the hill, she supposed some would find such a *folly* impressive. There was even an altar of sorts…

The journal tumbled to the floor as Daisy stood up quickly, slipping her feet back into her half boots. She grabbed for her shawl and a heartbeat later was hurtling down the servant stairs.

CHAPTER FIVE

VALENTINE WAS NO more than a quarter hour into his ride before he decided three things. One, the entire Fernwood estate could neatly fit inside the boundaries of Redgrave Manor at least five times. Perhaps six. Secondly, although actually first in the order of discovery, Charles Mailer was no judge of horse-flesh, clearly preferring showiness over breeding. The gelding he was aboard had been the best of a bad lot, which said little for the gelding and much about the rest of the stable.

Lastly, he was comforted to realize he'd have no problem explaining away any interest he might show now, or at dinner, in the stone circle—it was the only thing of even marginal uniqueness on the entire estate. Well, that and the horseshoe-shaped cliff, clearly created long ago by industrious folk who had quarried stone there for a time, but then abandoned the area.

He'd asked one of the grooms if there were any interesting spots he should visit on his ride, and was told maybe sir would like to take a peek at the queer stones his lordship had ordered built in the middle of the trees a couple of years ago. Valentine had longed to kiss the top of the man's head to have his suspicion confirmed, but refrained, only asking directions to the spot, a cleared patch of land surrounded by ancient trees. "But don't wander too far, sir. It be trees, and then the cliff, bang, with no warnin'. His lordship's first missus mistook where she was, and went over. Sad, that."

After pretending an interest in other areas of the estate, Valentine finally dismounted at the bottom of the tree-covered hill. With Piffkin's warnings ringing in his head, he slipped the sword cane from the saddle, ostensively to employ it as he entered the treed area and climbed up the gentle slope alongside the cliff, trying to imagine anyone so desperate as to fling herself over the edge and onto the sharp stones below, leaving behind two small children. He held a special compassion for children abandoned by their mother.

Of course, she might have fallen. People toppled off cliffs all the time, didn't they? No, they didn't. The woman had most probably jumped…or had had help. Valentine shivered as he imagined a broken body sprawled fifty feet below him. He could only hope she'd been already dead.

There was no sense in delaying this any longer. It was on to the standing stones. At last the trees gave way to a surprisingly large, cleared area. It all looked bucolic and romantic enough, he supposed, long grass and wildflowers nodding in the breeze that seemed to circle the ruin as if undecided whether to linger or move on.

Valentine pushed his hair out of his eyes and stepped inside the circle, heading for what was obviously some sort of altar. The grass grew thicker here, higher. He'd half hoped it would be trampled, showing signs of visitors. Then again, grasses could grow quickly between full moons.

His boot trod on something hard yet round and he nearly slipped. "That can't be good," he muttered to himself. "Not for a man with a strong imagination which, sadly, it appears I have."

Employing the sword cane, he prodded the area, bending the grass away to one side. Bones. Definitely bones. "How lovely."

"What? What did you find?"

Valentine would never say he had jumped out of his skin at the sound of Daisy's voice coming from behind him, but it had been a near-run thing.

He whirled about to confront her; she was standing a good six feet behind him, a pale blue shawl covering her hair and wrapped about her neck. She could have been a nun, an apparition of some Druid goddess. Mostly, she was an increasingly painful metaphorical thorn in his side. "What in devil's name are you doing here, sneaking up on me like that?"

"I frightened you?" Did she have to sound so... so smug. Yes, that was it. Smug. And exactly like a governess.

"Hardly," Valentine countered, once again brushing his blowing hair out of his eyes. "You damn near got skewered, actually," he said, sliding the swordstick partially out of its hiding place to emphasize his point.

The distraction didn't work.

"Oh, dearie me. I'm certain that's massively impressive when you show it off to your friends. Now I repeat, what did you find, Mr. Redgrave?"

Valentine smiled in spite of himself. "You sound very like one of my tutors years ago, when I presented him with a strange white frog I'd found in the pond. *Extraordinary indeed, Master Redgrave, but now if you'll please allow us to return to our sums.* I've just realized something, Miss Marchant, ma'am. It must be quite the adventure, teaching young minds who would rather you go stuff your head under the pump."

She readjusted her useless yet incredibly important-looking spectacles. "One does what one must do. If not always personally rewarding, it does allow one to eat," she said tightly. "Again, if you would show me whatever it is you've found?"

"Bones." There was no diverting her. "I found bones. I imagine there were more than simply bones, originally. That would explain why the grass grows thicker and higher here." As she opened her mouth to speak, he held up his hand to stop her. "Small bones. Probably a chicken, or a young goat."

"A kid," she said rather vaguely, her color, which

had been sadly missing there for a moment, flowing back into her cheeks.

"Your pardon?"

"A young goat is a *kid,* Mr. Redgrave. A female kid is further designated a doeling, and the males are bucklings. Once castrated, males are wethers."

Valentine was as near to speechless as he'd been in his entire life. "Why do you know that?"

"I know that, Mr. Redgrave, because I am a—"

He waved off her words. "Yes, yes, because you're a governess, and I suppose I'm suffering this education because I so doubted you and you're determined to drive the nail all the way in, aren't you? But I didn't ask you how you know, I asked you *why* you know. Why would anyone want to know that?"

She loosened her shawl, allowing it to fall onto her shoulders, clearly trying not to smile. He could see and appreciate her struggle as she answered: "It's probably of some interest to the goats."

"Especially the males," Valentine said, and then she did laugh.

God, what a sound, like sweet music. And her face seemed to light up, no longer frozen in what must be her idea of a raised-chin professional demeanor. Her eyes sparkled, her mouth was wider than he'd supposed, her teeth white and even save for one front tooth that slightly infringed on its mate.

Perfection was such a bloody bore.

When she attempted to cover her smile with the

back of her hand, she looked young and vulnerable and...not at all like a governess.

If this was what a single smile, a single laugh, could do to her, imagine how she'd look after what he was fairly certain would be her first kiss. She wasn't a great beauty; she was more than physically beautiful. She was Daisy Marchant, and very much her own person.

With thick, glorious copper hair that curled around his finger, hair that, when spread across his pillow, would be the eighth wonder of the world. The tip of his tongue tingled at the thought of running along that delightfully crooked tooth.

And you don't have time for this, he told himself.

But then she did something else surprising, although, if he considered the revelations of the past few hours, probably to be expected.

Daisy Marchant began to cry.

She didn't sob. She didn't make any sound, really. She just stood there, those huge blue eyes filling with tears that soon chased each other down her cheeks as she continued to hold her hand to her mouth.

"Miss Marchant," Valentine said, extending one arm toward her, not sure how she would react if he actually touched her. Crying women were a puzzle; she could push him away, she could throw herself into his arms and weep all over his lapels.

"I...I brought Lydia and William here for picnics. We did fairy dances. And all while..." She took off her spectacles to wipe at her eyes. "I didn't know."

He winced. There wasn't a lot he could say to that. He could barely look into those huge, blue cornflower eyes; they were too tortured, too sad.

"Is this…is this where they…did what they did?"

He hastened to reassure her. "No, unquestionably not. This would be where they have their ridiculous hellfire rites. To entertain their guests, I'm sure, and to impress the impressionable. It's isolated, yes, but much too public for what…what else they do."

Someone might hear the screams. One of the poor creatures could escape into the trees, or over the cliff. But he didn't say either of those things.

His mind, however, whispered something interesting to him: *You say* do, *but she said* did. *You're speaking of the present, but when she spoke, it was as if about something in the past. The extremely punctilious governess had made a mistake? Or had she?*

"Then where did they—" She stopped, either unable to finish the question, or belatedly realizing what she was revealing to him with her questions.

Valentine decided to ignore her mistake. "I would imagine indoors, somewhere. But that's not for you to worry about, is it? I know this has been a trying day for you, Miss Marchant, and it may be cruel of me to push at you. There are two things I must ask, however. Do you have any names for me? And, are you now ready to listen to reason, and allow me to have you removed to safety at Redgrave Manor?"

Daisy gave one last swipe at her cheeks with the

back of her hand, and replaced her glasses. "You seem almost unnaturally eager to be shed of me, Mr. Redgrave."

It was amazing. She could put him through an entire gauntlet of swiftly changing emotions in the space of a few minutes. Surprise, humor, shock, compassion...downright seeing-red anger.

"For the love of God, Miss Marchant—"

"I would thank you to leave God out of this, Mr. Redgrave. He certainly hasn't been involved up to this point. I'm not going anywhere."

"Because you came here for a reason," Valentine said, giving up all pretense. "I've already figured that out with my minuscule brain."

She bit her bottom lip, shook her head. "I don't wish to speak about this with you. I simply can't. If you don't mind, Mr. Redgrave, although to do so violates my feelings of privacy, I would rather give you my journal. My reason, and the names of a few of Lord Mailer's guests, are catalogued within. I'll mark the page where you should begin, and ask you to swear not to satisfy your curiosity by reading the previous pages. Your word as a gentleman, sir."

"You have it...Daisy."

"Thank you, Mr. Redgrave, but as we have serious business to confront, I would rather we two remain on a more formal basis. For you to address me as Daisy automatically relegates me to the role of subservient, and for me to address you by your given name hints at a friendship between us that is most certainly neither appropriate nor desired."

Valentine shook his head. It would probably be best if he didn't tell her how much he suddenly longed to rip away those hideous spectacles and plant a whacking great kiss square on her prunes-and-prisms lips. "As my grandmother would say, you're a pip, Miss Marchant. She'd enjoy watching you put me through hoops."

"I've no intention of putting you through hoops. I should only ask the same favor in return. We should separate now, and I will meet you to turn over my diar—my journal just outside the servant entrance behind the stables in a quarter hour. The full moon could be as close as this very night."

Valentine pulled a small silver disc from his watch pocket and looked at it closely. There were, in fact, three discs, all joined together at the middle, and each could be moved independently of the other. "Yes, it begins tonight."

Daisy stepped closer. "How can you know that for certain without consulting a chart? What is that strange thing?"

At last, something she didn't already know! He passed it over to her. "Just something I discovered in a shop in Bond Street. I'm assured the language is German, so it may have found its way here along with the first George. But the months are also marked with their Zodiac signs, so it's all read easily enough. You move the dials about, and the small openings reveal the days of the week, the phases of the moon, even the number of days in each month, the length of the days and nights."

Daisy was studying the disc, turning it round and round. "The *Calendar Ivmperpetuum*. Perpetual calendar, I imagine. And you're right, quite old. There's a date here, 1696. So if I slide the disk to the correct year, month and day— Ah, there we are. It's rather amazing, isn't it? Don't lose it." She handed the disc back to him. "Now, as to meeting again. A quarter hour. Are we agreed? Please don't dawdle."

And with that she was gone. Without another look toward the stone altar, or to him, for that matter. *Don't lose it. Please don't dawdle.* She was handing out orders now. "I told Piffkin she'd get in the way. And now she's gone and done it. *Dawdle?* God, she's wonderful!"

She was, precisely thirty minutes later, also late. Valentine didn't pace, like some anxious Romeo waiting to steal a moment with his Juliet—because that wouldn't be *appropriate* behavior—but he was beginning to worry. He was adequately concealed amid the fairly overgrown shrubbery flanking the servant entrance, but at any moment a servant could be popping in or out, and that would put paid to any secrecy, which couldn't be a good thing.

So where in bloody hell was she? This was why nobody in clear possession of his wits ever involved a female in his plans. Women were an unknown quantity, prone to improvisation, and a man worrying about a woman could end up a dead man in more ways than one.

He heard the latch depress and quickly stepped back against the wall, so that the opening door would conceal him.

Which would have been a sterling plan, save for the fact the door opened inward, leaving him exposed, looking the complete fool as he stood pressed up against the stones. All he was missing were the pointed shoes and the bells. If the rest of his day went as it had gone thus far, he might have to consider himself being punished for some unknown sin.

Still, when Daisy stepped straight out onto the path, the move put her in front of him; she had yet to see him.

"Oh, God, no. He's not here," she said, her voice barely above a whisper.

"I thought God hasn't been here all along," he said, stepping forward.

And then he had the surprise of his life.

"Valentine!" She took his hands in hers, squeezed his knuckles together with more strength than he'd supposed she possessed. He could have taken this fervent greeting as a sign of some growing affection for him, save that her fair complexion was once again almost deathly white against her copper hair. "It's gone. It's missing. I looked everywhere."

"The journal?"

She let go of his hands and glared at him. "Yes,

the journal. What else could I be talking about, Mr. Redgrave. It's gone."

"Valentine. A moment ago, I was Valentine. I still am, Daisy."

She sighed in exasperation. "All right, all right. Valentine. I had it out of its hiding place to look up the names for you. I was reading it when I...when I thought of something, and I believe I allowed it to fall to the floor unheeded as I left the room."

"Wonderful," Valentine commented, wincing.

"You don't have to pull one of your disapproving faces to remind me how unfortunate this is. But nobody comes into my room, not even to clean it. I was allowed a key when I applied to Lady Caroline for one. I always demand a key. Husbands and sons, you understand."

"Not really. I should think they'd be too terrified. Did you lock the door?"

"Please restrain yourself from questioning the obvious. Of course I neglected to lock the door. I was in a rush to follow you and— None of this is even vaguely amusing, Valentine. They'll know why I'm here."

"Then this *they* will know considerably more than I." He grabbed her hand. "Come along now like a good little governess, Daisy. You're leaving."

She pulled herself free. "No. I can't leave. Not without my diary. It has those names you need in it, remember? And...and memories. If—if I can't locate it by tomorrow morning, yes, then I'll agree to leave. I'll have no choice."

"And how do you suppose you'll locate it?"

"I'll simply have to ask people, that's all. For some reason, people find it difficult to lie to me."

"Imagine that," Valentine said, knowing he was being facetious. But he said it to her back, because the door was already closing.

DAISY LEFT THE servant stairs on the third floor and headed straight for the nursery, mostly because she had no plans to interrogate Lady Caroline or Lord Mailer about the missing journal. That left the servants, and the children.

Hoping for a simple answer, she wouldn't approach Lady Caroline's keeper, Davinia, unless left with no other option. After that interview, she'd have no choice but to remove herself from the premises without delay. Not to be too dramatic about the thing—was that possible?—she would first tie up her possessions in a blanket and drop it out of her window before speaking with Davinia.

She wasn't going to divulge her quickly devised plan to Valentine Redgrave, however, no matter how generous his offer to *protect* her. She didn't know where Redgrave Manor was located, but certainly it was some distance from Fernwood. She would take herself no farther than a few miles away, so that she could return at night and watch the comings and goings of Lord Mailer and his guests. She'd find where he'd taken Rose, and then…and then…

"One step at a time, Daisy," she whispered to herself as she hurried past the front stairs.

"You there, girl! Marchant!"

Her stomach sank to her toes, but she took a deep breath, turned about to look down at the landing, and dropped into a curtsy. "Lord Mailer, sir. I was just on my way to the nursery."

"Did I ask? Come down here."

He knows, he knows. I have to run. Now.

"Yes, sir."

As she descended the stairs, her eyes downcast, she could feel his gaze on her, raking her head to toe.

Her hand on the newel post, to keep her from trembling, she hoped, she curtsied yet again, poised to race past him down the next flight of stairs, to bolt out through the front door before he could order anyone to stop her. "Sir?"

"No. Still don't see it. He must have meant what he said, he felt some ridiculous need to apologize. Very well, that's all. You may go now. And keep those brats indoors the next few days. I don't want to have to see them, or my wife. They're all sick. Indisposed. Earn your bloody keep, Marchant. Understood?"

"Sir." Keeping her shoulders forward, her head down, she bobbed yet another curtsy and turned to return upstairs, careful to keep her hips steady as she climbed. When she reached the landing and turned around, Lord Mailer was gone.

She'd been so close to bolting, so close to giving herself away!

But what had he meant? He didn't *see it?* Didn't see what? But as she walked on, one possible answer came to her. She and Mr. Redgrave—Valentine— had been observed together, either last night or today, and he'd offered the excuse that he was apologizing for something he'd done? Ha! He had a lot to choose from, didn't he? But why should Lord Mailer care? Was he no better than Mrs. Beckwith and her other employers, believing she was out to seduce anything in pants? And what did the horrible man expect to see? Not a resemblance between herself and Rose, surely. He couldn't have stumbled on to that, could he?

Oh, where was the dratted diary? And where was Valentine, who would be able to tell her what Lord Mailer had meant? He only seemed to be underfoot when she *didn't* want him.

Daisy turned down the hallway leading to the nursery, to be greeted by the sound of William's howls. She stepped up her pace and entered the room in time to see Agnes, the nursery maid, apparently attempting to poke an apron-tipped finger into the boy's ear.

"What on earth?"

"Gots mud in his ear, Miss Marchant, even after his bath, and won't hold still to let me dig it out."

"I doubt I'd sit there placidly while you *dug* into my ear, Agnes. Isn't there another way?"

"Soakin' him head and ears in a water bucket, I suppose."

William's howls climbed a few decibels.

"Well, what do you suppose we stop for now, and consider other options. Is that all right with you, Master William?"

Whether the child understood the full extent of her words or not she couldn't know, but he certainly understood her tone. He grinned at her, slid off the nurse's lap, landed a kick against her shin and took off for his bedchamber on the other side of the nursery. Daisy knew she should correct the boy, tell him to apologize, but she simply didn't have the strength.

"I'll be takin' m'self downstairs for a cup o' tea and some time with m'feet up, ma'am, iffen you don't mind. Fairly wears me out, that boy does. How's the headache?"

"Go along, Agnes, and thank you for allowing me time for a lie-down. It was just the thing."

That left only Lydia, who was industriously drawing something as she sat at one of the low tables. Odd, she hadn't been laughing at William. She hadn't even been looking at him, or at Daisy, for that matter. She'd seemed genuinely concerned earlier, when told her governess had the headache, and all but ordered Daisy to her bed in an endearingly grown-up voice.

"Lydia? What are you drawing? May I see?"

The child didn't answer, so Daisy repeated the question as she walked toward her.

"Go away," Lydia said, curling her arm around the top of the paper and lowering her head over it, as if to hide the drawing.

Daisy smiled, believing she at last understood. "By any chance could you be drawing a picture of Mr. Redgrave? Is he wearing a crown, and perhaps bowing over the hand of a beautiful young princess? Oh, please let me see."

Lydia lifted her head for a moment, her face running with tears, and Daisy, alarmed, quickly snatched up the drawing.

It was nothing like she'd imagined.

"Lydia? Who is this?"

"It's *you!* You're a horrid, horrid person, and horrid people are *ugly!*"

"And apparently tied to a stake to be consumed by a trio of fire-breathing dragons." She laid the paper on the table once more, before squeezing herself onto one of the small, low chairs.

"It's not funny! You're a horrid, horrid person, and horrid people—"

"Yes, I think we've established what should happen to horrid people," Daisy said, extracting a folded handkerchief from her sleeve. "Here, blow your nose. It's dripping."

The child did as she was told, which Daisy had learned most people did when confronted with calmness and reason. "It might be helpful if you told me what I've done to incur your anger, so that I can apologize appropriately. Will you tell me?"

"You…you know what you did," the child said, then blew her noise noisily. "You lied. We're not ever supposed to lie. You said so."

Oh, dear. "And how did I lie to you? Because I'm prodigiously sorry."

Lydia blew her nose again, wiping at it rather ineffectively. Daisy rescued the handkerchief and dabbed at the child's face.

"You said you had the headache, and that's why we couldn't go back to the greenhouse to get the mud pies. We couldn't go outside *at all.* So I…so I took two of the prettiest roses from the bouquet and sneaked out of the room when Agnes was busy with Willie, and climbed up to the attic to give them to you so you'd feel better. And you know what, Daisy? You weren't there."

"Ah…"

"But I saw you. I climbed up on the window seat and looked out the window. I would be the princess in the tower. It's so very high up, you can see lots of things. I saw you. I saw Mr. Redgrave, too."

Daisy put her hands to her head and began rubbing at her temples with her fingertips. The standing stones weren't visible from the house; Lydia must have seen Mr. Redgrave riding away, and then her governess heading for the path leading up through the trees. That was the only possible answer. "I didn't see him. I…I went for a walk, Lydia, thinking some fresh air would aid my headache. Did you really think I was off to meet with your prince?"

"No-o-o-o… Yes… Didn't you?"

This lie was too big to be excused by crossing her fingers behind her back. But it was for the best. "No, Lydia, I did not. I suppose I could have come back to the nursery, to tell you I was going to take a walk, but was that really necessary?"

"No-o-o-o…I suppose I was being a silly baby."

Daisy reached over to squeeze Lydia's small hand in hers. "No, sweetheart, you most certainly were not. What happened to the flowers?"

Lydia raised her head and grinned. "I ripped them into little pieces and dropped them in your chamber pot."

Daisy laughed out loud. "One day you'll read Will Shakespeare, Lydia, and his declaration that a rose by any other name would smell as sweet. I think you may have discovered the singular exception to that rule."

"I don't understand. But you sound nice when you laugh. I'm sorry. I shouldn't have ripped the flowers. I shouldn't have taken this, either, I suppose."

So saying, the child reached into a pocket of her painting smock and pulled out Daisy's journal.

"Here, take it. I didn't know what to do with it, anyway. It was too thick to rip up and put in the chamber pot."

Daisy fought the urge to snatch her diary from Lydia's hands. "You…you didn't show it to anyone?"

"Only Willie." Lydia picked up her drawing and began tearing it into small pieces. "Do you want to see my drawing of the royal prince? I think I may have given him too much hair. But it's so pretty, isn't it? *He's* so pretty."

Daisy had a sudden flash of Valentine as he'd stood in the center of the stones, his long, strong legs spread, his narrow waist and broad shoulders, that so youthful, almost-pretty face made tolerable by that interesting hawkish nose...the full waves of nearly black hair that blew gently in the breeze. His dark-lashed eyes, almost amber in the sun, and filled to the brim with compassion. Caring. Concern. And maybe, just for a moment, something else, something warmer...

"Yes, Lydia," she said, slipping the diary into her pocket, "Mr. Redgrave is very pretty."

"Prettier than you," the child announced matter-of-factly, bending over another drawing. Clearly not all had been forgiven.

Daisy laughed again. It had been long months since she'd laughed; she'd nearly forgotten how. Yet now, in the midst of hearing proof of her greatest sorrow, somehow she seemed to be coming back to life....

CHAPTER SIX

PIFFKIN HELD OUT a small folded scrap of paper as Valentine frowned into the mirror atop the dressing chest, attempting to get his hair to behave.

"Your resignation, Piffkin?" he asked, amusing himself but clearly not Piffkin.

"Found it slipped under your door, sir."

Valentine glanced at it, one eyebrow raised. "Under the door? My, my, such dark intrigue. What does it say?"

The valet brought his posture up stiffly. "As if I would ever be so unaware of the confidentiality of my employer's correspondence as to— Oh, the devil with it. *Located. All's fine.* I'm certain you know what that means?"

"I do. It means we won't be getting rid of Miss Marchant just yet."

"You'll pardon me, sir, but I do not believe I can remember you having such limited influence with a member of the fairer sex. In fact, the mind fairly boggles."

Valentine made one last spread-finger stab at pushing errant locks from his forehead, and abandoned the mirror. "Yes, I can see where I'm a sad disappointment to you. I'm all but too ashamed to look you square in the eye."

Piffkin held up Valentine's coat so that he could slip into it, adjust his cravat and shirt cuffs. "I understand there will be additional guests at dinner, sir."

Valentine returned to the high dressing table to select a ring from the box Piffkin opened for him. "Well, that took you long enough. Or perhaps you didn't think I'd be interested?"

"That is rather open to question, yes. What with all these distractions."

"Have you ever thought of retirement, Piffkin?" Valentine asked, heading for the door. "You've a sister in Shropshire who'd love to have you, I believe."

"Millicent, yes. But first I'd have to find you another keeper, else I'd simply worry myself into a frazzle. Do you think you might apply to Miss Marchant? She seems to hold you in line very nicely."

The door to the hallway had closed before Piffkin could finish, actually, but Valentine could still hear the valet's laughter through the thick wood.

He entered the drawing room just as the first gong rang, calling everyone downstairs. Mailer was the single other person in evidence, striking a relaxed pose with one arm resting negligently on the mantel, a glass of wine dangling from his fingers. He might have pulled off the deception if his complexion wasn't unattractively splotchy, his other hand closed into a tight fist.

Valentine didn't subscribe to poking sticks at hornets' nests, but couldn't seem to refrain from taking a jab at Mailer.

"Good evening, mine host, good evening!" he called out cheerily. "What a glorious day I've had, Charles. A fine, refreshing ride on a singular mount, a delightful if necessarily short tour of your stunning, simply stunning, estate. So enjoyable. You're a stellar host, my friend, leaving your guest to his own devices. I do so loathe organized outings, insipid picnics and the like. Are you going to offer me wine, or continue to stand there like a…well, a statue of Bacchus, I would imagine?"

By now Valentine was close enough to the man to see that his eyes looked much too blue, because his pupils were tightly contracted. He'd seen this phenomenon before; the man had been eating, drinking or smoking opium. Everyone should have his little hobbies, he supposed.

In his checkered youth (that Piffkin, if applied to, would probably attest persisted to this day), Valentine had been coaxed into sampling an opium pipe. But he hadn't liked the sensation that came with it: the loss of control over his own thoughts, his speech, even the movements and imagined needs of his own body. Yet some, he knew, enjoyed all of those feelings, and sought them out to soothe, to excite the imagination, to empower—whatever excuse they could find at the moment the pipe called to them.

Mailer waved the hand holding the wineglass,

stumbling as the move had his arm slipping off the mantel. "Drinks table's over there. Help yourself."

Valentine put out a hand to steady the man. "Careful there, Charles. Already had your share, did you? I've been told more guests have arrived?"

"Oh, they don't all stay here. Visited and gone. Off to a party." He leaned closer. "*Private* party. And m'wife knows she is to remain in her rooms, as you demanded."

"Suggested, Charles. I never demand."

"Good evening, gentlemen. Am I tardy-*hee-ee?*" The question had come from somewhere behind Valentine.

"*Shhh,* he's not invited," Mailer whispered.

Apparently, neither had Mailer or Valentine himself been invited. And didn't *that* raise a few disturbing questions in his head. Had an unhappy Mailer been left behind—again, thanks to Piffkin's earlier suggestion—to act as chaperone while the others met and the new guests were considered for... for what? Membership? Blackmail? Elimination? It didn't help to be fanciful, but Valentine knew he had to consider any of those possibilities.

He turned toward the doorway, to see a tall, thin, rather awkwardly put together man of about his own age sauntering into the room, tugging at his cuffs. His rigout bordered on the ridiculous, his shirtpoints high and sharp...although the man's sad lack of chin would probably keep him from slicing himself as he turned his head.

"Frappton," he muttered under his breath, recognizing the man from the last time he'd attempted to visit Spencer Perceval. Frappton was the clerk to some minor undersecretary, and the man charged with denying Valentine access to his superior. That man was still three levels below the undersecretary who had the final word on who saw the prime minister. No wonder nothing was ever accomplished; everyone was too busy guarding the gates. Worse, Frappton couldn't seem to say more than three words without tagging on a giggle at the end. He was the sort of man other men just naturally longed to toss into a cupboard.

Most importantly, things could get sticky if Frappton said something inappropriate right now, such as *did you ever get to see the Prime Minister-hee-ee-ee?*

"Introduce us, Charles," Valentine prodded when Mailer said nothing, only leaving Frappton to stand in grinning discomfort in the center of the room, probably wondering if he'd left one of his most strategic buttons unanchored.

Mailer blinked, as if coming out of a dream. "Oh, yes, yes. Mr. Valentine Redgrave, I introduce to you—what was your name again?"

Valentine thought: *Caught between a pair of fools, with the initiative clearly up to me.*

"Frappton, my lord. Cecil Frappton. But known mostly as Frappton, sir-*hee-ee.* Don't you remember me, Mr. Red—"

"Frappton, Frappton," Valentine cut in quickly, walking toward the man, his right hand extended. The idiot took it, and Valentine gave the bony appendage a squeeze. A very *tight* squeeze, the sort that put a man's knuckles in much closer proximity to each other than is generally considered desirable. And he kept squeezing, even as he sent the man dire messages of worse to come with his eyes. But when he spoke again, his voice was light, friendly. "Do I remember you? I believe we've met, yes. Perhaps at one of the more tame balls last season? Is your lovely wife with you?"

Even an idiot can climb to some low threshold of understanding...or else Frappton decided he might one day wish to use his right hand again.

"Couldn't have been me, sir," he said, attempting not to grimace, which in a chinless man saddled with a prodigious overbite is not a sight to be encouraged. Valentine rather thought he most resembled a constipated rabbit. "No, I can't think we've ever met. Not ever, sir. And...and alas, I have no wife-*hee-ee. Ow,* sir?" he then whispered hopefully.

"Good man," Valentine confided, at last releasing Frappton's paw. Were rabbits' feet called paws? He'd have to remember to ask Daisy.

More loudly, he said, "Too bad, Frappton. But I'm convinced you'll make a grand prize in the matrimonial stakes. Charles, don't you agree?"

"What?" Mailer was in the process of seating himself, but halted with his backside in a state of limbo between upright and nicely cushioned when the gong rang a second time. "I suppose we have to eat now. Lady Caroline is sadly indisposed, so it will be only us gentlemen…and you, Frapworth. Shall we?"

Just in case Frappton couldn't open his mouth twice without landing Valentine's head on the chopping block, and as Mailer seemed most interested in the level of wine in his glass, Valentine took over the role of host, keeping the conversational ball in the air, and amusing himself by telling some fairly ribald jokes learned at his grandmother's knee or when she thought none of the children were within earshot (Trixie was never without a stack of dinner invitations heaped on her mantel).

Mailer roused at these witticisms, adding a few of his own that nearly put Valentine to the blush, most notably a trio of limericks that had Frappton giggling like a prepubescent schoolboy.

"No entertainment tonight, Charles?" Valentine asked after what had seemed an interminable dinner, as they lingered over brandy and cigars. Frappton puffed too frequently on his, in an amateur effort to keep it lit, and his complexion was turning visibly green, prompting Valentine to *hee-ee* silently. "I thought you had mentioned something about a party? That is why we're here, isn't it, Frappton?"

"Oh, not me-*hee-ee*," the man said, gratefully resting the cigar on the plate in front of him. "I'm only here at the request of my superior, the Honorable Mr. Harold Charfield. I fear he took ill on the journey here, and has retired for the evening-*hee-ee*."

"Really? Charles—I say, *Charles?* Is your household now a hotbed of sickness? Perhaps I should leave."

'You know damn full well m'wife— *Wright!* More brandy."

The butler stepped forward to refill his master's snifter from the decanter warming on a table near the fire.

"Ah, that's better," Mailer said, seemingly having had sufficient time to collect his wits and thus guard his tongue. "Now, what was it you asked, my friend? Something about sickness? No, no. Caro's riding the rags again. Takes to her bed like clockwork, every time. I doubt Charfield suffers the same complaint."

"Hee-ee-ee," Frappton tittered. That was excusable, for the fellow was an irreclaimable twit.

Charles Mailer, however, had all the sensitivity of a cockroach, and Valentine added yet another check mark to the list of reasons he would so enjoy breaking the man.

"In any event," he said, dropping his serviette onto the table, "please convey my wishes to Lady Caroline for a rapid recovery."

"Small chance of that. Women are of no use to a man when they're unclean. She'll reemerge once she's decent again."

Another check mark.

"Frappton? Is there any chance your Mr. Charfield will rise from his sickbed by tomorrow? Otherwise, Charles, I will have to make good my intention to depart this sad excuse for a holiday in the country. I've seen what there is of your quaint little estate, Frappton here is a dead bore—many pardons, Cecil—there's no one present from the gentler, more interesting sex and you're drunk. You promised witty conversation—again, Cecil, my apologies—and entertainment I would enjoy to the top of my bent. Thus far, Charles, I've had better times at the tooth-drawer."

Mailer opened his mouth to speak, but Valentine stood up, holding out his hand to stop him. "Frappton? What do you say we leave our host to slopping up his brandy, and take a refreshing stroll in the gardens? According to my *Calendar Ivmperpetuum,* sunset is no more than an hour from now."

The man perked up his ears, his nose nearly twitching with excitement. He looked no better as an excited rabbit than he'd done as a grimacing one. "I—I should like that above all things. May…may I leave the cigar here-*hee-ee?*"

"I would, it's inferior in any case. Charles," Valentine said, bowing, "by your leave?"

"Yes, yes, I'm off to bed soon m'self, if you two are settled. You are settled, aren't you? But I swear, Redgrave, you'll meet the remainder of the party tomorrow night. You, too, Frapply."

"Frappton, sir-*hee-ee.*"

"Whatever. It was Harold who invited you, not me."

"Come along, Cecil," Valentine encouraged, smiling at the hurt expression on the man's face. "You probably need some air to rid yourself of the effects of that cigar." *And a polite grilling about your Mr. Charfield. First the wife and kiddies, then Daisy and now Cecil-rabbit. He'd soon be rescuing whole villages, rather like Robin Hood.*

VALENTINE, CLAD IN black from head to toe, waved a cheeky goodbye to Piffkin, who was wearing a concealing nightcap as he maneuvered himself beneath the covers of his master's bed.

"Back facing the door to the hallway, Piffkin. There's a good fellow. Don't forget to say your evening prayers."

"This won't fool them if they *really* come looking, you know," the valet pointed out.

"A single candle, a dying fire in the hearth. Some gentle snoring wouldn't come amiss. Mailer's a lazy sot, he won't do more than poke his head in here to assure himself I'm asleep. Just make certain that nightcap doesn't slip off your shiny, betraying head."

Ignoring Piffkin's next grumble, Valentine stealthily made his way downstairs and exited the house via the French doors in the library. Mailer probably hadn't seen the library, or the inside of any book, in decades.

Now it was off to the servant entrance.

This time he was careful to hide behind one of

the overgrown shrubberies. He grabbed Daisy at the elbow as soon as she'd pulled the door shut behind her, and turned her around so swiftly they were chest-to-chest, with her breath all but knocked out of her.

Sometimes it was better when she couldn't talk, Valentine had decided. He took advantage of the moment to press a quick, hard, not at all satisfying kiss against her mouth, then took her hand and broke into a run that didn't end until they were inside the first line of tall, concealing trees.

"All right," he said, letting go of her hand. "You may feel free to berate me now. Only please keep it to a whisper."

"I wouldn't know where to begin," she told him, still attempting to catch her breath as she adjusted her spectacles. He saved her the effort by removing them for her and shoving them in his pocket. *Tonight the spectacles, tomorrow the bun. All good things come to the patient man. Shame I've never quite mastered patience....*

"Moonlight reflects off flat, shiny surfaces," he told her. It was as good a reason as any, since saying he longed to see her without the damnable things would only add to her "I wouldn't know where to begin" budget of complaints.

"How did you know I'd be... Oh, never mind. Of course you knew I couldn't stay away."

"So no credit forthcoming for brilliant deduction, I imagine. Very well, then I won't mention the

Ivmperpetuum Calendar showing both tonight's full moon and the time of sunset, the journal you've promised me and, last but certainly not least, your unnatural interest in my interests."

"*Calendar Ivmperpetuum.* You said it the wrong way round. As to the rest," she said, reaching into the pocket of her drab cloak, "here is the journal. You'll recall your sworn promise not to look at anything that comes before the place I inserted the marker."

"Sworn promise? I swore? Really?"

"Don't attempt to make light of this in order to ease my apprehension, if you please. You're not amusing."

"Good thing I brought my sword stick. Excuse me now whilst I step behind yon tree and throw myself on it."

"Valentine?"

His smile faded immediately. This was serious business. He knew it, she knew it. He just bloody well wished he knew why she was so adamant in remaining in such a dangerous situation.

"Yes, Daisy?"

"Do shut up, please," she said rather kindly. "I don't need to be coddled."

She knew what he'd been doing? How could she know? That was unsettling. "Good for you. But maybe I do. Please, Daisy, go back to your room. I know what I have to do, and I'd much rather not have to worry about you while I'm about it."

"You really think they're gathering tonight at the

stones? Even with you in residence? Why would they do that?"

And there it was. The question he'd been dreading. "I think they're voting me up or down, and perhaps another *guest* who arrived today. You know, Romans, the Colosseum, thumbs. That sort of thing."

Daisy put her hand on his arm. "Voting you up or down for what?" Then her eyes widened. "For *membership?* Oh, my God, Valentine. *You?* That's why you're here? To...to become one of *them?* And they believe you?"

He smiled slightly. "You don't have to sound as if that's so incredulous. However, after carefully building myself up as an interested *parti,* I'm here to infiltrate the Society and learn the names of the members. We can't stop what we don't know, Daisy. It's only logical."

"Is that what they call themselves? The Society? I thought you said they were a hellfire club, or organization, or whatever they call themselves. Not a coven, that's for witches. And you came here to *join* them." She put a hand to her head and turned about in a full circle, just to glare at him again through the darkness. "Downing Street," she said, accused, actually. "That's the *we* you just spoke of? Valentine, I will give you precisely three seconds to tell me everything, or I may just scream, and put paid to this entire venture."

"You wouldn't do that. You're whispering. Harshly, but careful to keep your voice low. You'd never scream, because then you'd never know what it is you feel this overweening need to know...and I wouldn't know what the devil you're still hiding."

Daisy exaggeratingly rolled her huge, marvelous blue eyes. "He chooses *now* to be logical?"

Valentine brushed at his left shoulder, hoping to dislodge Cupid—or at least some sort of small, interfering imp—who seemed to have taken up residence there at this most inopportune time.

The sky was getting darker, and the shadows cast by the full moon made it possible for him to see a path off to his right. "Does that lead to the standing stones?"

"Yes. It's how I take the children up there, and how I—"

This time he picked her up, so there'd be only one pair of feet swiftly but silently moving through the undergrowth, and didn't stop until he'd settled her on the ground a good twenty yards away, going down on his haunches beside her behind a concealing bramble bush.

"You think they're really coming, don't you? And they'll use the path?"

"She chooses *now* to point out the obvious?" Valentine responded. "Keep your head down, it's less than an hour until midnight."

"How do you know they'll come at midnight?"

"I don't. But as they most probably aren't here yet, it's either that, or they aren't coming at all. Can you please not ask any more questions right now?"

There was complete if rather injured silence for the next quarter hour, save for unanswered whispers coming from Daisy every few minutes.

"I suppose I should feel confident that you don't really wish to be one of them."

And within a minute: *"You don't, do you?"*

Followed a few minutes later by: *"That very improper kiss was meant to keep me from screaming, wasn't it?"*

And, lastly: *"Will they slaughter another chicken? Only men would think that the height of demonstrating their power. It isn't as if the chicken could take up arms and fight back. Did you just laugh, Valentine Redgrave? The strangest things amuse you."*

Finally, and not a moment too soon for Valentine, a light appeared in the distance. He felt certain he was seeing a smuggler's lantern, shuttered on three sides, so that only the path in front of the man carrying it was exposed. Those following the man were like a small herd of pachyderms, holding on to the back of the cloak of the man in front of him, as elephants held on to each other's tails with their trunks.

Only there were no elephants here. Only cloaked monsters whose exaggeratedly large heads bore the faint outlines of horns, false, strawlike hair, grotesque features that could be mimicking goats, lions, bulls and more. Valentine thought first of his *Calendar Ivmperpetuum* and the Zodiac signs on its face.

There was a sharp intake of breath from Daisy, quickly cut off as she clapped a hand to her mouth.

Once the last cloaked figure disappeared from
view—Valentine had counted six in all—she attempted to get to her feet. He pulled her back down.
"What? We are going to follow them, aren't we?"

"In a few minutes," Valentine whispered back
to her. "We already know Mailer is among them. I
could smell his sweat and brandy from here. He was
carrying the lantern, probably because he knows the
grounds best. I'll give you my perpetual calendar if
one of the others isn't the so lately indisposed Harold Charfield, the superior of the unsuspecting fool
I met at dinner tonight. Charfield. Burn. It fits as
one of the bizarre code names we've already discovered via that journal we found. Miner, Bird, Webber,
Urban and Cot and some others are dead. Post we
discovered, and perhaps now, Burn. Hammer still
unknown, and then we're at the end of our code, with
God knows how many more to locate."

"I'm convinced you know just what you're talking
to yourself about, if you'll pardon my poor grammar
at such a trying time as this. And, again, you keep
saying *we*. Since *we* isn't you and me, I need to know
more. If you and I both manage to live out this night,
I expect a full explanation tomorrow, complete with
time reserved for questions afterward."

"You're more annoyingly curious than my sister,
and twice as logical, which is no great help to me
right now." Valentine got to his feet, helping Daisy
rise, as well. "You won't do the sensible thing and
remain here? No, of course not. Just keep in the

forefront of your mind the sure knowledge that I will push you facedown in the dirt if you attempt to utter another word between now and when those bastards ahead of us are gone back under the rocks they came from."

"There's no need to get prickly, or profane," Daisy said in her best governess tone, but then she shut her mouth with a snap when he growled under his breath.

She was terrified, and for whatever reason, she seemed to need to talk when she was nervous. Valentine knew that as much as he knew she wouldn't back down, step away, even if he held a pistol to her head. The journal was burning a figurative hole in his pocket; he couldn't wait to read what she couldn't seem able to simply tell him.

Whatever that *it* was, he only knew he was going to fix it for her. He wasn't really a knight in shining armor, but he was a determined man. Kate would say this was her brother's natural response to a damsel in distress, but he disagreed. This was his response to a prickly, independent, annoying, headstrong young woman who not only refused to be impressed by him, but who had also clearly decided he was not the sharpest arrow in the quiver.

He had to get a handle of sorts on his reactions to Daisy Marchant. His family would pillory him otherwise, for one thing, and he was beginning to feel like the fourteen-year-old Valentine who used to stand on his head to impress the Redgrave cook's young daughter. What did he think he was doing, allowing her to come along with him tonight? It was the action of a man who could tell himself he knew she would simply follow him, anyway...while a small part of him whispered: *Show-off. How far will you go just to hear her finally say,* Oh, Valentine, you're wonderful?

"All right, we've given them enough time. Let's go," he said at last, figuratively pushing both the imp and his conscience into a mental cupboard and locking the door. "You stay behind me, walk when I walk, step where I step, stop when I stop. We're here to observe, nothing more."

"And if we're detected?"

"You should have asked yourself that question before leaving your room. It's too late now, because I can't have you out here alone."

She didn't seem to have a response for that. *Finally!*

He took her hand and they began the at-least two-hundred-yard slow climb to the clearing in front of the cliff.

CHAPTER SEVEN

DAISY BEGAN TO hear the dull, repetitious chanting when she and Valentine were perhaps halfway along in their slow, careful climb through the trees. It was a sound designed to make one's skin crawl.

They were only men in silly costumes. That's all. They weren't really beasts, or anything in the least mythical or unnaturally powerful or possessed by the devil.

They were just men.

Six of them.

Valentine was one man...and she was a distraction.

She shouldn't have come.

What if she coughed? What if she sneezed? What if she stubbed her toe in the dark and said *Ouch* before she could stop herself?

Valentine must be out of his mind, to allow her to put him in such danger. She ought to tell him... no, gesture to him. Point back the way they'd come, show him she was leaving. Her need to know what happened to Rose had clouded her judgment. The need to assure herself Valentine was safe had convinced her she could somehow protect him, be of use to him.

She'd have to think more about that latter reason tomorrow…if they lived to see tomorrow.

Valentine gestured, pointing to himself, pointing up toward the still unseen standing stones. Pointing to her, pointing to the ground. Making an almost ridiculously fierce face that told her he'd brook no argument from her.

This was it; there was no turning back now.

She nodded her agreement, and he turned about on his haunches, getting ready to rise to a crouch, she supposed, and move forward. Would she ever see him again? She took his hand in both of hers and he turned back to her, frustration in his eyes.

She kissed the back of his hand, hoping he understood what she meant: *Be safe. Come back.*

Strange. She'd always thought she was rather proficient when she and her charges played at charades, but this time she'd clearly missed the mark. Or so she thought when Valentine pulled her close and captured her untutored mouth with his own clearly much more experienced one.

His arms went around her, his tongue played havoc with her lips and tongue, and she was dizzy and near to breathless when he at last broke the kiss to whisper close beside her ear.

"We who are about to die salute you."

"That…wasn't helpful. Please be careful," she whispered back rather shakily, and then he was gone.

Daisy waited a full minute—she silently counted off the seconds—before she realized she wasn't going to be able to talk herself out of following him. No one had ever kissed her before, Lord knew if she'd ever be kissed again...so she was not about to let this silly, brave man get himself killed!

First checking to be certain her sharp sewing scissors were still safely tucked into her pocket, she began her slow move forward, staying just to the right of the line Valentine had taken.

Her heart seemed to be beating in time with the chants coming from above her. She could make out a few of the words now, and they were ridiculous. Pompous. Self-aggrandizing. Clearly meant to build up their courage and convince themselves of their great, devil-blessed power. *Full of sound and fury and signifying nothing.* If she didn't know what she now knew, she would think them overgrown boys playing at something they didn't understand, and who'd probably turn tail and run if their governess saw them and demanded to know what they were doing.

If only she could see them, but that would be more than useless—it would be unnecessarily dangerous.

The chanting stopped. There was nothing now but silence, and the sound of Daisy's breathing, which seemed unnaturally loud to her.

"All right, then, that's done. I'm sweating like a pig. I'm taking this damned thing off."

"Leave it, Post, you know the rules," another voice ordered.

Daisy strained forward, as if this might help her hear better. But she was already fairly certain the first voice belonged to Lord Charles Mailer. Mailer? Post? Ah, so that's what Valentine had been nattering to himself about—some sort of code names. Leave it to men to think up such nonsense and believe it brilliant.

Mailer spoke again. "What? Now you're taking on the job of that useless old idiot Miner? *I am the Keeper. There are rules.* What a bloody bore, may the traitor burn forever in our Unholy Master's deepest pit of Hell."

Someone laughed, then said, "Started him off flaming here, didn't we, to help him on his way? Him and his ladywife both. Shame about her, though. The things she'd do, and gladly. Never saw a woman so appreciative of my—"

"That will suffice. We're here to discuss this month's applicants, not indulge your fantasies about the size of your cock, which is largely wishful thinking in any case."

Daisy squeezed her eyes shut, wishing she could squeeze her ears shut, as well. Had that been a woman's voice? It had been, yes, even as the mask probably distorted the sound. One of the monsters was a *woman!*

"Sorry. Didn't mean to bring that up. Know we're not supposed to talk about it. So sorry."

Now the silence coming from the circle was tense, nearly deadly.

At last Mailer—Post—spoke again. "Mine's getting restless and keeps saying he's going to leave."

"I'd leave, too, if I was quartered with you," someone said. One of the men; Daisy couldn't really sort out their voices too well. Again, it must be the masks.

"He's sincere, Post? I wonder if this isn't all too convenient." The woman again.

"If you thought that, why did you have me go after him?" Mailer asked peevishly.

"We're still waiting, Post."

"All right, all right. He's seems genuine enough to me. Always going on about his brother. The earl, you know. How he's kept him on a leash and a poor pittance of an allowance, how he's just as much a Redgrave as him, how it's our own monarchy that keeps its foot on his neck with outdated rules, entails, entitlements and the like—on and on. He's more than hinted about his admiration of Napoleon and downright hatred of the Hanovers. Even some drivel about being descended from the Stuarts, as if that means a jot these days."

And again, it was the woman who responded. To Daisy, it was clear she was the one in control. "That's good, but hardly enough. Anyone can talk. We need to own him."

"I spoke with the madam at the brothel we visited one night. Redgrave put three of her best out of action. He's got unnatural ways, that's what the madam told me. She's had him barred from the place even though she said he tossed fifty quid at her feet, to pay for what he said were *damages*. And then there was the boy."

Daisy had both hands clamped to her mouth now, her eyes wide as saucers. *Valentine? They were talking about Valentine?*

"What about the boy?" one of the other men asked. "You can't stop there."

"We were walking back from my club," Mailer went on. "I turned down one of those scraggly beggar boys that come up on the quality all the time— you know the sort. Next thing I know, there's howls from the alleyway and Redgrave goes trotting off to investigate, God knows why."

"God knows nothing. Satan knows all."

"Yes, Burn, of course, just as you say, all hail to the king of the bottomless pit. I'm sure Post didn't mean anything by it," the woman said rather wearily. "Is there any way you can shorten this, Post? We still have the other to discuss." Oh, yes, the woman was clearly in charge.

"I was almost done. The beggar boy's master was caning him, for having failed, I suppose, and Redgrave put a stop to it, flashed a small purse and asked the master if he could have him. The beggar boy, you understand. His coach had been following us along the street for protection, and Redgrave had the boy lifted up next to the coachman, then bid his good-nights to me. I told him, I said 'Redgrave, you're a soft-hearted fool.' And he winked at me and said he wasn't, that he was a man with *appetites*. Left me standing there on the street with my jaw at half-mast, so eager was he to get home."

"Hmmm," the woman said, and Daisy could almost imagine her nodding her head, considering. "We don't need him ruining our women and pleasures, or that of our other invited guests. Do please keep that in mind."

"It was only the once, and I didn't actually *mean* to—"

"My comment wasn't confined just to you, Post. I was speaking to all of you. Our supply is not unlimited. We'll consider the latter then, for Redgrave. We've used a boy before, to great effect. Unless anyone has an argument to the contrary, Redgrave is approved. Burn, find me a boy before tomorrow night."

"How in bloody hell—cursed heaven—am I supposed to—"

"Do I have to think for all of you? You've had enough boys of your own, Burn, find a way. Now, tell me about this man of yours. Frappton, is it? Redgrave will come in handy thanks to his brother's estate. Why would we want your man?"

"You don't, I do." Daisy could now tell that the man named Burn was the one speaking. "I think I may have tipped my hand a bit with that last diverted shipment of boots. With City being so stupid as to walk in front of a dray wagon, we'll never know if he was about to take the blame for that one, or me."

"Then it really was an accident? You mean we didn't do that?" Mailer sounded relieved, almost joyful. "I mean, not that we would have had any reason to… That is…um, do go on, Burn."

"As I was doing before you interrupted, you mean? You're an ass, Post. If it weren't for this being the perfect place for the altar—"

The woman all but shouted his name. "Burn! You were asked to share your reason with us so that judgment can be passed."

"Yes, sorry, Exalted One. Anyway, the way I've figured the thing, I need Frappton to willingly put *his* hand to the next set of orders and forge my name at the bottom. He'll of course be caught out, thus effectively clearing me of all suspicion, as I'll be shocked past all bearing by this act of treachery and treason. Not that he's to know that part."

"Clever. So it's to be the usual test of loyalty after a night of unmingled pleasure he'll be hot to experience again, and then he conveniently puts a period to his existence, since you can only use him the once. He couldn't live to expose any of us."

"I thought a midnight leap into the Thames wouldn't come amiss for such a disgraced man," Burn said jovially.

"Then we're agreed. You may bring him tomorrow night. How best do we accommodate his tastes?" the woman asked just as if, Daisy's spinning mind suggested, she was inquiring into this Frappton person's wine preference.

Burn laughed. "Tastes? I wouldn't put it past him to be a virgin."

That statement was followed by snickers and general laughter, and then the sound of clapped hands, followed by immediate silence until the woman spoke again.

"I have disturbing news. There's good reason many of us are not in attendance this night, as they are of necessity occupied elsewhere. We are now informed Weaver did indeed fail. He's either dead or gone to ground, knowing the punishment for failure."

"And our shipment? The opium we requested?"

"Gone, disappeared. Hammer has been put in charge of those of us burdened with recouping our losses. That we know anything at all is that one of our French contacts managed to escape the attack. It took him some time to find his way to us, and we had to dispatch him, of course, once we had his news. We couldn't be certain he hadn't been followed, and preservation of the Society trumps all."

"Understandable. Can't have any of these fellows roaming the countryside, speaking their Froggie tongue," Post agreed. "Was he able to tell us what happened? Revenue officers? A storm?"

"Neither. He swore it was pirates, attacking both on land and at sea when the schooner attempted to run. *Pirates.* Clearly the man was both a coward and a fool. Still, fearing for his life, he actually jumped from the schooner and somehow made his way to shore, which is the only reason we know anything at all."

Burn asked: "And what do we know?"

Now the woman's voice became hard, her words quick and clipped. "Bonaparte foolishly extends his honeymoon even as his mistress gives birth, but should return to Paris soon. We know Masséna assumed command in Portugal, and have it on good authority that the next move is to successfully end the siege at Ciudad Roderigo in order to target key fortresses along the lines of Torres-Vedras. Viscount Wellington is rapidly gathering an Anglo-Portuguese army to confront Masséna, so that it is imperative we continue our efforts to disrupt supply lines and slow Wellington's progress. We can afford no more failures, as our credibility with the new emperor rests on our successes."

"You said we lost the shipment," another voice asked. "Can we take that to mean the gold heading for Bonaparte is included in that loss?"

"It does. Along with our schooner and landing parties. Sad to say, it was a complete rout. I need not tell you this is a crushing blow. We've barely any time before the new moon to gather enough gold coin, which will be difficult thanks to the loss of the opium, and with no real way to alert our French friends not to land in the usual place. We were foolish to keep our knowledge of his connections to the

French limited to Weaver. Turning Redgrave our way or blackmailing him with the boy alive to point a finger at him so that he hangs as a sodomite—the method doesn't matter, understood, as long as it leads to success. We need access to that beach one last time, and we have no reason to trust this Redgrave fellow but your assessment, Post. It isn't necessary, I hope, to tell you the consequences if you allowed yourself to be hoodwinked."

Mailer *hrummphed* with some bravado. "As you all know, I plan to live well into my ninth decade, and die in the arms of my latest mistress."

Now came a voice Daisy hadn't heard as yet, muffled by the mask, but definitely male. "What an ass you are, Post. Have you ever seen a ninety-year-old teat? Because that's the best you could hope to get."

They were little boys. Horrible, filthy little boys. It was the woman. Daisy felt certain of this. She controlled the others. She'd heard how many of them speak? Post. Burn. That last voice. Perhaps one other, earlier.

That left one. One who was there, masked as the others, but not speaking. Why? Because he had nothing to say, or because he let the woman speak for him?

Daisy couldn't be certain. She had no way of knowing if she was right or wrong…but it seemed logical to her that the woman would have a consort. Didn't all the most renowned villainesses of history have a consort? Or perhaps some variation on a witch's *familiar?* Someone physically stronger, able to dispatch those she condemned? A presence, albeit in the background, that reminded anyone foolish enough to challenge her that she was not without her protection?

She would have to ask Valentine his opinion… directly after he was done tearing a verbal strip off her hide for having sneaked up the hill to eavesdrop, of course.

Daisy came back to attention as the woman ordered the session closed. There was some foot shuffling, a final prayer having some slight connection to the Lord's Prayer, but horribly profane, and then the unexpectedly bright light from the lantern as it was held high and the descent begun.

She all but dug herself into the ground, counting slowly to one hundred, and then to one hundred again, before making her way back down the hillside, hoping to locate the spot she was supposed to have been inhabiting for the past half hour.

Valentine was already there, drat him.

"I should have tied you to one of these trees," was all he said as he grabbed at her hand and began pulling her back up the hillside. "You heard everything, of course."

Daisy hoisted her skirt so she wouldn't trip, and said nothing.

"Silence is as good as a yes, you know."

"I—I don't want to go back up there."

"Oh, no, Miss Marchant. In for a penny, in for a pound. You're not backing out now."

"Speaking of *now,* I don't like you very much right now," she told him as the stones came in sight thanks to the full moon.

"I'm not particularly in charity with you at the moment, either, so I suppose that makes us even. There," he said when they'd reached the circle. "Sit down right there."

Daisy's eyes grew wide. "On one of these stones? No, absolutely not."

"Sit. Down."

She sat down.

He sat down right beside her.

The gesture didn't make her feel any better, especially when he immediately jumped up again, swearing, and rubbing at his hip. "What in hell do you have in your pocket?"

Now she felt really silly. "My sewing scissors. To… I thought if I needed to…defend myself— Oh, stop glaring. Your eyes are positively shooting daggers in the moonlight."

"I'm not shooting daggers—I've been *stabbed* by one. I have never met a woman who can drive me so close to insanity, do you know that?"

"Yes, and I'm not proud of that, no," Daisy told him, twisting her fingers together in her lap. She tipped her chin toward the spot where the altar had been placed. "Is…is there anything over there?"

Valentine sighed, and went to look, poking at the

grass with his sword stick. "Chicken. No, I correct myself, it was a rooster. The obligatory sacrifice to the netherworld, I suppose. I don't think the woman is some sort of witch or true believer. This entire business of devil worship and the rest is nothing more than a sop to get her what she wants. She's humoring the others, even trapping them into doing her bidding. A woman. God, I never would have believed it, and neither will anyone else."

She couldn't seem to control her tongue. "So you noticed. I agree. Post—Lord Mailer, that is—finds all the ceremony fatiguing, I believe, but Burn—that would be your Mr. Charfield, of course—is more invested in all the…theatrics. I imagine some would find it all strangely empowering, rather like rousing war whoops before going into battle."

"War whoops?"

"Yes, done both to invigorate and terrify. I've read about the Native Americans, and the Saxons, of course. The Mongols. And the Vikings—stop shaking your head like that. You did ask. But to continue. I couldn't tell much about the others, and I don't think one of them spoke at all. Do you think that's because he's only a more minor member? I don't. I think he's her consort. No one can lead simply with determination. There always has to be a show of force somewhere. All the great leaders of history knew this."

Valentine rubbed at his mouth. "Sweet Jesus. I'm terrified you'll faint in fear, and you're turning this into a *classroom*." He returned to the fallen lintel stone and sat down once more. "So, you figured out the code."

She nodded. "Yes, but I think I'm done now, except to say you should be quite ashamed of yourself."

He turned toward her. "Because of—damn it, woman, I didn't *do* any of those things."

"No, but you thought them up, didn't you?"

"Not really, no. I, um, *borrowed* them from something I read. We found some journals the Society had been keeping, recording their—let's call them *exploits*—and picked from any number of possibilities. Look, I should probably start at the beginning."

Daisy wrapped her cloak more tightly around her. "Yes, I suppose so. I'm in no great rush to return to my room in any case. I wouldn't dare sleep, for fear of nightmares. Please, if you would, begin with *we*. Who are *we?*"

It took some time, and Daisy had to bite her tongue now and again, to keep from interrupting with a question, but at last she understood. Or thought she did.

We were the Redgraves, the entire family, including, unbelievably, their own grandmother, all of them out to aid the Crown and keep both old and new scandal away from their name. Their own grandfather had founded the Society, their own father had resurrected it some years later, and now persons unknown to them had invented their own version, their own aims and ambitions.

Jessica, the current earl's wife, had nearly been a victim of the Society, and it was her father, Turner Collier—his code name *Miner*, as colliers were miners—who had helped form this latest group. It was through meeting Jessica that Gideon, the earl, had learned about the Society, and it was Collier and his second wife who had been murdered by the Society, their coach then set on fire. *Started him off flaming here, didn't we, to help him on his way?*

Collier had been the *Keeper* of the Society rules and journals, second in command to Barry Redgrave—Valentine's father. The journals kept by each member ever since the first Society was active had all been found, but the *bible,* where Collier annually condensed *all* the information, had been destroyed by Collier himself before his death. The bible had been the key to understanding the journals, and contained a list of all members and "guests" by name as well as code.

The Redgraves had made much progress, but there was still so much to know before the Society could be destroyed.

Many of the members whose code names were culled from the journals were now dead, but clearly some remained alive, like Burn, and Post, and Hammer. And, also clearly, the Society continued to bring in new members, all of them set on handing the country over to Bonaparte in turn for whatever reward they coveted. They employed the same method of recruitment and entrapment, the hellfire club. And, probably thanks to Collier's knowledge of the area, had both adopted the rites and made use of tunnels and beaches at Redgrave Manor to carry out some of their plans. Until, having no further use for him, it would appear, the Society had him and his wife murdered.

The Redgraves believed the last of the Society to be active during their father's years as Exalted Leader or whatever he called himself were now all dead, either through age or execution, and there was no way of knowing the identities of any of the new Society unless they could break the code found in Collier's journal. Charles Mailer (Post) and Archie Urban (City), had been the last known code names the Redgraves knew, save for Hammer. Although the Society had many members, the inner circle wielded the power, limited to a Devil's Dozen of thirteen.

Prime Minister Perceval seemed to believe the Redgraves when Gideon went there to tell what he knew, but had then forbidden them to involve themselves: a request clearly ignored. Valentine planned to insinuate himself into the Society via Lord Mailer in order to gain information and hopefully destroy the Society from the inside, and when he looked at the governess in her drab gown, bun and glasses, saw the disdain and intelligence in her eyes, he'd assumed she was an agent sent by Perceval to watch both Mailer and himself.

"Me," Daisy said at last. "I still cannot imagine why you would have thought such a thing."

Valentine put a finger to his mouth. "*Shh,* I'm not done. Don't you want to know what's going on *now?*"

"But I already do, don't I? You're going to be invited to *perform* for them tomorrow night—and how you'll get around that I don't wish to so much as contemplate. Mr. Frappton, poor man, is going to be royally entertained—something else I don't want to think about—and then coerced into treason as a proof of loyalty, and then summarily murdered to protect Burn. The Society, thanks to its own bumbling—in my opinion, they really should have kept that Frenchman alive—are being forced to meet their French counterparts on Redgrave land one more time come the new moon, and that's when you'll have them. Because there aren't really pirates, it was you Redgraves. Pirates? What nonsense."

"Yes, what nonsense," Valentine repeated, grinning.

Daisy's mouth dropped open as she stared at him. "You can't really mean that's true?"

"As my sister's soon-to-be husband said, and all that he will say, is he gained assistance from a least-likely but exceedingly talented and proficient party. Some questions aren't to be asked, and I only hope Simon knows how to contact these men again. Now, if there are no more questions for tonight—I'm certain you'll think of others for tomorrow—I suggest we return to our beds."

He stood up, held out his hand, and she took it. "You don't think we were missed, do you?"

They began making their way down the path, Valentine in the lead.

"I hope not. I can't be certain Mailer won't check on me a second time, and Piffkin may have rolled over in his sleep, giving the game away."

"You put your valet in your bed to pretend he's you? You know, Valentine, that was rather brilliant. Not that anyone would think to come looking to see if I am in my bed."

"You keep the door locked, and as I've said before, I doubt anyone would dare…and that was before I knew about the scissors."

Daisy concentrated on her footsteps for a while before asking, "Who do you think that woman could be, Valentine? Someone called her Exalted One."

"But only the one time, did you notice that, as well? It would appear she has no code name. I wonder if those fools even know who they're bowing to, what with the masks."

"I still think she isn't the sole leader. I think there have to be two of them. A woman can be so easily overpowered. Physically." As she said the words, she had a horrible flash of Rose being grabbed by strong men wearing those awful masks. She gasped aloud, and couldn't stop herself from staggering as she felt the blood draining from her brain.

Valentine turned around at once, letting go of her hand and taking hold of her at the shoulders.

"What? Did you hurt yourself? Daisy, are you all right? You didn't stab yourself with those damned scissors, did you?"

"No, no. I'm fine," she said, but she couldn't look at him. It was dark enough beneath the trees that he probably couldn't see her face. Or her sudden tears.

"No, you're not. I can feel you trembling. You're so damn calm, and logical, reasonable—I should have realized the true effect all of this is having on you. You've led a sheltered life, no matter how independent you pretend to be. My God, the vicar's daughter, come face-to-face with a hellfire club. What could be worse?"

Knowing your own sister was one of their victims. Sensing her terror, forced to acknowledge her fate. Remembering the lessons of her father, dutifully searching for, but finding no forgiveness in her heart. Wanting them dead, wanting to kill them all. Rose. Oh, sweet Jesus, Rose...

Daisy couldn't hold herself together any longer. She broke down. Completely.

Valentine drew her to the ground with him, settled her on his lap as she held on to him with all of her strength, sobbed against his chest for what seemed like hours.

He loosened her bun, softly stroked her hair, her cheek, rocked her as if she were a child.

"I'm sorry," he said in a broken voice, over and over again. "I'm so, so sorry."

At last, she stopped; there simply were no more

tears to cry. She didn't feel better. She felt drained, empty. Hollow inside.

She said nothing as Valentine wiped at her face with his handkerchief, then put it to her nose and told her to blow, as if she were a toddler in the nursery.

"Good girl," he said bracingly, and somehow she smiled.

"And you're a good man," she told him, touching her hand to his cheek. "Thank you." She moved in closer, and pressed her mouth lightly against his.

He was so sweet. He held her, but only lightly. He stroked her hair again, somehow brought them both to their feet while not breaking the kiss. She felt his arms encircle her back, slid her arms around his neck.

They kissed. That's all. They simply kissed. At a moment like this, anything less wouldn't be enough, while anything more would be profane.

And the world would go on, wouldn't it? The world always went on.

"Come on," Valentine said at last, breaking the kiss, taking her hand once more. "Let's get you safely back inside before any of the servants stir in the kitchens."

When they got to the servant entrance, he pulled her spectacles from his pocket and put them on her, carefully wrapping the flimsy wires behind her ears. "You know, I'm almost beginning to like these," he told her, and then kissed her one more time. "I'll find you tomorrow, I promise."

She took hold of his sleeve. "Valentine? What about the boy? You can't let them…you know what I mean."

"They're sending Charfield, so I'll follow him. I'll see to it he fails. Just don't ask me how, because you may not want to know."

"I don't care what you do, not to any of them," she said quietly, wishing he'd kiss her again, but knowing they couldn't risk being seen together. "You're going upstairs, as well?"

"Either that, or for a dip in the pond, hoping the water is cold." He smiled at her look of confusion, shook his head. "You really have no idea what I'm saying, do you? I can't tell you how wonderful I find it that you are, for all your varied and sometimes astonishing knowledge, still less than proficient in some areas. Good night, my brave Daisy."

"Good night," she said, lifting her hand to rather weakly wave at him. She watched his shadowy figure in the moonlight until he was gone, her fingers to her lips, and then turned and headed for her bed. For the first time in a long time, she was eager to say her evening prayers, at last remembering what her father had taught her long ago: *you don't blame God, Daisy, for the sins and shortcomings of mankind.*

And life did, eventually, move on….

CHAPTER EIGHT

"MASTER VALENTINE, it's time you were dressed."

"Not yet, Piffkin," Valentine said as he sat in his banyan, still damp from his bath, turning yet another page in Daisy's journal.

"You're reading the parts you promised not to read, sir. I feel it necessary to point that out. You undoubtedly swore on your honor as a gentleman."

"Daisy says I did. I don't recall. Piffkin, listen to this. 'I know Rose is the elder of us two, but I have always felt myself to be of a more practical mind. Papa's last words to me were to take care of Rose, and I have always striven to do so. Her marriage relieved me of that responsibility for some time, but with Walter now gone these last months, may he rest in everlasting peace, Rose most naturally turns to me, and I am delighted we are so close once more. She will one day find love again, smile again, how could she not? I suppose some may envy her immense beauty, her thick blond curls, her sweet and gentle nature, but I cannot. We are who we are, and I have always loved her dearly. I can only worry about her choice to continue to reside in London while she is in such straitened circumstances, most especially while I am forced to remain in this position with the Beckwiths, so far away from her. I have moved in an older lady fallen on difficult times, Miss Hopkins, to bear Rose company, and will send funds whenever I can. I will only hope to find a position closer to London as soon as possible, perhaps even in London itself.'"

Valentine closed the journal. "That entry was over six months ago."

"Poor duckie, she has to feel responsible for the rest of it, what you read to me from the pages she allowed. It's a terrible thing when a parent charges a child with such heavy responsibility, and not at all fair, to my way of thinking."

"True. It was bad enough I was charged with keeping Kate out of trees," Valentine said, trying to shake the dark mood that threatened to envelop him once more, that had been pressing heavily on his shoulders ever since he'd read the journal last night.

"As I recall, you failed. Abysmally." Piffkin began busying himself choosing his master's outfit for the day. "But do go on. What are you thinking, sir?"

"I'm sure you know. Daisy is the most calm, clearheaded, single-minded and resolute person you could ever imagine, and that's taking into consideration her long overdue, I'm sure, bout of tears last night. Witness those journal entries we read, Piffkin. She set herself off with barely any information, yet managed to both track down Mailer *and* get herself installed in the household."

"Much to admire in the young miss, yes, I agree. Unless one chooses to call her pig-headed, and impervious to considering her own welfare. Sir."

"Well, yes, I'll concede you that one. But there's no denying we have to admire her courage. Imagining kidnapping, enforced servitude—as close as I imagine Daisy could come to saying *kept mistress*. She'd remained hopeful the woman was still alive, awaiting rescue. She's now convinced her sister is dead—how ironic that her name was Rose—and wishes only to find out what happened, and the location of the body so she can return her sister to their parents in some church graveyard. Now, no thanks to me, she's also got a head full of nightmares concerning *how* Rose died, and if I'm right, a belly full of determination to make those who killed her suffer. You know what this means, Piffkin."

"It means you're even more in charity with the brave Miss Marchant than you were, and with good reason. Perhaps even bordering on enchanted."

"Well, yes, I suppose it does, you old romantic you. I don't often kiss a woman and then walk away and leave it at that, but my only thoughts last night were for her, and not frightening her after she'd heard what she'd heard. Piffkin, if you also keep a journal you may want to make a special entry today. Your lifelong charge may be growing up—astonishing, isn't it?"

"I agree. And at only the tender age of five and twenty. Mind-boggling."

Valentine grinned at him. "But to get back to what last night and this journal has taught us, mostly this means I couldn't budge Daisy out of here with a battalion of soldiers at my back. She wants answers, she's looking for some sort of justice if not revenge, and she won't stop until she gets them both."

"She also wants the whereabouts of the corporeal remains of the body, as you pointed out earlier. Some people put quite a bit of store by things like that. Knowing where your deceased lie, visiting, bringing posies and the like. Not the dowager countess, though."

Valentine had no answer to that statement, at least not one he wished to share. There were too many reasons Trixie had always told him and his siblings that the dead should rest with the dead. Not only did the Redgraves never visit the mausoleum holding their ancestors unless a new one was to be shelved there, but they were warned Trixie would haunt them from the grave if anyone dared to bring her flowers and weep over her. *Strange how none of us ever questioned her; we were children, we simply accepted.*

"What time is it, Piffkin? I'm not even dressed, yet alone fed. Where's the tray I asked you to have sent up to me? I can't allow you to keep me captive here any longer, listening to you expound."

Piffkin bowed. "Forgive me, sir." Then he tossed Valentine's small clothes at his head.

Valentine was dressed in ten minutes, fed in another five and heading for the stables, a piece of buttered toast jammed between his teeth, before the clocks struck the half hour, Daisy's journal in his pocket.

Less than an hour after that, he stood at his ease, negligently propped against a stable wall, one leg bent, the sole of his riding boot pressed against the boards, his curly brimmed beaver set front over his eyes, a lit cheroot dangling from one corner of his mouth. Just another of those apparently indolent, charmingly incorrigible, damnably attractive Redgraves. Dangerous as a dandelion.

At the sound of approaching footsteps, he peeked out from beneath his hat brim to be sure he knew who was coming. He then inhaled deeply on the cheroot, and spoke around his exhaled breath, the blue smoke carried toward the newcomers on the slight breeze. "Well, hullo there, gentlemen."

He waited until the two men saw him lounging in the shade before pushing away from the boards, holding out his hand as he approached a tall, rather lean man on what seemed to be the wrong side of forty who was eyeing him owlishly. "Frappton, you'll not introduce me? Very well. Redgrave, my good sir. Valentine Redgrave, currently a guest, as are you, of Lord Charles Mailer. Frappton and I met at dinner last night, didn't we, Cecil, had us a lovely chat, but I was devastated to learn Charles's other guest was indisposed. You look hale and hearty this morning, and isn't that good news."

Frappton was looking at Valentine with eyes bulged out like a terrified fish, as if to say *You meant it? You really meant what you said to me when you snuck into my room late last night? Please don't let this be happening. Please.*

"Lovely-*hee-ee-ee*.... *A-hem,*" he managed in a strangled voice, then sank into a silence that probably felt as dark and lonely as the tomb to the man... and he was as yet to know the half of it!

"Charfield," the man said as he glared at his assistant, pulling his hand free of Valentine's. "Harold Charfield, and I was hardly indisposed last evening, but most happily occupied. Chas didn't offer you the same? How rude of him. There's nothing more refreshing after hours spent planted on your rump in a coach than to take an invigorating ride, I say. I like my fillies young and snug, if you take my meaning. How about you?"

Now Frappton looked ready to turn and run, or swoon where he stood.

"Charles knows I prefer to choose my own bedmates, and certainly never from the servant class. But, then, to each his own, I suppose. There's no accounting for tastes, is there?" Valentine responded brightly, suddenly not feeling at all conflicted about what he had planned for this fool. "Have you come to inspect the mounts? I've already chosen the best for the length of my stay."

Charfield's long, lean face had gone nearly purple at the insult, but then he smiled. "If there is a *best* among Chas's nags, I've yet to see it. I've brought my own, and am only helping Frappton here in choosing the best of the worst. Are you riding out this morning, Redgrave?"

"Already been, actually. But don't let me keep you two from your pleasure. There's a fairly impressive ring of standing stones you might enjoy seeing, clearly a tepid copy of Stonehenge or some such site. But mind the cliff, which rather sneaks up on one, as its edge is obscured by trees."

"Yes, yes, I've seen it on previous visits," Charfield answered shortly, clearly anxious to be gone. "And now good day to you, sir. Come along, Frappton. And don't whine to me again that you don't ride. Never heard such nonsense. We'll fix that, make a man of you before the day is out, I swear it."

Frappton looked desperately to Valentine (who only winked), before his thin shoulders drooped and he dutifully followed after his employer. A casual glance at the man's nearly nonexistent rump that was about to meet a saddle for the first time, and Valentine came to the conclusion Frappton wouldn't enjoy the evening's antics even if laid back on a dozen soft pillows. Not that he'd be there at all—even Robin Hood couldn't be expected to rescue so many in one fell swoop. The pack needed thinning, beginning with dear-*hee-ee* Cecil.

Valentine waited until the two men had entered the stables, and then headed toward the front of the house, neatly cutting into the trees where they ran near the gravel drive. A five-minute walk took him to the tree where he'd tied his mount. A person didn't always need a full battalion at his back, Valentine knew, a person oftentimes merely required a brain.

He'd already taken Mailer's borrowed horse and ridden to the small wayside inn where his coach and men waited. He'd given his coachie, Twitchill, some short instructions—thank God the Redgrave servants were loyal, and didn't ask too many questions. Then he had borrowed a mount from one of the outriders, leading it to this exact spot and tying its reins to a branch, before then returning Mailer's gelding to the stables in time to say his good mornings to Charfield and Cecil.

He couldn't be certain where the pair were headed—life was always a gamble when formulating a plan—but felt fairly comfortable in his earlier assumption labeling the former too lazy to distance himself too much from the estate and the latter too unused to horseback to last more than a mile or two in any direction.

That left the closest village to the west, so that's the direction Valentine turned his horse to, and set off.

KEEPING THE CHILDREN inside when the weather outside remained so pleasant was not an easy task, and gave Daisy yet another reason to loathe Charles Mailer. *Post.*

Lydia had finally settled in with her dolls, serving them "tea" from a set of exquisitely small china she'd informed Daisy had once belonged to her *real* mama.

William, however, was quite another matter. After a solid ten minutes spent banging one of his toys against a windowpane, screeching his displeasure at being locked indoors, he had disappeared when Lydia dropped one of the teacups and it shattered on the floor.

Soothing the hysterical Lydia, followed by the necessary careful clearing of the small sharp pieces had taken Daisy's full attention, what with Agnes gone downstairs to fetch the children's lunch.

Daisy had checked every room and cabinet in the nursery before giving in to the realization that the boy had somehow escaped and could be...well, most anywhere. She couldn't leave Lydia, who was still sniffling, and had to cool her heels until Agnes returned.

"Agnes, did you see Master William?" she got to ask at last, as the woman carried a heavy tray into the room. "Well, no, of course you haven't, else he'd be with you, wouldn't he? Please do take charge here, while I go locate the naughty scamp."

Naughty scamp. Indeed! Boys were a menace,

and they only got worse as they grew. Valentine Redgrave was surely proof of that!

Daisy stepped out into the hallway, rested her hands on her hips and considered her options. She could call out William's name as she walked the hallways, but that would only call attention to the fact she'd mislaid her charge. She could open every door, search every room, go floor to floor to floor, but that could take hours. He was a very small boy in a house with dozens, if not hundreds, of places for a very small boy to hide.

Lady Caroline was closeted in her own rooms, hadn't even called for Daisy let alone her stepchildren. Frankly, Daisy couldn't see William wishing to see his stepmama. Even very small children are seldom hoodwinked by patronizing women who feign an interest and affection they can't feel. Her husband must have ripped all the *caring* out of her, poor thing.

"He wanted to go to the greenhouse to make more mud pies," she reminded herself, feeling struck with inspiration. But how does one small boy get out of the house unseen? Not via the front stairs and the foyer, always inhabited by at least one footman. Not the servant door, only accessed by crossing the kitchens, always busy this time of day.

What did that leave? Daisy closed her eyes and concentrated, recalling which rooms had French doors. *The library. The drawing room, the morning room.*

"The library," she concluded, attempting to bolster her hope. "There could be people in the other rooms, but not the library. Nobody in this house has the least interest in the library. But is William that clever? The library *is* located closest to the greenhouse, and the children and I have visited the room on the pretext of Lydia learning about globes when I was searching hopefully for maps of the area. It is possible...?"

With nothing to lose but more precious time, Daisy set out down the servant stairs and put on her sternest I-will-brook-no-nonsense governess face as she squared her shoulders and all but marched her way toward the library.

And then, her hand on the latch, she hesitated.

What if she was wrong? What if Charles Mailer was on the other side of this door? Could William even reach up high enough to depress the latch of the French doors? Would he have shut this door behind him? Children of his age didn't close doors; they simply left them swinging as they pursued what it was they were pursuing.

Besides, if he had used the doors, he'd already be at the greenhouse, now wouldn't he?

Daisy made an about-face and headed for the kitchens and the servant door. "Good morning, ladies," she said as she leisurely walked past the cook and two scullery maids. "My, my, doesn't it smell wonderful in here. No, Sarah, thank you, I would love an iced bun, but not at the moment."

As governess, Daisy knew she was considered neither fish nor fowl in any household she inhabited. Not good enough to dine with the family or even the housekeeper and butler, yet too far above the other servants to sit in the servant hall. A governess by and large led a lonely existence, which was why she took great pains to cultivate the servants. Not only did most appreciate the attention, the compliments, but over time it also provided Daisy with treats. She adored treats.

Once outside, she picked up her pace again, only to find the greenhouse locked. William may have gotten this far somehow, but he couldn't have gained entry. That left two more choices—either a return to her first assumption, the library, or searching the entire estate, both inside and out. A monumental task.

She'd get the library out of the way, then move on from there.

Anxious and distracted, Daisy nearly missed the unexpected opening of the French doors as she cut across the flagstones and approached the library. Not wishing to have to explain what she was doing outside, and without her charges, she quickly stepped behind a tall potted shrubbery, praying she wouldn't be seen.

"There, fresh air. That's better. This room reeks of inferior cigars. I still cannot fathom why you allow him to run loose."

"But you approved him." The second voice belonged to Charles Mailer, the first to an unknown man.

"She approved him."

"Yes, but isn't she in charge? You said nothing when it came time for the vote. You *were* there, weren't you? I could have sworn…"

"*We* are in charge. But not everyone has to know what we know. It pays not to be too inquisitive. Let that serve as the only reminder you will receive. You've still got to explain your flit from London after City died."

"But I did explain," Mailer whined. "I thought we'd done something wrong. I thought Archie was… eliminated. I wanted to come here, where I could collect my thoughts, contact you. But it was an accident, the dray wagon? It wasn't the Society?"

"Spoken like a coward with a guilty conscience. You never did tell me why you thought we might wish to eliminate the pair of you. Would you care to do that now?"

"It was this fellow, this Simon Ravenbill man, the Marquis of Singleton. Bird's brother, remember? He was after Archie and me all the time. Always where we were, going so far as to tell our wives he was watching us. The cheek of the man! We did nothing wrong, Archie and me. Bird put a period to his own existence, we had nothing to do with it. We just thought…well, we thought maybe you thought we had become a, you know, a liability. And then Archie was dead. I told you that."

"You did. Did I tell you the marquis is now betrothed to the Redgrave girl?"

"My God, no."

"Your cursed God, yes. And quite friendly with all the Redgraves, down to being in residence at Redgrave Manor at this very moment. Being in residence the night we lost our last shipment to this supposed band of pirates. *Now,* you flame-headed buffoon, do you realize why we had you bring him here, hmm, and why he was so happy to help you convince him?"

"He's somehow onto us. We're going to eliminate him?"

"Not immediately, no. We have him, we may as well use him, hopefully more than once. Here, take this, as I'm through explaining myself to you. You know what to do with it."

Daisy wished she dared sneak out from her hiding place to see whatever the man had just given Mailer, but if she were caught she'd be of no use to Valentine at all. They were onto him. He had to be warned.

"I want to make mud pies, but I can't find any eyes."

Daisy thought her heart would burst through her chest. She turned around quickly, to see William standing directly behind her, his clothing wet, his hands and legs covered in mud. She went down on her knees and grabbed him at the shoulders, resisting the urge to shake him only by a great application of restraint. "Where have you been?" she whispered fiercely. "No, I can already see where you've been—come with me, now."

William stamped his foot, spraying mud and water on Daisy's skirt. *"No! I want to make mud pies!"*

"Someone's out there. Who's out there?"

"Demmed if I know," Mailer said, even as Daisy heard his footfalls on the flagstones. There was no running away, no hiding. She stood up, took one of William's hands in hers, and adjusted her glasses more firmly on her nose.

"My lord," she said, stepping out from behind the potted evergreen, to curtsy stiffly and say condemningly, "Your son is incorrigible, an abomination. I hereby hand in my notice, effective at the end of the current month, and wish you luck in finding anyone who could even attempt to control his devilish, contrary ways. I gladly forfeit any severance pay, but will demand a glowing letter of recommendation—*glowing,* sir—for all I've had to put up with dealing with this spawn of Satan. Are we agreed?"

There was laughter heard from inside the library. "An incorrigible abomination? Devilish ways, spawn of Satan. My congratulations, old sport, you've done at least one thing correctly, unless you were cuckolded, which were I you, I'd suspect."

His lordship looked at his son, quite nearly smiling, and rather clumsily patted him on the top of his head. He then glared at Daisy, who returned his look from between slitted eyelids, standing her ground like a Trojan (or at least she hoped so). She'd used the largest words possible, certain William wouldn't understand what she'd said about him, and purposely tossed in those references to Satan.

"Agreed," Mailer said at last, keeping his voice lowered. "I never wanted you and your prissy ways here, anyway. Now get my boy here cleaned up and get him a sugar treat. As many as he wants."

Daisy didn't respond verbally—she couldn't be certain her voice wouldn't quaver with relief—but only dropped another stiff curtsy and walked off with William's hand still in hers.

"Papa patted my head," he told Daisy as she walked toward the greenhouse once more.

"Yes, wasn't that wonderfully condescending of him," she said, grabbing up an oaken bucket she'd seen outside the greenhouse earlier, never breaking her stride. "You're a good little boy, or at the very least very good at being a little boy, and you will eventually grow into a fine, kind man. Always remember that, Willie."

"Yes, ma'am. Are we going to make mud pies?"

"Indeed we are, young Master William, once we're back in the nursery, indeed we are," she told him as they neared the thankfully shallow stream behind the greenhouse. She could see the indentation of William's small shoes on the soft bank.

She dipped the bucket into the water, dragging it along its muddy bottom, and then pulled it onto the bank to inspect its contents. "And learn all about tadpoles, as well, it would seem. We need to add more mud, though. Why don't you scoop some up with your hands?" she said, determined to give the boy a wonderful memory from this day. The child was probably going to need some of those.

VALENTINE HAD BEEN hidden from sight at the abandoned spinney, the agreed-upon location less than a mile along the road leading to the village, long enough to begin second-guessing his brilliance.

He pulled out his pocket watch, flipped it open, frowned at the dial and then looked up at the position of the sun in the sky, to double check the accuracy of the timepiece presented to him by Trixie upon attaining his majority. Because the gift was from his grandmother, the engravings on the watch didn't bear much close scrutiny, at least by the ladies. Daisy wouldn't approve…perhaps Piffkin would accept it as a reward for faithful service.

He smiled, realizing what his thoughts revealed, slipped the timepiece back in his pocket and remembered he was turning impatient.

Charfield must be slower off the mark than even Valentine had given him credit for, if he was taking this long even with Twitchill's help. It couldn't be that the coachman had lost his way; he'd had sufficient time to reconnoiter the area and remember its location.

"Yer lordship?"

Valentine all but jumped out of his skin. He'd been so busy watching the front of him, he'd forgotten to pay attention to the back of him. In the wrong situation, that could have been his very last mortal thought, he pointed out to himself as he turned around to see the young woman holding the hand of a boy no more than eight or ten.

"Good morning, miss," he said, taking off his hat and offering the woman an elegant, sweeping bow. "You would be Twitchill's new friend?"

The woman gave a toss of her head. She was young, probably no more than Valentine's own age, but she had the proverbial "ridden hard and put away wet" look to her of someone who had seen more of life than her summers would indicate. She held out a fairly filthy paw to show him the gold piece on her palm. "Don't need no more friends. What I needs is the mate ta this."

"Which you shall have, once you've completed the task Twitchill set before you. If you don't mind, I would like to hear you tell me what that task is, all right?"

The woman sighed. "Show up here at the spinney with m'brother, say m'good days to the gentry cove there, stand in plain sight until the large'un what gave me this coin and two others shows their faces, wait until the gentry cove tosses me the other coin, and then take Georgie here and run like blazes 'til we're home again. I knows that's right, 'cause he made me say it a dozen times. Now show me the coin."

"Excellent." Valentine pulled the coin from his

pocket and held it up to her. "Would you care to bite it?"

She looked as if she might accept his offer, but then shook her head. "This is havey-cavey business, ain't it?"

"It is. And if you should ever think to use Georgie here in any such way again, I'll know about it and you'll be the worst for it, understood? You shouldn't be doing it now."

"I shouldna worry my head about that, yer lordship. Hiram!"

Valentine heard the crack of a dry branch behind him, followed by the appearance of a red-shirt-clad trio of mountains with arms like tree trunks and fists like ham hocks. They didn't look too smart, but when you're that big, smart isn't always needed.

"Hullo there, Hiram," Valentine repeated, bowing, and then looking to the other two men, "and et cetera. Out for a stroll?"

"Wuz told I could bring m'other brothers along," the young woman said, grinning so that the gap between her two front teeth was evident…and repeated in the smiles of all four brothers. "Get yerself back in the trees, Hiram. You, too," she added, waving at the other brothers.

Valentine doffed his hat once more, this time finishing by wiping his forehead with his coat sleeve. "I must remember to thank Twitchill when I see him. My heart hasn't had such exercise in quite some time." Then his smile faded. "All right, I think we need to take up our positions now. Remember, when I toss the coin to you, you run off home…you and *all* of your brothers."

"I knows what this be about, yer know," she told him as she held tight to her brother's hand and walked to the dry well at the center of the abandoned spinney, putting the boy in front of her, her hands clamped on his shoulders. "The miller, he warned us all, after his boy comes crawlin' home a while back, all bawlin' and hurtin' an' tol' him how he come ta have a pocketful of coins. Sent Bertie off ta live with his granny, the miller did. Don't knows what happened, but it was terrible bad."

"There'll be no more Berties after today. I promise you. Now, quiet, the two of you." Valentine stepped back into the trees, hoping Hiram and his brothers didn't have their own form of justice in mind. He was having enough trouble controlling his own blinding anger.

An excruciatingly long five minutes passed, during which the girl sang an old ditty about a lovelorn lass and her brother dug for (and found) hidden treasure in his left nostril. Finally, three horses rode into the clearing, led by Twitchill, who held back branches so that an angry-looking Charfield and a near-to-weeping Frappton could pass through ahead of him.

Charfield was grumbling. "I still don't see why we had to come to this godforsaken spot to conclude our transaction. There are burrs on my jacket. Burrs!

This will cost you, my good— Ah. Well, now there he is. And with an added treat you didn't mention, did you? What say you, Frappton? Cleaned up a bit, she'd be more than good enough for you."

"Sir?" Frappton asked. Even from a distance of thirty feet Valentine could see the man's bottom lip trembling. "I really don't understand why—"

"No, of course you don't, never yet having the delight. But you will. All right, my good man, let's get down to cases. How much for the pair of them?"

"Twenty quid, and a twist of tobacco," Twitchill grumbled, "and you're robbin' me blind at that."

"Twenty quid? Are you daft, man?" Charfield swung his leg back and over his mount and lightly hopped to the ground. "For that, I'll need a personal inspection, now won't I?"

"Now," Valentine called out as he stepped from the trees, the gold coin already singing through the air. The young woman deftly snagged it, grabbed her brother's hand, turned about and they both ran as if the hounds of hell were after them. Which, in one way, they were.

Twitchill had dismounted, as well, and was now holding a wicked-looking coach gun pointed directly at Charfield's head.

"Charfield, we meet again. Do you know what's about to happen, or am I going to have to say something silly like, *Burn,* old fellow, the jig is up."

"What? What the devil is going— Put down that

weapon, you underbred scum. I order you! What's this? *Redgrave?* You...you *know?*"

Valentine sighed. "First he blubbers, and now he states the obvious. Cecil, you're looking a mite green about the gills. Are you all right?"

"I...I...I... *Oh, dear...*"

Twitchill had just very neatly tapped Frappton's employer on the back of his head with the butt of his weapon.

"Yes, precisely." Valentine skirted past the now-recumbent Charfield to approach Frappton. "Did you do as I instructed you last night?"

Cecil was looking down at his employer, bug-eyed. "When...when you came to my room? I...I... yes, I did, sir. Packed it all up and put it in the wardrobe, just as you said to do. Even added my nightshirt and cap this morning. But...but I cannot possibly remain on this horse all the way to London. I can't, sir. Please don't make me."

"He can't, sir," Twitchill agreed. "Sorriest thing you'd ever to want to see, him bouncing down the road and saying *ow, ow, ow* each time his rump said good-day to the saddle. I'll get him to the village and put him on the mail coach, if that's all right."

Valentine tried not to smile. "That seems reasonable, Cecil. My man Piffkin has undoubtedly already taken your case to my coach. Twitchill here will retrieve it and make sure it rides with you on the mail coach. Agreed?"

"Yes, sir. But...but what about *him,* sir?"

Charfield was just beginning to stir, moaning and holding a hand to his head as he attempted to sit up. Twitchill stepped on his chest, putting him back down.

"As I told you, Cecil, your employer here ordered you back to work while he extends his visit in the country, and that is what you're to say if anyone should ask. It's also all you want to know. Charfield—order Cecil back to London, will you? I don't think he's the sort who can lie with any authority."

"The hell I will! Ride to the estate for help, man. Go!" Charfield shouted, still struggling to rise, but not making any progress. The coachman was a very large man, with very large boots.

"Oh, no, no, no. That wasn't quite right. Twitchill?" Valentine prompted. "I think our friend here needs some encouragement."

The coachman's heavy boot was pressed harder against Charfield's ribs.

"All right, all right! Frappton…take your worthless ass out of here…go…go back to London."

"Well done, Burn. Splendid," Valentine said brightly. "You're off now, Cecil, and with a clear conscience. Or do you still doubt what I told you last night?"

Frappton mutely shook his head, then looked down at his employer. "You…you were going to make me look the traitor, and then *kill* me. And…

and the boy, what he said about the boy. Everything Mr. Redgrave said was true. I hope you hang!"

"And all said without a giggle." Valentine clapped politely. "Huzzah. Cecil, today you are a man."

"Thank you, sir," Frappton answered, sitting up somewhat straighter in the saddle. "Today I am a man-*hee-ee-ee*. Oh, dear."

"Practice, Cecil," Valentine said kindly. "Some things take practice. Twitchill, I'll have that rope now if you please."

The coachman tossed down a burlap bag containing two lengths of rope, among other things Valentine had requested.

Valentine's brother Maximillien had taught him several Naval knots, and one particular way of trussing up a captive that he applied now. He bound Charfield's ankles and wrists behind his back and then pulled another length of rope up through both and looped one end around the man's throat, bowing him backward as he secured both ends at the wrists. It wasn't a comfortable position, and struggling would only tighten the rope around his neck, but Valentine found he could not bring himself to care about the man's comfort.

While Valentine worked, Twitchill assisted Frappton from his mount and onto his employer's.

"Very neat, sir," the coachman congratulated his employer. "I should be getting back here in an hour or so, to take him up in your coach and deliver him all personal-like, with your compliments."

"Along with a note tied round his neck, yes." Valentine was now down on his haunches beside his captive, testing his handiwork. "No hurry in returning, though. Take time for a bird and a bottle. He's not going anywhere."

Twitchill and Frappton rode off, Twitchill whistling a tune while leading the outrider's horse, Frappton punctuating each step his new mount took with a steady stream of "Ow, ow, ow."

It was the little things that mattered, Valentine thought as he watched them go. Charfield's mount supposedly on the road to London, Frappton's mount back in the stables in Fernwood, alongside the mount Valentine had ridden out on earlier.

"Ah, isn't this lovely," Valentine said, making himself comfortable on the grass. "Just the two of us."

"You can't do this! They'll know I'm gone! Damn you, Redgrave, let me up. I'll tell you anything you want."

"Really? Or would you sneak a knife from your boot and plunge it into your own chest?"

Charfield was sweating profusely now. "Why… why would I do that?"

"I don't know," Valentine said as he checked the man for any hidden weapons. "Because you'll hang in any event, I suppose. Or perhaps because your fellow traitor Weaver—or should I say Webber—managed to snatch a pistol from one of his captors and turn it on himself."

"Christ."

"Christ? Not Satan? Yet just last night you seemed so fervent a believer."

"That's all hogwash, and you know it. Comes in handy, I'll give you that. Look here, Redgrave. I know what you want. You want information, and I can give it to you. I'll give you all of it. Just let me go."

"What? No offer of money? Riches beyond my wildest dreams? Unlimited licentious pleasure in the arms of a dozen willing virgins? The seat of honor to the right of Bonaparte when he dines in triumph at the palace? I'd had such hopes. Damn, you disappoint me."

"Yes, yes, that, too! Anything you want!"

"Thank you, but no. As you must be well aware by now, I'm having some jolly good luck finding out everything I need on my own. Care to try again?"

Charfield was a traitor—for whatever reasons he deemed important—but he wasn't stupid. "You're one of those bloody idealists, aren't you," he said accusingly. "Incorruptible. Doing it all for king and country. But that means you won't kill me, either. I'm too important to you, alive."

Valentine reached into the sack once more, to retrieve a pistol he then calmly aimed at his captive's head. "And there's where you'd be wrong. I'm *doing this* as you said, for family, Burn, and family trumps all. You stepped on the wrong tail, you see, when you and your little group of merry pranksters first put foot on Redgrave land. I don't need you. I've got *Post,* don't I? In fact, you're rather in the way."

He cocked the pistol.

"But…but that man said he's taking me somewhere."

"That was said only for Frappton's sake. Me? I simply want you out of my way. See that well behind us? Dry, deserted. It will be a long time until anyone finds your bones. Not the insects, though. They'll undoubtedly find you very quickly."

Charfield stared at the pistol. A dark wet stain began spreading in the area of his crotch. "But… but I don't want to die."

"There aren't many who do." Valentine knew he had him now. "But I can be a reasonable man. Tell me what you know, quickly, before we're missed, and I'll see that you're delivered to Perceval intact and breathing, I suppose you'd like to say—if not quite dry. I imagine you'll hang, but if you sing to him the way you will now sing to me, perhaps you'll be allowed to live out your days in the Tower."

Less than thirty informative minutes later, as he still had much to do, Charfield was gagged, a black hood over his head, and Valentine was on his way back to the stables on Frappton's mount.

Poor Charfield. He believed he was being taken to Perceval, to strike a deal that would save his miserable skin. In truth, when the captive was relieved of his hood, the first face he'd see would be that of Simon Ravenbill, Marquis of Singleton.

Stupid, gullible, clearly minor player in the Society Harold Charfield. As if he'd hand the man to an uncooperative, only half-believing Spencer Perceval on a platter, so he could conveniently disappear to save the Crown a trial (or a messy explanation). No, no. Not when the Redgraves might still have need of him.

CHAPTER NINE

DAISY HAD WORRIED Agnes would throw up her hands in horror when she saw both William and the bucket, but she hadn't counted on the nursery maid being country-born and bred, and therefore delighted to show off some of her expertise in both mud-sculpting and tadpole rescuing to the clearly dazzled children.

Nearly two hours of giggles and creativity had followed. With a myriad of hopefully human figures, three-legged horses, long-tailed cats and other delights made of the good clay mud from the stream lined up on a tray placed on the windowsill to dry, Agnes had shooed Miss Lydia and Master William off to bathe them in the tub filled with hot water from the kitchens…and Daisy had at last made good her escape.

And she'd known just where she had to go.

As Valentine's rooms were in the guest wing, away from most of the hustle and bustle of the household, she hadn't expected to be stopped and questioned as to just where she was headed, and that proved to be the case. Still, she looked up and down the hallway, and then up and down the hallway again, before rapping on the door she knew was his.

"Mr. Piffkin?" she asked a moment later, when the door was opened a crack.

"Miss Daisy, I presume," was the answer, just before the door opened a bit wider and she was unceremoniously yanked inside and the door shut behind her. "He said determined. I said pig-headed. I suppose we both were right. With all respect, Miss Daisy, what in blue blazes are you doing here?"

Now that her arm had been released, Daisy brushed at her sleeve and stepped past the bald-headed man, heading farther into the room before turning to face him. "My impression, Mr. Piffkin, gained through things Valentine has said to me about you, is that you are both friend and keeper. He needs both at the moment, plus the information I have for him. Where is he?"

Piffkin looked at her for some moments. Uncomfortable moments. "Levelheaded, not at all missish or silly. Direct. Tolerant of his ways and more than capable of tugging on the reins when needed. No flaming beauty, I suppose, but a sweet, intelligent face a man would feel comfortable growing old with. Yes. I would never have thought it, frankly, but you're just what he needs. Perfect. Very well, Miss Daisy. Master Valentine is out stirring up mischief. I wouldn't frown so. He's quite accomplished at it. He'll turn up."

Daisy was left speechless. But not for long.

"That…that was all quite interesting, Mr. Piffkin. But you and he don't know what I know. They're onto him. I overheard Lord Mailer and an unknown man discussing him in the library, and then the unknown man handed something to Mailer, telling him he knew what to do with it. I've spent the last two hours imagining all sorts of things. A ceremonial knife these monsters place some sort of stock in somehow? A small, easily concealed pistol Mailer can slide out from his cuff when Valentine conveniently turns his back? All manner of things. He has to be warned, Mr. Piffkin, and we must all three of us leave here immediately. And Lady Mailer and the children, of course. I won't leave the children behind."

Now it seemed to be time for Piffkin to go in search of his tongue.

He rubbed at his shiny pate, as if to warn his brain it needed to be completely alert. "Onto him. I knew this was all going much too smoothly, but he said Lord Mailer had swallowed his story whole. Clearly someone else did not. I'm not half done carrying out my instructions…" He looked at Daisy. "Are you quite sure, miss?"

"I see no need to argue the point, Mr. Piffkin, as I know what I heard. And it's more than two hours since I heard it, so we shouldn't be standing here, wasting time. You see, what I don't know is if Mailer believed me about why I was outside the library in the first place. What did Valentine tell you to do? Perhaps I can help."

Piffkin spoke even as he began packing up Valentine's belongings.

Some of what he'd been instructed to do was already done.

Cecil Frappton's tapestry traveling bag was already at the small country inn, with no trace of the man's presence left behind, and the clerk probably already safely halfway to London, while Harold Charfield was headed elsewhere.

Valentine's evening dress had been pressed and laid out, and a hot bath had been ordered for five o'clock, as it was important to continue the charade that All Was Well.

A note had been delivered to Harold Charfield's valet just ten minutes earlier, informing him to pack and be ready to leave in the coach as soon as possible, to meet up with his employer back in London.

"Why?" Daisy asked. She was following along, but just barely.

Piffkin lifted a stack of undergarments from one of the drawers and held it close to his chest, his back prudently turned to Daisy as he shuffled sideways over to the portmanteau and quickly stuffed said intimate apparel inside. "A messenger direct from the prime minister intercepted Mr. Charfield, the clerk, and Master Valentine as they were out riding, and Charfield commissioned Master Valentine with informing his host and valet that he and

Mr. Frappton were heading straightaway to London—Charfield on his horse, the clerk put in irons and stuffed into the nondescript black coach the accompanying soldiers had brought with them—and with no time to waste returning here. And, of course, for his coach and valet to follow. It would seem a major discrepancy has been discovered within Mr. Charfield's office, and the clerk suspected of treason."

"But…but why would Mr. Frappton's bag already be gone? Surely the valet would also be charged with packing the man's bag."

"I'm going to offer to do that actually, helpful fellow that I am. No one will realize the clerk is not traveling with Mr. Charfield."

Daisy began to feel more hopeful. At least so far, Valentine's plan, if his plan was to save Mr. Frappton and be rid of Mr. Charfield, was working quite well. He was bloodlessly removing some of the players from the field, that's what he was doing, which would greatly enhance his chances of success.

"Clever. To Lord Mailer and the others, the obvious conclusion is that Charfield is worried something he's done on orders of the Society has been uncovered. He and his fellow conspirators will be too alarmed to look deeply into Valentine's story. But if Valentine has yet to return?"

"The valet won't be concerned with such details of timing, and our mutual charge is exceedingly clever with a credible lie. Plus, for all we know, he is already downstairs, informing his lordship of the latest events, and will be upstairs shortly. With your permission, I'm off now to lend assistance to my fellow gentleman's gentleman, offering to transport the bags down to the coach in order to speed its departure rather than to wait for lazy footmen. If you'd be so good as to remain here, I'm certain Master Valentine will be delighted to see you upon his return."

"You're even going to carry the bags? Oh, yes, to make sure he doesn't notice Mr. Frappton's isn't among them."

"In part, Miss Daisy, yes. If, as Master Valentine said, things somehow had gone sideways this morning, he didn't want any evidence of the clerk's presence left here to be discovered. The man, according to Master Valentine, already has enough on his plate simply being Mr. Frappton. But mostly, I'm to be sure the coach departs without one of Mr. Charfield's bags, as well."

She racked her brain for an explanation, and believed she'd found it. "Oh. You mean the one holding his cape and horrible mask, don't you? To show as King's Evidence before the Bench, I suppose. Or Valentine may believe he might have a use for both."

"I doubt there will ever be a trial, Miss Daisy, not for any of the Society. Such a thing might alarm the king's subjects, along with staining the government. When the Society is gone, it is gone. It will simply disappear."

Daisy headed to the nearest chair, and sat down.

"You…you're saying Charfield is dead? I probably should have asked that sooner."

Piffkin halted with his hand on the door lever. "Better the bird in the hand, Miss Daisy. If all has gone as planned, the man will be an unwilling guest at Redgrave Manor before midnight tomorrow. Now, if you'll excuse me?"

Daisy nodded absently, her mind whirling in several directions at once as she came up with her own agenda. She had to pack her meager belongings and toss the bag out the window, just as she had planned previously. She had to insist upon seeing Lady Caroline, somehow get rid of the snooping Davinia and convince her to leave with the children. The children themselves would be eager for any outdoor excursion, so they wouldn't present any problems, and it would be easier to order Agnes to accompany them than to leave her behind and possibly blamed for their disappearance.

Not everyone would be able to pack and take bags with them. Such a procession of trunks would certainly be noticed, not that there was time to pack those bags in any case. No, Lady Caroline and the children would have to leave with only the clothes on their backs and Lady Caroline's pin money. It was different for Daisy, and for Agnes, as well. Their possessions were few, and not so easily replaced.

Yes, that was neat. Orderly. A natural progression. Thankfully, no one seemed to much care what went on within the nursery, Lord Mailer often going weeks between so much as seeing his children, and Lady Caroline was indisposed, and not to be expected to go down to dinner.

Daisy wondered for a moment if Valentine had anything to do with the convenient absence of Lady Caroline, and then dismissed the idea. Mr. Piffkin put a lot of credence in his employer's abilities, but it seemed unreasonable to credit anyone with that much power and foresight.

Well, no matter. She couldn't simply sit here and stew, now could she? What was most important was getting them all safely out of here. She stood up and walked over to the wardrobe, intent on packing up the remainder of Valentine's belongings, quoting quietly, "'He that fights and runs away, may turn and fight another day; but he that is in battle slain—'"

"'will never rise to fight again.' Tacitus the Roman, I believe."

A neat stack of carefully pressed neckclothes hit the floor, ruining a good hour of Piffkin's best work with the pressing iron. "Valentine!"

She who always thought very carefully, didn't think at all. She simply turned and ran across the chamber, to all but throw herself at him.

"Well, now," he said, wrapping his arms around her, "other than being very nearly strangled, isn't this a lovely welcome."

She pulled slightly away from him, her arms still locked around his neck. "Oh, do shut up, Valentine," she told him, blinking back tears.

"Shut up? Or shut up and kiss me? Perhaps even *please* shut up and kiss me? Yes, I like that one best."

His smile was a delight. His amber eyes sparkled with mischief from between long, black lashes. His dark, windblown hair framed his face almost lovingly. He smelled of leather and horseflesh and sweet grass and sunshine. He was truly the most handsome, even beautiful, man in creation.

And he was smiling at her. He was holding her. He was about to kiss her, Daisy Marchant, nobody. Daisy, she of the beautiful sister. Daisy, with the practical brain and the sometimes sharp tongue. Daisy, with her unimpressive bosom, her narrow hips, her drab outdated gowns and her nonexistent prospects.

He was smiling at *her*.

And now he was slanting his head slightly and moving closer, and she was closing her eyes, and she was slightly opening her mouth for a reason she didn't understand, and he was touching his mouth to hers, and nibbling at her bottom lip, and smiling against her mouth, and drawing her closer as he somehow freed her hair from its pins, and she was raising her hands, her spread fingers sliding into his warm waves of ebony, and—

"Master Valentine, that will be enough. Appearances to one side, Miss Daisy didn't come here for that. Release her at once."

They sprung apart like a pair of guilty children, Valentine's expression caught somewhere between sheepish and outraged, Daisy heading for one of the window embrasures to hide her blushes as she twisted her hair back into its tight bun.

"Taking on the role of duenna now, Piffkin? I'll have to alert Consuela that you've usurped her position. Perhaps she'll allow you to borrow her castanets."

Thanks to long years spent learning self-control, Daisy, hair once more tidy save for a few errant curls she could feel hanging loose at her nape, left her refuge and returned to stand beside Valentine. "I'm all right, Mr. Piffkin, thank you. Who's Consuela?"

"One of my deceased mother's servants still at Redgrave Manor. I'm half Spanish which, some would say, is also an explanation for the Redgraves' wild, reprobate ways," Valentine explained as if by rote.

Daisy blinked as a discomforting thought struck her. She'd just been kissing a man she'd just barely met and knew precious little about. That wasn't like her, not at all. "We really don't know one another, do we, yet here we are together, knee-deep in skullduggery. Isn't that strange."

Valentine grinned an unholy grin. "For some, I suppose. But not for a Redgrave. It must have something to do with our honest faces, our air of gravitas, our obvious trustworthiness."

"No, I don't think it's any of those," Daisy countered thoughtfully, and Piffkin hid a laugh behind a cough.

"Piffkin, if you've been entertained enough for the moment? What's going on?"

"I believe you must ask that of Miss Daisy, sir, but I do know your self-proclaimed brilliance has put you in some danger."

"And just when I was busily patting myself on the back. Daisy?"

Valentine listened intently as Daisy recounted all she'd heard while standing outside the library, not mentioning how she'd happened to be there, but keeping only to the pertinent parts. "I can't be certain the other man remained completely unsuspicious of me," she ended, "although I doubt Lord Mailer is any the wiser."

"If he became any the wiser on any head, he'd make a tolerable doorstop. All right, I have to get you gone from here."

"I concur— Oh, don't look so surprised, Valentine. I'm not a fool. We *all* need to be gone from here, now. You most especially, as you've really put yourself in a pickle, now haven't you? How do you propose we go about it? I already have most of a plan in mind, but I know you'll disagree with at least half of it and wish to add your brilliance. But do hurry, as someone may remark on my prolonged absence from the nursery."

Somewhere behind them, Piffkin chuckled.

"You have something to add, Piffkin?" Valentine asked.

The man put down the small black leather bag

he'd carried into the room with him. "Me, sir? No, sir, nothing, not a thing. Everything's *perfect*."

Daisy could feel her cheeks reddening again as Valentine placed his hand on the small of her back and ushered her into the dressing room, closing the door behind them.

He looked at her for a long time, various emotions coming and going on his face, before he finally spoke again.

"I read your journal. Here, you should have it back."

"Oh," Daisy said quietly, looking at the thing as he held it out to her. She took it, quickly slipped it into the pocket of her gown. It was all she had left of her sister. "That...that seems so long ago. I mean, that I gave it to you."

"I'm sorry, Daisy. I'm so, so sorry."

She nodded, unable to speak.

He took her in his arms, pressing her cheek against his chest. "You know she's gone, don't you? You know we're not going to find her."

"I know. I've probably always known. He killed her, didn't he? She was so lonely, she always needed to be loved, protected. He lied to her, tricked her. He lured her here, and then after he...and then they killed her."

She looked up at Valentine, seeing him through a veil of tears. "Do you know how much I long to scream? That's silly, isn't it? But I long to just be alone somewhere I can scream and scream and..."

She bit her lips together between her teeth, and shook her head, knowing it would aid nothing to lose control. "Why, Valentine? Why her? Why anyone? Is the world really this cruel, this twisted?"

"I don't know how to answer that, Daisy. I wish I did."

"My father would say we must abhor the sin but love the sinner. That seemed so easy in theory, even reasonable. When Rose and I were children, we didn't know what real evil is. Not us, and probably not Papa, either. I only know I can't forgive it or those who perpetuate it. Does that make me terrible?"

He kissed her forehead. "That makes you human, Daisy. Evil people, truly evil people like those in the Society...they're not human. They still walk on two legs, but they're not human any longer, having banished humanity from their souls. They're self-created monsters. We're fighting a war against monsters."

"But...but can they win?"

"No," Valentine said firmly. "I won't believe that. You know I was with Charfield this morning. And I saw him for what he is, beneath his evil, beneath the mask he chose to hide behind. And do you know what I saw?"

Daisy shook her head.

"Fear. Cowardice. A willingness to betray his comrades in a heartbeat in order to save his own neck. Kate's fiancé believed the man he caught at Redgrave Manor chose death over betrayal, but he was wrong. He chose a quick death over the hangman, that's all, and took the coward's way out. That's how we'll defeat them, Daisy, through their greed, their ambition, their evil and, at the heart of it all, their cowardice, as they turn on one another, destroy one another."

She managed a wan smile. "Because, in the end, good always triumphs over evil?"

Valentine grinned. "And because we're smarter than they are."

Daisy lifted one eyebrow.

"More determined?"

The other eyebrow went up.

"Luckier?"

"We'd better hope so, *Master Valentine*," she said. "Thank you, by the way. I promise not to go all weepy and missish on you again."

He ran a fingertip down her cheek, then watched intently as one escaped curl all but wrapped itself around his finger. "You're never missish."

"That's true. I'm perfect," she said, this time smiling in earnest.

Valentine frowned, and looked toward the door leading to his bedchamber. "Why does the idea you and Piffkin have cried friends make me suddenly nervous?"

"I'm sure I have no idea," Daisy told him, stepping out of his light embrace and taking up a seat on the very edge of the slipper chair in the corner of the room. "Now, what do we do next? I'm already convinced my plan of gathering up Lady Caroline and the children and all of us then simply racing hotfoot away from here holds no immediate appeal for you, although my vote is we flee and return another day. Only please tell me you aren't thinking of doing anything too heroic. And by that, I mean heroically dangerous."

"I need you all safely away. Far away," he said quietly. "If I don't present myself in the drawing room before dinner, they'll be after us in a heartbeat. Therefore, you are now commissioned General-in-Charge of removing everyone to the inn—it's less than a mile so the children can manage it, and Piffkin knows the way. I will give you the time to do that, and be put in a hired coach that will head for Redgrave Manor. Once I'm certain I've given you enough time to be safely gone, I'll excuse myself via one means or another, and make my way to the inn, taking up Charfield's not-too-shabby bit of horseflesh and employing an alternate route to the Manor, just in case I'm followed. We'll all meet again there in two days. Simple, yes?"

"I suppose so. But please explain the part where you *simply* excuse yourself from the drawing room."

"I would, if I knew that part," he told her, putting out his hand to assist her to her feet. "Now go back to the nursery, Daisy. As you said, you'll soon be missed."

"In a moment. First I think we have to go over your brilliant plan one more time. With one minor change. Or did you really think you could be rid of me so easily? Oh, and then I think you could probably kiss me again."

"GOOD EVENING, CHARLES," Valentine called out as he entered the drawing room before the first gong had rung for dinner, wishing to speak to the man alone. "Will it just be us two again this evening, now that the esteemed Mr. Charfield has been called back to London? Quite exciting that, I have to tell you. A half-dozen nattily-clad soldiers charging toward us. Frappton looked guilty as sin when they clapped on those irons, although hanging him might prove problematic—with the noose slipping up and over his nonexistent chin. Or is it still the chopping block for treason?"

"I wouldn't know," Mailer replied absently, pouring himself a glass of wine. His hand shook, and the rim of the decanter almost danced against the rim of the glass. "Six of them, you said, and a coach? That...that sounds excessive."

"An impressive escort, definitely. Rather like an honor guard. Or at least a guard of some sort. But enough of our absent friend. You didn't deny we'll be boring ourselves spitless for a third interminable evening. Please say it isn't so."

Mailer seemed to remember he was Valentine's host. "No, no, I assure you, we'll still be a jolly enough group. Only the two of us for dinner here,

I'm afraid, but then we'll move on to the real adventure I've been promising you."

Valentine sat down and crossed one long leg over the other at the knee, the picture of an unsuspecting man at his ease. "Promising, yes. Providing, no. Charfield told me about his evening. A servant girl? I believe your idea of entertainment is thus far underwhelming, Charles. Tell me more about this *party* you're so certain will make up for the delay. You may begin, if you please, by explaining why I must travel to it. Is it even your affair at all? I had assumed you were in charge."

Come on, come on, Post. Let me hear how you plan to coerce me, use me. Even if now you simply plan to kill me. Please, take your time. And while we natter on, Piffkin and Daisy are already removing your wife and kiddies to safety.

Mailer seemed more than willing to expound. After all, what dastardly villain doesn't enjoy boasting of his nastiness, especially to his prospective victim, who wouldn't survive to repeat any of it?

The man took up a seat on the facing couch after placing a glass of wine on the table in front of Valentine, who slanted the contents a quick look, half surprised the contents weren't fizzing.

"I told you about the conversations, our determination to change the face of England forever, and you'll learn more of the *how* of that as we meet with the others. An England with the land and money and power in the correct hands, brilliant hands, and not simply passed on by something as chancy as birth order. We aid the emperor in attaining his goals, and in turn he aids us in achieving ours."

Valentine picked a bit of lint from his breeches. "It's called *quid pro quo,* Charles. I just recently learned that somewhere. Working with men who share our enlightened view of the world. I admit this interests me, as I am not a man without ambition, yet considered a near child by my older brothers, and not recognized as a man of worth. You and I, Charles, we're kindred spirits, and too long denied."

"All that will change. All of it. *You* will be the master of Redgrave Manor and all that goes with it. My cursed brother will be applying to *me* for an allowance. We have the emperor's word on that."

"Yes, yes. But I must admit I'm more intrigued at the moment by the prospect of this *entertainment* you've hinted at so broadly. Three days without an outlet for my passions thanks to you—I could be a monk, for God's sake. The *outlets* will be prostitutes, I imagine. You're certain they're clean? So far, Charles, the only thing worse than cooling my heels here could be returning to London with a dose of the clap."

Mailer laughed. He seemed to have located his bravado again, if not his courage. "Oh, they're clean. My woman sees to that every time. And willing, most of them, eager to indulge your every fantasy. I like the unwilling ones myself. Whores only play the parts, but the unwilling ones? That's where the true pleasure lies. Pleasure the like of which you've never known in the tame brothels of Piccadilly. Those will come later, but for tonight, with not all of us able to be in attendance, we make do with the whores. They're all quite convenable. What's your appetite? Pain? Pleasure? Men? Women? Both at once? Watching? Charfield likes to watch. Looks the fool at times, standing over some writhing Cyprian performing for him, panting and drooling and using himself like a bloody pump handle. I like blondes, myself. *True* blondes. Sweet and silky. Like licking iced cakes."

Valentine was amazed he'd yet to leap across the table and choke the man with his own cravat. "You're describing an orgy, Charles," he said disdainfully. "I'm not a performer at Astley's."

Again, Charles Mailer laughed. Valentine longed to never hear that laugh again.

"Ah, a shy one. Many are, at first. Some always. They never show their faces. Everything else, you understand, but not their faces." There was that laugh again. He sat forward, cupping his wineglass between his pudgy fingers. "Here's the thing, my friend. Have you ever heard talk of Dashwood's Hellfire Club? Not that his was the only one, but your dormitory mates must have whispered about it at school. Met in a cave, the way I heard it, held unholy rites and diddled the naked women draped in their laps while spouting poetry and politics and drinking themselves senseless. Virgin sacrifices some say, along with plans to overthrow the king, but no one could ever prove it."

"I know what a hellfire club was, Charles, and never believed the half of what I heard. So now you're telling me you worship Satan? What? Dress up like horned devils and drink goat blood, dance naked under the moon with your cocks dangling like undercooked sausages, that sort of nonsense?"

"But there's a reason for it all, don't you see? Rutting gives us strength, the ancient Greeks and Romans—one of the two, at least—knew that. And… and it creates the most intimate *bond* between us that can't be broken. For others—not you, God knows not you—who share our dreams and interests, we offer pleasure for favors. Like…like Charfield's man— Fratby, was it? A night with us and he'd do anything we asked, just so he could return for more pleasure. Do you see now, do you understand now?"

Valentine stood up, wanting to distance himself from the wine, which might be drugged, and from his thoughts, that ran back to his own father and grandfather performing such rites with the Society, using those rites to gather a small army of highly placed traitors. He supposed it had been so since the beginning of time, and might always be so—sex as a lure, and then as a weapon. How many empires had risen or fallen, not because of a Cleopatra or an Aphrodite, or even Homer's Helen of Troy, but because a man felt some overpowering need to feed his twisted belief in his own powers?

His mother, his grandmother, Daisy's sister and how many countless more were there, would there be, if the Society wasn't stopped? Women used to bolster a man's opinion of himself, women subjected to all manner of horrors and physical degradation, so that the men could feel powerful. Women abused, even killed, employed as tools to seduce and even blackmail other men into helping the Society. And, if the man's ambition led to disaster, it was always the women left with the blame.

No wonder his grandmother heartily despised men.

And yet, in this incarnation, the leader of the Society was a woman. How would Trixie react to that, once she was told?

But Mailer was waiting for an answer.

"Thank you, Charles, but no. If you'd told me this at the outset, I wouldn't be here at all. Hellfire club? I wouldn't so lower myself as to…" He turned back to face his host, who was looking concerned, nearly frightened. Clearly what they'd planned for him was planned for later, at this so-called *party*. Mailer must be afraid he'd failed, and there were punishments for failure. "Masks, you said? No one would know who is whom?"

Mailer hopped to his feet. "Yes, yes, masks. And…and capes. Here, let me show you." He rushed to a wooden chest beneath one of the windows, only to return holding up a large, vile green head fashioned to resemble a scaled serpent with a flat, diamond-shaped forehead and red forked tongue, a similar green scale-designed silk cloak over his arm. "There, see the eye holes? You'd be looking through those, just as if you *were* the snake." He used both hands to move the mask from side to side. "Sliding and slithering, even biting your way through a sea of bare, perfumed flesh. I designed it for you myself. Isn't it ingenious?"

It wasn't difficult for Valentine to arrange his features in a sneer of disgust. "It's ridiculous."

Charles seemed nonplussed for a moment, but then smiled. "Oh, you misunderstand. The mask is just for the procession and a bit of silliness before we really get down to cases."

"Procession?" Valentine repeated, unfortunately as a mental picture formed in his mind. Women forced to watch as a line of grotesquely masked monsters entered by torchlight, naked beneath their cloaks, probably chanting gibberish, and then moved among them, choosing their partners, their victims. He'd never set foot in another masquerade ball. Never.

"There *is* an order about things, yes. Pomp and ceremony, to add to the excitement and the fear, you understand. But then the masks come off."

This was it, Valentine's best chance to avoid the *party*. Thanks to Charfield, he already knew its location. Now he knew the rest, and could plan his timing accordingly once he was certain Daisy was on her way to Redgrave Manor. He had no coach, no Twitchill, but he would have one of the Red-grave outriders. One should be enough...especially once the Society was otherwise occupied with their whores. *And,* he thought with an inward smile, *highly unlikely to be armed.*

"No, Charles. I already told you. Thank you very kindly and all of that, but I decline to make myself a spectacle."

"But here, look." An obviously sweating Mailer reached into his pocket and withdrew a wad of black silk. "See? You really need to see this," he said, holding up what looked to be a snug hood with two long tails of silk obviously meant to be tied behind the head to secure the thing. "Here, try it on. Several wear them, at least at first. Your own mother wouldn't recognize you. Oh, sorry. Shouldn't mention your mother, I've been told that. But you know what I mean." He looked toward the hallway. "Damn, got to hide this."

Mailer quickly tossed the snake head and cloak behind the couch. "Yes, Wright, what is it?"

"Beggin' your pardon, my lord, but you asked for another decanter. I'll just show the boy here where to put it down and we'll be gone."

Valentine didn't bother turning around as the footsteps faded into the hallway. He'd knowingly put himself in a corner, but not without a way out. An unlocked window in his chamber and a sturdy drainpipe awaited him, along with the stubborn Daisy and two of the Redgrave outriders carrying a satchel filled with weapons who would meet him on the path just inside the trees.

"There's no need to try the thing on, Charles. You've convinced me," he said, picking up the wineglass, but then hastily replacing it on the table, its contents still untouched. He put his hands to his waistcoat and began to scratch himself. "Damn. Of all the bloody times for— Charles, give a look," he said as he frantically unbuttoned his waistcoat and shirt. "Is it—damn, of all the bloody times!"

Mailer was goggling at Valentine's exposed chest in horror even as he backed away, a high compliment to Piffkin's expertise with putty and paint. "What... what *is* that? You're all welts and spots."

Valentine pulled his shirt closed once more, as too much scratching directly on his skin could dislodge bits of Piffkin's masterpiece, and picked up the wineglass again; he rather enjoyed teasing Charles with the wine.

"Oh, for the love of God, man, put your eyes back in your head—they're hives, not the plague, although I've been *plagued* with them all my life. But I will attempt strawberries, anyway. My fault, all my fault. I'll be covered in them if I don't plunge myself in a cold tub. That keeps them away. *Damn,* they itch! Have dinner sent up, will you, Charles? I'm certain I'll be fine before we leave."

"At half-past eight. We leave then. But...but you didn't try on the mask." Mailer nearly bleated the words. Clearly the man had been given a mission.

Valentine recommenced scratching. "Charles, don't be an ass."

Something sharp poked Valentine in the small of his back. "Charles can't help being an ass," a deep male voice commented from behind the couch. "Happily for the rest of us, we learned that long ago. You were going to let him leave, weren't you, Charles?"

"But only to bathe. He…he's got these *things* all over him…."

Valentine's mind was working furiously. It hadn't been Wright and a footman who'd entered the drawing room. It had been Wright and another person, and when the butler left, the other man had remained, having ducked out of sight behind a chair or some such thing. Clever. And stupid of him, not to have bothered to turn around when the butler entered. But that was over, the damage done.

Now to get himself shed of the man and the knife. And he needed to do it before the man eased his way around the couch and closer to him. At the moment, he was rather off-balance, and that favored Valentine. It was the only advantage he had.

Mailer had both hands curled into fists and jammed against his mouth, so that Valentine could barely understand him when he spoke. "You've a knife. But…but, Hammer, we're not supposed to kill him."

"Post—you blabbering *idiot!*"

Yes, Post was an idiot, and wasn't that fortunate. The knife suddenly didn't trouble Valentine so much.

With a quick, jerking motion of his right hand, Valentine aimed the contents of the wineglass toward the source of the voice directly behind the couch. Just as quickly, he bent his knees, swiveled to his left while snapping the stem of the thin crystal glass from its bowl with his thumb and forefinger, turning the now sharp stem into a weapon. By the time he'd turned enough to face the man Charles had called Hammer—no more than a split second although it felt like hours—the man's still extended knife arm presented the perfect target.

Plunging the stem into the inside of Hammer's beefy wrist set the man to howling even as the blow sent the knife flying across the room.

The black-silk-hooded man Mailer had called Hammer pulled the crystal stem from his wrist, and then screamed in horror. The stem had, with the greatest good luck, sliced through an artery. Blood spurted out in an arc with his every heartbeat. Hammer clamped his other hand around the wound, yelling for Mailer's help.

If these two had any talent other than perverse ambition, Valentine knew he'd have had no chance against them. But they weren't soldiers, weren't even particularly brave. No, they were the sort of puffed-up schemers who had others do their fighting for them.

Yet desperation must have given Mailer courage

because, just as Valentine was reaching toward his boot and the knife hidden there, he launched himself at Valentine's back with the force of a charging bull. Already off-balance and half-tangled in furniture, he went down under Mailer's more considerable weight, pinned between the edge of the couch and an overturned table.

Mailer's knee pressed into the small of his back as the man—what was he trying to do? The silk mask? Why was he shoving it at his face, rubbing it on his face, pressing it against his nose and mouth?

Valentine's every muscle tensed as he attempted to buck Mailer from his back. He held his breath, refusing to breathe, but now Hammer had unhelpfully pressed his boot against the side of Valentine's head.

Not the wine. The mask. Something had been soaked into the mask. He had a moment's remembrance of his initial assessment of Mailer—a buffoon, but tread carefully! *How had he forgotten his own advice? He had to get up. He had to get out. Daisy was waiting for him. She'd wait forever, or attempt something brave and stupid. Daisy! Ah, God, Daisy!*

Valentine attempted to jackknife his body, hoping to tumble Mailer off his back, but this time his muscles didn't fully cooperate. He was running out of air. He needed to breathe. His brain, his heart, his lungs, every last cell in his body, all were demanding he breathe....

CHAPTER TEN

DAISY REMEMBERED LOOKING into the hand mirror that was all she had left of her mother, marveling at her own reflection. She had barely recognized herself. She'd always been the *other* sister, the plain one with the white skin and curly copper hair, too tall, too thin and gawky next to Rose's petite but curvy frame. And definitely too bookish and serious.

She'd seen a softness about her now, around her eyes, her mouth, something she hadn't quite understood but easily concluded had something to do with the way Valentine looked at her, as if she wasn't only passable, but passably pretty.

If she'd thought about it, if she'd had the leisure of time to think about it, she would probably conclude he liked her, quite a lot. Perhaps almost as much as she liked him, because she did care for him, oh, so very much. Even in the midst of all this horror and ugliness, he had the power to stir her senses as well as her mind. She believed she might now have at least a small inkling of the joy Rose had found with her Walter. And in time, God willing, she would forget the rest of it, banishing evil and replacing it with good.

She'd wrapped the mirror in her extra petticoat, placed it in the very center of her tapestry bag before closing it and carefully dropping it out the window. She'd earlier done the same with Agnes's few belongings, and now leaned out the open window far enough to assure herself both bags had landed safely behind the shrubbery.

Looking back, it all seemed to have happened so long ago.

Daisy had then gone downstairs to the nursery, where a willing Agnes waited, both her beloved charges dressed and eager for an adventure. Agnes was going to take them to a secret stream to catch *real* frogs, which only came out when the sun was going down. They had to be very quiet, though, or else one of the other servants might hear them, and they'd all be shooed back upstairs to the nursery.

Piffkin and a pair of outriders, as planned, already awaited them on the path through the trees. There, they would wait for Daisy to bring Lady Caroline along, and would then set off immediately for the out-of-the-way inn, Piffkin in charge. The outriders would remain, to watch over Daisy until Valentine was safely out of the house, mounted on Charfield's horse and on his way. That had been her single request: to be allowed to wait for him before she and one outrider moved on to the inn, the other riding with Valentine. He'd seemed almost flattered, until she'd added that she wouldn't trust him not to do something foolish if he didn't know she was there, patiently waiting for him.

Daisy had kissed both children, given the nervous Agnes a bracing hug and watched as the trio headed for the servant stairs. She'd held her breath, watching from her attic window, until Piffkin had emerged from the trees, hustling them to cover.

Everything had been going exactly according to plan.

All that had been left was for her to return to Lady Caroline's chamber, as the woman had insisted on packing at least one small bag, and they also would be safely away.

The woman had been difficult to convince, so great was her fear of Lord Mailer, but Daisy had managed it, just as she'd managed to avoid Davinia, who had been conveniently absent, completing some special chore for Lord Mailer.

She'd knocked softly at her ladyship's door and then quietly stepped inside. Lady Caroline had been standing in the center of the room, her smile sickly, her hands twisting together in front of her.

"You're ready?" Daisy had asked, looking about for a traveling bag and seeing none. "You said you were going to pack a few belongings."

"I changed my mind. What if we're caught? Charles would be so angry. He could kill me."

Daisy had attempted to hold down her temper. "He wouldn't do that."

"He killed his first wife. He took her up to those

terrible stones and pushed her over the cliff. He said her scream was the most exciting thing he'd ever heard."

They were wasting time, but Daisy had felt she needed to know more. "He *told* you this? Why?"

"I…told him I didn't want to…to do it anymore. I couldn't bear doing it anymore. That's when he told me. About her scream and…and how if…if I wouldn't *delight* those horrible men anymore then… then I could delight him with…with my scream." Lady Caroline's words had come more quickly then, nearly tumbling over themselves. "He even dragged me up to the stones, to pretend he was going to push me over the edge. He made me promise I'd always obey him. It's easier to obey. Don't you see? I have to think of myself."

"So do I. I wish I had time to argue some sense into your head, but I don't." Shaking her head, Daisy had turned her back on the woman only to feel a heavy bag come down over her, pinning her arms to her sides as she was wrestled to the floor.

"Don't struggle," Lady Caroline had cried from somewhere above her. "I had to protect myself… you see that, don't you? It…it won't be so bad, not if you cooperate."

"You fool!" Daisy managed even after Davinia— it had to be Davinia—began all but smothering her through the rough burlap. She'd twisted her head about, trying to avoid the pressure, her frantic kicks fruitless as they struck nothing but air.

"Don't fight them, Daisy. Especially not Charles, when it's his turn. I saw one fight, and he put his hands around her neck as he took her and...and when he was done she wasn't moving anymore. Don't fight, Daisy, don't fight. Please, I had to do it, I had to save myself. But you don't have to die. You'll see. You'll learn. Some even begin to enjoy it. Stop fighting!"

Where Daisy had found the strength to dislodge the larger woman she didn't know, but she'd found it. Now Davinia was on her back, and Daisy, strad-dling her, had managed to rid herself of the burlap sack. She saw the world through a red haze of rage. Charles Mailer had killed her sister. Those monsters had watched as he'd killed her sister. Lady Caroline had watched, as well, and most probably this woman scratching at her now, trying to be free.

Without conscious thought, Daisy had raised her clenched fist and driven it down sideways into Da-vinia's face, as if she was pounding on a tabletop. Not once, not twice, but over and over again. She had the strength of a thousand men, the fury of an army of banshees. Blood spurted from Davinia's nose, and that didn't stop her blows. Nothing would stop her, not until the woman let loose her tight grip around Daisy's back. She had to let go, why didn't she let go?

But then Lady Caroline, timid, pathetic Lady Car-oline, had grabbed hold of Daisy's bun, wrenched back her head, and pressed a wet cloth over her nose and mouth.

"Hold still!" her ladyship shouted. "I told him you're a virgin. He hadn't thought of that. He's promised to let me go when I bring you to them. I'm the one who deserves saving, not you. You're just another nobody like the others. They're making the altar ready for you now. Stop fighting me!"

They were handing her over to the monsters. She was going to die before she'd ever been able to live. Tears of hate were replaced by those of regret as Daisy felt herself slipping away into oblivion, never to see Valentine again, never to know happiness....

VALENTINE WAS WRONG again. Charles Mailer was both an idiot *and* stupid.

Even as he believed himself mere heartbeats from having to inhale a damning breath, he could feel Mailer's grip on him easing. The man had been holding the mask. He'd even pressed his hands to his face when Hammer entered the room and put the knife to Valentine's back. The mask was in Mailer's hand now, as he attempted to rub it against Valentine's mouth and nose.

Mailer was older and heavier, but not stronger. He'd had too many good meals, moving his jaws up and down probably the extent of his physical exertion. Because he was breathing rapidly, nearly panting with effort...and every breath he took included at least a hint of whatever in hell the mask had been soaked in.

Now, with a sigh, Charles Mailer lost consciousness, his full weight collapsing across Valentine's body, the hand holding the silk dropping away from Valentine's face.

With a final upward heave of his back, Valentine dislodged the man's weight, then pulled back from his position between the sofa and overturned table before Hammer could lift his foot, sending the man tumbling backward, unable to save himself without having to relieve the pressure he was holding on his injured wrist.

Exhaling in a rush to draw in clean air, Valentine half crawled to the French doors, once more holding his breath. He pulled himself upright with some effort, slapped down at the handle until it finally gave way and, bent nearly in half, staggered out onto the flagstones.

His legs weren't fully cooperating and his mind was swimming, but he knew what he had to do. The path lay to his left, and so did the stables. One hundred yards, no more. Yet he felt as if he was walking through waist-deep water, with miles and miles to go.

Daisy. Have to get to Daisy. Have to get her safely away.

Still breathing only when his body forced him to do so, he somehow reached the stables, where he fell to his knees and dunked his entire head and shoulders into one of the horse troughs, rubbing his hands over his face to rid his skin of anything that was left of the solution from the mask.

When he at last raised his head, one of the young grooms was staring at him, wide-eyed.

"Sir?"

Valentine flashed the groom a lopsided grin. "Drunk…drunk as a…as a wheelbarrow. Canya… canya help a man up? Ah, tha's better. De-demon drink. Here." He fumbled in his pocket for a coin. "Didn't see me, y-hear. There's a g'lad. Shames me all hollow, it does." He lifted one shaking finger in the general direction of his lips, wavering where he stood. "*Shhhhh*…didn't see me."

He staggered off in the direction of the tree line.

"Yes, sir. But…but the Manor lies *that* way, sir."

Valentine pulled himself up straight in the exaggerated way only drunks believe lends them an air of sobriety. "I know that," and then continued on his way, heading straight for the trees. Each step was still an effort, but his mind was clearing.

His right. He had to turn to his right now, make his way into the trees and turn left to find the path.

Right, no, left. No, right…right?

No matter. He was out of sight of the manor house, safe within the trees. He simply had to keep moving. Daisy was waiting.

Never disappoint a lady. Especially this one. Just keep moving. Hold on to the trees. Take a step. Take another. Another…I'm coming, Daisy, I'm coming.

"Mr. Redgrave, sir. It's Luther, sir, over here. You just stay there. Here I come. We'd about given up. Are the ladies behind you? Mr. Piffkin said there was to be a pair of ladies."

DAISY LOOKED INTO the mirror, and wondered who was looking back at her. Then, losing interest, she closed her eyes and let her chin fall forward onto her chest.

Something was wrong. What was wrong?

She remembered being so very sick, vomiting again and again into a basin someone held for her. She remembered that, and the pain that had threatened to blow off the top of her head. The single time she'd attempted to look at her surroundings, she'd nearly screamed when light as bright as the sun poked knives into her eyes.

Someone had given her something to drink, something sweet and cloying. The pain began to ease almost immediately, and her body seemed to float. She didn't open her eyes now only because it was simply too much effort. She'd rather float.

Hands had touched her, arms had lifted her, eased her down in a warm tub. *Ahhh. Wonderful.* She remembered that. She'd allowed her head to loll on her shoulders as she was soaped, and rinsed, and lifted once more, only to be wrapped in warm toweling and laid on a cool, smooth pallet.

Yes, she'd been sick. And Mama had given her a bath and put her back to bed. *I miss you, Mama....*

And still, she'd floated. A smile curved her lips as something warm was poured on her stomach and hands began smoothing the liquid all over her. From her shoulders to the toes of her feet, she was being warmed by the liquid, the many hands.

Daisy's eyes had flown open and she attempted to push herself up, but then someone said *Give her more* and she tasted the cloying muskiness on her tongue again and her sudden panic had melted away. She had melted away, floated away, disappeared in a lovely *poof.*

Yes, she remembered. But wasn't there more? Wasn't there still something she'd forgotten?

Somebody took hold of her shoulders, shook her.

"I told you—look at yourself!"

"No," Daisy said, her voice slurring. "Not me. Want to sleep…"

The slap, both the sound of it and the pain it caused, nearly toppled Daisy from the chair, but someone roughly steadied her. "Open your eyes! Look at yourself!"

It's easier to obey.

Daisy worked to open her eyes, raising her eyebrows several times before her eyelids would cooperate…and there was a stranger in the mirror again.

This time the stranger was a doll. A porcelain-headed doll, with wild copper curls, eyes as black as midnight, cheeks and mouth red with paint. It had been clothed all in flowing white veils somehow held together between its breasts with a garish golden brooch in the form of a rose in full bloom. A diamond winked at its very center.

A rose. There was something about a rose...no, not a rose. Rose.

"How much did you fools give her? She should be awake by now," the same voice said: a woman's voice, and exceedingly angry. "I want her awake, aware, when he sees her, when we give him his marching orders. See to it. Have her downstairs in one hour."

There were mumbles, coming from somewhere behind Daisy. She paid them no attention. She was remembering now. *Lady Caroline. Rose. Valentine.* She drew in a short, sharp breath, all the haziness gone in an instant. *Valentine. She had to get to him. He was waiting for her.*

A door opened, then slammed shut.

"Thank God she left. What will we do, Davinia? She's so angry."

"Not at us," the maid answered. "We did what was right. It's that fool of a husband of yours. He let the new gentleman get away, and we'd all better hope they find him soon. That's one too many mistakes, you know."

"What...what does that mean? He's to be eliminated? But what about me? I...I could have gotten away from here. I didn't have to tell him, not if he's going to be dead. What happens to *me?*"

Daisy was becoming more awake by the moment,

but felt it best to continue the way she was, slumped in the chair, all but asleep and unresponsive.

"They still need this place. They still need the stones. Me and you, *my lady,* we'll do just fine, as long as you do what they say."

"Oh, I will, I will. I'll do anything they say. Anything!"

"Good. Start by helping me lock this one in the preparation chamber, and then pray she's alert in time for the ceremony. If there is one, if they catch him. Hammer swears he'll come back for her. Then come with me while I check on the others. One or two of them might need some of our special drink if they're to put on the show we want him to see."

What was Davinia talking about? She was talking about Valentine, wasn't she? And about her...how he'd come back for her. She was in a nest of spiders, helping them weave a web to ensnare Valentine....

Daisy allowed herself to be rudely lifted beneath her shoulders and half carried, half walked into another room, then pushed into a large wingback chair.

"There. She'll keep until they want her. Now come with me."

"Davinia? I don't think you should be the one giving orders. Once Charles is gone, I will truly be the mistress of Fernwood. You just said you need me, remember? You must show me respect."

Daisy dared to peek up at the two women, just in time to see the maid turn around at the open doorway and sharply box Lady Caroline's ears. "There's your *respect,* you stupid cow."

The door closed on Lady Caroline's howls of pain and a key turned in the lock, throwing the small room, and Daisy, into darkness.

She waited until she was certain the two women were gone, and then sat up, took several deep breaths of heavily perfumed air, and decided she could chance standing up. Her eyes had adjusted to the dim light and she believed she could see the outline of moonlight against a pair of closed draperies.

As she tugged back the heavy draperies one at a time and secured them with their tie-ropes, the full moon illuminated the room just enough for her to see she was in a dressing room of sorts. There was only the single door, the chair she'd been dumped on, a full tub sitting in the middle of the room, scattered piles of damp toweling and a single dresser with several glass bottles and vials arranged on top of it.

So this was the preparation room. Had Rose been here? Did they only bring virgins here? And what did it matter? She simply needed to be *out* of here so they couldn't use her to trap Valentine, use him to do something against his will. Nothing else mattered.

Well, one other thing mattered.

She also needed some sort of decent covering. Even with only the moonlight to illuminate the room, she could see her naked body beneath the filmy material. How ridiculous, and most certainly impractical. Escape was her plan, but she wasn't about to make a spectacle of herself while she was about it!

What did she need to do first?

She looked up, to see the ceiling was slanted. All right. She was in an attic, but not the attics of Fernwood; those ceilings were covered with plaster. This one was raw wood, and supported by huge wooden beams. But where was she? Looking out through the uncovered window confirmed she wasn't at Fernwood. She was only a single story above a strange landscape made up almost entirely by moonlit rocks.

She had no idea which way lay the manor, or the waiting Valentine. If he was still waiting, which he most probably was not. He'd search for her, she knew that, just as the Society knew that.

She doubted he'd search for her in an attic.

"Stop it. Your mind has already spun in too many circles tonight," Daisy warned herself, partly only so she could hear her own voice, pressing her palms against her temples. "You heard them. Mailer had Valentine in his clutches, but he somehow escaped. So he's not waiting for you, he's looking for you, while they search for him. Just think. Calm yourself, and think! God help me, there has to be an answer."

She looked around the room once more, hoping to see something she hadn't seen before. Tub, chest, chair, windows, draperies.

Draperies?

God helps them who help themselves.

Yes, Papa, I remember.

It was one thing for brave, valiant Valentine to take another go at playing the knight in shining armor, but she couldn't just sit here as if she was some princess in a tower and then lower down her hair to him. She was no princess. She'd been on her own since the age of seventeen, and she had learned to fight her own battles. She'd even found her own way to Fernwood. There were dozens, hundreds of things she couldn't do, but she should certainly be capable of getting herself shed of an attic!

"I wonder if I'm intoxicated, because I'm feeling awfully brave," she mumbled as she dragged the chair over to one of the windows and climbed up onto it.

CHAPTER ELEVEN

PIFFKIN HELD UP Valentine's sopping wet jacket and gingerly sniffed at it. "Laudanum, yes. But also something more. Besides the smells of vomit and wet horse, of course." He then tossed it into the bushes. "You do realize that jacket is ruined."

"Stubble it, Piffkin," Valentine said, raking his fingers through his hair as he sat on the ground, which, thankfully, seemed to have at last stopped moving. "Why are you here, anyway? You're supposed to be at the inn with the children, with Robert and Luther here."

"Yes, sir, but there was a change of plans. I decided to send Robert off with the children, as I thought Luther sufficient once I was also here. The children are safely with their nurse, supposedly investigating the pond behind the inn. They're hunting amphibians, sir. *Frogs.*"

"Frogs." Employing the trunk of a thin scrub tree to aid him, Valentine climbed to his feet. "I'm not even going to ask whose idea that was. So where are the ladies? And, no, don't answer that, Piffkin. I know where they are. They're up to their necks in trouble." He reached into his waistcoat pocket before remembering it was empty. "What time is it?"

When Luther had first asked his question about Daisy, Valentine had gone cold to the marrow of his bones, and wretchedly sober. But his body had taken longer to recover from the effects of whatever in hell Mailer had been trying to make him breathe. The sky had gone completely dark now, but full of stars abetting the light of the full moon. He'd add the helpful shine reflecting off Piffkin's hairless pate, but this was neither the time nor place for levity.

And while Valentine hadn't been doing much more than holding on to the ground for the past quarter hour (to keep it steady), his mind had been racing: fighting panic, considering options, cursing himself for a fool for not having come up with a better plan. Thinking about Daisy…fighting panic.

"Nearly nine, sir," Piffkin said, having consulted his new pocket watch. Then he looked at Valentine, and frowned.

Valentine knew the look, and ignored it. Piffkin really had to stop worrying like a hen with only one chick. "All right. Nine. They begin at nine, although I may have put somewhat of a crimp in that. Luther, it's more than time we were off."

"And me, Master Valentine," Piffkin put in as the trio headed down the path to where the outrider had left the horses. "I'm going with you. Someone has to watch over you."

Next thing he knew, his keeper would be pulling a set of leading strings from his pocket.

"Thank you for that sterling vote of confidence, Piffkin, but no. We don't have to travel far, only to a cottage of sorts hidden in the trees below the cliff. But it will be quicker if we take the horses, and we only have the three mounts. Correct, Luther?"

"Yes, sir, Mr. Redgrave. One for you, one for her ladyship and the last for me."

"There, you see," Piffkin said rather triumphantly. "Three horses. I can ride, you know. I'll more than keep up."

Valentine kept walking. "No, you won't. I've known you all my life, and I've never seen you ride."

"You only know me all of *your* life, as you say. I had a life before your grandmother made you my charge, unbelievable as you may find that. I'm perfectly capable of riding a horse."

"Piffkin," Valentine pointed out as they neared the waiting horses, "Luther here was to ride his own horse, I was going to take Daisy up with me as far as the inn, but since I've already seen Lady Caroline ride in Hyde Park, we provided the third horse for her."

Piffkin nodded quickly, as if anxious to be moving again, rather than talking. "And I will ride her horse. It's this one, correct?"

"Yes, Piffkin," Valentine said as the man circled the bay mare, most probably in search of a stirrup.

"That one. The one with a sidesaddle strapped to its back."

Luther snorted. "Shall I help boost him up, sir? I'll be sure to mind his skirts."

Unbelievably, as his heart was filled with fear for Daisy and feeling a blood lust rising in him for any member of the Society he found, Valentine laughed.

Piffkin left the mare and walked over to point a finger at the outrider's smiling face. "You may snicker, young man, but Mr. Redgrave here is always the better man for a chuckle or two, isn't that correct, Master Valentine? We'll find Miss Daisy and her ladyship, and we'll do what must be done. Not by worrying and blaming yourself, and not by knocking on their door and politely turning yourself over to them—and I know you were thinking just that—but by being the man I know you to be. Although I would like to put forward the idea we *walk* to this cottage that isn't so far away. Giving you more time to clear your head, as it were."

"Thank you, Piffkin. I was about to go charging in there like a mad bull, wasn't I? I could have gotten us all killed. I promise you, I won't just hand myself over to them in exchange for Daisy."

The manservant shrugged. "Not your fault, sir. Between whatever they were rubbing on your face and fearing for your lady love, there's not many a man who'd have his brain straight."

"Daisy is not my lady love. She's in this mess because of me and it's up to me to set things right."

"As you say, sir. Why, that touching embrace I walked in on was probably only something you did out of a sense of duty. Buck her up for the trials to come and all of that. Good on you, sir."

"Piffkin, I swear I'll— Never mind."

"Yes, sir? You were about to say, sir?"

"Enough, you've made your point. Luther, those pistols are loaded, correct? Hand me a pair and let's be on our way. Piffkin, I probably should ask. Do you shoot as well as you ride?"

"If at least one of us is being truthful, about the same, sir, yes. But I do have this." He reached into his pocket and drew out a—

"What in bloody hell is that?"

"My best crimping iron, sir. I hope you're correct and we'll soon be able to recover the remainder of our belongings, but I couldn't risk my best crimping iron to Dame Chance. It will make a tolerable weapon, if necessary."

"No wonder you and Daisy get along so well. I must be out of my mind. Come on, we head this way. And God help us all if I can't come up with a course of action between here and there."

He already knew his first order of business, and that was locating and rescuing Daisy and Lady Caroline. The Society hadn't wanted him dead, had believed they'd lured him here while also somehow knowing he wanted to be here, so they'd obviously had a plan for him, had intended to use him in some way, so that it stood to reason they also now needed Daisy alive to use to bend him to their will.

"And if *that* didn't make my head hurt, I suppose I must be better," he muttered to himself as he led the way uphill through the trees, to the standing stones.

"Sir?" Piffkin asked from behind him.

"I was thinking out loud. They had me, but they lost me. Now they have Daisy. Their only option now is to use Daisy to get me to do whatever it is they wanted me to do all along. Correct?"

"It would seem so, yes. You're saying they know you aren't on your way back to London, happy for your escape."

"They somehow know I wouldn't leave here without her, yes. Do you know what I think that means?"

The older man was huffing and puffing a bit, but Valentine pretended not to notice. "Please enlighten me."

"I think it means Lady Caroline betrayed her somehow, either deliberately or by accident. I'm only surprised the children got out safely."

"I will say her ladyship doesn't care much for the children, sir. Agnes, their nurse, told me as much as we walked to the inn and Miss Daisy went off to fetch her ladyship. She kept referring to them as those *poor little souls*."

Valentine looked back over his shoulder at Piffkin. Something wasn't right, and he had a feeling whatever it was, it was important. "But you all were to leave together, Lady Caroline and the children."

"Her ladyship was at first reluctant, fearing they'd be caught, and then insisted on some time to pack a few belongings. I last saw Miss Daisy at her attic window, watching as the children joined me in the trees. Then she was off to fetch Lady Caroline while Luther here sneaked across the lawn to gather up the baggage Miss Daisy tossed out her window. When Miss Daisy didn't appear, Robert escorted the nurse and the children to the inn, and Luther and I waited for the ladies, and for you—and I won't apologize again for that. I know your head hurts, sir, but why must we go over and over this?"

Valentine thought about this as they covered the quarter mile to the standing stones, running it all over and over in his mind. He arrived at a conclusion.

"Until and unless Daisy tells me otherwise, consider Lady Caroline one of the enemy," he said at last as he stood at the edge of the cliff, knowing it would be impossible to see the roof of the cottage, as he hadn't been able to see it in full daylight. But Charfield had told him where it was, and how to get down to it. God help the man if he'd lied; because if he had, Valentine was going to take him apart, piece by piece.

"There's a path to our left, gentlemen, the same one used by the Society when they leave off killing chickens to go have their fun. I doubt there will be more than a half dozen opponents inside, one of them a woman. She'll most likely be the only woman wearing a mask…or much of anything else. Luther, keep your mind on business, understood, and then prepare to forget anything you see."

"Yes, sir, I'll do my best."

"If you see a weapon drawn, Luther, fire. And shoot to kill. Don't hesitate. That includes the woman."

"Sir?"

Valentine ignored him. They'd turned another corner in the path that kept curling back on itself through the trees, each turn taking them a level lower, toward the flat, stony land below, the floor of the abandoned quarry. He held up his hand to stop the other two, and went down on his haunches. "There it is. Clever, I suppose. See it?"

Beside him, Piffkin squinted into the darkness. "Not at all, sir."

"Charfield told me it was built half into a natural cleft in the quarry wall, with the roof itself camouflaged with stone from the quarry. But that's it, I'm certain of it. I don't see any guards, which makes sense."

"How so, sir?"

"Three reasons. One, whoever can be is out hunting for me. Two, whoever's inside thinks they're safely hidden. And three, thank God, we're either smarter or luckier than they are. I believe Daisy hasn't as yet decided which one. Let me circle around to the front while you stay here. There's probably only a single door, which will make things easier, as they truly have their backs up against the wall. Once I have the lay of the land, as it were, I'll come back to you and we'll decide what to do next."

Piffkin nodded his bald head. "Agreed."

Valentine grinned. "Difficult as this may be for you to contemplate, I wasn't applying for your permission. Luther, give me your jacket. This white shirt is too visible in the moonlight."

'My mum made this for me, sir."

"Then I'll be doubly certain not to get blood on it."

Yes, I'm definitely feeling better. Daisy's close, I just know it, Valentine thought as he made his way down the remainder of the hill, leaving the twisting, switchback path in favor of the cover of the trees.

Even if the now nicely decimated Society was going to stick to its ritual, they only could have gotten as far as their damn procession and posturing. He'd be content to wait until they were all naked and vulnerable before crashing down the door, but with Daisy somewhere inside, he'd rather spare her that sorry spectacle. He wouldn't even imagine her as a part of it, not when it was so obvious they'd be using her to draw him in.

He crept out from the trees, holding on to the stone wall as far as it went until his hand touched wood and he came away with a splinter the size of a nail. Clearly they'd built themselves no great palace. The *cottage* as Charfield had called it, once Valentine had reached a corner, was longer than it was wide. About halfway down, he could make out a single door with a narrow window on either side. Uncurtained, as the light from inside cast square shadows on the ground outside. A second story displayed several windows, one of them just above him.

All right. A single entrance, a single exit. Luther and Piffkin at the windows, pistols and crimping iron at the ready, and himself kicking down the door. But first, he wanted to go have a look through one of the narrow windows.

Suddenly Valentine's body tensed as he heard a sound coming from somewhere. But where? And there it was again. A soft, kicking sound. Both his pistols drawn from his waistband, he attempted to make himself invisible as he hunkered down, looked to his right, then to his left.

"If you'd consider looking *up,* Valentine? No, wait, I forgot. Don't look up. Just catch this."

Naturally, he looked up, just as something heavy and damp landed on his head.

"What in bloody hell…?" he whispered as he pulled off what seemed to be a large sheet of toweling. He rose to his feet and slid the pistols back in his waistband.

Daisy was above him, hanging above him, doing her best not to swing about in circles as she slowly lowered herself down some sort of improvised rope, her apparently bandaged feet dangling beneath bare legs and white, billowing— What happened to your clothes?"

"You should pretend not to notice," she countered, managing to make her whisper sound absolutely *prim* as he raised his hands to catch her as soon as she dropped closer to him.

"Daisy," he hissed. "Let go."

"Only if you don't look. I was hoping to get down with no one noticing, decide where I am, and then go looking for you. This is embarrassing. Close your eyes."

"For the love of God," Valentine pleaded quietly. "Let's go. I won't look."

Touch, but not look. Imagine, but not look. Dream, but not look. Oh, hell, just one more quick look....

And then he grabbed onto her bare calf, smooth and soft, and even slippery with some sort of oil, halting her slow rotation, and obediently, reluctantly, closed his eyes. And then he had both hands on her narrow waist. And then her slick, perfumed body was sliding down the length of his, and was just as suddenly gone.

Now her whisper was more of an order. "Keep your eyes closed."

Valentine didn't need his eyes, only his hands. But he decided discretion dictated he shouldn't point that out.

"Yes, that's a brilliant idea. That way I'll be spared seeing the brute sneaking up behind me with a heavy club."

"Oh! I didn't think of— There's nobody else out here. All right, you may open your eyes now."

Much of her remained all but bare beneath the filmy white silk, but now the damp toweling sheet was wrapped tightly around her middle, denying him sight of all the best parts, not that he'd say that to her. Her hair reached well past her shoulders, loose and wild with curls, and even in the near dark he could see that she'd been painted up to resemble a— No, he'd probably be wise not to mention that, either.

"Very fetching," he soothed quietly, touching her hand, the one that wasn't clutching a bunch of toweling in what seemed to be a death grip. He'd kiss her, but she'd tell him this was neither the time nor place, and she'd be right. They had to get out of here; explanations could come later. "They didn't hurt you?"

"No. But if I ever get my hands on Lady Caroline or Davinia or that horrible woman, they shouldn't count on me not to hurt *them*. Where are we?"

"Quietly, sweetheart, they're not all that far away. To answer your question, we're below the cliff. As you may have deduced by now, I was about to rescue you."

"I'm sorry," she said, patting his cheek commiseratingly. "I'm certain you would have done it exceedingly well, too."

Valentine couldn't be positive, but he thought he may have blushed. "Yes, thank you. Now, if you're quite ready to get out of here? I've got you, I've got two more names thanks to your journal, I've got Charfield already on his way to being tucked up at Redgrave Manor. All in all, we've done remarkably well, with only a few unfortunately glaring missteps. However, the remainder of my army consists of an old man with a crimping iron and a near lad named Luther who doesn't want me to get blood on the coat his mum sewed for him. Would you care to have it, by the way? The coat?"

"In a moment. I mean, we'll leave in a moment, but no, let Luther keep his coat. I want to see what's happening inside. Have you taken a look?"

"I was about to, but then something else came up, or should I say down."

She rolled kohl-darkened eyes at him. "I *said* I was sorry. Come on."

"I'm not complaining, mind you," Valentine whispered as she dragged him along the front of the building, "but when did you get so brave?"

"I'm not brave, I'm terrified. Oddly enough, that seems to make me very, very angry."

"And reckless?"

"Possibly."

"I'll be sure to inform Piffkin. He'll have to watch over the both of us."

Daisy looked back at him over her shoulder, pushing her wild curls out of the way. "You go first. I'm suddenly not so certain a vicar's daughter should see this."

"Nor a governess." He squeezed her hand and, careful to keep low, moved toward the narrow window closest to him, then stood up, pressed his shoulder against the outside wall, and turned slightly, to peek through the glass.

"Sweet Jesus," he hissed.

He could have been looking into a stable, and perhaps he was. The quarrymen could have used this building to house their mules a century before. It was one large room, a rude wood floor covered with a scattering of rugs and piles of pillows, and free-standing candelabras, a dozen or more couches and chairs, and not much else. A long red carpet ran down the center from front to back, the area behind some sort of raised altar nothing but the stone that made up the wall of the quarry. There were a few bits of wooden apparatus here and there, shackles hanging from one wall, a set of stocks, what looked to be a whipping stool. There was a flight of stairs off to his right. Not quite a cave, but not a pleasure palace, either.

Nothing like the gold, marble and other grandeur that couldn't hide the implements of sexual perversion Simon told him had existed inside the recently discovered hellfire chamber their grandfather had constructed at Redgrave Manor.

Valentine didn't know if that made it better or worse, that the ugliness was much easier to see here.

He counted the men in the room, which was easy enough to do, as they were all sitting around a low round table not more than fifteen feet away from the window, taking turns puffing on some sort of communal smoking device. *Opium pipe,* Valentine told himself. *Perhaps they think it gives them courage.*

Four of them wore black. Black silk clothing, capes and masks. The fifth, Charles Mailer, was bareheaded, still dressed in the evening clothes he'd worn earlier, in the drawing room. He appeared terrified. As Valentine watched, Mailer reached for the smoking pipe, only to have one of the others snatch it away from him. That man had a thick white bandage extending from his cuff. *Hammer.*

Who were the others, and where was the woman? The table was round, giving Valentine no easy clue as to who was in charge.

He saw the women, counting six of them, gathered on the far side of the room. They were all dressed—or undressed—in the same fashion as Daisy, and they appeared to be waiting for something to happen. One appeared to be sleeping. Three were playing cards. Two of them held hands.

Valentine snuck back to where Daisy waited for him

"Not a jolly bunch. There's really nothing to see. I think I've interrupted their plan for this evening," he whispered. "Be careful if you still want a look. The men are at a table near the window, and the women are gathered in the far corner to your left."

Daisy nodded, biting her bottom lip, and made her way to the window on, he now realized, feet wrapped and padded in toweling sheet. She was practical even under fire, he'd give her that. Under fire, and underdressed.

Rather than peek in from the side, she crouched down, placed one hand on the windowsill and slowly raised her head.

He knew when she looked at the men, and when she turned her head slightly, he knew she was looking toward the women. And looking. And looking.

Valentine crept over to her. "Come on, that's enough."

She didn't seem to have heard him.

"Daisy, we have to get out of here."

He tried to take hold of her hand, but she was gripping the windowsill with white-knuckled fierceness.

"It's her. I…I can't be certain. My own sister, and I can't be sure. But I think it's her. It's Rose."

"*Shhh,* sweetheart," he warned her, fearing she might stand up, call out her sister's name or God only knew what. "Come on, we're here too long. We'll think of something we can do, and then we'll— What in hell?"

The hooded members at the table had just stood up in unison, leaving Mailer seated, his chin quivering as he imploringly looked from one to the other and then the next. Then, as he watched, and Valentine watched, each hooded member held out his right hand, drawn into a fist, thumb out to the side. At some signal Valentine couldn't hear, one after one, the fists were turned, the thumbs pointing down.

When Hammer's was the last thumb turned down Valentine could hear Mailer's scream through the glass as the men flanking him on either side grabbed his arms and hauled him to his feet, tugging at his jacket as if to rip it off. *"No! No-o-o!"*

Mailer struggled to remain where he was, but it was clear enough to Valentine. The others were dragging him toward the door even as they tore at his clothing. Someone barked out an order. The women left their corner and followed, lingering only long enough to retrieve lanterns and some of the over-size masks.

"Poor bastard. Let's go," Valentine said, grabbing up Daisy at the waist and running with her as if she was a sack of meal thrown over his shoulder, running as fast as he could until he'd turned the corner of the building and made his way back to the path. "Piffkin, Luther. Into the trees. Go!"

But Piffkin was already on his feet, and in the midst of removing his jacket. "Miss Daisy," he said, offering it to her.

"Take it," Valentine ordered, and she reached out to grab it even as she was carried away from the path. When he thought they'd gone far enough, he turned away from Piffkin and Luther and put her down, shielding her as she buttoned herself into the wide black jacket that reached to her knees. "Again, very fetching," he said, kissing her nose. "Now, down, and not a word from anyone. Not a sound."

CHAPTER TWELVE

DAISY TUGGED ON Valentine's sleeve. "It's her. I know it's her. I think I'm sure now. It's Rose."

"Quietly. We can't help her if we're captured."

She felt hot tears running down her cheeks, and wiped at them with a sleeve of Piffkin's jacket, for the cuff was a good six inches longer than her arm. She had an odd, completely inappropriate thought: as her nose had also insisted on running, she'd probably ruined the valet's jacket. She very nearly giggled. What could be more *inappropriate* than being out-of-doors, all but naked, and in the company of three men?

None of that mattered.

Rose is alive. Rose is alive!

"I know. *Shhh*." Valentine's arm was around her shoulders, holding her close against his body.

Had she spoken aloud again? She hadn't meant to do that. Or perhaps he'd noticed how badly she was shaking. She nearly apologized, but as he'd probably only *shush* her again, she attempted to keep her mind on the fact they were all hunkered down in the bushes for some reason. Among them, she couldn't help noticing—painfully—at least a few covered in thorns.

"Listen. Here they come."

Daisy did as Valentine said, and listened. *Then* they'd go get Rose.

Was it Rose? Or had she seen blond curls and her imagination had done the rest? With all that paint on their faces, except for hair color, the women all looked disturbingly, anonymously alike. Rather like china-headed dolls, not human at all. Maybe it wasn't Rose, but only wishful thinking.

Daisy felt physically ill. If only whatever Valentine was hiding them from would happen, and she could go back, take another look.

At first, all she heard was some sort of mumbling, possibly a chant. The sound was low, and definitely intimidating. The sound grew louder. Someone was coming, the Society was coming. They were going to pass right by them as they hid in the trees.

Would Rose be with them?

Please let them have left her behind. Just let these monsters go on their way and leave Rose behind.

The chanting grew closer, louder, and now Daisy could make out the words.

"Hear us, Satan, hear your servants. We bring you one unworthy. Hear us, Satan, rejoice in your servants. We offer you one unworthy. Hear us, Satan, hear—"

Daisy clapped her hands over her ears, attempting to block out the macabre words. But nothing could block the sound of the screams, the pleas, the hysterical sobbing.

"Mailer," Valentine whispered next to her ear. "I believe he's to be punished for his failure."

"They're going to kill him? *Sacrifice* him? But... but we can't let them do that." She looked at Valentine through the darkness. "We can't let them do that, can we?"

"I find I don't have a problem with it. He had to know this could happen. As Trixie once warned us, you choose your bed and then you must lie on it. Or, in this case, I suppose, your altar, as I'm fairly certain that's where they're heading. Now look, but don't cry out. The women are leading the procession. They appear to be somewhat drugged, don't you think? Almost in a trance. Take your time, Daisy, as you look at them."

Their diaphanous draperies all but glowing in the moonlight, the women made their way along the path in pairs, each holding up a small lantern. The light and shadow caused by the lanterns made them into broken dolls, and nearly as frighteningly macabre as the men once again wearing their hideous oversize masks.

"Cor," the young man Valentine had called Luther breathed, and Piffkin clapped a hand over his eyes.

Daisy's heart was pounding; she could barely catch her breath.

And then: "There. The last pair. She has blond

hair. See her? Oh, God... *Rose.* It's truly her. Has she been here all this time?"

"Steady," Valentine warned her. "They aren't going to hurt her, not tonight. They've got other business."

That *other business* could still be heard above the repetitive chanting as the men came into view. Naked as the day he was born, his arms strapped to his sides, his ankles bound, Mailer was being carried along the path by four Society members. "Stop, stop! Please stop! Put me down! Hammer, you know me. You know I'm as good as my word. Fernwood—it's yours. You can have it all! All my money, every penny. Anything, just name it. One vote! For the love of God, man, I only need one vote!"

"Hear us Satan, hear your servants. We bring you one unworthy. Hear us Satan, rejoice in your servants..."

"*No!* Axbridge, damn you, I brought you into the Society. You'd be nothing if not for me. Anybody, anybody! What do you want? What do you want! The children? Take them, they're yours. One of you must want them, damn it! You can have them. They're young, trainable. *Take them!* Just give me one vote. Please, oh, God, please, somebody, just one vote!"

"Hear us Satan, rejoice in your servants. We offer you one unworthy..." The chanting began to fade and soon all that was left to hear were Mailer's sobs and curses.

"Risk yourself in an attempt to rescue that heinous lump of offal from his fate, Master Valentine, and I will personally leap on you and hold you to the ground until the inclination passes."

"He's not the one we're going to save, Piffkin. Did you notice the blonde woman with the others?"

"I can't say as I had my eyes open, sir."

Daisy leaned across Valentine to lay a hand on the valet's arm. "She's my—"

"Good friend," Valentine broke in as Daisy hesitated. "Miss Daisy's very good friend. That's why she came to Fernwood, believing her friend to be here. Isn't that right, Daisy?"

"Yes," she agreed, nodding furiously. She couldn't be sure Piffkin didn't know the truth, if Valentine had told him the contents of the journal, but for Rose's sake, at least, they would all pretend in front of one of the Redgrave servants. "My very good friend. I'm so very happy to have found her."

Now it was Piffkin's turn to nod. "I understand. Clearly it is our duty to rescue her from her unfortunate dilemma. Sir? I believe damsels in distress are within your bailiwick?"

Everyone looked to Valentine.

But he was looking elsewhere, as if his eyes could follow some sound the others had missed. "Quiet. Horses."

Daisy turned her eyes to the path, and was soon rewarded by the sight of two horses, one ridden, the other being held by its leads, picking their way up the path. Both had traveling bags strapped behind the saddles.

"Ah, the woman. I wondered where she was," Valentine said. "And riding astride. Sadly, also cloaked and masked, as we'll probably have to let her go. I wonder who she's taking with her. Luther, come with me."

Daisy watched as Valentine tucked his pistols more firmly into his waistband and headed uphill, Luther behind him, preferring to cut through the underbrush rather than follow the path's switchback route. Then she looked at Piffkin, and in her best governess voice commanded, "On your count if you please, Mr. Piffkin, as he didn't expressly order us to wait here."

He smiled at her, and then held up one hand, raising first thumb, then index finger, middle finger, etc. "Now should be sufficient, Miss Daisy. Modesty suggests I precede you."

Daisy looked down at herself; the mercifully lengthy jacket, the all but transparent white draperies below. "Yes, thank you."

"I meant mine, Miss Daisy."

Cheeks most certainly flaming, she let him take the lead.

They stayed to the path, for which she was grateful, as she was certain her bare legs were already bleeding from being scraped against the undergrowth, her unbound hair tangled with burrs. "We're observing, Mr. Piffkin," she told him. "Valentine wouldn't want us to distract him."

She felt fully confident in Valentine, certain he wouldn't fail her, convinced he could do most anything he set his mind to doing. He might not do it the way she would approach the same problem, but she never doubted his success.

She should probably remember to say that before he could scold her for disobeying him. Again.

They progressed along the path, following faint shafts of moonlight that filtered through the leafy branches, and then halted completely when they heard the sound of voices up ahead.

Loud, angry voices, all but tumbling over each other. It was impossible to know one from the other, save for the woman.

"You're taking Scarlet? You're leaving? Why?"

"You question me? Don't any of you listen? The woman escaped. We're *all* leaving."

"Not Post! He's the cause of everything. We voted! The rules demand the Forfeit of Manhood."

"Eager, aren't you, Hammer," the woman said archly. "So ready to step into his place in the Inner Circle."

"Hammer's right. We must finish unless there's a reprieve, that's the rule. Post told us, when he told us about Bird."

"Bird cheated us, he cheated Satan's justice."

"Post endangered us. It's our right!"

"That's true, we're entitled to the ceremony. The women are already here."

"Fools!" the woman shouted in fury. "There's no time for your opium-riddled pleasures. Post, stop that bleating, you demean yourself and your former station in the Circle. Your fellows have tried and judged. Your cock is forfeit. Gentlemen, hold him down."

"No! Let go of me! Don't do that. Keep your hands off me! Don't touch me! Stop! You can't do this!"

"Now would you look at that. He's about standing up on his own."

"*Silence!* Have your fun if you must, but then be on your way."

Mailer was sobbing. "Wait! You have a vote. You can stop this. I'm loyal! I've always been loyal! Exalted One, just one vote!"

"He does only need one vote."

Daisy sucked in a breath. That was the voice, that last one. The voice she'd heard in the library. *Scarlet.*

The woman answered. "He's known, and therefore useless. No reprieve!"

The man named Scarlet laughed before answering. "You want to be the one who does it, don't you? The road can wait another minute. Here, use my knife."

"You know me so well," the woman nearly purred.

"But…but what of the women?" Daisy knew it was Hammer who'd asked the question.

"Must I think for all of you? This sanctuary is lost to us. Dispose of them, they're no longer necessary. Hammer, step aside."

Daisy began to run. Barely able to make out the path, she pushed past Piffkin and ran, and stumbled to her knees, and got up and ran again.

She heard a scream, a terrible scream suddenly cut off, and clapped her hands to her mouth as she froze in place for one horrified second. And then she ran on.

"Daisy! Daisy! Stop. I've got her. Look, look, I've got her. See? Here she is. No one was paying the women any attention, so we pulled them one by one into the trees. I've got to go back and help Luther, as I don't think he knows what to do with them. You'll hear our pistols, but don't worry, we're only hastening the panicked bastards on their way."

"Rose?" As Valentine set down his slight burden, Daisy put out her arms to her sister, gathered her unresisting body close, kissing her face, her hair, drawing her into a fierce embrace. She released her only to look at her again in the dim light, still only half believing the miracle she'd prayed for had actually occurred, and then unbuttoned the jacket, enfolding Rose inside along with her. "Rose, it's me. It's Daisy. Rose? It's all right. You're all right. You're safe now."

"Here, Miss Daisy. It will be better if you each have a garment."

Blinking to clear the tears from her eyes, she looked at the offered shirt, and then to its owner.

Piffkin had smallclothes still covering him, a sort of sleeveless vest that buttoned at the neck and all the way down his ample stomach. He looked, at the least, uncomfortable, and also seemed to be blinking rather furiously. "Are you quite sure?"

"I am that, yes, Miss Daisy."

"Mr. Piffkin? Are you by any chance crying?"

"Not at all, Miss Daisy, most certainly not. I'm, in fact, feeling extraordinarily jolly, considering my charge is up at the top of that cliff, possibly shooting people."

Rose had yet to say a word, but just allowed herself to be held. But now she spoke. "She…she…and then they all stabbed their knives into him. He's really dead, isn't he? You'll check for me, please? You'll make certain? He needs to be very dead…"

Daisy did her best to soothe her sister, stroking her hair, rocking side to side as if comforting an infant. "He is, sweetheart, I'm certain he is. You're all right, everything's all right now. I'm going to take you away from here, just the two of us again, and it will be as if none of this ever happened. I promise, Rose, I promise. It's me. It's Daisy. Rose?"

But Rose said nothing.

Piffkin rather noisily blew his nose into a linen square he'd produced from somewhere on his person. "It's that drug, miss. They gave it to Master Valentine. I'm certain she'll soon know who you are. In the meantime, may I suggest we retrace our steps to await Master Valentine at the bottom of this infernal hill I refuse to climb again? I'll then search about inside the building, in hopes of locating...*ahem*...locating something more suitable for you ladies to wear."

LORD CHARLES MAILER and his lady wife were laid to rest in the small fenced area that was the graveyard at Fernwood. Davinia, no last name apparently known, was buried without ceremony on the other side of that fence. No marker was planned for her grave.

Mailer and Lady Caroline should have by rights been buried beside Davinia, and not in hallowed ground, as theirs had been a murder carried out by a spurned wife, followed by her suicide (the story Valentine had thought safest).

Lord Mailer's brother didn't seem to care to ask the truth surrounding Davinia's death, and although the tragedy of a murder and suicide might be a difficult pill to swallow, Valentine had decided it beat the truth all to flinders. There were the children (and the family reputation) to protect, so as far as the rest of the world was concerned, the couple had succumbed to the same short, violent illness.

Valentine had discovered the bodies of the two women when he and Piffkin entered the stable turned hellfire club in search of clothing for Daisy and Rose and the other women. Her ladyship's throat had been neatly sliced, and the servant lay facedown beside the altar, a large knife in her back. She certainly did favor knives, this Exalted Ruler.

To the observer, it seemed the servant had dispatched her mistress, most probably on orders, and then, undoubtedly to her unhappy surprise, had been assisted from this mortal coil, as well.

Clearly the so-called Exalted One had been displeased to learn of Daisy's escape. When that woman decided to cut her losses and run, thinking it better to fight another day, she didn't believe in leaving any loose ends dangling behind her.

"Again, thank you, Mr. Redgrave," the earl said, taking Valentine's hand in both of his own as they stood outside the manor house and pumping it up and down mightily. "I always knew Chas's braggadocio about all the women he bedded would do him no good, but I never suspected things would end this way. There's always been suspicion his first wife also took her own life, you know. I'm only sorry you had to be visiting here at the time of this great tragedy, although you've been all that is kind. And discreet."

"And will continue to be so, my lord, on my honor as a gentleman. I can only be glad I could be here for the children," Valentine said, retrieving his hand. Mailer quite resembled his brother physically, but there the similarity ended. From the moment he'd ridden the ten miles to the earl's estate several days previously, and met him and his wife, he'd known Lydia and William would be in good, loving hands.

"I'll be departing myself for London as soon as the equipage is brought round."

The two men bowed to each other before the earl descended the few steps to his coach, where his wife and the children awaited inside.

"Goodbye, my prince!" Lydia called, leaning nearly halfway out the dropped window.

"One moment," Valentine called up to the coachman. "I nearly forgot something." He turned and stepped inside the doorway to take the large bouquet Piffkin handed him.

"My princess," he said as he handed the bouquet up to a clearly delighted Lydia, and then stepped back to sweep her a courtly bow. William was too engrossed with his trio of caged frogs to even wave his farewells as the coach pulled away.

"You've ruined the young miss for all other gentlemen, you know," Piffkin said from behind him. "She's fated now to search the whole wide world for another one like you, doomed to failure, as there is, thank the Lord, only the one."

"I do set a high standard, don't I?" Valentine shot back, grinning as he stripped off the black mourning band that had encircled his upper arm and shoved it in his pocket. Now if Daisy could only be won as easily as Lydia. "You're certain Luther is on his way?"

"He is. As soon as he's satisfied the fires he laid have taken hold. You're certain we aren't setting off a conflagration?"

"Hardly. The bloody place is surrounded by rock," Valentine pointed out as his coach pulled into the circular gravel drive, Twitchill up on the box, Robert and two other Redgrave outriders cantering along behind. "Fire worked for Simon, remember. Besides, can you think of a more fitting end for a hellfire club?"

"For the structure below the cliff, sir, or the entire Society?"

"Both. Ah, and here comes Luther. How is he faring after all the excitement, by the way?"

"After accepting the grateful thanks of those highly excitable Cyprians before seeing them off back to their London cribs, sir? I'd say his mum will find him a highly changed young man."

"For the better, do you suppose?"

"Not for me to judge, sir. But he did mention a certain young barmaid at The Eagle, and how he thinks he knows now what she meant when she suggested he take her out walking, and then winked at him."

Valentine threw back his head and laughed before walking over to open the door of the coach and let down the steps. He approached carefully. Rose clung to Daisy whenever a man was present, but she seemed to make exceptions for Valentine, who had rescued her, and Piffkin, who treated her as if she was the most innocent of lovely young damsels, addressing her as Miss Rose, and constantly appearing with gifts secured in the nearby village. Chocolates, sugarplums, pretty ribbons for a bonnet he discovered, on and on.

Valentine had teased the man, saying if Piffkin weren't forty years Rose's senior, he would have to ask him his intentions. And for the first time in his memory, his valet had demanded an apology.

"Ladies? Good morning to you both, and don't you look fine as ninepence. And happy to be leaving the inn behind at last, I'm sure."

"How were the children when they left?" Daisy asked him as Rose treated him to a shy smile and then ducked her head so that her bonnet all but hid her face. She looked somewhat worn and tired, but there was no denying she was an exceptionally beautiful young woman.

"They're anxious to live with their cousins. How's...?" He indicated he meant Rose with a lift of his chin, rather than ask the question aloud. The questions. Was she all right? And, was she all right to travel with Piffkin and the maid Daisy had chosen from the Mailer household to accompany her to Redgrave Manor?

"We're doing very well, thank you. I wanted to speak with you about our traveling arrangements, however. I don't think—"

Rose put her hand on Daisy's arm. When she spoke, Valentine always had to lean in close to hear her, as he did now. "Piffkin and I will do nicely together, really. And he assures me Cloris is a more than adequate chaperone. Please, Daisy, don't fret about me. You've worried more than enough. It's only for two days. Piffkin says there's no more need to cry, that I've cried enough. We've all cried enough this past week, and Piffkin says once I'm at Redgrave Manor I can feel safe among friends and remember who I once was and once again am, and plan the rest of my life. Isn't that right, Piffkin? I believe I said it all correctly."

"Exactly so, Miss Rose. But if we're to make our planned destination for this evening, we'd best be on our way."

As Daisy frowned at her sister, Valentine held his breath. He'd never heard Piffkin's name so many times in so few breaths; the man deserved a substantial rise in wages…perhaps even a kiss on top of his bald head.

"If you're certain," Daisy said at last. "I'll see you tonight." She leaned over to give her sister a kiss on the cheek followed by a fierce hug. "I love you, sweetheart."

"I love you, too, Daisy." Rose leaned across her sister and looked Valentine directly in the eye. "Thank you again for taking care of her, and for saving me and for—for everything Piffkin told me."

Daisy looked to her sister, to Valentine and then back to Rose. "What *everything* has he told you?"

"Not now, Daisy," Valentine interjected quickly, holding out his hand to her. "It's time we were on our way. I doubt highly anyone is watching us after all this time, but lingering here still isn't advisable."

One more hug, one more exchange of kisses, and Daisy was standing beside Valentine on the gravel drive, smiling bravely as she waved at the departing coach, the outriders, including Luther, tagging behind, leading Charfield's mount. Like the Exalted Leader, Valentine believed in leaving no loose ends untied.

"What *everything?*" she asked him, the brave smile hastily reformed into an inquiring frown.

"Uh-oh," Valentine said instead of answering, shielding his eyes as he looked in the direction of the standing stones. "Smoke's rising above the trees. It's time we were gone."

"Yes, but— Let go of my hand, Valentine. You're all but dragging me. Good lord! What on earth is that thing over there? That's my bag strapped to the back, isn't it?"

"Along with one of mine, yes."

"We—we're going to ride in *that?* I'd rather cling to the top of your coach."

Valentine nodded to the groom who was holding the bridle of one of the pair of showy bays in the traces of Charles Mailer's ridiculous red racing curricle with its garish yellow wheels.

"A request from the earl. Since I arrived here with his brother and have no transport, I've been asked to deliver this horror to Tatt's for their sale. There's bound to be some young idiot who'll think it all the crack. If you want to keep your face pressed into my shoulder the entire way to London, I'll understand.

I may never live it down, myself, if I'm seen up on this monstrosity."

"London? But…but we're going to your brother's estate. We're going to meet Rose at night, but just ride separately because the coach would be too crowded and Mr. Piffkin needs a seat of his own because of his…that is, at his age."

"And I couldn't see Cloris riding up with me, and you felt sorry for me because I'd have to ride alone. You forgot that part."

"I did not forget that part. I *regret* that part. And stop grinning at me like the village idiot. We're not going to London, Valentine. I can't go to London, Rose expects me."

"Piffkin and your sister seem to have established some sort of special relationship these past days— one I've learned not to question—and she obviously trusts him. He's going to tell her we'll be slightly delayed but will meet up with them at the Manor."

"Delayed because of this *monstrosity?* I agree. I'd rather walk."

He climbed up on the springy seat and the groom handed him the reins before assisting Daisy. A coin flipped to the groom, they were on their way. If neither of the showy horses broke down or stopped to admire their reflections in every stream they passed, Valentine believed they could be in Cavendish Square just after dark.

At least now they were moving, and Daisy was

entirely too sensible to attempt to jump down from the seat. It was time for the truth.

"We'll be delayed because we're going shopping. At my expense, as it's my idea. No, my demand. Fetching as your gowns may be to those with a discerning eye, I think you and Rose will be more comfortable at Redgrave Manor clad in gowns less reminiscent of the schoolroom or, for her, the months of her captivity. I know my grandmother's always said a woman can never be the worse for a few new gowns and fripperies. In fact, I'm going to put Trixie in charge of you, so I hope you've sufficiently regained your stamina. I believe she often points her parasol at her coachman and shouts *charge* when her destination is Bond Street."

"That's highly amusing, even intriguing, but I won't be distracted. If you're set on emptying your pockets, there must be a village near your brother's estate where I can easily find materials to make up new gowns for both Rose and me. I'm a fairly accomplished seamstress. I made this gown myself, just recently."

He looked over at the gown. White collar tight around her throat, long sleeves with white turned-back cuffs. Buttons running down the front of the thing, and large pockets in which governesses often carried stubs of chalk, small slates, a short ruler and an extra linen square in case one of her runny-nosed charges hadn't thought to provide her own. She probably had made extra collars and cuffs, for whenever one set needed washing. Eminently practical. "Very, um…well sewn. It's brown."

"Yes, brown. A perfectly acceptable color for a governess. Thank you for thinking of Rose, and I agree she should be rid of anything having to do with these last months, but I really don't see a trip to London as necessary."

"I do. Oh, and there's no more need for these." He reached over and relieved her of her spectacles, tossing them over his shoulder, onto the roadway. "You haven't figured this out yet, have you, my genius?"

"Apparently I have not." She sat very straight on the seat, looking forward. "Enlighten me."

"I want to introduce my fiancée to my grandmother. There'd be the devil to pay if she isn't the first to know. Other than Piffkin, of course, who has already wished us happiness. You don't really think you and I would be riding unaccompanied in this circus wagon of a curricle otherwise, do you?"

There was a silence so solid Valentine had been told it at least metaphorically could be sliced with a knife. There was a silence so portentous one might feel the need to bow one's head in prayer. There was a silence so eerie that same person might not be able to resist turning himself about to see who or what might be sneaking up behind him on tiptoe.

And then there was Daisy's silence, that beat them all hollow.

"Daisy?"

She turned her head toward the scenery beside the road.

"I should have proposed, shouldn't I? Done the down-on-one-knee business and the rest of it? Kate will have my head on a platter, as she's always saying we Redgraves are the most unromantical people on earth. But God knows you're a practical sort, and it's obvious, isn't it? I've kissed you, more than once. That's enough in itself. And then that night, the filmy— Your, how do I put this? Your unfortunate *déshabillé?* Marriage is the only sensible solution."

She mumbled something he couldn't quite hear, but her tone wasn't promising.

"Pardon me?"

"I said, if that's the case then I shall marry Mr. Piffkin, as Luther is too young. It's not as if you're the only one who saw my *unfortunate déshabillé.* There's no great need for you to be the one to make such an obvious sacrifice."

"I can't see your face, but that last was said with a sneer, wasn't it?"

At last she turned to face him.

"A terrible sneer, yes, you should rejoice you missed it. At least I'm not half-hearted, nor am I hiding behind some sort of silly society rules and conventions. And…and if I am to be considered compromised, what should Rose be doing? Taking herself to a nunnery for the remainder of her days?"

"Because of what the Society did to her? Why should she be punished for what they did?"

"Exactly. A few kisses to one side, why should we be punished for what the Society attempted to do to me? Or with me. Or whatever it was they planned."

"I'm fairly certain they planned to parade you in front of me, and then give me some dastardly deed to carry out, something they'd thought up when they still believed I wanted to be one of them. I think they simply amended the plan wherein I commit the same dastardly deed in order to have you back or you'd pay the consequences. To be frank, I believe they may have suggested a virgin sacrifice or some such rot. In a way, Daisy, you should be flattered the Society thought I held you so high in my regard. So being married to me would be a punishment?"

"Don't twist my words, Valentine. It would be a punishment for both of us. You didn't deliberately see me in my unfortunate... I'm not going to repeat that."

"I knew I wouldn't do this right," Valentine said, pulled nearly into a ditch by the showy pair as the mail coach went racing by. He really should be concentrating on the road ahead, instead of trying to remember what stupid thing he'd said that had begun this less than helpful conversation. "Do you want me to tell you I love you beyond reason? I could do that, but we'd both know that isn't possible. As you said yourself, for all we've been through, we barely know each other."

She smiled at him, and somewhere inside he felt something break into small pieces. "I think you're too much the gentleman for your own good. Didn't Mr. Piffkin say rescuing damsels in distress is in your bailiwick?"

"Yes, Kate's told me that a time or ten herself. However, if that's the case, let me press my gentlemanly advantage. There's also your sister to consider. She may be much improved from the night we first found her, but what happened to her isn't something someone gets past all that quickly. She'll be more than simply accepted at Redgrave Manor. I know my family. She'll be cared for, most assiduously, I'm sure, by Trixie. She'll have the time she needs to put the past behind her. As my fiancée's sister, there's no questioning why she stays with us indefinitely."

Her question surprised him, but not for long. After all, Daisy was a commonsensible person.

"You live at your brother's estate?"

Valentine considered the question from her point of view. He was a younger son, the youngest son at that. Some would think him the poor relation, sponging off his brother's largesse, holding out his hand for his quarterly allowance. Or lazy. Or both.

"I don't believe I live anywhere, actually, having never seen the need," he admitted. "I spend time at Redgrave Manor, or at the mansion in London, and sometimes with Trixie, when she laments that she's just an old woman, alone in the world. But for the most part, I've been traveling ever since I left school. Scotland, the Continent, Greece, even Russia. First on a Grand Tour, and then on the occasional assignment for the Crown, although you could pretend not to have heard that part."

"Happily, yes."

"You'll probably want a residence of your own, won't you? An estate, and perhaps a town house or at least a flat for the Season? My brother Gideon may have inherited the earldom, but thanks to our mother's dowry and Trixie's financial brilliance over the years until Max and I reached our majorities, he and Kate and I are probably what you would term odiously wealthy in our own rights."

"You could be rich as Croesus and own a dozen castles and it makes no difference. I'm not marrying you, Valentine."

"Even for Rose?"

She lifted her chin. "Shame on you. And before you say anything else, the subject is closed."

Silence you could slice with a knife. Profound and even portentous silence. Eerie silence.

He'd forgotten one.

The *guilty* silence that remained throughout most of the entirety of the journey, including one decidedly unpleasant stop for luncheon, was so loud inside Valentine's head he was tempted to clap his hands over his ears to keep it out.

But now they were close to London, and to Trixie, who never failed to sniff out every secret. Not that a blind man wouldn't notice if Daisy still refused to speak to him. She'd never needed those spectacles in order to be taken seriously. Oh, no. Miss Daisy Marchant could probably successfully halt a charging elephant in its tracks with just a glance.

God, how he adored her. He didn't know why he did, which was one of the reasons he hadn't declared his undying love or whatever women expected to hear, but he adored her. She was everything he never knew he wanted or needed.

He shouldn't have lied. He shouldn't have said he didn't love her, believing she'd find such a declaration difficult to swallow on such short acquaintance. Instead, Cupid had conked him over the head with his shovel, and Valentine had used it to dig a hole and toss himself into it.

Now what? Maybe Trixie had an idea.

Wait a moment.

Trust Trixie to have an idea even marginally connected to common sense? Was he out of his mind? Was that what love did to people?

"Daisy?"

"No," she answered shortly, holding on to her bonnet in the breeze.

"You didn't know what I was going to ask."

"I don't *care* what you were going to ask. The answer is no."

He pushed on, working under the premise he may as well be hung for a sheep as a lamb: "I care for *you*. Very much."

Silence.

"I said, I care for you, Daisy. Very much."

She looked over at him, and then looked away. "You're impossible."

"Not really. Anything's possible, if you just apply yourself. I'm going to apply myself to hearing you say yes. You won't be able to resist me."

"I'm resisting you now, with barely any effort."

"Ah, but you're weakening. Resistance is futile when I apply myself. Just ask Piffkin."

Now, unfortunately, he had her full attention. "That's it, isn't it? Mr. Piffkin told Rose that you wanted me alone with you so that you could propose. That's why she didn't object to traveling without me. She'll be expecting me to be delirious with happiness while feeling her own future secure. I told you how she's terrified of being penniless and alone. And you did it all on purpose, didn't you?"

"Not really, no," he answered honestly. "I'd foolishly thought you'd see reason and say yes. But now that you've pointed it out to me, I suppose you could come to that conclusion. I think a July nuptial would be pleasant, don't you?"

Silence prevailed once more, but this was even one more variety of silence, and almost enjoyable. This time the silence was because he felt he'd rather left Daisy with nothing to say. Not that he wouldn't pay for his momentary victory at some point, which was another reason he adored her.

CHAPTER THIRTEEN

IT WAS THE bone structure, Daisy concluded. Many a young debutante was apple-cheeked and fetching, or shy and winsome and winning. Youth didn't last, and superficial beauty faded along with it. But not bone structure. That was forever, and the dowager countess of Saltwood had been sculpted by a master artist.

Her brow bones were high and clearly defined above huge, bright eyes, her nose thin and straight; patrician, one would suppose. And that jawline was a marvel, only slightly square, and with no sign of allowing the flawless skin covering it permission to sag.

Trixie Redgrave was petite, curvaceously slim, wore her blond hair in becoming ringlets strung with jewels and, good Lord, painted her toenails. She reclined on a one-sided lounge chair fashioned of white brocade satin, her gown a marvel of pleats and tucks of blue silk that perfectly matched her eye color. Her slim throat and wrists and fingers were adorned with diamonds and aquamarines that dazzled beneath the light of the several chandeliers in the drawing room at Cavendish Square.

The ring on her negligently dangling right hand,

her right arm perfectly posed along the back of the single side of the lounge, held a diamond as large as the proverbial goose egg.

Daisy was certain she was seeing a well-practiced pose. She mentally conceded it was a most effective one.

Trixie arranged the last bit of pleat over her bent knees. "Ah, and now that's over, my dramatic entrance. Impressed?"

"Possibly overwhelmed, my lady," Daisy answered honestly from her seat on a soft-bottomed damask chair that was helping her forget the curricle seat. She'd been sitting here primly for more than an hour, taking an occasional small sip from a glass of lemonade at her elbow, before her ladyship had floated into the room on the scent of something elusive but delicious, and had risen only to curtsy before the dowager countess arranged herself daintily on the lounge.

"No, you're not. If anything, you're faintly amused. I believe we'll rub along quite well. I apologize for keeping you waiting, Daisy—I'll call you Daisy because Valentine does—but all of this takes more than a bit of time to accomplish, and I was only stepping out of my bath when told of your arrival," Trixie said with a sweep of her arm that indicated her person, head to toe. "Even the chandelier above our heads is fitted with specially made candles that cast a faintly pink glow. Harsh lights and sun directly on your skin are a woman's worst enemies, especially as you age. A lesson my granddaughter steadfastly refuses to learn. You've been made comfortable?"

"Yes, my lady, thank you. I'm both fed and rested. Val—Mr. Redgrave has gone out, I believe to Grosvenor Square, where he hopes to see his brother Mr. Maximillien Redgrave. His note promises his swift return."

"Val's on a fool's errand if he's looking for Max. Richard and I only just returned to town ourselves yesterday, but as far as I know, the boy is still being exceedingly good at being a very bad boy on the Continent. I imagine that's a hum and he's really gone to see Lord Perceval, most probably to rub his nose in some grand accomplishment, which would do Spencer good, to my way of thinking. Valentine has had a grand accomplishment, hasn't he? Other than you, my dear, whom he suggested I will enjoy greatly. I believe you're to be *my* grand accomplishment. Have you ever worn pink? With that particular shade of red hair, the effect could be stunning."

"I'm a governess, my lady. Pink of any shade is out of the question."

"Yes, but a governess no more, correct?"

"To hear your grandson tell it, yes. I strongly disagree."

There was a faint, one might believe amused cough from the doorway as the butler entered, carrying a single glass of wine on a silver tray. He bowed over the dowager countess and she accepted the glass. "Thank you, Soames. Delightful, isn't she?

Not his usual sort at all, which may account for some of the attraction. Either that, or our prayers have been answered and our little boy has finally grown up. This should be grand fun."

Daisy considered her options. Stomping from the room in high dudgeon was briefly considered, but just as quickly abandoned. Pretending she hadn't heard or understood was ridiculous. Which left changing the subject entirely her final option. Unfortunately, she could think of only one other subject.

"The statues lining that imposing curved staircase leading up from the street, ma'am. When I noticed them upon our arrival, Mr. Redgrave informed me there's a story behind them, although many wish there were fig leaves in front of them."

"Val in particular. My late and exceedingly unlamented husband had the commissioning of the statues. Fig leaves are the invention of the prudish, you know. The ancient Greek and Roman statues these were carved to represent were meant to be a celebration of the heroic male. They're works of art. That's what I tell those who ask. But to be honest, it's great fun to see my male guests embarrassed by the truth. There's really nothing less impressive than, shall we say, an *uninspired* manhood."

"Trixie, you promised!"

Daisy watched as Valentine all but stomped into the room in much the way she had considered stomping out, and laughed. "Don't climb up into the boughs, for goodness' sake," she told him. "I'm a governess. I've studied anatomy."

"Not the way this one has," Valentine grumbled, kissing his grandmother's prettily offered cheek and then sitting down beside her as she tucked her bent legs a bit more to provide him room. "I haven't returned a moment too soon. Next you'll be regaling Daisy with one of your many exploits."

Trixie began lightly rubbing her hand up and down Valentine's upper arm. The shared affection was wonderfully obvious. "Which one, pet? Do you have anything particular in mind?"

"I've got several I'm still attempting to *banish* from my mind." He turned slightly to look at his grandmother more closely. "You're going out? At this hour?"

"Would you listen to him, Daisy? They're all the same, too. As if they were the adult and I were the child. Yes, dear, I'm going out. Richard and I are promised to Imogene for a late dinner with her son, Simon, the Viscount Roxbury, you know. I believe I'm to assist her in marrying him off. Or was that in *not* marrying him off? Yes, that's it. Imogene is in no hurry to become the dowager viscountess."

"Whatever. Surely you can cry off, Trixie."

"I could, but you'd only want to keep this poor girl sitting here while you tell me how you met, what you did and how much trouble you've caused the Society, while she clearly longs for her bed. Don't you, dear?"

"Thank you, ma'am, yes." Daisy did her best to not allow her shock to show. The dowager countess knew Valentine and his brothers were hunting the Society—and approved? She looked to Valentine, and smiled sweetly. "Perhaps you and I can have a dish of tea before I gratefully retire."

"There, it's settled, even as I recognize Richard's footsteps on the stairs." Trixie gave Valentine a small push to dislodge him and got to her feet with an alacrity not usually shown by ladies of a certain age. "You'll both breakfast with me tomorrow at ten, in my rooms."

As Daisy got to her feet, dropping into a curtsy, Valentine lifted his grandmother's hand to his lips and kissed her. "Tomorrow at eleven, right here. I've heard enough about your bedchamber to not want to see it."

"I told you, Daisy. A prude. Honestly, I don't know where I went wrong with the boy. Behave yourselves if you must. Goodnight, children, I'm off!"

"Well, that was more than faintly excruciating," Valentine said after procuring himself a glass of wine from the drinks table. He downed half its contents in two gulps before leaving the glass behind as he returned to stand in front of Daisy. "Let's go upstairs to your chambers and talk."

"I think not."

He tried a boyish smile. "I promise to behave myself."

"I don't. I'm still longing to box your ears. You're much safer here. Your grandmother wishes to see me in pink."

Valentine put his hands behind his back, considering the idea. He couldn't see Daisy in pink. He'd rather gotten used to her in brown, which was not at all possible anymore. "She wanted my sister to stop wearing her riding habit to the dinner table. Would you care to guess who won that battle? A word of advice, Daisy. Let her win if losing isn't all that earthshakingly bad, because there will be times you need to win."

"And yet you wonder why I wonder why you brought me here. She's marvelous, really, your grandmother. But perhaps just in small doses?"

"I can't explain Trixie to you, because we're none of us able to see inside her head. But I already told you that my grandfather began the Society. You already know Mailer routinely turned his wife over to the other members of the Society. Now, much as I'd rather you not, think what that implies. Trixie was my grandfather's perhaps fourteen-year-old bride— she really never says the same age twice. My father took up the reins in his turn, until my mother shot him. We can't ask her why she did it because she's dead, but I believe we can all guess why. Trixie, my mother, the wives of all the members, they were handed around at those damn *ceremonies* like party favors."

"Valentine, stop, please."

"Not yet. My grandmother, my mother, your sister and only God knows how many more, all victims of the Society. We're involved because we feel responsible for much of what happened in the past and because this third incarnation of the Society has dared to use Redgrave land for some of its activities. And yes, because no one knows of our family's past involvement, and we'd prefer to keep it that way. *Now* do you agree to go upstairs to your chamber so we can speak more privately?"

"I agree to allowing you to continue as you escort me to my chamber, but that's all." Daisy was doing her best to assimilate everything Valentine had just told her. Most striking, and most sad, was that his mother had murdered his father. "You didn't witness it, did you? Your father's demise?"

Valentine took her hand in his; he could tell she was feeling sorry for a little boy now grown. "No. It happened a long time ago, when I was still in the nursery with Kate. I really don't remember either of them. Trixie has been the only constant in any of our lives. Trixie, each other and Redgrave Manor."

"All of which you now consider to be under attack." Daisy was surprised to find herself on the stairs; her legs must have moved of their own volition. "You can't allow the Society to be traced back to its source. You're not working for the Crown, or

Lord Perceval. You're working for the Redgraves. No wonder you were so upset when you believed I was sent to Fernwood as some sort of spy, or something."

"You make a tolerably good spy, by the way."

They'd turned the corner at the top of the stairs, and headed down the hallway. "But I gave up too soon. I stayed at Fernwood hoping to find evidence against Lord Mailer, but I had already told myself Rose was lost to me. I may never forgive myself for that. My loss of heart. If you hadn't come along?" She sighed as he opened the door to her chambers. "If you hadn't come along, Valentine, my sister very well could have been dead by now."

She looked around the chamber. "And why are you still here? Is there more I don't know?"

"Indeed there is." Valentine took himself over to the high tester bed and rather gracefully launched himself onto it, landing on his back at the same time he tucked his bent arms behind his head against the pillows. "Mailer kept a journal. Remind me never to do anything so silly, please. At any rate, I discovered it in his study once he was dead. He had plans for your sister."

He patted the mattress next to him. "You may want to sit down."

"I believe I'd rather stand." Daisy couldn't take her eyes off him. In her bed, or at least *on* it. Lying there in all his handsomeness and tousled hair and devilish smile, his ankles crossed, completely at his ease. How wonderful it must be to have such confidence in oneself, to be able to give oneself over to relaxation. She'd never felt capable of letting down her guard that way; not Miss Proper, Miss Straightback, Miss Prunes and Prisms. "You're still the only one here who considers us betrothed. Now tell me about Lord Mailer's plans."

Valentine jackknifed into a sitting position, his long legs dangling over the side of the bed. "He made a mistake a few months before meeting your sister. In…in the throes of passion, some might say, he managed to choke the life out of one of the female participants. Although titillated—or so Mailer believed—the Society frowned on such a waste of good… Well, we'll forget that part."

Now Daisy did sit down on the nearest chair, as her knees were threatening to give way beneath her. That could have been Rose's fate. "Oh, that poor woman."

"Yes. They told him to find one woman for himself, keep his hands off the others, and if he lost a second one he could damn well amuse himself by himself— I'm sorry, Daisy. I'm trying, badly, not that there's a good way, to explain why he took some time to get to know Rose. Because he knew he wasn't going to just use her, but keep her."

Daisy dipped her head. "She told me he was the only one, but I doubted her. I thought it made her feel less…less, I don't know what. And how he'd *visit* her whenever he was in residence on the estate. Other than he, Davinia was the only person she saw between…between meetings. She told me the days were so long, that it was no one but Davinia sometimes for weeks on end, that she'd almost begun to look forward to Mailer's visits, just to see another human being."

"Mailer believed himself in love with your sister. But he couldn't figure out how to get rid of Lady Caroline," Valentine told her. "His first wife had supposedly slipped and fallen from the cliff, although many thought it either suicide or murder. Those avenues were closed to him. He considered poison, a fall on the stairs. Much as she feared the meetings, I'm sure her ladyship feared Rose more, for she had to know she was looking at her replacement. Passing his wife around to all and sundry, while keeping himself only to Rose."

Daisy raised astonished eyes to Valentine. "He was going to *marry* her? Is that what you're saying?"

"That was his plan, yes. I would have thought Rose had told you."

Daisy shook her head. "Never. After that first night, when she wanted me to make certain he was *very* dead, she never mentioned his name again. Perhaps she didn't know his plan." She got to her feet, unable to sit still, and approached him, laid a hand on his arm; she didn't think twice about touching him; it only seemed natural. "Thank you for telling me all of this, Valentine. About Rose, about your family. You do know you can't be held responsible for what happened in the past, before you and your siblings were even born."

"But Trixie is alive. Until a recent rash of what we'll politely call accidents, many of my father's contemporaries were still above ground, and several of them had actually kept up the Society after his death. For purely *social* reasons, if I can be excused for that description of so-called devil worship and indulging their perversions. Gideon believes one of the new members they recruited saw what my grandfather and father saw, and not only came into the Society, but quickly took charge of it."

Daisy was becoming more and more aware that the two of them were alone in this lovely room, the only light from several flickering candles and the small fire in the grate. She'd been alone with him before, but this was different. She didn't know why, but it was. She was even having trouble concentrating on what he was saying, being much more interested in watching his mouth as he said the words.

"Daisy?"

"Oh. Oh, yes. What did this new leader see?"

"Power. Position. Wealth. And although those in charge in France changed over the decades, the central theme of the Society remained the same. Collaborate with the French, bring down the monarchy, and be handsomely rewarded for their treason. At the moment, the Society is using the beaches at Redgrave Manor to smuggle gold and information to France, and bring back God only knows what to

England. My father's contemporaries knew about the landing beach, the caves, the route inland. If the Society is exposed, the Redgrave name goes down with them. Trixie goes down with them. She enjoys her scandalous reputation, even encourages it, but could never overcome the real truth were it to get out."

She knew what she was about to say would betray her, but she said it, anyway. "You and your siblings aren't going to stop until the Society is completely destroyed, and you might have done it, if you'd been able to capture the woman and her consort. I didn't help you, I was in your way. I could have gotten you killed. Valentine? I'm right, aren't I?"

He touched a hand to her cheek, smiled down at her upturned face. "I'm sorry. I was attempting to imagine this past week and more without you there to scold me, keep me in check, astound me with your courage. Looking back, I wouldn't have had it any other way. Especially when I was told to look up, and saw you descending into my arms like a goddess from above. I wouldn't change those moments for the world."

"We weren't ever going to mention that," she reminded him quietly.

"And I've tried. But it would seem I can't control my dreams."

"I looked horrible. I saw myself in one of the mirrors, you know, and I looked like some sort of perverse doll. And by the time we returned to my prison to locate my clothing, my face was nothing but a smear of black and red and my hair was a rats' nest of burrs and…and…stop looking at me that way. You know how I looked."

"I still wanted to kiss you. Nearly as much as I want to kiss you now. More than kiss you. Much more than kiss you."

He moved closer, and she put her palms against his chest. "Valentine, don't…"

"Don't what, Daisy? Don't want you? Don't imagine holding you, touching you. Feeling you move beneath me as I watch the wonder dawn in those beautiful eyes? I love your eyes, they're like windows to your soul. You were right to hide behind those spectacles, because your goodness shines so clearly someone less scrupulous than me would have taken advantage of you long ago."

"Valentine, don't say such—"

His arms were around her waist now. "Don't tell the truth? The first time I saw you all I could think was how I needed to see you with your hair down, so I could run my fingers through your warm curls. Take your hair down for me, Daisy. Please."

She looked into his eyes, and couldn't say no. Her hands trembling only slightly, she reached up to pull out the restraining pins. Her hair fell below her shoulders in its usual unmanageable curls.

Valentine smiled as if she'd pleased him.

She gave her head a small shake, which probably only accentuated its wildness; she simply had too much hair.

He brought his hands slowly up her back, his fingers spread, teasing at the delicate, oddly responsive skin of her nape, and then disappeared into her hair, his fingertips moving in a slow, massaging motion that sent tingles running all the way down her back. He pressed his thumbs behind her ears, then traced their outline. All of this done while watching her, intently watching her, perhaps memorizing her features for some reason known only to him.

"You're beautiful."

"I am not. I've never been beautiful."

"You are to me. You're the most beautiful woman in the world. It's all there, in your eyes."

He leaned in and kissed her, his mouth warm and sweet with wine, and she decided the lady doth protest too much. If the man wanted to see her as beautiful, why would she want to persist in pointing out his error?

His mouth still clinging to hers, he bent down and scooped her into his arms, carrying her over to the bed.

Daisy reluctantly broke the kiss, nearly gasping for air. Her clinging arms giving the lie to her words, she said, "I don't think we should—"

"Ah, sweetheart, but I think we must, and I think we both know it. There's only one way to forget the sordid side of what men and women can do to each other, and that's to learn the beauty, and begin looking forward."

Her heart skipped a beat. He was saying what

she had been thinking ever since he'd come into the room with her, that there was only one real way to erase the unnatural and replace it with—what had he said? The beauty? Yes, that was the word. How could he know?

"That does seem logical, I suppose."

His smile had its usual effect on her. She melted. "And my Daisy is always logical. Be a dear and pull back the coverlet, so I can put you down."

"Valentine, we're both completely dressed. We couldn't possibly…"

He was nuzzling her neck. Was that nuzzling? Yes, she was certain that was the word. Nuzzling was…nice. At least parts of her body she'd previously never paid much attention seemed to like it. And she supposed he was right, what they were about to do was inevitable, and had been since their first kiss.

"You're being logical, again."

"I have to be. This is my best gown."

"An incriminating statement concerning your wardrobe if I ever heard one." Valentine put her down in front of him. "I particularly dislike these buttons. Let's be rid of them."

"Valentine…"

He kissed the tip of her nose. "You're right. We'll start with my jacket." He opened the buttons and enlisted her assistance in tugging off his right sleeve. He made short work of the rest. And his waistcoat.

Then he slid off his cravat and raised his hands to open his top shirt button.

She could see bits of dark, curly hair in the soft candlelight.

"I...I can do that," Daisy heard herself say. He was so handsome. No, so beautiful, so perfect. He put the statues lining the stairwell to shame; sculptors would have wept to have the privilege of having him pose for them.

Yet he was flesh and blood, and as she slid the buttons free of their anchors, she could feel his soft hair tickling at the backs of her fingers, watch his chest rise and fall...feel his heartbeat, his rather rapid heartbeat.

When she got to the last easily reachable button she stopped, dropped her arms to her sides. She had no idea what to do next.

"My turn," he whispered, already busy with her plain wooden buttons. Whatever had made her think she needed so many of them?

She felt the back of his knuckles against her bare skin, realized his expertise in loosening the plain laces of her modest chemise, gasped aloud when he slid his hands inside and cupped her unimpressive breasts.

Daisy bent her head forward, resting her brow against his bare chest. Perhaps she was wrong. Perhaps he felt he was being kind, in the same way he'd insisted they marry. "We shouldn't..."

His hands went back to her buttons, until he'd

opened them below her waist, and then he helped her ease the gown from her shoulders so that it puddled around her legs. He bent and helped her off with her shoes, leaving her legs clad in cotton stockings. He was probably used to seeing silk, and lace. But he didn't seem to mind.

Still, she instinctively gripped the sides of her chemise closed over her breasts, watching as he rid himself of his shirt.

The candlelight loved him. It must, to so wonderfully define his long, lean muscles, the skin she ached to touch. She found it difficult to swallow.

"You look as if you're cold," he said, running his hands up and down her bare arms. "Are you cold?"

"No," she said, and then shivered. Not with cold, but for some other reason she didn't understand. If she were forced to put a word to it, she realized what she was feeling was desire. The desire to touch, to be touched in return. She'd long ago resigned herself to returning to her Maker as innocent as the babe she had been, never believing anyone would ever care about another nearly invisible governess.

Valentine's smile was so sweet she briefly considered ordering him to leave, because it was evident he saw straight through her. But if he said he believed he could see into her soul, she may as well abandon any thoughts of being a woman of mystery.

"Not cold, then, but modest. Here, let's take care of that."

Before she could protest, he'd reached past her,

turned down the coverlet, and she was deposited nearly in the middle of the bed. Valentine reached for the buttons holding his breeches and she immediately turned her head.

This was happening. It was really happening. And it was wrong. She should stop him. She should stop herself, because men were full of needs, but women should know better. She should know better.

Several long moments later, he came down beside her, managing to drag the bedding up to cover them both to the waist. A marvelous feat, neatly accomplished, save for one thing.

"Ouch! You're leaning on my hair!"

He hastened to raise his elbow and she pulled her hair free, lifting her head so that she could sweep her hair all up and behind her against the pillows. She was about to twist it into a knot when Valentine stopped her.

"No, please don't," he said, taking hold of her hand. "It looks wonderful, like a living fan."

"Or a highly embarrassed peacock," she grumbled, pretending she wasn't lying in a bed, Valentine lying beside her, his head propped against one bent arm, smiling at her.

Still, it was nice that he laughed at her poor joke.

"You know, Daisy, I'm much more accomplished at this than I would appear to be so far."

Daisy sought protection the only way she knew how: with words. "Bumbling or wonderfully clever, you do realize I wouldn't know the difference."

"Ah, how you ease my mind. However, as the spell of my stunning expertise has been most definitely broken and you're wondering what possessed you to have me next to you like this, may I suggest we stop talking so I can kiss you again."

How did he know she wasn't feeling half so amorous as she'd been only a few minutes earlier, and much more apprehensive? Was that natural for a woman? She had no idea.

"If you believe it would help."

"I do," he said, shifting on the bed, the two of them now sharing the same pillow. "All you have to do is say stop, Daisy. I want you, but I would never hurt you. I want you to know how much I need you in my life, not as an obligation, but because I know I'd never find anyone else like you, not if I searched for a thousand years."

Daisy felt tears pricking at the backs of her eyes, even as she turned slightly toward him. "I suppose that's very sweet of you to—"

He took her mouth with his again, only this time so much more intimately, coaxing her senses with teeth and tongue, retreating and advancing until she put a hand on his shoulder to keep him close. He had magic in his mouth, turning her from reluctant maiden to eager participant.

Never really taking his mouth from hers, he began touching her body. Easing the chemise strap from her shoulder, sliding his fingertips lower, finding her breast, seeking out her nipple for extra attention, rubbing it with the faintly rough pad of his thumb.

Now it was she who broke the kiss as she gasped for breath, shaken by her body's reaction to this intimacy. He seemed to take advantage of the moment to begin kissing the length of her throat, the slight indentation above her collarbone. And then lower.

As he held her, as he lifted her, he brought his mouth down over her nipple, drawing it into his mouth, caressing it with his tongue.

There was nowhere for her to go, nothing for her to do but concentrate on the pleasure coursing through her body. She tensed and melted at the same time, longing for his touch, the rasping pleasure of his tongue.

And more.

So much more.

Her chemise was completely open now, the laces somehow undone, and Valentine shifted again, so that his hand was free to explore her other breast, bring it to life, as well. She knew her nipple had gone hard, as if straining to be noticed, and when he began lightly pinching it between thumb and forefinger she felt as though he'd found some secret connection between her breasts and the dull, almost pulsating ache that had begun between her thighs.

But when he moved his hand down her belly, sliding beneath the now untied waistband of her petticoat, she suddenly panicked.

"Stop," she said quietly. "Please stop."

He did as she asked, and she sighed in relief.

She could feel the weight of his hand, his palm resting on her lower belly. It felt good. It felt nice. She felt safe.

He went back to kissing her. Her forehead, her cheeks, her mouth. He nuzzled at her ear, coaxing yet more shivers when he traced her ear with his tongue, as his warm breath tickled at her, and she began to feel liquid again.

"Daisy, sweetheart, let me tell you what I'm going to do, and you can tell me if I may, or if I should stop. All right?"

"You must think me an idiot," she said, closing her eyes.

"*Shh,* nothing of the kind. I want to touch you, Daisy. I want you to feel, just a little, what it would be like if I could make love to you. But I can't do that if you keep your legs so closely together."

"I…I can't."

He continued in that same soft, encouraging voice. "Do you trust me, Daisy?"

Her bottom lip caught between her teeth, her eyes tightly shut, she nodded.

"You're covered, sweetheart, I can't see anything. I won't even try to look. I promise. I'm going to move my hand now, and I'll stop if you tell me to stop."

She let out a long, hopefully relaxing breath, and nodded again. But her thighs remained tightly, protectively together.

She felt his hand moving again, drifting over the skin of her lower belly, a fingertip exploring her navel even as he captured her breast in his mouth once more.

That was nice. That felt good.

He ran his hands over her thighs, into the nest of curls, and then retreated once more to her navel. She dared to open her eyes, to see his dark head bent over her, the sweep of his lashes against his cheeks as he licked at her, teased at her, she could fancifully believe, very nearly worshipping her body.

Yes, there had to be more. She willed her body to relax, even as he lowered his hand once more to the apex of her thighs. Where she felt so tight, so unnaturally warm, even liquid. So very nearly needy.

She heard her own voice above the pounding of her heart. Not saying *stop*. Not really saying anything. Just a low, wondering whimper.

He was massaging her now, pressing the heel of his hand against her, holding and moving all of her so that the skin between her thighs moved, as well. Easing her, relaxing her, until his middle finger slipped lower, and she felt the shock of his touch against her impatient flesh.

He was whispering in her ear again. "Open your legs for me, Daisy. Your body knows, and it wants you to let me in."

She turned her head away from him. And willed her thighs to relax.

"Yes," Valentine breathed as his hand slipped

lower. "That's it, sweetheart, that's what we both want. Now I'm going to touch you, learn you because I want to find all your secret pleasures. Your body's ready, Daisy, easing my movements, smoothing the way. Feel it? Your body knows there's more, so much more. Pleasure you can't even imagine. Draw up your knees for me, Daisy. Open yourself to me. Trust me."

"I…I can't. I can't. Oh, God, what are you doing?"

She knew how moist she was, and it embarrassed her, no matter what Valentine told her to the contrary. She was losing control, had lost control of her own body. She wanted to grind her teeth, wanted to lift her bottom so he could *do things* to her, whatever he wanted.

Like now. He was holding her slightly apart, and stroking at her very center, and a switch seemed to turn deep inside her, unlocking her last inhibition.

She bent her knees, and dug her heels into the bed, and lifted herself up, desperately afraid he'd move his hand, lose the secret place he'd found, leave her hanging on some precipice, never knowing what it is to fly.

"There," she heard herself say. "Yes. Just there. I can't…I can't…"

He was everywhere, even inside her. And she gave him everything she had, everything she didn't know she had to give. Her body began its own dance, unbidden by her, and she cried out her pleasure, her wonder.

"Hold on," Valentine whispered tight against her ear, and then he plunged his fingers deep inside her, breaking through the barrier that marked the line between unknowing spinster and true womanhood.

She hurt, she burned, but he stayed with her, stroking her, soothing her…and then moving on top of her, nestling himself between her spread thighs, guiding himself to her, inside her, filling her. She felt him move, slowly at first, and then with urgency creeping into his every thrust, until he clasped her tightly to him and she felt his release.

His back was damp against her palms, evidence of his exertion, and she kissed his slick shoulder, licked the salt from the side of his neck.

What he'd done to her…what she'd given him. There was nothing else in this world more important. Not money or power or station or jewels. Nothing. Everything she ever wanted or needed was right here, collapsed and breathing heavily in her embrace.

He really did *care* for her. He really did see her as a desirable woman. Right at this moment, she certainly did *feel* like a desirable woman. Wasn't life amazing?

"You're a good man, Valentine Redgrave," she told him in awe.

Being Valentine, he lifted his head and smiled down at her. "I can be even better," he promised her shamelessly. "Just give me a few minutes to recuperate."

And then tremendously loud bells began to peal in the attics two floors above them, followed hard by the sound of running feet and servants calling out: "Fire! Fire in the main foyer! Down the servant stairs, everyone—fire, fire!" and someone was pounding on Daisy's bedchamber door. "Wake up, miss! Fire!"

CHAPTER FOURTEEN

VALENTINE KNEW THAT of all the fears those who lived in London faced, be it thieves, cut-purses or cut-throats, or even slop buckets being emptied overhead by a careless maid, there was one that stuck deep in the hearts of anyone who heard that single word: *fire*.

Nearly all of London had burned in the fire that had begun in Pudding Lane in 1666, and several sections of the city had met the same fate again and again over the years. There was always a lack of easily accessible water, and by the time a brigade could be formed to fight the blaze, often all that was left of an entire block were stone chimneys and smoldering ashes.

Daisy had leaped out of the bed, tripped over her untied petticoat, rallied quickly, and been buttoned into her chemise and gown by the time Valentine had pulled on his breeches, thrust his arms into his shirtsleeves and located his second shoe.

He grabbed her hand and together they raced to the door, throwing it open and then shutting it firmly behind them. "This way," he told her, and they headed toward the rear of the tall rather than wide mansion and the servants' stairs that led all the way down to the ground-floor kitchens.

Halfway down, they were met by servants on their way up. "Fire in the kitchens, sir," a footman yelled. "A lantern thrown through the window and spilling on the tiles."

"A lantern? Valentine, that means—"

"I know what it means. You," he said, grabbing the footman by his lace cravat, "stand firm right here. Let nobody up these stairs. The front stairs are also burning. Cover your mouths and noses, and wait for my summons. Come on, Daisy!"

He kept hold of her hand as they ran down two more narrow flights, smoke rising toward them as they went. He could have grabbed the footman instead, but the lad seemed terrified, and if he had to choose someone to stand firmly at his back and remain cool under fire, there was no one he'd rather have with him than the unflappable Daisy Marchant.

They stumbled a bit at the bottom landing, where the stairs curved into the kitchens, and then he pulled Daisy to her knees, hopefully to keep them below the worst of the smoke.

The fire in the center of the brick floor had all but died on its own, but not before having found several new homes in the curtains, an old tapestry rug tacked to the wall and a pile of folded linens stacked on a long wooden table. Another few minutes and flames could reach the wooden ceiling, and the mansion would be beyond help.

"Where's the pump?" she asked, and then went off in a small paroxysm of coughing.

Valentine slapped her on her back as he attempted to get his bearings. He'd spent many an afternoon in these kitchens, peeling vegetables as punishment for something or other he'd done wrong, never letting on to Trixie that the cook very much favored him and he'd spent most of his time slathering butter from the huge crock onto buns hot from the ovens, or licking sweet icing from a wooden spoon.

"This way. Hold on to my leg."

She could have made it to the door leading out to the mews, saved herself. But not Daisy. Daisy grabbed on. If she was afraid, she didn't show it. She'd simply put her faith in him, just as she'd done upstairs, in what seemed a lifetime ago now.

And he'd be damned if he'd ever do anything to prove her trust in him unfounded. It was a hell of a time for an epiphany, but Valentine knew himself to be a better man because of one Daisy Marchant.

The pump was a large one, set above a trough sink. He primed it and began to pump, even as Daisy ripped two strips from her petticoat and wet them. She handed one to him and then tied the other around her nose and mouth.

Without a word, they knew what had to be done. Daisy took over the pumping while Valentine lined up buckets stored beneath the trough. When the first was full, he took a deep breath and crossed the kitchen, to douse one set of burning curtains. By the time he got back, the second bucket was full.

They kept their small chain going until there were no more flames, but only dark, choking smoke. It was safe to throw open the door and windows without feeding the fire.

Still with the cloths tied around their faces, they called out to the servants hovering on the stairs, waited until they were all down in the kitchens and then raced up a single flight, Valentine intent on helping whoever might be attempting to douse the fire in the foyer.

Again, they were met with smoke, but no flames.

The butler, Soames, was leaning against the stucco wall at the head of the curving staircase, using a small brush he'd probably procured from his pocket to swipe at some offending soot on his sleeve. His unruffled demeanor did a lot to calm Valentine's concern.

Valentine pulled down the rag that had covered his nose and mouth as Daisy did the same. "I take it the fire's out?"

"Yes, sir. A pair of lit lanterns and a bladder of oil, all tied together and tossed inside when George, here, opened the door to a rather commanding knock. Don't hang your head, George. It's not as if we can see *through* the door, now is it?"

"How did you manage to put it out, Soames?"

"Smothered it, sir, as it was oil. Water wouldn't have done us any good, no good at all."

Still holding Daisy's hand, Valentine walked over to the decorative balustrades and peered down at the foyer below.

He shook his head. "Those are two of the Aubusson carpets from the drawing room, aren't they? The rather priceless Aubusson carpets from the drawing room, won by my grandmother in a private wager with the Prince of Wales?" And then he took a chance Soames may not be as unflustered as he appeared. "Do you happen to know the nature of the wager itself? She never told us."

But one didn't remain the butler to the dowager countess long by speaking out of turn. "I'm sure I couldn't say, sir, and also that the family should be happy in its ignorance. Very tightly woven carpets by the way, and quite heavy. They worked like a charm, although I fear the marble floor may be forever stained. There's soot everywhere. It will take a week or more just to clean the crystals on the chandelier. There are over six hundred of them, you understand."

"Politely chastened, am I, Soames, and the subject neatly changed? Still, it was worth a try." Valentine turned his attention to the previously unadorned statues, now mantled in black, smoky soot. "I'll grant you have a mess on your hands, but your quick work saved the mansion."

Behind him, Daisy cleared her throat. "I believe you *all* to be heroes, and I commend you. If you'd be so good as to summon your housekeeper and all the servants, Mr. Soames, I will take things from here. Let them begin by throwing open every last window in this establishment. We're in for a long night, I'm afraid, but together we'll get through it. Oh, and if there's any more lemonade, I'd very much like the taste of smoke banished from my mouth, as would everyone else, I imagine."

As Soames looked rather bug-eyed, Valentine quickly jumped in to save her. "Actually, Miss Marchant, I think the first order should be to have the grooms arm themselves and stand guard around the mansion for the remainder of the night."

"True, Mr. Redgrave, and eminently practical. We have been attacked, haven't we. Does this sort of thing occur often in Mayfair? Well, no matter. This mess won't clean itself, as my mother was fond of saying, so let's get to work."

And then, in the totally unaffected way of a woman who placed practicality above most everything else (apparently even above returning to what had been their recently shared bed), Daisy managed to tame her riot of curls and twist it into a knot at the top of her head. She had all the qualities of a warrior queen; she just didn't know it.

Valentine had to restrain himself from kissing her.

"Yes, miss, but—"

"I believe Soames is trying to say he's in charge, he and the housekeeper, and after that, the cook."

"Oh, I'm so sorry, Mr. Soames. I'm afraid I'm unaccustomed to standing idly by while others work. Of course you're in charge. If you'd just tell me how I can be of assistance?"

"Thank you, miss." The butler bowed. "If I may be so bold as to correct you, sir, I had been about to apologize for the possibility there is no lemonade prepared, and suggest a small, restorative glass of wine for the young lady while she's waiting."

Soames, you dog, you, you're under her spell now, as well, aren't you? "Splendid idea—a glass of wine for everyone, from major domo to pot boy, and then to work. Miss Marchant, if you'd be so kind as to come with me for a moment?"

Valentine took her hand and pulled her into the drawing room, shutting the double doors behind them. Then he turned and looked at her, couldn't stop looking at her. Her hair was still a mess, long, tight ringlets falling in her face, around her nape. From her forehead to halfway down her nose, her skin was gray with soot from the kitchen fire, her eyes looking twice as blue. Her brown gown was misbuttoned rather badly, the bodice and skirt sopping wet from working the pump.

He was so damn proud of her he felt his own buttons might burst.

"How are you?" he asked her.

"Reluctantly ready to take you up on your offer of some new gowns, I suppose," she said, smiling faintly. "I'll never be able to get the smell of smoke out of this one. How are you? You look quite dashing, you know. Your hair adorably awry, your face most attractively streaked with soot, as if you'd applied it while peering into a mirror. Your shirtpoints still wonderfully starched, a credit to Mr. Piffkin, I'm sure. You could be a pirate, standing at the bow of the ship. I, on the other hand, have probably never looked worse. How do you suppose that is? That one person can look so attractive, no matter what the circumstances, while the other—"

"I think you're beautiful," he told her, walking toward her.

"Yes, yes, it's all in my eyes. Thank you. You know, Valentine, I'm beginning to think you believe yourself besotted, or some such thing. I am *not* beautiful. My sister is beautiful. Your grandmother is beautiful. Goodness, Valentine, *you're* beautiful."

"Now that's embarrassing."

"Forgive me. *Handsome.* Granted, I don't send little children screaming for their nurse, but I am not beautiful and I wish you'd stop saying I am. You make me uncomfortable."

Valentine was doing his best not to laugh. Laughing, at this precise moment, would not be a good idea. "May I at least say you make love beautifully?"

Daisy opened her mouth, frowned, closed her mouth again. She looked at him rather intensely, as if to assure herself he was serious. "I do?" Then she shook her head. "Oh, I do not. Do I?"

"I'm not about to issue a complaint," he told her,

at last unable to hold back his smile. "I brought you in here, however, to ask how you're feeling."

"Feeling? I'm fine. I wasn't even slightly singed."

"I'm not talking about the fire, sweetheart." Now he was the one feeling uncomfortable. "Look, Daisy, it was your first time, and sometimes—"

"Oh. That. I suppose I'm a little… That is, now that I have a moment to think about it, I— But I'll be fine. Although a bath would be wonderful, wouldn't it?"

"In so many ways, yes." He was smiling again. She was again trying to be practical. And, he supposed, attempting to treat what they'd shared an hour earlier as some sort of— Ah, hell, what did she think about it? As they'd had no time to discuss the thing, he really had no idea. He didn't want a critique, but he'd like to think he hadn't bungled the thing, even if he hadn't been more nervous in his life.

"But not until the foyer is at least partially put to rights. Your grandmother may return soon, and she shouldn't be greeted by such a terrible mess." She tilted her head to one side. "How are we going to explain this to her? Will she know it's the work of the Society, aimed at the two of us? Do you think they've been watching for our arrival? Why didn't they attack us along the road? How do you suppose they knew we were here? Oh, and do you think the fires were meant to kill us, or to warn us? After all, if they'd waited another few hours, the entire household probably would have been asleep."

"One question at a time, please, although you're right, it would have been much easier to attack us on the road, even logical." A thought struck him; Daisy had this way of asking just the correct question— that perfect question must have been somewhere in that litany of questions—and it had sparked some in his own mind. It was almost as if she was his muse... or somehow opened up some better part of himself. "Unless... Daisy, we're going to allow Trixie to tell us what she suspects. Volunteer nothing."

"I don't understand. Could you be more— Oh. Are you saying the attack *wasn't* meant for us? That it was meant for your grandmother? But why would anyone wish to harm your grandmother?"

"As we've just been talking about it, I can think of several reasons." Valentine's mind was racing now, the fire itself relegated to the past. "She was there, at the beginning. She knows things. People, places, secrets no one should know. She's been a great source of information for us, but she's had to   let's say *talk* to several people recently, in order to gain some of that information. It's never smart to delve too deeply into how Trixie does what she does. On top of that, my brother Gideon still believes she hasn't told us all she knows, not that anyone can blame her."

"I'd want to forget it all. I can't even imagine how difficult it is for her that her grandchildren now know what it was like for her when your grandfather was alive."

"She's been extremely brave ever since Gideon

approached her with what he'd learned, if not always immediately forthcoming. She and Richard—you've yet to meet him, but rumor has it my grandmother is actually in love—were traveling somewhere, doing only God knows what, until returning here yesterday. If she said something along the way, asked the wrong question, wasn't as discreet as she believes herself to be?"

"You have quite the interesting family, Valentine. The more I hear, the more I wonder why I'm not walking about with my jaw at half-mast. Is there more?"

It was probably the smoke making him slightly giddy; he'd inhaled more than his share of it, because he opened his mouth and, before he could think better of it, said, "Well, although it's one of the things we'll never bother mentioning to Trixie, we did misplace our father's remains for a few decades, but we've got him safely tucked up in the mausoleum again. Come on."

While her mouth actually was at half cock, he took her hand and led her back to the upstairs foyer, to find Soames waiting there with a tray holding two glasses of wine.

"Thank you," Valentine said, handing one glass to Daisy and then downing his own immediately before replacing the glass on the tray. That's when he noticed that she'd drunk all of hers, as well, as if she'd been thirsty and the contents were nothing but flavored water. As he doubted the vicar's daughter had ever so much as tasted wine until now, this could prove interesting. "I believe Miss Marchant has decided to leave you to it and only asks that hot water be brought upstairs so that she might have a bath."

The butler bowed, eyeing the empty glasses; yes, he'd been butler to Trixie Redgrave for a long, informative time. "Begging you pardon, sir, but anticipating just such an outcome, I already took the liberty of ordering up tubs for you both."

Daisy was blinking rather rapidly, which could be thought to be a reaction to the smoke, although Valentine thought differently. He could remember his first glass of wine—sipped, not gulped—and how warm and pleasant he'd thought the experience.

"Oh, you shouldn't have. That's too much trouble right now, what with—"

"Ignore her. She has no idea how worse for wear she looks."

Soames looked at the floor. That, at least, had to be something new to the man. "Sir."

Halfway up the stairs, with her hand still in his, she whispered, "I said I'd thank you to stop prosing on about how beautiful you mistakenly think I am. But that doesn't mean you have to say I look as if I've been dragged backward through a hedgerow." Then she stumbled on the stairs.

"Women," Valentine said, scooping her up to carry her the rest of the way. "There's no pleasing you, is there?" He put her down in front of the door to her bedchamber, normally Kate's when she kept

Trixie company, which they all took turns doing, always grumbling they'd be more comfortable in Grosvenor Square, but always genuinely delighted to share special time with their grandmother.

He put Daisy down and delivered a quick kiss to her pouting mouth. "I'll be back in twenty minutes. Make certain the maid is gone and the door unlocked."

"Yes, we do need to talk more about the fire, don't we? But twenty minutes? That's impossible. I'll barely have the smoke out of my hair by then. Valentine? Do you have any idea how I hate it when you make pronouncements and then just turn and walk away from me?"

Already partway down the hall, he turned and blew her a kiss, then kept on walking. He was certain she'd figure out what he meant on her own, eventually.

Piffkin had the ability to anticipate Valentine's most every need, but Piffkin was on his way to Redgrave Manor, so there were no fresh clothes laid out in the dressing room. Valentine dismissed the manservant waiting (but not anticipating) for him, believing himself capable of bathing and dressing himself. Making do with shirt and breeches, deciding against hose and shoes and banyan, he and his still-damp hair were on their way back down the hall in only a little more than thirty minutes.

He couldn't chance the efficient Daisy not to already be out of her tub which, to his way of thinking, would be a crying shame.

He knew the layout of Kate's room, having spent hours there with his sister when they were younger, the two of them lounging about on bed or floor, discussing everything from the silly to the deadly serious.

He lightly rapped on the door he'd long since abandoned opening without knocking first, and then stepped inside, locking the door behind him.

"Daisy?" he called out softly in the dimly-lit chamber, already on his way to the dressing room and the large tub kept behind a screen in a corner of that room. The door was slightly ajar, and he believed he could smell the fresh scents of lemons and violets. "It's me, Valentine. Is your maid gone? I want to come in."

"Yes, I've rather figured that out. If you don't mind, I'd prefer you didn't."

It wasn't an outright order to go away...

"You're still in your tub, aren't you? All covered with bubbles, entirely modest?"

"As I don't bathe in my clothes, no, I'm not *entirely modest.* Is this what happens to normal people, Valentine? Do something once, and then be unable to think of anything else? Even with a house nearly burnt down around one's ears? Because it's very disconcerting to— Valentine! I didn't give you permission to— Oh, I don't believe you. What are you doing now?"

"I believe the exercise is commonly called re-moving one's shirt," he told her as he stood beside the tub, envying the bubbles that clung so lovingly to her fair skin. "I'm going to assist my lady in the washing of her hair."

He watched her as she watched him strip off his shirt and drop it on the floor beside him, her eyes going slightly wider at the sight of his bare chest. "Please put your shirt on again. It's...distracting."

"I'll assume you mean my chest, and not my shirt." He turned toward the low table arrayed with a half dozen bottles of differing shapes. "Which of these do you use to wash your hair?"

She was holding a large sea sponge in front of her breasts now. "Those aren't mine. I use the same lye and wood ash soap I use to...to wash the rest of me. It's still in my bag, in the bedchamber. I don't know whom all those bottles belong to, just that Sara poured two of them into the tub. Go away, Valentine. Please."

"Homemade soft soap? We must have something better than that here." He was already busy uncork-ing and sniffing the contents of the bottles, decid-ing he liked the smell of lemon best. "We'll use this one," he said, pouring a goodly amount into his palm. "Duck your head under the water to wet it. Or should I be looking for a pitcher of water here somewhere?"

"You're not going to go away, are you, even know-ing how embarrassed you're making me. I suppose

I should be practical, as sitting in this water until it freezes over and the bubbles disappear certainly isn't the answer. The pitcher is for rinsing the soap out afterward."

And with that, she took a breath and sank beneath the surface, coming back up with her face and hair dripping with water and bubbles, even as he found himself torn between admiring what she'd done and wishing the high-sided tub wasn't quite so long or so deep. That was Kate's fault; she'd demanded a tub like Trixie's, one she could "stretch out in, not sit with my knees up to my chin."

As Valentine recalled the thing, nobody had told her *why* Trixie's tub was, well, large enough to fit two people inside. But perhaps now that Kate had found her Simon, she understood.

"You look a whole other person," he said now, marveling at how Daisy's curls remained, even though sopping wet. They were simply plastered to her head now, her exquisitely shaped head, her nose shiny from what had to have been a good scrubbing, her thick, water-darkened lashes resembling small, slightly curled spikes, her perfect fair skin glowing a bit from the heat of the water.

If she were a sugarplum, he would eat her up in one delicious bite.

"Here we go," he warned as she continued to cling to the sea sponge. He knelt down behind the tub and slid his soap-slick hands over the crown of her head.

He felt a strange tingle rise up his arms, and fan

out across his shoulders. All he was doing was rubbing soap into her hair, yet there was an intimacy about the thing that both startled and pleased him.

"Ummm," Daisy said as he lightly rubbed at her temples. She closed her eyes and leaned back her head. "That's…nice. I imagine this is all in aid of seducing me?"

"You imagine correctly." He rose up over her enough to be able to bend forward and kiss her damp lips, and then sank back onto his knees, applying himself to his job once more. "How the devil do I get soap on all of this? Half of it's still hanging into the tub."

She instructed him how to scoop up the length and plop it on top of her head, and then apply more soap and "Just squeeze it, don't rub it, or I'll be combing out a rat's nest of tangles for a week."

Valentine attempted to do as she instructed, but what she asked was impossible. In his mind, he had pictured a romantic, sensual interlude. In reality, he was getting sopping wet, Daisy's hair was constantly attempting to elude his fingers when not tangling around them, making a jangled mess.

"There's got to be another way," he said, not sounding romantic at all, and he knew it.

"There is, but not with you in the room, although I normally wash my hair over the washbasin," she told him, reaching up one hand to check on his progress. "Oh, no. Valentine, stop. Please, just stop. Go into the other room and let me finish."

He gave up on what he knew to be a bad job, another romantic dream shattered, and got to his feet. But he felt fairly certain all wasn't lost. "And then I can seduce you?" he asked her cheekily.

And the vicar's daughter-cum-governess answered calmly: "Yes, Valentine, and then you most certainly may seduce me. Now go away."

Which made him more eager than if she'd purred something inane like, "Oh, darling, take me, take me!"

He left, but did not go far. He made it only to the other side of the door, which he carefully left ajar a few inches, telling himself it was mere curiosity that had him watching her, to see how she did something as mundane and yet complicated as wash her hair.

To his surprise—and delight—she first ducked beneath the surface again. She reemerged face-first, her head tipped back, her hair falling straight down her back. He caught his breath as she continued to rise, going up on her knees in the deep tub, exposing her body to him nearly to her waist.

She raised her arms, gathering her hair at her nape, and twisted its length, squeezing out much of the water, and then draped it all over one shoulder before leaning over the tub to take up the bottle he had used and pouring some into her hand.

She had such a long back, her spine straight yet dipping in at her narrow waist. The flare of her hips was subtle, exquisitely delicate. And mind-blowingly enticing.

Ah, now he understood. *Start at the scalp, and work your way down*. The process was purely practical. Not that this phenomenon kept him interested for more than a few seconds. No, he was too busy watching how her small, perfect breasts rose and fell as she worked the soap into her hair, completely relaxed in her nakedness because she believed herself unobserved.

Valentine could almost convince himself he was witnessing living art, rather like Botticelli's *Venus Rising from the Sea*...but then Daisy surprised him yet again.

She stood up.

She reached for one of the pair of earthenware pitchers on the table beside her.

She lifted the first pitcher and slowly poured its contents over her head.

Water and clinging bubbles, cascading down her body, sliding between her breasts, gliding down over her amazingly flat stomach, arrowing toward the juncture of her thighs.

Valentine was finding it difficult to breathe, and when she repeated her action with the second pitcher, he knew it was either turn away or betray his presence. He eased the door completely shut and took several deep, calming breaths (which, truth to tell, did very little good if he had hoped to calm his libido).

By the time he heard the door open, he had strategically placed himself on the hearthrug, his damp shirt drying as it hung down from the mantel, held there by a heavy brass figurine. He was in the act of stoking the logs with the poker when Daisy sat down beside him, a large bath sheet wrapped around her, another smaller one tied turbanlike around her head.

"Sara laid out one of your sister's nightrails and dressing gowns for me, but they seem rather pointless, don't you think? You've already seen me like this. Oh, good, Sara put out my combs, as I'd asked her. I told her I like to dry my hair by the fire when I can."

He looked at her, wondering what the devil was going on. One proposal, one bedding, a single glass of wine, and suddenly everything was fine, perfect, no need for convincing her she wanted him here?

He'd never understand women. He doubted anyone ever would, even other women.

And most especially this woman.

But he'd ask, anyway. That's what made him a man. Men were always asking questions they probably shouldn't ask.

"Are you all right?"

Daisy was unwrapping the towel and easing it from her head. Her wet hair smelled like lemons and there were golden sparkles among the dark red curls. She pulled her hair away from her face, lifted it and let it fall past her bare shoulders.

"What could be wrong? I've been told in a most businesslike way that I must marry, have been relieved of my virginity, nearly been roasted alive, been told I'm beautiful by a man who seems to have said it enough to believe it and accosted in my bath by that same matrimonial, amorous, clearly delusional half-naked male who just five minutes ago peeked at me as I was rinsing my hair. All in less than a single day. Oh, and I've had my first taste of wine, and admit to feeling slightly muzzy, but I believe fatigue also may play a part in that. I've decided I may as well enjoy all of it. Except for the roasted alive portion, of course."

Valentine had begun smiling halfway through her recitation. "Of course. I can see you might not wish to repeat the almost roasted alive portion of today's entertainment. Now what?"

She was working one of the combs through her hair. "Isn't this nice? I wonder what was in that bottle, as it's clearly superior to my soft soap. My hair is barely tangled. Oh, you asked me something, didn't you? I suppose that's up to you, isn't it, Valentine?"

"Why me?" he asked in some amazement. When had he lost control of his planned seduction? Because clearly he was no longer in charge; Daisy was making all the moves.

Except her next words contradicted that.

"Because clearly I'm no longer in charge of my own life."

"Is that so?"

"*And,* I suppose, because I didn't come to your bedchamber to watch you while you were in your tub."

"You make a valid point, Miss Marchant." Suitably chastened, he picked up the other comb and motioned for her to turn her back to him. Mimicking her movements, he began combing the hair on the right side of her head. It felt like silk between his fingers. Unable to resist, he raised one damp lock and watched as it curled around his finger, like a living, breathing thing, binding him to her forever. "Wait a moment. You *knew* I was watching you?"

"Not immediately, but once I did, I certainly wasn't going to shriek in alarm and drown myself, so I pretended I didn't." She turned back toward him, taking his hand in hers, relieving him of the comb. "Valentine, I have no idea what's happening between us. We barely know each other, we've been rather busy with hellfire clubs and rescues and hoping not to get ourselves killed. I have, however, come to see the sense in your proposal."

He let go of her hair. Maybe he was wrong. Maybe he didn't want to hear this. "The sense in it, I see. By sense, I imagine you mean practicality."

"Rose is going to need more than I can possibly give her on my own. And she'll be safe at Redgrave Manor, you said so yourself, and I believe you. And Mr. Piffkin is amazing with her."

"You aren't a governess anymore, Daisy. Soames is Soames to you now, and Piffkin is Piffkin."

"He will never be less than Mr. Piffkin to me. I owe him so much. You can have no idea how gentle he was with Rose at the inn while we waited for you to conclude your…your business at Fernwood. He always seemed to know exactly what to say to her, and when to not speak at all, but only stay close by if she might need him. And that doesn't include how actually revelational he was to me prior to Rose's rescue."

"Revelational? In what way?" *God, even Piffkin knows her better than I do…and apparently she knows Piffkin more than I ever have. I need to think about all of this at some point. But not right now.*

Daisy lowered her head for a moment, but then looked him straight in the eye as she cupped his cheek. "I'm good for you. I don't completely understand why, but I am. And…and you're good for me. To me. From the beginning, I've known you're a good man. Well," she said, smiling, "except in the very beginning, when I worried perhaps you might be mentally unhinged."

Valentine chuckled in agreement. "You can safely forget that now, I hope. But you've made me curious. Why am I good for you?"

"We don't have to talk about that now," she said as she twisted her hair at the nape of her neck and it obediently wove itself into a long, curly rope.

"True," he said, running his finger down the center of her chest, stopping at the knot she'd tied between her breasts. "However, I find I want to. Why am I good for you, Daisy?"

She averted her head. "You, um, you make me understand why I'm here." Then she looked at him.

"Oh, I don't mean here, in Cavendish Square. I mean *here*. Here at all. Alive at all. I'd never really given the matter much thought beyond the obvious. I've always simply done what had to be done, what was expected of me. I did my duty. I—I don't know how to explain myself, but I know what I mean. I've always been an exceedingly solid and sensible person. A worker, I suppose you'd say. Someone had to be, once our father died, and that someone was me. Too tall, too thin, too smart, too plain, but eminently sensible. And yet now?"

She raised her chin ever so slightly. "Now, thanks to you, I'm a woman. You think I'm pretty, and desirable. And I like it. I'm not certain I know exactly what I'm admitting, but I'm not ashamed to admit it. You've made me see…possibilities. But understand, I know I'm not perfect. One could also say I'm at times too practical. Annoyingly common-sensible. And perhaps prone to…to a certain stiffness of tone."

"One could say that, yes."

"I don't laugh often."

"You probably haven't had too much to laugh about these last years. But that's one of the things I plan to change. At least once people aren't trying to kill us."

She summoned a small smile. "You're humoring me now, aren't you?"

"Absolutely. Come here."

Valentine pulled her onto his lap and pressed her

damp head against his chest, realizing he had an all-but-naked woman in his arms, and wasn't feeling at all amorous, yet strangely, wonderfully *complete*. He bent and kissed the top of her head and she snuggled more against him, her nearly bare legs tucked up, her body all but melting against his.

She trusted him. With her life, with her body, with her future. Piffkin was right, she was good for him. She made him want to be the man she thought he was. She allowed him to see why *he* was here, why he'd been born. He'd been born to be the man Daisy Marchant believed him to be.

"This is nice," she told him. "I feel as if all my worries have washed away in my bath, or some such thing. I don't remember when I've felt so relaxed. You're a good man, Valentine. I can't say that enough."

"I'm a better man than I was two weeks ago. But you'd be wise to never count on me to be *too* good."

Daisy laughed at his words, the sweet, delightful sound pure music to his ears, and Valentine felt his heart swell. *By God, I've gone and turned romantical. We're falling like dominos, that's what we Redgraves are doing. First Gideon, then Kate...and now me. Banged over the head by Cupid's shovel. Another rascally Redgrave, tamed, domesticated. Thank God there's still Max. Cupid would need to drop an anvil on Max's head, probably repeatedly....*

The mantel clock chimed twice, rousing him from his thoughts, and he realized that, as he'd been thinking, Daisy had grown very quiet, her body more and more molding against his.

The hour was late, the warmth from the fire cozy and relaxing, and they'd definitely had a busy day. It would be so easy to rest his back against the wingchair behind him, his arms full of soft, clinging, sweet-smelling female, and simply glide into sleep.

"Daisy?"

Her only response was to slide her arm farther around him and sigh into his shoulder.

Yes, he thought as he carefully maneuvered himself to his feet and carried Daisy over to the bed, *I'm a much, much better man than I was.* He laid her down on the soft mattress, relieved her of the damp bath sheet and, after only one rather long, satisfying look, pulled the covers up to her chin.

She sighed in her sleep, and seemed to reach out her right arm across the mattress as if in search of something. Someone. *Him.*

Valentine looked to the door to the hallway, remembered he'd locked it. He looked to the fireplace, where his shirt hung, drying. Putting one and one together, he should don the shirt, unlock the door and take himself off to his own chamber.

Or he could walk around the bed, climb in beside Daisy, gather her close (she had been searching for him, hadn't she, or she might be cold, having lost the warmth of the fire, the warmth of his body?) and wake in the morning to an armful of warm, hopefully still-willing woman.

"All right," he whispered aloud as he headed for the other side of the bed, "so perhaps I'm not *that* good."

CHAPTER FIFTEEN

"Valentine? *Valentine*. Valentine, you have to move. I can't get up, you're lying on my hair."

He opened his eyes. Daisy was right. He was behind her, his body following the outline of hers, his arm draped over her bare waist and his nose was rather buried in her thick, still faintly damp curls. No wonder he'd been dreaming of lemons.

"Nice," he murmured, pulling her closer to what was rapidly becoming his morning arousal. "You really can't move?"

"No, I can't. Not that I have anywhere to go. I'm naked."

"I know."

"But you're not."

"An oversight easily mended," he assured her even as he slid his hand around her breast. Began stroking her nipple with the pad of his thumb. "I'll have you know I didn't touch you, not that I wasn't tempted." He whispered the next words against her ear. "Sorely tempted."

"A gentlemanly behavior you abandon at dawn?" she asked him, even as she bent her head as far as she could, exposing her long, slender neck to his light, trailing kisses.

"It appears that way, yes. I've never before spent the night with a woman. It avoids...complications."

He raised his head, releasing her hair as she turned toward him. "Would you consider it to be even more *complicated* considering you have also awakened under your grandmother's roof?"

He could see the laughter in her eyes. He'd seen so many emotions there, but the twinkle he saw now had to be considered his favorite. "You're right, of course. You've thoroughly compromised me. Shame on you."

She pressed her palm against his chest. "I don't know that I feel at all ashamed. In fact, Mr. Redgrave, I believe I'm feeling rather proud of myself. Daisy Marchant, seductress. A rare accomplishment for a vicar's once probably uninspiring daughter."

Valentine slid his hand along her side, enjoying the dip of her waist, the flare of her hip. "You *inspired* me from the beginning. Daisy? I want you to know you don't have to marry me. Well, yes you do. But if you'd said no, we Redgraves would have taken care of Rose, anyway. You do know that, don't you?"

"Yes, I realized that at once. It was the fact that you didn't consider the offer as some sort of leverage over me that was so wonderful. You're a good—"

He put a finger to her lips. "Don't say it. I swear Daisy, I don't ever want to hear you say that again.

I keep expecting you to then pat my head and send me off to play with my toy soldiers."

"You can't stop me. You're a good— Valentine!"

He'd flipped her onto her back and come down on top of her. "I warned you. Say it again, and there will be consequences."

She smiled up at him as he laughed, because he could see a hint of devilishness now in her beautiful eyes. "You're a—" She couldn't say more because she became lost in a paroxysm of giggles as he set in to tickling her. She slapped at him ineffectually, twisting provocatively beneath him as she tried once more: "You're— Oh, stop, Valentine…."

He'd seen her smile. He'd heard her rare laugh. But giggles? Pure, unaffected delight? Silliness, the sort she'd probably left behind in her childhood, before her spirit was all but squeezed out of her by the hand life had dealt her? No worries, no fears, no need to stand completely on her own. Never again. She'd never have to face life alone again.

Valentine made a vow, right there and then. She'd laugh at least once a day, until the past was no more than a long ago memory, with the *now* and the *future* the only things that mattered. Their *now,* their *future,* together.

"Valentine?"

He'd stopped tickling her. He was simply looking at her. Her eyes intent on him, her hands tightened on his shoulders.

"Valentine?" Her voice wavered slightly.

"Daisy," he countered, barely able to breathe. There was no question in his voice, only certainty. She was his *now,* his *future,* his reason for, as she'd said, *being here.* He had to tell her.

But perhaps she already knew.

He watched as a tear escaped her eye, to run into her hair. She opened her mouth slightly, raised her head from the pillow just enough to show him her willingness, perhaps even her own dawning realization that something important had just happened between them, was happening between them.

They came together in a kiss that said everything that had to be said, and more. He slid his hands beneath her upper body and held her tight against him, rolling over onto his back, taking her with him, their mouths still melded together.

He ran his hands up and down her back as she cupped his head, as her hair cloaked them, as their tongues dueled…as they strained to be closer. Closer.

He'd die if he couldn't have her. Be deep inside her. Give everything he had to give, take anything she would willingly offer.

Daisy pushed herself up, her delicate spine bowing as she twisted her hair so that it all fell over her left shoulder. She pushed her palms against his chest, maneuvered her way down his body, her gaze never leaving him, even as she sat back on her haunches on his thighs, her hands going to the buttons on his breeches.

It was too much. Her inexperienced touch was

about to drive him over the brink. He'd never felt more aroused, more urgently driven toward completion. He was a raw youth again, and in danger of losing control.

He pulled her toward him, rolled her onto her back once more and settled himself between her thighs. She was so ready for him, taking him in, scissoring her legs up and over his back to hold him to her, in her.

Summoning all the command over himself he had managed to retain, Valentine pushed himself up on his hands and looked down into her face. Then, slowly, oh, so slowly, he brought his mouth down on hers. Holding himself completely still inside her.

Until she began to move beneath him, grind herself against him, and he was lost.

And yet, forever found.

DAISY WASN'T CONVINCED her ensemble, borrowed from Lady Katherine's amply supplied wardrobe, quite suited her. She was more accustomed to grays, to browns. But Sara had assured her the cap-sleeved pink morning dress was just what the dowager countess had explicitly ordered laid out for her. The softness of the material, the lovely mint-green leaves embroidered stem-to-tip just beneath her bosom, the overskirt of the same deep pink material that reached three-quarters of the way around her, adding fullness to what was otherwise a fairly slim skirt, the pink satin slippers that, with a minimum of tissue stuffing, had fit her so well had been too difficult to resist. Impossible to resist.

And if that made her a silly, weak woman, then so be it.

Sara had proved a marvel with the curling stick, taming Daisy's wild ringlets into long smooth curls concentrated behind her left ear and secured with pins. Daisy had protested only at the end, when Sara advanced on her with a soft brush and a tin of fragrant pink powder, but relented when the maid promised a ladylike blush to her cheeks would add sparkle to her eyes. "Lady Trixie says if God didn't give you everything, there's always the shops."

Daisy was still smiling about that remark, one she believed was probably typical of the dowager countess, as she headed toward the drawing room Soames had directed her to when she came down the stairs. Then again, she had only lately crawled out of the bed she and Valentine had shared this morning. She was so in charity with the world she could smile at most anything.

But first she had to stop and admire the miracle that had taken place after she'd gone upstairs to her bath.

"Saving a lingering smell of smoke," she said as she stood at the balustrades and looked down into the main foyer. A circular rug covered the marble that had been scorched, fresh flowers were displayed on the large drum table and the statues lining the stairs had been returned to their former unadorned glory. "It's as if the fire never occurred at all. My congratulations and admiration, Mr....um, Soames."

"Thank you, miss," the butler said, bowing. "There remains much to be done. The chandeliers, a fresh coat of stucco on the walls, we'll be quite overrun by workmen and ladders and the like, I'm afraid. Both here and in the kitchens. Her ladyship will be removing to Redgrave Manor until all is set to rights."

"Sensible," Daisy said, nodding. "Mr. Redgrave and I will also be out from underfoot as soon as possible. You are a marvel, Soames. Her ladyship is a lucky woman to have you."

The butler straightened his spine, clicked his heels together and favored Daisy with another, this time deeper, bow. "The miss is too kind."

"The miss is exceedingly grateful for your kindness and discretion," she said, feeling her powdered cheeks flushing naturally.

She entered the drawing room, still lovely, although missing two very large carpets, to find her ladyship occupying the same chaise she had reclined on the previous evening, while Valentine rather melted into a couch, his booted feet crossed at the ankle and resting on the low table in front of him. He hastened to his feet, waiting as Daisy curtsied to Trixie before motioning for her to join him.

When she sat down, arranging her borrowed skirts around her, he took her hand and lifted it to his lips. "You're beautiful," he whispered, but apparently, as age had done little to her ladyship's physical appearance, it had likewise shied away from fiddling with her hearing.

"Most definitely, pet. I knew that shade of pink would be perfect for her."

Valentine was still looking at Daisy, stroking her hand. "The most beautiful woman in the world."

Daisy turned to smile at Trixie. "I'm not, you know, although he most certainly is the most handsome man in the whole of England, at the very least. But, as he refuses to be dissuaded, I've at last decided to humor him."

Trixie clapped her be-ringed hands in clear delight. "Oh, I see I m going to love you, young lady. Look, he's blushing."

"If you ladies are done poking fun at an innocent and apparently hapless man? Daisy, I was just now asking Trixie if she might have any notion as to who attempted to turn us all into cinders last night."

"And I was just responding that I believe the blaze was meant for him after he made such mischief for the Society at Fernwood, as I believe myself to be universally loved and admired," Trixie countered neatly. She toasted him with her wineglass. "And the shuttlecock is on its way back over the net to you, pet. I can keep this up all morning."

Daisy could sense Valentine's frustration. Clearly his plan wasn't working. She herself was more accustomed to the direct approach, although she wasn't entirely against the role of amused observer as these two volleyed back and forth.

"All right, let's try it this way," Valentine said, once again sitting back at his ease, pulling Daisy back with him and lifting his feet onto the tabletop once more. He really favored his comforts and, she had to admit, she could get rather used to not forever sitting erect, as if one had a board strapped to one's back. Although, at this moment, she believed he was mostly using her in an attempt to convince the dowager countess he and his questions were harmless. "After the fire at the dower house, you and Richard didn't come straight here to Cavendish Square, correct?"

"There wasn't a fire, Val, there was a conflagration." She smiled at Daisy. "The entire pile burnt to the ground, and beyond. If I were a romantic, which I'm not, I would say it burnt halfway to hell. It was magnificent." She turned back to Valentine. "I've heard from your brother, and he and Jessica are going to have both tennis courts and a croquet lawn in its place."

"Wonderful," Valentine answered flatly. "Where did you— Damn, who let these two in here?"

Two small, plump yellow dogs with rather black, smashed-in faces had come bounding into the room, the pair of them heading straight for Valentine, yipping and yapping and attempting, it would seem, to climb him. "Gog! Magog! Down. You hear me, *down!*"

"What very *different* names they have. Oh, stop, Val. They're excitable, I agree, but obviously harmless."

"They'll be *hairless* in a minute," he responded as one of the pair began nipping at his shiny Hessians.

Ah, well, do what you do best, Daisy told herself. She snapped her fingers, twice, and then said in her most stern governess voice, "Gog, Magog. Down. At once. *Sit.*"

The two dogs immediately aimed their rumps at the floor, their pink tongues lolling, their tails thumping against the marble floor, their eyes trained on Daisy in case she should ask something else of them, anything at all.

"How the devil did you do that?" Valentine asked, inspecting the damage to his boot. "They don't listen to anyone."

"I don't know," she told him, dipping her head slightly since he seemed able to see things in her eyes, perhaps even small fibs like the one she'd just uttered. "People—and dogs—just seem to want to obey me. I suppose they know I mean what I say and will brook no nonsense from them."

"I believe I've just seen my future," Valentine said glumly as his grandmother laughed in delight.

"You may laugh, my lady, but enjoyable as it is to see Valentine flustered, it's time for us to get down to cases."

"Oh, such a matter-of-fact tone you have, Miss Marchant. First my dogs, and now me? Very well,

Daisy. Clearly you two have a broadside prepared between you. Fire away."

"Yes, ma'am, thank you," Daisy responded, even as Valentine briefly lifted her hand to his lips. "Now, I believe your grandson was inquiring as to where you traveled after leaving Redgrave Manor, and before returning here yesterday. Please enlighten him, and then you and I will go shopping. I would value your opinion if he's to outfit my sister and myself from head-to-toe, which he has promised. He brags he's nearly odiously wealthy, and I've never before shopped without pinching every penny until it squealed. I'm looking forward to emptying his pockets."

"Ha! Orders, followed hard by bribery? The stick, held out to dangle the carrot? And you think that's going to work with my grandmother? Trust me in this, Daisy, the best have tried and—"

"Richard and I were driven to Canterbury, where we met with the archbishop, who happened to be in residence, and were married by special license by the man himself, after which we retired to a lovely inn just outside the city and celebrated our nuptials in the customary way. I'll accept your congratulations, pet, the moment you can lift your lower jaw back into place, since you've ruined any chance for Richard and me to surprise the family."

She held out her left hand, to show the simple gold band on her ring finger. It had rather been lost amid the diamonds.

"Married? You're *married?* But that's wonderful. Mostly unbelievable, but wonderful!" Valentine was on his feet in an instant, to bodily pick up his petite grandmother and swing her in a circle as if she was a young girl before kissing her on both cheeks. "Where's Richard? I want to shake that man's hand and toast the two of you. *Married?* How many times have I heard you vow to never marry again?"

Trixie had her hands on Valentine's shoulders. "Yes, yes, but it seems love has a mind of its own. Now put me down before you wrinkle my gown. But first swing me about again. Ah, that's lovely. Daisy? Might I have a kiss from you, as well?"

Daisy happily obliged, marveling at how small and delicate this powerful woman was as she hugged her, the matriarch clearly held in great affection and perhaps awe by her family. "Forgive me for ruining your surprise, ma'am."

"Trixie. I'm Trixie, remember? And truth to tell, I've been all but bursting to tell someone." She sat down once more and took up her wineglass. "But now, back to cases. Richard and I went nowhere but Canterbury, spoke to no one but dearest Charles— the archbishop, dear—quite frankly stayed in our rooms at the inn, and then came directly here. The only other people I spoke to were Kate and Simon and a few of the longtime tenants at the Manor, which means we're back on your side of the court, Valentine. Tell me more about your adventure at Fernwood. Obviously you've been quite busy."

"And reasonably successful, yes."

"I'd consider your rescue of Daisy's sister to be your greatest coup."

"Oh, yes, ma'am—Trixie. I...I had thought her lost to me."

Trixie nodded. "We'll discuss your sister on the way to Bond Street. For now, since Valentine here is in such a hurry, I believe I need to hear the names. You do have names for me, don't you, pet?"

Valentine returned from the drinks table with a glass of wine in one hand, a glass of lemonade in the other—he'd earlier told Daisy only fools drink water in London—and retrieved a folded piece of paper from his jacket pocket.

"You already know Charles Mailer, now deceased. From what we overheard, it seems he had been one of the current Devil's Thirteen, the innermost circle of the Society. Hammer, a code name we already knew, will be taking his place. As he was pleading for his life, Mailer called him Axbridge, reminding him it was he who had brought him into the Society in the first place. Hammer, ax. As we've said, not an elaborate code."

"Axbridge," Trixie repeated thoughtfully. "I know no— Ah, wait a moment. Remember, pet, memberships also were often passed along in the family, which is why the code names were always connected to the surname. Baron Terence Conway introduced his son Stephen to the Society during your father's time. The elder Conway was then left to his gout and hassock, and his son Stephen took over both his place and code name. Stephen was mad for gambling, and ran through his inheritance with considerable speed. Worse for the Society, he'd sired only daughters, and began marrying them off one after the other to fairly lecherous old men in exchange for considerable dowries."

"Trixie, is this leading anywhere?" Valentine asked, but Daisy could see he was listening intently.

"Yes, dear, it is. It was a scandal at the time, but only a nine-day wonder, however, as something else came along to take everyone's attention elsewhere." She gave a graceful wave of her hand. "Perhaps Lettie Lade riding bare-breasted around the Serpentine, or rumors of our dear King George precariously balancing on the balustrades at Buckingham dressed only in his bathrobe, and shouting gibberish? Something like that."

Daisy kept herself occupied (and her burning cheeks averted), by leaning forward to scratch the dogs behind their ears.

"Trixie…"

"Yes, yes, I'm getting there, but in my own time, pet, if you please. I have a multitude of memories to sort through in order to find the one I want. Ah, now I have it."

"We're so relieved. I thought we might have to listen to you recount yet again Casanova's visit to England, and how he chased you everywhere but you refused to be caught. Poor fellow left the country the following year a crushed and disheartened man, never to be the same again. Isn't that how it went?"

"Oh, darling, I lied about that. I was barely out of leading strings when that overly amorous buffoon came to England. But it was a lovely story, wasn't it, and I'm certain I had an exceedingly good reason to tell it."

Daisy decided she would never again believe herself to be bored, not as long as she resided with the Redgraves.

"Now, pet, where was I? Ah, yes. Stephen's finances dropped lower and lower, his remaining daughters younger and younger. Comely girls, all of them, by the way. The scandal was the marriage of the youngest, barely fifteen as I recall, to the son of a screamingly wealthy private banker in the City hoping to boost his family up the social ladder. One Giraud Axbridge. His sad bride perished in childbed a year later, and not only was Axbridge forced into mourning for a year, but he was no longer received at the highest level upon his return to society. With no more daughters to put on the auction block, it's always possible Stephen offered the grieving widower something else in return for a fresh infusion of funds."

"The Society." Daisy was confused. "But it was Lord Mailer who brought Hammer into the group."

Trixie nodded her agreement. "Baron Conway was never one of the Devil's Dozen, and I doubt Stephen was, either—he's dead now, by the way, so don't bother to go looking for him. Another unfortunate fall down the stairs, as I remember, leaving behind a widow of no more than eighteen. No one was shocked that he fell. After all, he was a wild drinker, constantly in his cups."

"Another accident," Valentine interrupted. "We should add him to the list of older Society members who met such sad ends in the past year, leaving such happy widows behind."

"Yes, I suppose so. I'm sorry I didn't think of him earlier. But back to Axbridge. Stephen would have made the initial suggestion, but it would be left to one of the inner circle to issue the actual *invitation*. And remember, I'm only saying you might consider him. He must be edging toward fifty now. What else? Ah, yes. Mother French, father English, if you believe that matters, and I would assume so unless told otherwise."

"A banker could be invaluable to the Society. He's got to be our man. Trixie, you're a marvel," Valentine said, bending down to kiss her blond curls.

Daisy felt Valentine's excitement. She was excited, as well, but that emotion was tempered by concern. Valentine looked ready to go chasing hotfoot after the man who'd recently held a knife to his back, and that could be dangerous.

"What are you going to do?" she asked him.

"Nothing rash, I promise you. I only want to get close enough to see if our Mr. Axbridge is sporting a bandage on his right hand and wrist, and then I can definitely put the face to the man. Once I'm positive he's who we think he is, he'll keep until we can get together with the others and formulate some sort of plan. In the meantime, why don't you two brilliant ladies head off to the shops?"

"In a moment, Valentine," Daisy said, "as I believe you've forgotten something. Someone tried to burn down this house around our ears last night. Or are you now convinced it was Axbridge's work?"

"Yes, pet. Have you made other enemies during your time in the country?" Trixie asked.

"Oh, he's made several," Daisy told her, smiling up at him. "Haven't you, *pet?* We just don't know who they are."

"We've got some names. We've even got one of them, Harold Charfield, a medium-size cog in Perceval's offices, locked up tight at Redgrave Manor. I imagine Simon is having some fun, questioning him. Charfield, Trixie. *Burn.*"

"Yes, another code name. And the last we know, correct?"

"We've got two others possibilities, thanks to Daisy, as she wrote down the names of guests that visited Fernwood. But I'm rather afraid the names are false, created specially for the occasion."

"There is one more thing we learned, in addition to another code name," Daisy said, surprised Valentine hadn't mentioned it, either. She spoke to Trixie. "If Valentine hasn't yet told you, it would appear the leader of at least the small group that met at Fernwood is a woman. They called her the Exalted One."

Trixie had been taking a sip of wine, and coughed, nearly gagged. "A *woman?* But that's…that's impossible. A woman couldn't be in charge of the Society. Women are their *victims*."

"Not this one," Valentine told her. "I think she's harder than any of the men. In fact, they seemed nearly terrified of her."

"I'd say *good for her,* if the Society wasn't such an abomination," Trixie told them consideringly. "A woman. Why on earth did I never think of that? There was a time I held them all in the palm of my hand."

"I would chance it to say such a thing never occurred to you because you aren't a monster," Daisy told her. "She murdered Lord Mailer herself, and followed it up by coldly telling the members to dispose of all the women, as well, including my sister."

"And, lest we forget, she personally dispatched Mailer's wife and servant," Valentine added. "I believe she's the most dangerous of them all."

"Fascinating. Both ambitious and filled with hate. Disdainful of the men she leads, controls. And completely bereft of morals. I wonder if she participates in the ceremonies. As the aggressor, certainly. I wonder, does she carry a whip?"

"When we find her, I'll make certain those are the first two questions asked," Valentine answered tongue-in-cheek, putting down his wineglass. "Since we still have no idea who tried to turn us to crisps, I'm off to the City. You two enjoy yourselves buying out all the shops and we'll meet here at five. And for God's sake, don't corrupt my fiancée."

"Yes, Valentine, just as you say," Trixie told him sweetly, rolling her eyes at Daisy.

"Wait, Valentine," Daisy said as he boldly leaned down to kiss her. She may not have been kissed in her first twenty-two years but, with his help, she was certainly catching up quickly. "You didn't tell Trixie about the Exalted One's consort. The code name."

He winced. "Wasn't going to do that," he warned quietly.

But it was too late. "Consort? Perhaps the brawn behind the brains? How delicious. I must hear this."

Valentine signaled for Daisy to say what she had to say, which she did, although now she worried he had left off telling her something important. "She called him Scarlet. That would be another code name, wouldn't it?"

It got very quiet in the drawing room as grandmother and grandson looked at each other.

"A simple code," Trixie said at last, her voice dull, lifeless. "Burn for Charfield, Post for Mailer, City for Urban. Turner, Jessica's father, was Miner, for Collier. The code names often passed down father to son."

"So I was right to think what I've been thinking?"

"Yes, Val." Trixie sighed, suddenly looking more her age. "Father to son. It's the correct code name, although they much preferred Exalted Leader or some such drivel. Your father and grandfather both. Scarlet, for Redgrave."

"But…but that's impossible," Daisy said anxiously. "Isn't it?"

"I don't believe it possible, no, but the question begs to be asked. Where's Max?"

"And now you've asked it, as I've just asked myself, both of us already knowing the answer. I already told you Richard isn't here. I've asked him to chase down Maximillien, hoping he's still in Ostend, and bring him back. All the rest of you are too well known by the Society at this point."

"Hence our retreat to Redgrave Manor," Daisy said, nodding her agreement, relieved the uncomfortable moment was over. "Valentine tells me there's a moat."

"Valentine exaggerates, although just barely. But back to our problem. Max, to my eternal chagrin, never cared much for the silliness of Mayfair and is rarely in England at all since reaching his majority. Although I don't foresee him carrying his own name with him as he picks up the torch against the Society, he is the logical choice since we don't want Spencer involved."

"There is such a thing as coincidence," Daisy offered, knowing the woman had meant Prime Minister Perceval. She'd rather like an army at their backs, personally. But she supposed the Redgraves had been on their own too long to ask for help. "I can think of several English names beginning with red. Redburn. Reddell. Reddick, Red— Well, there must be dozens of names that begin with red."

Apparently Trixie had another idea. "Both your grandfather and father sired enough bastards in and around Saltwood to— Oh, God. Valentine, is it possible?"

Daisy looked to them in turn, feeling much like a living shuttlecock herself. "I don't understand. Is what possible, Trixie? Valentine?"

He sat down beside her once more. "Just a moment, Daisy. I think you'll understand soon enough. Trixie said she'd been speaking to some of our tenants, and retired servants, as well, I suppose, while she was at the Manor. Who, Trixie? And what were you speaking about with these tenants?"

The woman was kneading at her temples. "Let me think. Mildred, our old cook—she asked about you, pet, and if you still had such a sweet tooth. Faith, Hope and Charity. You remember the Miller sisters. Spinsters all, and happy tending their gardens now that they're not working in the dairy house, although I swear the butter has never been the same. They adore hearing me tell them that. Smithy. And Angus Cooper, of course. He and your grandfather were lads together, which Angus never fails to remind me. He will insist on calling us all his *family,* which is very sweet. God, Valentine. Is it possible?"

"Angus. Father to Hugh, who is father to Liam. Dozens of Coopers, as a matter of fact. Three generations of Coopers on Redgrave land. And dozens of Redgrave byblows, as you just said. Is it possible, Trixie? I've begun to believe most anything possible."

"Both Charles and Barry would hump anything that sat still long enough or was slow and defenseless enough to catch— Ah, forgive me, my dear. I will say the most outré things at times. I came of age in a much more open, plain-speaking time. You'll grow used to it."

Daisy's mind was whirling. "Yes, ma'am. But would they know of the Society?"

"Angus was a fine stone mason in his prime, Daisy, he and his brothers, his sons," Trixie continued, shaking her head. "All that marble, all the work that went into Charles's ungodly creation— everything. My husband certainly didn't build all he built on his own, nor did he lug the furnishings there by himself. True secrecy is never possible. We've never spoken of it, Angus and I, not in all these years, as if none of it ever happened. But, yes, the Coopers in particular must have known something about the Society, perhaps even about my late husband's ridiculous notions."

At least Valentine had found time to tell her about the "ridiculous notions." Charles, Earl of Saltwood, had believed himself to have royal blood, and wished to be the Stuart put back on the throne of England by aiding France. Clearly the man was mad. Just as clearly, he and his son had been madly dangerous.

Valentine broke his silence. "The knowledge of the caves, the underground meeting room, the smuggling, repairing the stone maze on the beach. It's more than probable they did their share of snooping when the master wasn't at home, finding the journals and bible, touring the *ceremonial* chamber. Everything makes sense now, how this new incarnation of the Society seemed to know so much."

"He'll do that," Daisy explained. "Talk to himself as he works something out in his head. I suppose someday I'll get used to that, too. Valentine? We're still here, you know."

"Sorry," he said, squeezing her hand. "Trixie, do you remember what you and Angus spoke of during your visit?"

"Nothing that seems important, I'm afraid. Angus and I were sharing some of his best homemade mead and reminiscing about long-ago days," Trixie told them. She was massaging her right temple now, as if the area pained her. "I wish Richard were here. He accompanied me, carrying my basket of gifts, and might remember more of the discussion. Ah, wait a moment. I may have, no, I know I did. I said something to Angus about us probably being the last two people still aboveground to remember those bygone days. Why did I say that? Did I put my head in the lion's mouth, saying that? I can't believe this, Valentine. I don't want to believe Angus Cooper would want me dead."

"Neither do I, but we can't dismiss the possibility

out of hand, even if the chance is equally high it was Axbridge or one of the others last night."

Trixie sighed. "You don't believe that, do you?"

"No. Sadly, I don't. They had too many opportunities to kill us at Fernwood, or on the way here. I— We've all always seen Redgrave Manor as our refuge. When Barry died, when we were nearly drummed out of society. With enough land around us, with loyal servants who had been with us for generations. It would be a hell of a thing if we'd built our refuge with the enemy already inside the walls. But it makes sense now, doesn't it? That this new Society operates on Redgrave land. We've attempted to tie them to us in some way, telling ourselves they learned about our land and history from Jessica's father, but the connection seemed tenuous at best. But this?"

"A dog always comes back to his vomit, I've heard it told. Only, if we're right, pet, this dog never left, but has been right there all along. What if they've been watching our every move? What if Kate and Simon had gotten too close? Would they be dead now? And this Charfield you spoke of—they would have seen him arrive, know he's our prisoner. We're getting closer, we've become a danger to them. Valentine, my heart's sick at even the thought we could be right. We're not the pursuers any longer. We're the pursued."

Valentine slapped down hard on his thighs and got to his feet. Clearly he'd made a decision. "Ladies,

I suggest you limit your shopping to materials and whatever trimmings go with them, and trust a local seamstress to the gowns themselves. We need to leave for the estate no later than tomorrow at dawn. As you said, Trixie, Kate and Simon are there, feeling themselves safe. Them, and our Mr. Charfield, who may not be as uncomfortable in his confinement as we'd hoped."

CHAPTER SIXTEEN

"MY COACHMAN, a groom up on the box and two hanging on behind, plus a pair of outriders, and none of them Coopers. All for the short trip to Bond Street, although we'll make slow progress at this time of day. My grandson does nothing by half measures, does he?"

Daisy, her mind instantly going to the pleasurable hour she and Valentine had spent together that morning, felt herself coloring slightly. "I believe you could be safe in saying he's quite thorough, yes." *After all, she'd been thoroughly kissed, thoroughly caressed, thoroughly aroused...and most definitely thoroughly satisfied.*

Trixie smiled rather knowingly. "You do know you don't have to ride facing backward, my dear."

"Forgive me, I just naturally took the rear-facing seat. Don't tell Valentine, please, or I'll only have to suffer another homily about the differences between a governess and a fiancée. Truth to tell, I rather like seeing where I've been."

Trixie displayed a small, ladylike shudder. "Spoken like a young lady with a clear conscience. You're quite the level-headed creature, aren't you? Do you love my grandson?"

Daisy didn't know how to answer that unexpected question. She hadn't even asked it of herself, and Valentine certainly had not volunteered any such declaration of his own feelings. "We're to be married."

"Not germane. In today's society, marriage more than not has little to do with love. Debt, wealth, social position, the cachet of a title, the need for an heir. Marriage is more than often a trade, or a bargain struck."

Daisy shifted uncomfortably in her seat. "You've heard about Rose," she said quietly. "I would have and will do anything to keep her safe and protected, but Valentine neither demanded nor offered marriage in exchange for helping her. Especially when it would be only Rose and I who profited from such an arrangement. He has nothing to gain. Although—" she paused to take in a breath, and gather her courage "—he did say that I've thoroughly compromised him."

"Ha! Leave it to Valentine to take the shoe and neatly put it on the other person's foot. A talent inborn in the Redgraves, I believe. Good for him. And let me tell you, my dear, I know that boy better than he knows himself. He does nothing unless he wants to do it. He may not always at first understand *why* he wants to do it, but he'll figure it out. I will tell you that, upon his arrival yesterday, he informed me I was about to meet the most wonderful, kind, brave, intelligent, fearless, challenging, beautiful woman in the world. I may have missed a few of the attributes he assigned to you, as he went on for a good five minutes, barely taking a breath. I half expected to come downstairs last evening to see a marble statue of Venus, wearing a halo while neatly juggling a sword, a book and possibly a rescued chimney sweep."

"Venus couldn't juggle, she has no arms." Daisy began to relax. "He's a good man, although it has been recently brought home to me that I'm not to tell him so, even though it's true. I believe, at the heart of it, Valentine's rather modest."

"Valentine? Modest? Well, I do believe you've answered my question, just as he answered it last night merely with the look on his face. You're besotted, the pair of you. This is merely a suggestion, but one of these days you probably ought to tell each other. You'd be amazed at all you gain when you give your heart away. I know I was."

Daisy lowered her head to hide her blush. "Yes, ma'am. I...I'll be sure to do that." Then she looked out the side window, to see the same haberdashery shop she'd been seeing for the past ten minutes. "We're not moving at all, are we?"

"I think we've made major strides," Trixie told her, her smile adding a sparkle to her eyes. "But now I need to hear about your adventure, and your rescue of your dear sister. It is she, you realize, who may be the one to finally bring down the Society. How fitting that her name is Rose. Almost prophetic."

Daisy remembered the rose pin employed to hold her ridiculous transparent robes together, and told Trixie as much.

In turn, the dowager countess explained the meaning of the golden rose employed by the Society to signify a member's success at deflowering a virgin during one of their ceremonies. "Both my husband and son had rather extensive collections."

"I didn't know. At least Rose was spared that. She was already a widow when Mailer tricked her into traveling with him to his country estate. In fact, Rose said he never shared her with the other members, but kept her all to himself, kept her prisoner in that terrible place."

"How odd. Perhaps, in some twisted way, he cared for her. Mailer's wife must have been terrified she was about to be replaced."

Daisy felt the need to share her thoughts with Trixie. Perhaps this woman who'd been in the position both Lady Caroline and Rose had occupied, would make her understand.

"Yet in the end, Lady Caroline decided to stay, rather than to trade her social position for freedom, and ended by losing her life, and Rose is ashamed she didn't take her own life, but instead *allowed*—only Rose could use that word and think it sensible—Lord Mailer to keep her as his imprisoned mistress. Frankly, I don't understand either of them. Lady Caroline happily sacrificed both Valentine and me, along with the futures of her stepchildren, and Rose insists on blaming herself for what Lord Mailer did to her."

"Fear makes people do things they would never otherwise believe themselves capable of—the will to survive trumping any other consideration. As for your sister, I understand Piffkin has taken her under his wing?"

The coach finally began moving forward once more. "He's marvelous with her, yes."

Daisy nodded. "He would be. He was there when my husband…passed. One might even say instrumental to me in those turbulent days. I offered him anything he wanted, but he turned me down in favor of a gold coating on his tooth. Years later, he asked to assume the care and feeding of young Master Valentine. You can trust Piffkin with your sister, with your life if need be. I know I long ago trusted him with mine, and that of my grandson."

"He armed himself with a crimping iron the night we rescued Rose. And then stripped off his coat and shirt to preserve what was left of our modesty. Mostly, I do believe Mr. Piffkin would kill for Valentine, if necessary, or throw himself in front of a sword or pistol to save him. I'm quite impressed with him."

The dowager countess smiled even as she reached up to grab the strap as the coachman turned a corner a bit sharply. "And he with you, obviously, or I would have heard by now. Oh, don't look shocked. When it comes to my grandchildren, I hold the reins loosely, but I do hold them. Until Richard, they've been all I had, all I loved in this world. In other words, Daisy, you have my blessing, you and Valentine. Who knows, with three of my grandchildren settled—I despair of Max—and with Richard by my side, I may just give up this hurly-burly life of mine here in London and retire to Redgrave Manor to become a doddering, devoted great-grandmother. In fact, I'm fairly looking forward to corrupting another generation of—"

Daisy reacted instinctively as the door of the slowly moving coach was thrown open. She reached out for Trixie's hand, fearful the older woman might topple out of the coach, and pulled her toward herself.

As a result, the knife-wielding intruder missed his target, the blade plunging to the hilt in the quilted velvet squabs rather than Trixie's chest.

There was a frustrated curse, the booming report of a carriage gun, and the intruder fell facedown between the two women, a prodigiously large portion of his back blown away.

Instantly all was chaos. Women on the street shrieked and fainted, gentlemen struggled holding up their female charges or shouted impossible nonsense in that way crowds have of providing much in the way of noise but little in the way of assistance. Carriage and saddle horses reared, attempted to bolt.

Aeons later, or so it felt to Daisy, although it could not have been more than five seconds, one of the outriders appeared in the opening now partially clogged by the assailant's body.

"He came out of the alleyway, my lady, runnin' full-tilt. We none of us could believe what we were seein', and then we couldn't stop him in time. I had no choice but to shoot. No choice at all, ma'am. Are you ladies all right?"

"That might have been your first question, Jackson," Trixie told him, using her handkerchief to wipe at bright red blood spattered all over her gown, "*before* offering your excuses. Yes, we're perfectly fine, thanks to Miss Marchant's quick thinking. Now kindly do me the favor of removing this clearly deceased creature lying on our feet. Wait! First turn him over, let me see his face."

"But, ma'am, you don't want to—"

Trixie was clearly shaken, although she struggled to retain her composure. "Another word of advice, young man. Never tell me what I want. Just do it."

"Do as she says," Daisy told the appalled servant in her quiet, brook-no-nonsense way. "Immediately after you retrieve the man's knife, please. It's dreadfully in the way."

"I shouldn't be doing this, miss. This is a bad thing to do."

The body was turned face-up, revealing a youth of no more than eighteen or twenty, barely a man at all.

"Sweet Christ in His heaven," Trixie breathed. "No." She began shaking her head in useless denial. "No, no, no."

"I told you, ma'am. You didn't want to see this. None of us wants to see this."

"How could they do this?" the dowager countess asked as she bent over to close the boy's eyes, employ her handkerchief to ineffectually wipe at the blood that had run from his mouth. "If they felt it was necessary, why did they send you? Damned cowards." She grabbed at the strap and leaned halfway out of the coach. "Are you out there? Are you watching? *Bastards! Look what you've done!*"

Daisy motioned for the outrider, now openly weeping, to remove the body, and then scooted over to sit beside Trixie. Her outburst over, she now sat staring, dry-eyed, at nothing. "Who was he?" she asked gently, sliding her arm around the slighter woman.

"The last person anyone would ever suspect of attempting to harm mc, or anybody. Liam Cooper. Dear, not-too-clever Liam. Angus is…was his grandfather."

There was the sound of something heavy being put in the boot, where it could be concealed beneath a leather tarp. Liam's body, most certainly. Trixie bent her head and began to cry.

For the first time, Daisy noticed the swarm of curious onlookers all but surrounding the coach. Her eyes narrowed, her expression stern, one by one she pulled up the leather panels on the windows, blocking their view, locking in the smell of freshly spilled blood and the sound of Trixie's sobs. She banged the side of her fist twice against the front side of the coach and called to the driver to move off before putting her arm around the dowager countess and drawing her against her shoulder.

The coach was on its way once more, not to the shops, but back to Cavendish Square, leaving behind a new Redgrave scandal, this one about to bloom in blood spilled on Bond Street.

VALENTINE HALTED IN his pacing as Daisy entered her bedchamber. "How is she now?"

"Much better than she was when you first spoke with her. Oh, Valentine, it's as if her entire world has just been knocked out from beneath her. That boy. He was so young..."

Valentine took her into his arms, pressed her head against his chest. "That *boy* nearly murdered my grandmother, and would have if you hadn't thought quickly enough to pull her to safety. After you convinced Trixie to go upstairs, I went out to the mews. Jackson and the others told me what happened. They told me you're a heroine, and extremely brave. Oh, and pluck to the backbone according to Jackson, taking charge the way you did. I'll thank you for that all the days of our lives."

She pulled away from him slightly, to look up in his face. "But it's not true. I had no idea what was happening. I only grabbed Trixie because I reacted as a governess when the door suddenly sprung open, as if she were one of my charges about to topple from the coach. I only shake when I remember that, if I hadn't taken the backward-facing seat, as I always did as a governess, I would have been sitting beside her and only put out my arm to keep her in her seat. If I'd done that, she couldn't have moved before the knife struck home. If I saved your grandmother, it was only by accident. I'm no heroine."

He kissed the tip of her nose. "You are if I say you are. You took charge when most would panic, and got the coach the hell out of there before the Watch could show up and demand answers. I dealt with them when they showed up on the doorstep earlier. There's nothing we can do to fix what happened today, which I'm sure is already the talk of every dinner table in Mayfair."

"Your grandmother leaned out the opening and shouted something, as if she knew someone was watching. Mostly I remember her calling them bastards, and telling them to look at what they'd done. Just as if there weren't a throng of people already gawking at the coach after the boom of the carriage gun drew their attention."

Valentine shook his head, not at what Trixie had shouted, but at the pain she must have been feeling to have so lost control over her reaction as to needlessly expose herself to another potential attacker. He tried to imagine her, her gown red with

Liam's blood, demanding those who'd sent him to confront what they'd done. As his mind conjured up the scene, and Trixie's grief and outrage, he reconsidered. Whoever saw and heard her probably didn't stop running until they were halfway back to Redgrave Manor. Or they'd never return there again, which would just make it more difficult to find and destroy them.

Because they'd be found, and they'd damn well be destroyed.

"We're Redgraves," he said at last. "We do nothing by half measure, I suppose. But Gideon will handle the gossip in his own haughty way, as he's done with the other scandals, as we've had our share. Tongues will wag until Gideon comes to town and visits a few of his clubs, and then the talk will vanish— *Poof!*"

"For Trixie's sake, I hope you're right. Are you certain?"

"Yes." *No, this is no nine-day wonder. And, win or fail—or die—no one will ever know* why *it happened.* "The problem we're presented with now is more important, and it lies in the miles between us and the Manor. Will Trixie be up to traveling tomorrow?"

Daisy walked over to the bed and climbed the two stairs next to it to seat herself on the edge of the mattress. "I don't know. She wants her husband, and he's supposedly bringing your brother back here with him. If he finds him."

At last Valentine found a reason to smile. "She always knows where we are. Her network of spies would put Perceval to shame. We all know that, just as all of us pretend we don't. Poor Kate has had a near battalion of *watchers* quietly looking out for her all of her life. I've got Piffkin, or at least I did until he deserted me for your sister. A few years ago Gideon negotiated down to Thorndyke, his butler in Grosvenor Square, and Dearborn at the Manor. So you can rest assured, if she says Max is in Ostend, then that's where he is. I'd tell you that's a port near Brussels, but you probably already know that."

"I do. I don't suppose you wish to know it was originally called Testerep, and is only a few hours' travel by boat if the weather is fair. A man could conceivably make the journey and return to England in the same day. And you don't mind? Not that I've just shown off my vast and varied knowledge, but that Trixie has set spies on you all."

Valentine hopped up beside her on the bed. "Not as much as I did a few years ago, a hot youth longing to kick over the traces, although knowing Trixie would find out if I went too far probably kept me from doing anything *entirely* stupid. Now I can't help but wonder if she's always feared the Society. She does know enough to make her dangerous."

"Perhaps too dangerous to strike out at her. Not to be too dramatic, but is it possible she warned them she'd written everything down in a memoir of sorts, to be published if she were to come to any harm?"

"You're right, that is dramatic. But entirely possible. I can't think of anything that would force her to part with that information, unless I consider the four of us."

"I'm certain she considered the same possibility." Daisy leaned her head against his shoulder. "Poor thing. I hope you weren't too much of a trial to her."

"Yes, you can see how worn and gray she is. But now that she's turned me over to your watchful care, I'm sure she'll sleep easier."

"I'm not going to be your *keeper,* Valentine. I'm going to be your wife."

He slipped one arm beneath her knees and lifted her fully onto the bed with him. "But I need a keeper, Daisy. Only think of the trouble I could get into, without you to guide me. Or better yet, think of the trouble we two can get in together. Although, just to be different, next time you can rescue me."

"I rescued myself, at least partway. You only just happened to be there when I…when I…"

"When you were letting yourself down from the window, having no idea where you were, where you should go, and not exactly appropriately dressed for a trek to the nearest village. Although I will say the men in the local taproom wouldn't have complained."

"All right, Valentine. You rescued me. My brave knight in his shining, no, his borrowed coat. But we're not going to talk about that anymore."

"Maybe not you, but I'll probably mention it from time to time. I may even include it in *my* memoirs."

He attempted to reach behind her back, to free her buttons from their moorings.

"Valentine, you can't be serious. Taking me to bed, at a time like this? You do remember what happened today, don't you? The danger your grandmother is in, the danger we're in?"

"I remember. But I have loyal men stationed all about the mansion, and there's really nothing we can do until morning, is there? I'm attempting to distract myself before I fall into a pit of despair. You could cooperate, you know. Perhaps turn over for me so I can get at these bloody buttons?"

Daisy laughed. No, she giggled, and then flopped over onto her stomach. "Just be careful. I've already ruined one of your sister's gowns today. I doubt she'd be delighted to have a second one consigned to the dustbin."

He worked diligently on the buttons while silently cursing the seamstress who had thought a gown needed so many; clearly the woman was an old maid with no idea of the trouble she was causing the men attempting a smooth seduction.

"Kate wouldn't even notice. Thanks to Trixie's love of the shops, she's got more gowns than she can count. Here, in Grosvenor Square, at the Manor. Yet she nearly lives in riding habits and boots. If you think I'm the despair of my poor grandmother, wait until you meet my sister. There, that's the last of them, on both gown and chemise. You can easily slip out of them now, under the covers if you like, and I'll join you in a moment."

"But I don't want to move. And my shoulder aches. I think I may have wrenched it earlier, when I reached for Trixie. I think I'll just lie here for a while. Now that I'm down, I've realized how tired I am. Besides, you never told me if you saw Axbridge, if he's our man."

Valentine was standing beside the bed, wreaking a fair amount of havoc on his evening's attire as he stripped it off. Daisy was still on her stomach, her long back with its delectable *sloop* exposed in front of him. As for dealing with the rest of the gown—as he'd said, Kate had dozens and dozens.

"Oh, he's our man, definitely. He's got the arm in a sling at the moment."

"I hope the wound is quite painful. And throbs incessantly," Daisy said, turning her head to look at him, her expressive eyes widening when she realized he'd managed to get himself completely naked. But she didn't look away, just as he hadn't looked away when she'd stood up in her bath.

That was encouraging. She was getting used to him. But she still wasn't shedding her clothes.

"He was coming out of his private bank when I saw him. I fought off a sudden urge to bump into his arm unintentionally once he stepped onto the flagway, and then look him straight in the eye and apologize if I'd caused him any pain, but I refrained. I should receive some sort of credit for that, shouldn't I? Perhaps even a reward?"

"Pass me your slate and some chalk, and I'll draw a star on it, for excellence. Valentine? What are you doing?"

He had climbed back onto the bed and was now straddling the tops of her thighs. "I'm ministering to your painful shoulder. Which one is it, by the way?"

"The right one. Ouch! Oh, never mind. That actually feels rather good."

"I agree," he said, kneading at her shoulders in between running his hands down and up the length of her spine. "You've got a beautiful back, you know."

"Thank you. A little more to the left, if that's possible?"

"Thank you? You're not going to protest because I said you're beautiful?"

"As I told your grandmother, I've decided to humor you. Why, I probably have a *gorgeous* back. Do I have a gorgeous back, Valentine?"

To answer her, he bent over her and began trailing kisses down her spine. He felt a slight quivering of her skin as he reached her waist. *Ah, she has so much to learn, so much I long to teach her.* He moved his hands down her one last time, and slid them beneath her lower belly, working his way toward her center, easing her thighs open…all while kissing and licking at the soft skin just below her waist.

They both heard the sound of ripping silk; he'd strained the fabric until one of the seams had split.

"Oh, Valentine," she moaned, "and it was such a pretty... Oh. I...um...where are you going?"

He'd moved down her body, now straddling her at the knees. "Ridding you of the rest of it, as I've never considered patience to be a virtue," he said, and suddenly the gown was nearly in two pieces, and the silk chemise, as well. The short cap sleeves of the gown still encircled her upper arms, and the gown hadn't ripped quite to the hem, and he was suddenly remembering every gift he'd ever received from Father Christmas. Daisy was the best gift of all and he was unwrapping her.

Valentine leaned forward over her once more, placing kisses on her neck and shoulders, skimming the outline of her body with his hands, his knuckles brushing against the sides of her breasts, his arousal now skin-to-skin against her glorious derrière.

"I'm not going to hurt you, Daisy. I'd never hurt you. Just put your weight on your elbows, and come back toward me. Yes, Daisy, like that, just like that."

He grasped her hips and lifted them, his knees now between her thighs, his manhood against her now and straining to be closer, be inside her.

She was ready for him and he slipped inside her, holding her tight against him, using his hands to rock her hips even as he began to move. He rocked her, feeling her surrender, recognizing her own need, perhaps even her surprise. Keeping one hand on her hip now that she'd found the rhythm, he used his other hand to spread her, to run his finger over the very center of her, feel her harden, swell with desire even as she buried her face into the pillows to muffle her small cries of pleasure. Pleasure he gave her, pleasure he took in return.

Perhaps, in a few years, he would take it slower, allow the passion to build. But not tonight. She was so tight, and he was so ready, and he knew the time had come.

He began to move faster, pulling her toward him, thrusting into her, quickening the pace as he marveled at her liquid heat. Faster. Deeper. More, more. More.

"Hold on, Daisy, just hold on," he managed as his heart pounded and his mind deserted him and it was nothing but the ever-accelerating of his thrusts, one coming right on top of the other; faster, faster, nearly beyond his control.

Daisy cried out and he felt her body clench and unclench around him as he drove deeper, even faster...until he felt himself nothing but a blur of movement and the building, teeth-grinding need for release. He knew she felt that release when it came, as his seed pumped over and over against her womb.

They moved as one as they collapsed onto the mattress, Valentine sprawled on her back, Daisy all but gasping for air beneath him.

They were good together, better than good. They were amazing. Made for each other. Fashioned to complete each other. Their hearts even raced in unison.

"I love you, Daisy," he said against her ear. "I

want to marry you because I love you. I think I have from the first. That's why I kept wanting you to leave…because if you didn't go then, I'd never be able to let you go."

She didn't say anything, and he disengaged himself and half rolled himself onto the mattress, keeping one leg lightly lying across hers. "Daisy?"

"Did Trixie tell you to say that?"

He hadn't known what to expect if he made a declaration, but it certainly wasn't this. "No. Why would you ask that?"

Daisy somehow managed to turn onto her side, oddly to suddenly look completely covered, as the sleeves and bodice of her gown were still intact. "Because she told me I should tell you. As…as I'm clearly besotted. So are you, according to her. She said we should talk about that."

"And now we're talking about that?"

"Yes, I suppose so. Thank you for loving me. I love you back."

Valentine smiled in real amusement. "You love me back. How long have you known you…love me back?"

Her expression remained deadly serious. He wanted to kiss her all over, and then start over again. "Since late this morning, while we were on our way to Bond Street. I'd never before considered myself to be the sort of person who'd ever fall in love, let alone marry. But you would persist, wouldn't you."

He stroked her cheek. "Redgraves are also stubborn."

"And brave. And kind to children. And foolish. And funny. And quite good lovers."

"How would you know?" he asked, recalling an earlier conversation between them. "You've only had the one, remember?"

"Because I know I could never bear to have another man touch me. I could never...*do* what you and I just did, not with another man. I can give myself to you without fear, without shame. And as Trixie so wisely pointed out to me, I have so much to gain when I give away my heart. I'm glad I could give it to you."

Valentine wasn't the sort who humbled easily, but he was humble now, in the face of all that Daisy had revealed to him.

"I love you," he said, easing himself against her, touching his mouth to hers before pulling away slightly, to look into her soul-revealing eyes. "But you do realize we can never tell our children the story of how we met."

Daisy laughed, and his heart swelled, and Cupid finally took his shovel and departed to bang some other thickskulled man over the head. Eventually the remainder of Daisy's ruined gown found its way to the floor, and the fire slowly burned down in the grate, and two very lucky people slept in each other's arms, the world successfully held at bay at least until they awoke.

EPILOGUE

THE COOPERS WERE gone from the estate. Every last man, woman and child: over forty in all.

Coopers had been part of the estate for more than a century, generation after generation serving the Redgraves, taking wives and husbands from the local population. Born on Redgrave land, died and buried on Redgrave land. Giving birth to more than a few Redgrave bastards.

Only Angus Cooper had lingered until the day of Liam's burial, to kneel beside his grandson's grave, his gnarled, crippled hands crushed into fists around some of the freshly turned dirt. Redgrave dirt.

Everyone else had already returned to the Manor. Valentine and Daisy, hand in hand behind Rose and Piffkin. Simon with his arm around a weeping Kate. Gideon and Jessica, physically supporting her half-brother, Adam, who had just lately formed a friendship with Liam. Richard Borders leaving only reluctantly, but not moving more than ten yards away from his wife.

Trixie stood vigil with Angus, finding it impossible to leave him, yet knowing she had no words of comfort for him.

Only questions.

She lifted the heavy black veil up and over her black straw bonnet. "I can only imagine you were left behind to deliver some sort of message, some sort of threat. As it was me one of you attempted to kill, I convinced the others it was my right to hear what you have to say. You can speak freely, and then you may just as freely leave."

"I'm only here to pray for my grandson's soul."

Trixie heard bitterness in the man's voice. Anger. And, perhaps, accusation. If she were to have any chance at answers, she'd have to tread carefully.

"Please don't lie to me, Angus. We were friends, or at least I believed we were. I know how much you adored Liam."

The old man slid the handfuls of dirt into his pockets and got to his feet. "No more talk. I only stayed to tell you that you can't stop what's coming. Not this time. You especially were meant to know your enemy before you died, and now you do. This time your meddling will have been for nothing."

Trixie had been alive a long time. Nothing much had the power to shock her, not anymore. But she hadn't expected this.

She fell back on bravado, for it was all she had.

"We aren't doing so badly, Angus. No matter who began this or why, we'll end it. And we will win. I promise you that."

"We've had enough of Redgrave promises, too."

Aware of Richard's nearness, Trixie spoke softly,

fiercely. "What promises are those? The same insane promises Charles made, that Barry made? A return of the Stuarts? You know that never would have happened. My husband and son never spoke sense, they spoke greed, and treason, and sexual perversion, and only playacted at royalty to cover their true motives."

"The Stuarts? This was never about the bloody Stuarts for us. No more questions. My grandson is dead. Kill me now, or leave me to grieve."

She put her hand on his arm. "Grieve? You should be angry. *I'm* angry. Someone filled that young boy's head with lies and hate, and then deliberately sent him off to die as some...some sort of *calling card* meant to terrify us. Whether he succeeded or not, Liam was dead the moment he was sent to kill me. I didn't kill him, Angus, the Redgraves didn't kill him. One of his own carries the blame and the shame."

He wrenched his arm free of her grasp. "Liam chose the short straw. I would have gone in his place, but I'm too old now, too slow. You kept your secrets, all these years. You protected yourself, destroyed anyone you believed could harm you. I never thought you'd betray yourself, but how else could your grandson have gotten so close? It was all you. It always has been you."

"You left me no choice. Yes, I told them what I know, even as it nearly destroyed me. I protect my own, Angus, at any cost to myself. You send yours out to die," Trixie said, shaking her head as she backed up several steps. "I didn't choose this path, the Society did, from the very beginning. I won't allow you to blame me for Liam's death."

"*Death* is all over you, and has been since the beginning." The old man climbed up onto the seat of the ancient wagon and took up the reins. His belongings, such as they were, piled up behind him. "The great Lady Saltwood. You murdered your husband to be free of him. You were protecting your son from his papa's evil ways, you told yourself, didn't you? But when Lord Barry turned out to be his father's son in spite of your—"

"Trixie? Are you all right? Come along with me now."

"I'm fine, Richard," she called out quickly, willing her voice steady. "Only a moment more, I promise. We're just saying goodbye."

Angus looked out over Redgrave land and the enormous, sprawling buildings that were Redgrave Manor. There was satisfaction in his eyes at what he saw, perhaps even love. "It was our work built all this, not yours. This time it will be different. Twice denied, but not this time."

"What does that mean?" Trixie asked, her heart pounding. "Did Charles promise you something for helping with his damned Society? Did Barry? Do you Coopers think you're *owed* something? What are you owed?"

And then the answer struck her, staggered her

where she stood. "You're doing what they tried to do, aren't you? You're plotting treason, not in exchange for a crown, but for the promise of Redgrave Manor? God, man, is that what all this is about?"

Angus released the brake of the farm wagon and flicked the reins so the single horse in the shaft began a slow walk toward the path to one of the gates.

Trixie hiked up her skirts and ran after him. "Angus! We're not through! Angus, come back here!"

"Let him go, darling. He's an old man, and harmless," Richard said, huffing and puffing as he caught up with her, for he was a man on the shady side of sixty, with too many good meals behind him. "Come on, let's go back to the house and find us both a cup of tea."

She nodded, unable to speak, and they started off.

Down the hill. To the tables set out on the terrace, where Valentine and Daisy waited. Where Kate and Simon waited. Where Gideon and Jessica and even her silly brother, Adam, waited.

Where everyone waited for Max.

* * * * *

With Redgrave Manor virtually under siege, it is left to Maximillien Redgrave to locate and destroy the Society, once and for all. But when the search finds him unexpectedly crossing paths with an old love, he can't be certain if she'll prove friend or enemy. Can he risk his family, his country, his heart and life, in the pursuit of the woman he's never been able to forget? Find out in What A Hero Dares, *the thrilling and passionate conclusion to the story of those scandalous Redgraves, coming soon from HQN.*

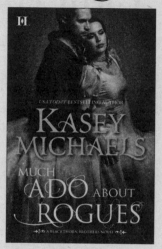

**Loving the enemy is one thing.
Trusting the enemy is quite another.**

New York Times Bestselling Author

CANDACE CAMP

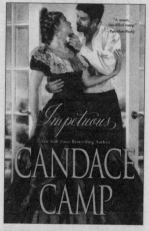

In the late 1600s, Black Maggie Verrere was engaged to marry
Sir Edric Neville in an effort to unite their two families. Instead she eloped to
America with another man, and the famed Spanish dowry vanished along with
her. The two families—the Verreres and the Nevilles—have hated
one another ever since.

Now, 150 years later, another Verrere woman seeks the dowry.
Cassandra Verrere has no hope of providing a future for her younger siblings,
or for herself, unless she recovers the treasure. Unfortunately her path to its
attainment requires the help of a Neville—the disarming Sir Philip. With an
ancient feud marking their lineage, Cassandra cannot imagine trusting him.
But the true challenge may be in trusting her heart not to fall for him.

Available wherever books are sold!

From *USA TODAY* bestselling author

NICOLA CORNICK

Lady Lucy MacMorlan may have forsworn men and marriage, but that doesn't mean she won't agree to profit from writing love letters for her brother's friends—letters that become increasingly racy as her fame grows. That is, until she inadvertently ruins the betrothal of a notorious laird…and a tempting suitor from her past.

Robert, the dashing Marquis of Methven, is onto Lucy's secret. And he certainly doesn't intend to let her have the last word, especially when her letters suggest she is considerably more experienced than he realized….

Available wherever books are sold!

Be sure to connect with us at:

PHNC741

REQUEST YOUR FREE BOOKS!

HARLEQUIN® HISTORICAL:
Where love is timeless

2 FREE NOVELS PLUS 2 **FREE GIFTS!**

JULIETTE MILLER

**In the midst of a Clan divided, two unlikely allies
must confront the passion that binds them...and the
treachery that may part them forever.**

To secure her family's alliance with
the powerful Clan Mackenzie,
Stella Morrison has no choice but to
wed the notorious Kade Mackenzie.
Unable to ignore the whispers that
surround him, she resigns herself to
a marriage in name only. Yet as the
fierce warrior strips away Stella's
doubt one seductive touch at a
time, burgeoning desire forces her
to question all she holds as truth.

Leading a rebellious army should
have been Kade's greatest
challenge...until conquering the
heart of his reluctant bride becomes
an all-consuming need. Now more
than ever, he's determined to find
victory both on the battlefield and
in the bedchamber. But the quest for triumph unleashes a dark threat,
and this time, only love may prove stronger than danger.

Available wherever books are sold!

Be sure to connect with us at:
Harlequin.com/Newsletters
Facebook.com/HarlequinBooks
Twitter.com/HarlequinBooks

KASEY MICHAELS

77764	WHAT A LADY NEEDS	___ $7.99 U.S.	___ $9.99 CAN.
77610	A MIDSUMMER NIGHT'S SIN	___ $7.99 U.S.	___ $9.99 CAN.
77433	HOW TO BEGUILE A BEAUTY	___ $7.99 U.S.	___ $9.99 CAN.
76764	WHAT AN EARL WANTS	___ $7.99 U.S.	___ $9.99 CAN.

(limited quantities available)

TOTAL AMOUNT $ _____
POSTAGE & HANDLING $ _____
($1.00 FOR 1 BOOK, 50¢ for each additional)
APPLICABLE TAXES* $ _____
TOTAL PAYABLE $ _____
(check or money order—please do not send cash)

To order, complete this form and send it, along with a check or money order for the total above, payable to Harlequin HQN, to: **In the U.S.:** 3010 Walden Avenue, P.O. Box 9077, Buffalo, NY 14269-9077; **In Canada:** P.O. Box 636, Fort Erie, Ontario, L2A 5X3.

Name: _____
Address: _____ City: _____
State/Prov.: _____ Zip/Postal Code: _____
Account Number (if applicable): _____

075 CSAS

*New York residents remit applicable sales taxes.
*Canadian residents remit applicable GST and provincial taxes.

HARLEQUIN® HQN™
™ www.Harlequin.com

PHKM1013BL